STEPHANIE FAZIO

STEEL FOR 5

Syafant Press

Syafant Press

New York, New York

Copyright © 2021 Stephanie Fazio.

All rights reserved. No part of this book may be reproduced in any form or by any electronic or mechanical means including information storage and retrieval systems, without permission in writing from the author. The only exception is by a reviewer who may quote short excerpts in a review.

Cover designed by Keith Tarrier

This book is a work of fiction. Names, characters, places, and incidents either are the product of the author's imagination or are used fictionally, and any resemblance to actual persons, living or dead, business establishments, events, or locales is entirely coincidental.

Stephanie Fazio

Visit www.StephanieFazio.com

Printed in the United States of America
First Printing: January 2021

Library of Congress Control Number: 2020912781

ISBN 978-1-951572-18-1

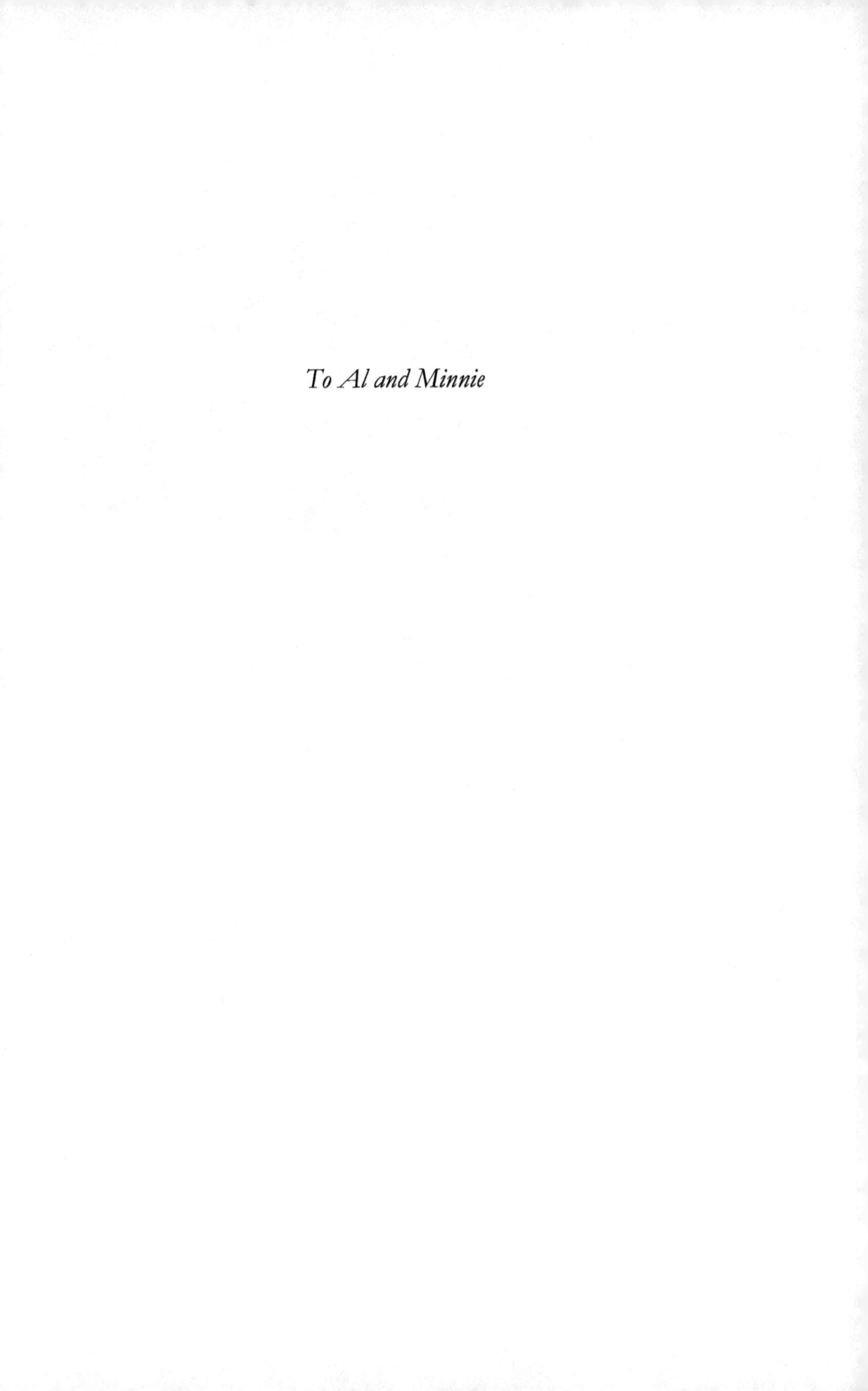
To Al and Minnie

CHAPTER 1

Calling all units. Backup needed at 522 Bulweather Street. We've got a Super Mag Pyro threatenin' to burn the retirement home down. Fire and paramedics stand by.

Oh jeez.

Oh my God.

Get the hell outta there!

"The whole place is burning," Smith reported as he plugged his headphones in, cutting off the police chatter.

"How many people still inside?" Graysen asked, his voice far cooler and more controlled than any of us were feeling.

"All of them," Smith replied grimly. "Residents, plus all the nurses and other staff who were working."

Kaira swore.

"We've got this, team," I assured everyone as I methodically cracked my knuckles. "Can we get some pump-up music going in here?"

Six groans filled the van when Michael turned on a soft rock station.

"Why are you smiling?" Smith asked me, his tone laced with suspicion. "You're about to run into a burning building."

"Precisely," I countered. "This is the most exciting thing I've done all day."

I gripped the handle on the door as the van careened down the road. We were heading straight toward the plume of orange flames. Even with the windows up, the reek of smoke filled the air and made my eyes water. The rest of the Seven began stripping off their coats and sweaters. I blew on my fists.

My fingertips began to tingle. Normal flesh took on a silvery hue as the titanium spread up my forearms and encased my bones. The cool metal brought down my body temperature and calmed the furious tempo of my pulse. The nervous tapping of my foot stilled.

"Stop here," I ordered Michael, who was driving.

"Catch ya on the flip side, Bri," Yutika told me, completely unconcerned by the fact that I was about to race headlong into an inferno.

She had good reason for her flippancy. There wasn't much—including fire—that could hurt me. I was a Level 10 Steel.

As soon as I felt the van beginning to slow, I wrenched open the door.

"Bri—" Kaira began, but I didn't wait for her to finish. I didn't need to be a fire fighter to know there wasn't a moment to spare.

I jumped out of the van.

Sparks shot up as my titanium skin scraped the pavement. I rolled four times before leaping up. There were small divots in the pavement from my fall, but my skin was untouched. I felt nothing except determination as I dashed toward the burning building.

The fire hoses were already at work. Jets of water were pummeling the building on all sides. Any normal blaze would have been extinguished by now, but this was no ordinary fire. It belonged to a Level 28 Pyrokinetic who could create a ten-alarm fire at the snap of his fingers…and had. Normal Pyros could start a fire or make an already-burning fire more powerful. But a Super Mag Pyro?

No amount of water was going to make a dent in this blaze. The building was a gonner. All anyone could do now was get out of the way and wait until the fire ran out of fuel.

I burst past the fire trucks, ambulances, and police cruisers.

"You can't go in there," a fireman exclaimed. "Are you insane?"

"Wouldn't you like to know," I replied, throwing him a wink over my shoulder.

I'd always had a thing for firemen.

There was no more time for pleasantries. I raced into the building.

Flames leapt toward me and died the second they met with my titanium skin. My clothes fared less well. I managed to bat out the fire before my outfit was completely incinerated.

If tomorrow's headlines featured a scantily-clad picture of me rescuing people, A.J. would never let me hear the end of it.

I didn't bother with doors. Instead, I barreled right through the walls until I found a group of five elderly people huddled beneath a mattress. They were all choking and drenched in sweat, but the mattress was keeping the worst of the flames at bay.

"Come on!" I pulled the everyone behind me, using my body to shield them.

It was slow going. I had to hoist one woman onto my hip like an over-large toddler. I used my other hand to yank a man along behind. The man was coughing too hard from the smoke to hold himself up.

"Stand back," I warned the people behind me before kicking right through the brick wall.

Cold October air filled my lungs, which were screaming for oxygen. The sharp odor of burnt plastic and other lovely carcinogenic fumes made my nose sting. Thick, black smoke poured out of the building and disappeared into the night sky.

I ushered the old people out as fast as I could. As soon as they were surrounded by paramedics, I went back in.

Realizing the upper floor wouldn't last much longer, I ran up the stairs. The steps were concrete, but the magical fire was eating them up the same way normal flames devoured wood. It took some tricky acrobatics, but I made it up to the second floor.

I screamed myself hoarse as I ran from room to room, searching for survivors. I didn't let myself linger next to bodies that lay stiff in their beds from smoke inhalation. I raced on until I found people cowering under bedframes or crouching in their tubs.

I darted down the burning stairs and practically threw the retirees at the waiting firemen.

"Get outta there!" a fireman called up to me. "This place is about to blow!"

Just a few more…. I could save a few more people.

I sprinted out with an unconscious woman slung over my shoulder. We'd barely made it outside when every window in the building exploded. Glass shards sprayed in every direction. Blue-and-purple flames erupted out of the open windows and lit up the sky. The police and firemen dove to the ground. The cop car nearest to the building began to sag as the exterior melted right off its frame.

There was a crash as the building's second floor collapsed.

"No!" One of the retirees reached out a trembling hand toward the building. "My wife's still in there!"

My heart sank. No one inside could have survived this kind of heat. Except for the one who had caused it.

I caught the man around his waist before he could barge back into the building.

"Debbie!" he yelled. "Debbie, oh God. Debbie!"

The man crumpled against me, sobbing.

I'm sorry! I wanted to tell the man. *I'm so, so sorry.*

But being sorry wouldn't bring the man's wife back. So, I held him more tightly as I stared at all those burned-out windows. I couldn't stop myself from counting them…and thinking about all those people who would never walk out the front door.

Before I knew it, I was extricating myself from the old man and going back toward the building.

"It's too dangerous!" a fireman shouted, reaching out to stop me.

I easily slipped out of his grasp. Michael would Whisper to the firemen and cops to make sure no one tried to follow me inside.

My titanium skin didn't register temperature, but I could sense how hot it was. Cinders glowed with magical heat. Even though the fire had already devoured most of the building, flames still crackled on the floor's charred remains. I shielded my eyes against the floating ash.

There was nothing to see except rubble. In just a few minutes, the blaze had eaten away at everything. My eyes watered as fire turned to smoke. My throat burned. While my exterior was titanium, my insides were still normal.

I shielded my nose and mouth with my arm as I moved deeper into the building.

"Help me."

The cry was weak, but I'd definitely heard the male voice. Someone was alive.

"Where are you?" I cried. Hope and panic surged through me.

I barreled through the remains of a wall that was barely standing. It crashed behind me in a flurry of embers. I hardly noticed. I swiped ash from my hair without slowing as I raced from one burned-out room to another.

"Where are you?" I called again. With my raspy voice and soot-covered skin, I felt like something out of a nightmare.

Movement caught my attention. I hurried forward, heedless of the remaining ceiling beams that could come down on my head at any moment.

I burst through the building's far wall. Even though I was in some kind of alley lined with dumpsters, the air seemed gloriously clean compared to the noxious fumes within the still-burning building.

"Please. Help."

I came to a screeching halt as I caught sight of the voice's owner.

A boy was sitting on the ground. His knees were drawn up to his chin, and his whole body was trembling. He looked up at me through tear-swollen eyes.

I went still. If I hadn't known better, I'd have thought the kid on the ground was an innocent bystander. With his twiggy limbs and the soot smudged across his cheeks, he didn't look capable of any crime worse than talking back to grown-ups. But I knew better. For the first time, I was grateful Smith had made me memorize every detail of the Super Mags' files.

I was standing in front of the Pyro who was responsible for this inferno.

"You." I clenched my hands into fists. Power flowed through my veins. I crossed the distance separating us in two leaps. "Do you have any idea what you've done?!"

I grabbed the back of the boy's shirt and yanked him to his feet. His head snapped back like a ragdoll.

I expected the Pyro to hurl flames in my face. Instead, he sagged in my grip. The Pyro hellion didn't look at me with anger or defiance. His eyes were dull. He seemed broken.

His shaking hands drew my attention.

"Shit," I gasped as acid flooded my mouth.

The boy's hands were burned almost beyond recognition. Patches of black, scaly skin were punctuated by oozing red blisters. His hands and forearms looked more like raw meat than human skin.

"What the hell happened to you?"

Part of the deal with Pyros was that they couldn't be harmed by fire. Just like I wouldn't be able to knock myself out with my own titanium fist. Not that I'd ever put it to the test….

The boy who had burned down an old age home and killed dozens of people began to sob.

"It's gone," he cried. "It's gone. It's gone. It's gone."

"The building?" I asked, staring at the smoldering remains. *What the hell did he expect would happen?*

"No." The boy let out a soft whimper. "My magic's gone."

CHAPTER 2

We stood within sight of the burnt-down retirement home as emergency personnel flurried around. I calmly gave my statement to the cops, all the while pretending like the anxious fluttering in my stomach wasn't making me feel like doing a thousand push-ups.

Twenty-seven people were dead.

Maybe if I'd moved faster…searched harder….

"That's all we need, Ms. Hammond. Thank you for your time."

A few words from Michael ensured the Seven of us could stay through the Pyro's arrest and interrogation. I stood off to the side, trying to be discreet as I bounced on the balls of my feet in abbreviated jumping jacks.

I excelled at the *doing* part of things. I still hadn't mastered the waiting around part.

"One of the Super Mags cut her leg," the Pyro told the Mag detective, scowling when his handcuffs clinked against his bandaged hands. "I hadda get a first aid kit, and the old people home seemed like they'd have one."

"Did it ever occur to you to go to a store and just buy one?" the detective asked dryly.

The Pyro glared at the woman. The detective took a step back, but no flames came spouting out of the Pyro's bandaged fingers.

"Those nurses shouldn't have fought back!" the Pyro growled. He looked down at his bandaged hands and seemed to deflate. "I guess I panicked."

We all turned to look at the smoldering remains of the retirement home. Blackened beams and sooty ash were all that remained.

"You're going to rot in jail for a long time," the detective told the Pyro with satisfaction. She'd been searching for the Pyro ever since he'd burned down MagLab and escaped with fifty other Super Mags. "You're barely thirteen, and you're already a mass murder. The world will be better with you locked away."

A sense of righteous justice flared through me. Now, this maniac would never hurt anyone else again.

"I'd like to know about what happened after the fire," Graysen told the Pyro.

The detective stiffened. I wasn't sure if it was because she felt like Graysen was stepping on her toes or because she didn't like Nats. Either way, she knew enough to keep her mouth shut.

"Someone dragged me outta the building." The Pyro scowled. "I couldn't see anyone, so I don't know who it was. I got stuck with something sharp—a needle, I think. And then my magic stopped working." His voice broke and his shoulders sagged. In spite of the still-smoking heap of rubble in front of us, I couldn't help but feel a little sorry for the kid.

The Mag paramedics on the scene confirmed that the Pyro had been injected with the Magical Reduction Potion—MRP as we now called it to save syllables.

The vile potion was developed by Edwardian Remwald's Alchemists in MagLab, and the different gradations of MRP could take away a Mag's powers temporarily or permanently.

The Pyro had been injected with the permanent kind.

"It's like the others," Kaira said in a low voice.

About a month ago, one of the Super Mags had been playing with her doll in the park when she was injected with the MRP. The same thing had happened to another of the kids a few days later. And now this.

Someone was injecting the Super Mags with the Magical Reduction Potion. Whoever it was must be incredibly stealthy…and either really smart or really stupid. So far, no one had been able to find out anything about the attacker's identity, even though the cops and other Super Mags were on the hunt.

"I'm gonna get that…that *magic ripper*!" the Pyro snarled as the detective led him to her cruiser. "I'm gonna find that sonuvabitch and burn him down to dust!"

"Without your magic, you won't be burning anyone or anything again," the detective told him as she unceremoniously shoved him into the cruiser.

The boy's retort was lost as the detective slammed the door shut.

"Magic ripper," Yutika said. "That's a good name. We should totally use it."

"Totally," A.J. agreed.

We watched as the righteous detective turned on her siren and sped away with the Pyro.

It was good the Pyro had lost his magic. The retirement home hadn't been the first time he'd used his fire to kill. In the process of breaking himself and the other Super Mags out of MagLab, he'd killed dozens of people.

Yet, the thought of someone stealing away my magic shot so much fear through me that I was left gasping.

Besides, it wasn't like the magic ripper had just gone after the Pyro. They had attacked innocent Super Mags, too.

"We better head home and deal with this," Kaira said, her mouth twisted in a grim line. "Reporters are already blowing up my phone."

"Agreed," Graysen said as he texted on his own cell.

"I'll see if I can track down this magic ripper," Smith said. His head disappeared behind the screen of his laptop, which he was balancing on one palm.

"Yutika and I can go talk to some of the other Super Mags," Michael offered. "See if they know anything that'll help us find this mystery person."

"I guess that leaves us," I told A.J. My thoughts were already racing ahead to how I intended to spend my first night off in months.

Over the last four months, we'd all been consumed with helping Kaira and Graysen set up their new administration as Co-Directors of the Alliance. After the election, our entire posse had moved into the Director's mansion. We'd had about two seconds to settle in before our collective skills were put to the test.

Every time I thought about how I and six other twenty-somethings were running the city, I got heartburn. And then I got back to work, since there was never any shortage of that these days.

It was a true marker of how busy we'd all been that A.J. hadn't even started talking about Halloween costumes.

Guilt nagged at me; the only reason I had a night off was because twenty-seven people were dead. Still, that fact didn't take away from the tingling sense of anticipation building in my limbs.

Finally, a voice sighed in the back of my mind. Finally, I could do something about the mystery that haunted my dreams and called to me like a siren. Finally, I might be able to get some answers.

The perpetual weight that rested between my shoulder blades eased a fraction.

"Oh, no you don't." A.J. narrowed his eyes at me. "You have your ass-kicking face on, and I have a date with a jacuzzi and a pumpkin latte."

I had an ass-kicking face? *Sweet.*

"Not anymore, you don't," I informed him. "We're going grave robbing."

CHAPTER 3

The fall breeze washed over my bare arms, which would have been covered in goosebumps if my skin was just skin. The silver of my bare titanium arms shone pale in the darkness. With my magic, I didn't feel the burn of muscles or exertion from all the digging I was doing. I could have dug all night without getting tired.

For just a moment, the wind pulled away the rotten earth smell and replaced it with the scent of a campfire. Somewhere nearby, people were roasting marshmallows and stargazing. While I was digging up graves.

"Is this your idea of a joke, Bri Hammond?"

I looked up. A.J. was peering down at me from the edge of the six-foot hole I'd dug. He wore a hat with a miner's lamp, which illuminated one of his patent faux-leather loafers, tapping away in irritation.

"What are you talking about?" I asked, annoyed that A.J.'s butter-yellow suit was pristine, while my outfit was covered in dirt.

Sir Zachary let out a playful yip. His outfit—a yellow jacket that matched A.J.'s suit—was as filthy as mine. Our little dog wagged his tail as he nosed around the fresh-turned earth.

"Bringing me to a graveyard, under a full moon, a week before Halloween…?" A.J.'s voice got high at the end. "I'm getting the heebie jeebies. If it wasn't for my incurable loyalty and perpetual good cheer, I'd do my digging from the car."

As a Level 10 Telekinetic, A.J. was capable of doing just that. Lower level Telekinetics had to be right next to an object to make it move. A.J. could control inanimate objects that were miles away.

I'd been watching his shovel work furiously beside me for the last hour, while A.J. reclined on his checkered picnic blanket and sipped his spiked pumpkin latte.

"Well," I drawled. "If you weren't so worried about our public image, then I'd be glad to dig up these graves in the middle of the day."

A.J. squeaked. "Do you know how hard I've worked to portray us as semi-law-abiding Bostonians?"

Legal, but with a twist was our joking, private motto. Our public one, which had gotten Kaira and Graysen elected, was *Get shit done*.

Even though Kaira and Graysen were now the most powerful people in Boston, defiling graves was still a crime.

Imagine that.

A.J. did have a point about the Halloween spooky stuff, although I'd never admit it to him. There wasn't much that could take me down, but it was admittedly a tad creepy being out here in the dark. I was usually a total sucker for scary stuff—roller coasters, horror movies, and haunted houses were my jam. But there was something about digging up a grave in the wee hours that filled my mind with images of ghosts and vampires. And zombies...*oh my*.

My shovel hit the hard-plastic exterior of the biohazard container I had known would be buried here. I leaned my shovel against the dirt wall and used my titanium fingers to pry the container out of its earthen cocoon. A.J. adjusted his miner's lamp helmet to illuminate the box as I pried it open.

"Anything?" A.J. asked from the top of the hole.

"Nope."

Just as I'd expected, the container was empty.

The container held a faint plastic-y smell. The inside was devoid of bones or whatever else would have been left behind if it had held a corpse like it was supposed to.

I leaned back against the freshly-dug hole, not even caring that dirt and earthworms were probably taking up residence in my long hair.

Before Kaira and Graysen became Directors, we'd been investigating Mag Subject 6, the Invisible and Mind Melder Super Mag who was murdering Alliance officials. He'd been the one to tell us that Mags were being kidnapped and enslaved to produce the Magical Reduction Potion.

And my niece, Lilly, had been one of the enslaved Mags.

The only person who knew where the slaves were kept had died before I could get the information out of him. Now, I was stuck in this purgatory where I didn't know whether Lilly was dead or alive, and I didn't have any way of finding out. All I could do was dig up the rest of the graves on the list of Mags who shared the same profile as Lilly in the hopes of finding a new lead.

"Get the Agent S and come on out of there, baby girl," A.J. said in a soft voice.

I realized I was crying and hastily wiped my eyes with a semi-clean corner of my shirt.

My tears, which had become titanium the moment they left my eyes, turned into solid, silvery balls. They struck the ground with soft thunks, looking like beads resting atop the soil.

I furiously kicked the offensive tears underneath the dirt. Those gleaming silver tears were just a reminder of my failure…a reminder of another problem I wasn't able to solve.

Like I could ever forget.

I'd destroyed three punching bags just this month out of a lack of more productive means of working off my frustration. If I kept it up, the Alliance would need to add a budget line called *Bri blowing off steam.*

I grabbed my shovel and began to dig again. I estimated I had three more feet to go before I reached the crate of Agent S I expected to be buried here.

Agent S was a strange, green substance that was toxic to everyone and everything…except me. It was also the main ingredient in the Magical Reduction Potion. Ex-Director Edwardian Remwald had planned to use the MRP to force all Mags in the city to go to war against the Nats.

My shovel struck wood. I carefully extracted the crate of Agent S. Before I bent down to lift it, the crate floated into the air. It landed with a gentle thud at the top of my ten-foot hole.

"Thanks," I called up to A.J.

I pasted on my *all is good in the world* smile and forced the tension out of my muscles. I didn't like anyone to see evidence of my weakness, even my best friend. And A.J. had a sixth sense for knowing when someone was upset and trying to hide it. I had to be strong. I had to be…well, steel.

Chuckling to myself at the tiny witticism, I scooped up Sir Zachary. The dog, who was snuffling around in the dirt and chewing I-didn't-want-to-know-what, gave me a dirty kiss on the cheek. Cradling him in my arms, I clambered back up the steep wall of the hole.

A normal person would have slid right back down to the bottom. In my titanium form, I scaled the crumbly surface as easily as a monkey climbing a tree.

Unlike less powerful Steels, who were made of other metals, my titanium skin was lighter and more flexible. More importantly, there was pretty much nothing that could hurt me when I was in this state. Fire and ice didn't bother me. A Super Mag having a tantrum had struck me with lightning a few weeks back, and I hadn't even felt it. Acids and poisons also had no effect.

It was the reason why I was the only one of the Seven who ever got within touching distance of Agent S. I had learned the hard way that Agent S and cashmere sweaters didn't mix.

I was pretty sure Smith would never recover from the scandal of seeing what was likely his first non-digital set of boobs.

When I got to the top of the hole, I found four other crates waiting beside the one I had unearthed.

A.J. directed his headlamp on the crates while I pried off the lids.

Each crate was identical to the ones we'd unearthed from other graves. They all contained rows and rows of glass vials filled with Agent S.

I'd seen the effects of the MRP firsthand when Cora, Kaira's sweet youngest cousin, was injected with a syringe full of the potion. I could still see Cora, sitting on a park bench and clutching her pink backpack as she sobbed. Before the Magical Reduction Potion, Cora had been an Inanimate Illusionist. Now, she would never use magic again.

I lifted one of the vials. The green liquid stuck to the side of the vial that was touching my hand. Even though gravity should have pulled the Agent S down, it stubbornly stayed as close to my body as it could get. It was like we were opposites sides of a magnet.

For some reason we hadn't figured out, Agent S was attracted to my titanium skin. It burned through everything else.

"You better stand back," I told A.J., who was already putting distance between himself and the crates. He whistled to Sir Zachary, who padded over to him.

Once they were far enough away, I put the vial back in the crate. Then, I lifted the entire thing and threw it into the grave. I used enough force to deepen the hole several feet. The ground beneath us shuddered slightly from the impact.

I heard the crack of wood and tinkle of glass as the vials shattered. The green liquid that oozed out sparkled in the moonlight. It hissed and sent up a burst of green-tinged steam as it burned deeper into the ground.

Since we'd told the rest of Boston about the MRP, the safest way to ensure its key ingredient didn't wind up in the wrong hands was to destroy it.

Whoever was going after the Super Mags' magic somehow had access to the Magical Reduction Potion. One criminal playing God in our city was one too many.

I threw the next crate down, and then the next, and the next.

Past experience had taught me that if I was too close to the Agent S when it was released from its vial, it would cling to my titanium skin and refuse to let go. That was how I'd discovered I was as ticklish in my titanium form as I was in regular skin…and inadvertently revealed my greatest weakness to all of my friends.

"What do you think, hon?" A.J. asked, as he refilled the grave without so much as touching a shovel. The particles of dirt just zoomed back into the hole at lightning speed. "On to the next cemetery?"

I nodded, bowing under the crushing weight that had settled on my shoulders. I knew what we'd find at the next cemetery…the same we'd found in the twenty graves we'd already dug up.

"We're going to solve this mystery," A.J. promised me as he tucked an arm around my waist. "We're going to find those slaves and figure out exactly what happened to Lilly."

Sir Zachary wagged his tail and nuzzled against my leg.

I only wished I shared their optimism.

* * *

A.J. stifled a yawn as we got out of the van. I was instantly awash with guilt. I was dragging A.J. all over Boston to dig up graves, when he should be catching up on some much-needed sleep.

"I'm sorry," I began, but A.J. waved away my apology.

"Nonsense," he said. "Fresh air is good for the complexion."

We followed the path until we reached the first grave on the printout Smith had given me.

A prickling sense of unease climbed up my spine as I looked at the grave.

I glanced at Sir Zachary to see if anything seemed off to him. He was avidly watching an earthworm as it wriggled back into the dirt.

I didn't hear anything, but that didn't mean we were alone. The cemetery was bathed in shadows that flickered and took on a life of their own. I turned my face into the wind. That was when I caught a smell I'd gotten so used to it hadn't registered at first.

Freshly-dug earth.

It hadn't rained recently, and there was no reason for the smell to be so strong, unless—

A.J. let out a muted protest when I pulled off his miner's helmet and pointed the lamp onto the grave.

The light left no room for debate. Someone had already been here.

A.J. toed a small pile of dirt the gravedigger hadn't bothered to push back into place. "What are the odds?"

"Of someone randomly digging up a grave that's been here for three years?" I chuckled darkly. "Nil."

I shone A.J.'s light all around the area. On my second sweep of the light, I caught a glimpse of something peeking out of the dirt. Hurrying forward, I grasped the tiny paper before the wind caught it.

It was a gum wrapper. Fire-hot cinnamon flavor, according to the label.

I pocketed the wrapper, because I didn't feel like getting one of A.J.'s lectures about littering. Finding no other clues about who might have been here and why, I grabbed my shovel and got to work.

It went quickly, thanks to the dirt being loose from whoever had already been here and A.J.'s shovel working steadily beside me. Even Sir Zachary helped, although his little paws didn't accomplish much.

A few seconds later, A.J.'s shovel hit the biohazard container. It was higher up in the hole than it should have been—maybe only a couple of feet. A quick examination of the container showed that it hadn't been disturbed.

A.J.'s announcement of "Nothing here except environmentally unfriendly plastic," came just as my shovel hit the edge of the Agent S crate. Again, it wasn't buried as deeply as the ones in the other graves had been.

As soon as I lifted the crate, my stomach plummeted. It was light.

Too light.

I knew even before I wrenched off the lid what I'd find inside.

The crate was empty.

CHAPTER 4

I t took us an hour to investigate all eight remaining graves on our list. Every single one of them had already been dug up. And their crates of Agent S were empty.

There were no other clues about who had dug up the graves, but it was obvious the Agent S-robber had known what they were doing. None of the other graves in the cemetery had been disturbed. That meant our thief had known exactly which graves to target.

My mind was a whirlwind of unanswered questions.

By the time A.J., Sir Zachary, and I got home, it was close to midnight. Despite the late hour, the mansion was bustling with activity.

When we'd moved in, I had been less than thrilled about taking up residence in Edwardian Remwald's old home. I'd proceeded to change my tune when I learned I was getting my own bathroom…with heated floors and fog-proof mirrors.

Sir Zachary made a beeline for the kitchen, where a warm, yeasty smell was wafting. Yutika had made a dog bed for Sir Zachary next to the refrigerator, since he spent so much time in the kitchen with Ma.

"Bri Hammond!" The booming voice was accompanied by a hard thump on my back.

Adam, Graysen's crew teammate, shook out his hand as he gave me a sheepish look. "Ow. I always forget how hard your skin is."

"So sorry." I blew on my fists, transforming my body back to regular skin before I slapped him on the back in return.

I could transform without blowing on my fists, but it took more concentration. In nature, oxygen made titanium brittle. When combined with magic, the oxygen in my breath made it easier to activate and deactivate the hardness of my titanium skin. Plus, it looked cool.

I felt my magic retreat back inside me. It hid just beneath the surface, waiting patiently until I called on it again.

Now that I was back in my regular skin, I couldn't keep from shivering. The house was heated, but not well enough for my choice of tank top and cut-off jeans.

"How do you manage to be so pretty even when you're covered in dirt?" Adam asked, batting his eyes at me. He sat back down at the long kitchen table with the rest of his crew team and Kaira's two cousins.

"Flirt." I grinned at him.

My appearance could best be described as cute. My blonde hair and hazel eyes were nice enough, but I had none of Kaira's head-turning effect. If she were to walk into the room right now, all of the crew guys would be picking their jaws off the floor.

My round face and five-foot-two-in-heels height made me look younger than my twenty years. It was why I chose outfits that accentuated my decidedly-adult physique. I also made sure my hair and makeup were always pristine—well, when I wasn't digging up graves.

"Bri isn't into you," Desiree, the older of Kaira's two cousins, informed Adam bluntly.

"That's okay," Adam told her. "I'm just killing time until you get old enough to date."

Desiree rolled her eyes, but I could tell she was happy with the compliment. If she'd actually been offended, we would have been deluged by one of her rain storms.

Yutika had created all of the furniture in the house with Desiree in mind. There was a great deal of vinyl and waterproof lacquer.

It had been a strange few months living with Desiree. Not long ago, she had joined the UnAllied and almost gotten us killed. She was also the reason why Cora was now magic-less.

The rest of the Hansley clan was still working to repair what Desiree had broken. I wasn't Desiree's biggest fan, but I had to admit she seemed to be really trying to make amends. She was still moody and difficult, but she wasn't as angry as she'd been. Strangely enough, she'd been spending a lot of time with the Super Mags. Those interactions seemed to be doing more for her maturity than anything else.

Adam winked at me before going back to his conversation with the crew guys.

Just six months ago, a Nat flirting with a Mag would have been unthinkable. But that just went to show how much the city had changed in a short time. Plus, Mag or Nat aside, he had a great body.

Adam and I had fooled around…twice. The first time, we'd blamed the lackluster experience on a few too many of A.J.'s mango margaritas. After the second time, when we'd both been sober and gone a whole lot farther than just kissing, we'd accepted there was no spark between us.

Adam had been more puzzled by the revelation than I. Guys liked me, and I liked them back. The only problem was that it never went much further than that.

There was never any fire or passion. Never any of those looks that I caught Graysen and Kaira making at each other.

"What are you up to?" I asked the crew guys, as I doled out high-fives and fist-bumps.

"Oh, you know," Adam said absently. "Helping Cora study."

"Yeah right." Cora, Kaira's youngest cousin, giggled. She was sitting between two of the guys with books spread out in front of her. She was definitely studying, but the guys seemed more intent on distracting than helping.

Graysen's crew friends spent most of their weekends at the mansion. According to them, they came to help with any Alliance grunt work. And to advise the new Directors, since—as the guys liked to constantly and humorously point out—neither Kaira nor Graysen were college grads.

We all knew the real reason behind the crew guys' magnanimous presence. They came for Ma's cooking.

Ma Hansley, Kaira's mother, had taken on the challenge of cooking for everyone in the mansion. The more mouths she had to feed, the happier she was.

"How's it coming, Cora?" I asked the younger girl, giving one of her braids a playful tug.

"Not the best." She frowned at her open textbook. "I can't get my practice test scores higher than 265."

"You will," I assured her.

Cora was only thirteen, but she was determined to ace the Nat entrance exam for the Boston School of Magical Unity. After she'd been injected with the Magical Reduction Potion and lost her magic, she'd put all of her efforts into studying for the BSMU's entrance exam for Nats.

I gave Cora a one-armed hug, conscious of the dirt covering my bare arms.

I waved hello to Kaira's Grandma Tashi and Smith's father, Oliver. They were both sitting on barstools and looking at a large art book. Neither of them was especially friendly, but they both became downright chatty when they got to talking about art together. Smith thought it was weird. I thought it was sweet.

The rest of the Seven were gathered in our official meeting room…otherwise known as the family room. There were three large couches that were big and comfortable enough to sleep on, as well as several love seats that were upgrades of the bean bag chairs we'd had in our old house. A fire crackled in the grate. Old-fashioned Tiffany lamps were perched on every end table. The air also smelled like vanilla, thanks to the candles I'd bought during a recent online shopping spree. The floor-to-ceiling glass windows that looked out onto the sprawling lawn were tinted, so we could see out but no one else could see in. The glass was also bullet-proof. I could punch through it, but it would take several hits.

Yutika and Michael were cuddling together on one couch. Yutika was busy sketching something that could have been a car or a new toy for Sir Zachary—it was impossible to tell until her drawing actually turned into whatever she'd wanted it to be.

Smith was sitting on the love seat that Yutika had made especially for him. It had a built-in desk that allowed him to work on three laptops at the same time. There was even a cup holder for his cans of grape soda, which he drank like water.

Kaira and Graysen were on one of the other couches. Graysen was lying with his head in Kaira's lap as he scanned a law textbook with tiny print and way too many pages. Kaira was typing on a tablet with one hand, while idly running her fingers through Graysen's hair with the other.

"Hail the conquering warriors," Yutika said when she caught sight of us.

I pushed past my failure-laden exhaustion and offered up a grin.

A.J. kicked off his loafers and settled onto the couch next to Michael. Not wanting to get my grime all over the furniture, I just plopped on the floor.

"How'd it go?" Kaira asked, putting down her tablet and giving us her full attention.

Graysen sat up and rolled his shoulders, wincing a little. Kaira wasn't even looking in his direction, but she reached for the ibuprofen and glass of water on the table for him. His lupus was clearly acting up.

I still couldn't believe the two of them were married. It was just such a grownup thing to do. Although, compared to everything else they'd achieved, marriage seemed like less of a big deal.

"We've got a problem," I said.

That got everyone's attention. Even Smith looked up from his computers.

Quickly, I filled them in on what A.J. and I had found at the cemetery.

"Do you think it's our magic ripper?" Kaira asked.

"Or someone working for the magic ripper," Graysen added.

"Or a copycat," Smith pointed out. "Or someone totally unrelated. A gum wrapper isn't exactly enough evidence to start making arrests."

The man had a point. If I'd known whose door to bang down, I wouldn't have let the pesky problem of evidence stand in my way. I cracked my knuckles.

"Ughhh," Kaira groaned. "We were so close to getting the Super Mags to fully trust us before this MRP-wielding fool got in our way."

The Super Mags had been hanging around more since Kaira and Graysen began pushing laws that would give them equal rights in Boston. We'd lured them to the mansion with the promise of Ma's home cooking.

I'd convinced the kids to stay for the Alliance meetings that concerned them by offering cartwheel and backflip lessons.

Now, with this magic ripper on the loose, they didn't trust us to keep them safe.

"I guess this answers the question of where the thief is getting the Magical Reduction Potion," Graysen said heavily, raking a hand through his already-tousled hair.

"You think he's making it himself?" Yutika stopped drawing and stared from Graysen to me.

"Why else would he be digging up Agent S?" Smith challenged.

I was only half-listening to my friends' argument. I was thinking about the Agent S slaves.

"Maybe whoever is injecting the Super Mags with MRP knows something about the slaves," I said.

Maybe they knew something about Lilly.

The mere possibility made my pulse pick up until I couldn't sit still. I paced around the room.

"Well, as long as we're at a dead end on the magic ripper mystery," Smith said, "I figured out something about our list of Mags with missing files."

I stopped pacing.

"What?" I asked, my voice coming out a little breathy.

"Since there's no records or tracking information," Smith explained, "I did a thorough search of their family tree. Then, I built a program that compiled all of the information, and—"

"Just spit it out, Smith," Yutika said. "You're killing us with the suspense."

Smith looked at me. "Every dead Mag on that list has at least one Steel in their extended family."

My jaw went slack. I stood there stupidly as words refused to come.

Of all the things he could have said, I hadn't expected that. Steels weren't rare, but we also weren't common.

Magics' abilities weren't generally the same as their parents, but we often shared similar magic to an extended family member. My aunt on my father's side was a Steel, although she was only a Level 1. She was an iron Steel, which meant that her skin was dense and clunky…and far less strong than mine. She refused to attend family functions, since my magic overrode hers and made her powerless. My dad liked to tell me it was karma for all the times his sister had beaten him up when they were kids.

Swallowing past the lump in my throat, I said, "Lilly was a Steel, too."

My brother, Brent, had been over the moon. As a Combat Mag and an athlete, he was all about the physical magic. It had come as a surprise to the family when, five years earlier, Brent announced that he was in love with a Bleeding Heart.

Bleeding Hearts were able to sense other people's feelings and empathize as though the emotions belonged to them.

Brent was the exact opposite of gushy and emotional, so my parents and I had been skeptical…until we'd met Sarah. She was his perfect balance in every way.

As soon as they found out Lilly's magic, Brent hadn't been able to shut up about how their daughter would have his brawn and Sarah's kindness. That had been mere hours before the doctors announced that Lilly had been exposed to DAMND, the fatal disease that Mag-Nat babies supposedly carried.

Thinking about my family brought a familiar rush of guilt and regret. It had been too long since I'd called anyone in my family. It had been even longer since I'd visited.

For all my willingness to run into a burning building, I was too much of a coward to drive across town and face my family's heartbreak.

"You okay?" A.J. whispered, giving me a small nudge.

I flashed him the same smile that had gotten my cheer squad to State Finals two years in a row. "Never better."

"I'll call some people who used to work in the Magical Marking Office," Graysen said, breaking through the helpless direction of my thoughts. "See if we can get them to reach out to all the missing Mags' families. Maybe we'll learn something new."

I gave him a nod, thankful that he was focusing on useful next steps. What I needed now more than anything was answers.

"I'll help you," Kaira told Graysen, standing up and stretching. "In the meantime, the rest of you should go to bed. Busy day tomorrow."

Five hours of sleep was a luxury, and one my body was crying out for in spite of my mind's turmoil.

We moved in a pack to the elegant double-sided staircase that led to the upper floors. The mansion was three stories, with more than enough bedrooms to accommodate all of us.

Sir Zachary, sensing that it was bedtime, skidded around the corner and leapt into A.J.'s waiting arms.

"Time to get you into your jammies," A.J. told the dog, who licked his face.

A.J. blew us a kiss as he turned off to the master bedroom on the second floor.

Since the master bedroom had been Remwald's, none of us had wanted to take it…except A.J. According to A.J., it wasn't the room's fault that a nasty man used to sleep there.

My bedroom was at the far end of the third floor. I'd decorated it with photos of the Seven and my family in happier times. Yutika had created a shelf for my old wrestling and cheerleading trophies.

I had started a cork board for all of the clues about the Agent S slaves, but it had looked too pathetic with just a few notes tacked onto it. So, I'd put the cork board in the back of my closet…out of sight, but never out of mind.

My desk was covered with job applications for Kaira and Graysen's security detail. There were also barely-legible notes from Smith that he thought were too sensitive to put in an email. I had passwords for high-security clearances on sticky notes that I kept telling myself I needed to memorize before Smith found them and had an actual cow.

My bed, with its satin sheets and teal comforter, beckoned to me.

"Just need a quick shower, and then I'm all yours," I said, giving the softer-than-clouds mattress an affectionate pat.

The best part about my bed was that it no longer shared a wall with Kaira's. I was over the moon for Kaira and Graysen, but I didn't miss hearing their twice- and sometimes three-times-a-night sexcapades.

There had been a few-week overlap between Graysen and Kaira getting back together and our house being destroyed. During that time, the poor insulation between our rooms had served as a nightly reminder of what I was missing. It wasn't their endless love that I wanted for myself. I envied their passion.

As I showered and got ready for bed, I thought about how it was probably good that I had so little free time. Me, plus free time, was a recipe for trouble.

CHAPTER 5

I lurched out of bed at 5:00AM on the dot, just as my screeching alarm filled the room.

There was a *tap tap tap* on my window. The woodpecker who had visited me every morning since we moved in was standing on my ledge. Most of the time I enjoyed our morning ritual, except on the rare weekend when I wanted to sleep in.

"'Morning Herbert," I said through a yawn.

The name had just seemed right for the little bird. No idea why.

Herbert gave my window another tap and flew off.

I put on the outfit I'd laid out the night before. Tailored slacks, a playful-but-professional peach blouse, and a fitted blazer.

Most people looked at my petite figure and saw nothing but the cheerleader I'd been in high school.

The gleeful little devil inside me loved that moment when someone realized just how powerful I was…usually when they were about to be on the receiving end of my fists.

I straightened my wavy blonde hair and then curled the ends. Pearl stud earrings, a quick swipe of coral lipstick, and an extra coat of glittery gold nail polish completed the look. Because even heads of security needed to have a little fun.

As usual, I was the first one downstairs. Ma wasn't in the kitchen, but the table was set for breakfast. There were bowls with fresh berries, platters with melon slices, and a bowl full of clementines. There was also a coffee cake, homemade donuts, bagels, and a note from Ma directing us to the metal warming dishes on the counter. Each one of the serving dishes was labeled, like we were in a five-star restaurant. There was a tofu scramble with vegan sausage, as well as eggs benedict for the non-vegan crowd.

I grabbed an apple and vegan cinnamon donut and headed for my office.

I suppressed a groan at the stack of mail that A.J. had left for me. As the new Directors' self-appointed lead strategist, publicist, and fashion consultant, A.J. had the most eclectic job title of the Seven. One of his responsibilities was going through the new Directors' mail and flagging any potential threats for me and Smith to follow up on. There were little sticky notes attached to each of the open letters. A.J.'s flawless cursive noted things like "See paragraph 2. Also please observe the unibrow in self-enclosed photo. Can we expense a complimentary home-waxing kit to send?"

In spite of A.J.'s flippant notes, I had seen his face after going through our friends' hate mail. I got the sense that the prejudice Kaira and Graysen faced for their untraditional marriage hit a little too close to home for A.J. When I'd offered to take over the task for him, A.J. had just waved me off and told me to stop being a mother hen.

I heard the tinkling of dog tags, and then my faithful second-in-command came trotting down the stairs.

"Morning, Sir Zachary."

Our little dog wagged his tail so ferociously his butt wiggled. He was wearing a dog-sized Red Sox jersey and already had his bedazzled collar in his mouth. I put on his collar, and together, we headed outside.

Sir Zachary took care of his dog business and chased birds, while I checked in with the security guards stationed all around our extensive property.

While we walked, I sent out a message over the group chat I had with the Directors' personal security team. This afternoon, Graysen and Kaira would be throwing out the ceremonial first pitch for the final Red Sox game of the season. The Red Sox, which was the only mixed Mag-Nat baseball team in the country, was playing an undefeated all-Mag team from Orlando.

Not even the Slaughters could defeat America's oldest pastime.

All the seats in the stadium were sold out, and I was getting anxiety at the thought of all those people and possible threats. Even though most Bostonians loved Kaira and Graysen, my friends had their share of enemies just like any leaders who were trying to do something revolutionary.

They'd overturned the second high law in the city of Boston, which had caused quite a stir country-wide. Some territory rulers were following our lead and allowing Mags to take out their trackers. Most of the Nat-run territories were threatened by the shift, and the US government was sending out the Enforcers in droves to put down the unrest.

After we'd publicly humiliated the US government with the Boston Enforcement Party scandal, they'd kept far clear of Boston.

I was halfway through my donut and email inbox when A.J. popped his head into my office.

"Looking good, button. Photo op with the Globe on the lawn in five."

He was gone again before I could reply.

"And freshen up your lipstick," A.J. called over his shoulder. "It looks better on your pouty lips than on that better-be-vegan donut!"

I stuck my tongue out at him, even though he was already gone.

Muttering a few choice curses, I did as A.J. had commanded. I checked to make sure there wasn't anything in my teeth and went to the appointed meeting, typing out email replies on the way.

"And where are Smith and Michael?" A.J. demanded as a dozen people with cameras tramped onto the lawn.

"What I don't get is why you're surprised," Yutika told A.J.

It was true. Whenever the press arrived, Smith and Michael disappeared. I imagined the two of them hunkering down in some underground tunnel they'd build to escape from the media attention.

Becoming public figures was a drastic change for all of us. I'd spent the last three years unMarked, which meant I'd had to avoid any kind of attention that might get me caught. It was a complete reversal to be constantly in the public eye.

While it was mildly uncomfortable for all of us except Graysen, who seemed to have endless patience for interviews and meet-and-greets, it was downright torture for Smith and Michael.

I noticed a cameraman loitering on the edge of the crowd who wasn't clicking away with his camera. He also kept looking in Yutika's direction. I was about to go full titanium bodyguard when Kaira caught my eye and winked. She mouthed *Michael.* I instantly relaxed.

I gave her a subtle thumbs-up and smiled for the cameras that were flashing spastically all around us. I answered a few questions about the Pyro's recent stunt with the retirement home, giving the polite-yet-vague answers I'd discussed with Kaira and Graysen.

I stepped back, keeping a hawk's eye on the Directors as they were grilled by the reporters.

"Ms. Hansley, how does it feel to be the youngest Director ever?" a breathless reporter asked.

Kaira lifted a shoulder. "You'll have to ask my husband." She turned to smile at Graysen.

"You're younger?" Yutika asked Graysen, sounding intrigued.

"I'm the one conducting this interview, if you don't mind," the reporter said in a haughty voice.

"By almost a year," Graysen told Yutika.

"Ohmygosh, Kaira." Yutika giggled. "You're a cradle robber."

I didn't hear the rest of their conversation. My phone chimed, and when I glanced down at the screen, my blood ran cold. It was a text from Smith.

911.

"Seven," I said in a calm voice, even though my thoughts were racing a million miles ahead. "Get back into the house. There's an important call for Kaira and Graysen."

It was our secret code for *get the hell inside NOW* without stirring up the hornet's nest of reporters.

Michael turned his unblinking gaze on the group of reporters, who were circling Kaira and Graysen like vultures.

"Leave," he said in a soft voice. "You got everything you needed for your interview, and you don't remember anything going wrong."

Nodding in placid acquiescence, the reporters packed up their equipment and headed back to their vehicles.

I started power-walking across the lawn as another text came through.

Intruder climbing the East Gate. Armed with a handgun and an axe.

Kicking off my heels, I began to run.

I blew on my fists. Strength coursed through my hands and ran down my forearms.

I'd heard others describe their magic as a rising heat within them. For me, it was the opposite. Cool power washed over my skin as flimsy flesh and bones were replaced by smooth metal. When I was titanium, I didn't have to second-guess myself. Every other substance crumpled and shattered when it came up against me. I felt invincible.

I tasted metal on my tongue. Its sharp tang filled my nostrils. Calm spread through me as I felt the steady, even thrum of my magic.

I was silent as I raced across the property. Even though I was sprinting, my heartbeat was slow and even. My muscles were relaxed. I was solid metal, but I felt as loose and flexible as a rubber band.

I was never more alive than when I was titanium.

Ping. Ping, ping, ping.

A bullet, and then three more, struck my chest.

The shooter had good aim. The bullets struck the spot right over my heart…and bounced off. I smiled.

The woman—a Combat Mag, if the muscles bulging from her bare arms were any indication—leapt off the top of the fence. She held out her axe as she threw her considerable weight at me.

I let her come.

There was a sharp clang as the axe blade struck my skin and shattered. Tiny slivers of the blade repelled backward, away from my unmarked skin.

The Combat Mag hissed in a breath as one of the shards sliced her forearm. Blood bloomed across her pale skin.

Steel…1. Combat Mag…0.

With a feral screech, the Combat Mag pulled back and punched me in the face. She howled as the bones in her fist cracked.

I was bored. This woman was like a hammer, while I was a tank.

"Are you finished?" I asked.

"You're protecting abominations," the Combat Mag panted. "They'll pollute this city with their devil spawn."

She pulled a knife out of her boot and stabbed me. The blade broke off against my jugular.

"I don't like when people trespass onto my property," I said, wrenching the woman's arms behind her back. "And I *really* don't like bullies."

The Combat Mag's eyes watered. I gentled my hold…just a little.

When I was younger, I'd needed to learn how to hold myself back so I didn't accidentally kill anyone. I was never more aware of how dangerous my magic could be until Subject 6 had taken over my mind and made me almost murder my friends.

That memory still haunted me, and made me gentler with this trespasser than I might have been otherwise.

"Okay?" Michael asked, breathing a little hard after his sprint from the house.

"Oh, yeah." I patted the Combat Mag's shoulder, making her wince and curse. "She's all yours."

Sadly, we had this routine down pat. I texted my person in the Mag unit of the Boston Police Department, while Michael hunched down to stare into the Combat Mag's eyes.

"You will never come back here," Michael said in a soft and unyielding voice.

"I hate them," the woman told Michael, giving him puppy dog eyes.

Michael pointed to the security booth nearest to us. To the Combat Mag, he said, "Go stand over there. Don't move until the police pick you up."

Like me, I knew Michael was holding himself back. He could turn this woman into Kaira and Graysen's biggest fan with just a few words.

Using our magic to take advantage of those who were weaker went against a core tenant of Kaira and Graysen's administration. So, we stuck by our faithful motto of *Legal, but with a twist.*

With a longing look in Michael's direction, the Combat Mag started her walk of shame to the security booth.

I sent a text out to the Seven as we walked, letting them know the coast was clear. Smith met Michael and me as we headed toward the house.

"It's time to rethink this Red Sox game," Smith said irritably. He glared at me, like the whole thing was my fault. "There's no way we'll be able to monitor the entire baseball field. You need to convince Kaira and Graysen to just say what they need to say from the house."

"Kaira and Graysen do have to go out in public occasionally," I told our Techie, bending to give Sir Zachary a pat when he delivered one of my shoes, now covered in slobber, to me.

"I could replace them with holograms that'll be so convincing no one will know the difference," Smith suggested.

"Holograms can't throw out the ceremonial first pitch," I pointed out.

"Well, maybe Yutika could make robots that look like Kaira and Graysen. And then—"

I gave Michael a *help me* look.

"You know Kaira," Michael told Smith, interrupting his monologue. "She's going to go out with or without our permission. At least this way, she tells us her plans so we can prepare."

"Fine." Smith pointed a finger at both of us. "But when this baseball game turns into a stampede and all of you get trampled, don't come complaining to me."

Noted.

I blew on my fists to pull the magic back from my skin. My blood was pumping, but in a good way. I loved my job. It made me feel competent and capable…the exact opposite of how I felt whenever I thought about my failure to find out what had really happened to Lilly and the others.

⁎ ⁎ ⁎

My security team was already waiting for me inside the gate Yutika had created when we moved in. I'd hand-picked these men and women from an array of the best private contractors in the world, whom Smith had tracked down and convinced to come to Boston. They were all wearing Red Sox gear, but the casual clothes wouldn't fool anyone. These were professionals. I got curt nods before my team went back to sweeping our vehicles and pouring over the printouts of Fenway Park.

"Anyone have any questions?" I asked, as Yutika came onto the driveway with an armful of headsets and mikes.

Given how drastically our job descriptions had changed over the last five months, surprisingly little about our operations had changed.

"Well, don't I feel popular?" Graysen grinned at the congregation of security personnel as he and Kaira came out of the house.

"Don't let it go to your head," Kaira told him as we all piled into the fleet of vehicles Yutika had made for us.

Kaira was stunning in a Red Sox-themed dress ensemble. She'd been growing her hair out, and her twists reached halfway down her back.

On the drive to Fenway Park, we all joked and chatted the way we always did. We put in our earpieces and clipped mikes onto our lapels so we'd all be able to stay in contact even when we were separated.

It was only when we neared the baseball field that my anxiety began to spike.

This was the largest and least-protected venue we'd attended since Kaira and Graysen's election. The Combat Mag's attack on our house had made me more squirrely than usual, or maybe Smith's paranoia was rubbing off on me. Either way, I was overcome by a rush of foreboding. There were too many people…too many ways for all of this to go wrong.

I looked at the people outside the tinted windows. All of their smiles seemed sinister. Their hands reached into pockets that might be hiding any number of weapons.

Smith's holograph idea was sounding better and better.

I opened my mouth to make that very argument a second too late. Graysen had opened the door and stepped onto the street. He was waving and saying something to the crowd that was pressed up against laughably flimsy police barriers. Seconds later, Kaira was at his side, leaning across the barrier to sign a kid's baseball cap.

"Nice knowing you," Smith said morosely.

Swallowing my growing sense of unease, I flipped on my mike and got out of the car.

CHAPTER 6

I stood at the edge of the field, my heels sinking into the soft grass as I scanned the area for threats.

"Kaira and I are so grateful to be Bostonians," Graysen said into the microphone. He raised his and Kaira's clasped hands. "None of what we've accomplished would have been possible without all of you."

"And we're just getting started," Kaira added.

Thunderous applause filled the stadium.

"You guys are killing it," Yutika said into our earpieces.

"Turn a little to your left," A.J. ordered. "And give the cameras a G-rated smooch."

"I assume that was to Kaira and Graysen," I said, grinning at the blushing security guard standing next to me.

"I thought it was for me," Yutika said. "Michael, get over here."

"Like you'd ever keep it G-rated," Smith said.

"Can we focus?" Michael asked in a gruff voice.

I split my attention between Graysen and Kaira, the chatter in my earpiece, and the surrounding crowd. The stadium could hold 37,755 people, and I was sure there wasn't an empty seat in the place.

"Minor issue in the bleachers," Michael said in my ear. "It's been taken care of."

"Drug deal going down behind the Green Monster," a member of my security team said. "Want me to deal with it?"

"Not unless it becomes a threat to Kaira and Graysen," I replied to the woman, who had been a consultant to the Mag cops' narcos unit before we'd snagged her.

"Roger that," she replied.

Everything seemed to be going smoothly. Kaira and Graysen had reminded the entire city of why they were the best pair to lead us into a new, better future. They were getting laughter and cheers as they good-naturedly teased each other. They even managed to sneak in a few previews of the new laws they'd been working on.

In spite of all the Alliance red tape Kaira constantly complained about, she and Graysen had brought about more changes in the last few months than any of the previous Directors had during their entire tenure.

The two of them walked to the pitcher's mound hand-in-hand. Graysen stole a kiss just before the ball left their joined hands. The crowd erupted in cheers.

The kiss cam overhead was featuring Nat-Mag couples who, thanks to Kaira and Graysen, no longer needed to hide their relationships.

Kaira and Graysen came to join me at the edge of the field as the game got underway. My security team moved in, not blocking them from view, but there as a silent warning.

If you want to get to the Directors, you'll have to go through us.

There was a deafening roar as the first home run was scored. The screens told me it had been by one of the Mag players on our team.

Nice.

Using the binoculars Yutika had made for me, I scanned back and forth across the bleachers. All at once, my gaze caught on movement in the crowd that didn't match the cheering and peanut-throwing madness of everyone else.

"Michael, right field box," I said into my mike. "Actually, change that. They're coming onto the field."

I watched the group shove their way past police and other park employees. Even without binoculars, it would have been impossible to miss the voluminous red hair and lime-green mumu dress.

Valencia Stark.

"Cheat-ah!" Valencia hollered in her obnoxious Boston accent. She pointed at the Mag player's name flashing on the scoreboard. "Cheat-ah!"

"Oh, wonderful," Kaira said, rolling her eyes.

Graysen moved protectively in front of her as his friendly gaze turned predatory.

"Stay here," I ordered both of them.

I blew on my fists and strode out to meet Valencia. Unsurprisingly, Kaira and Graysen were right there with me.

All Seven of us had a penchant for running headlong into danger, and becoming Directors hadn't made Kaira and Graysen any more concerned with their own safety. Their heroics gave the twitchier members of my security team—Smith and me included—constant ulcers.

The only reason I wasn't hauling my friends' asses back to the van was because Valencia was no longer a true threat.

Right before Kaira and Graysen's wedding, we'd tricked the Enforcers and UnAllied into facing off against each other. One of the Enforcers had injected Valencia with the MRP. In one fell swoop, Valencia had lost her magic and leadership over the UnAllied…a group that hated Nats. The UnAllied had disbanded after Kaira became the first Mag Director.

For several, blessedly-peaceful weeks, Valencia had disappeared from the spotlight. And then she'd reemerged…no longer anti-Nat. Now, she was anti-Mag.

She had a few followers, but mostly, the only ones who paid attention to her were comedians and sub-par talk show hosts.

Valencia and her small group were chanting something. As we got closer, their words crystalized.

"Keep Boston Natural. Keep Boston Natural. Keep Boston Natural!"

Graysen made a sound of annoyance.

"Valencia Stark," Graysen called in a clear voice. "Don't you have anything better to do with your time than to interrupt a baseball game?"

I tensed as she reached into her pocket. But instead of drawing out a weapon, she produced a megaphone.

"Baseball is for humans," Valencia shouted into her megaphone. "And Mags aren't human!"

Booing and jeers filled the stadium. The few isolated pockets of applause were quickly silenced.

If the crowd started throwing beer down at Valencia and my outfit got ruined, this lady was going to have hell to pay.

"Director Gald-ah," Valencia said into the megaphone, a little out of breath from all her chanting. "I'm here on behalf of the Nat Preservation Association."

Yutika turned her guffaw into a barely-concealed cough. I didn't look at her, because if I did, we'd both lose it.

I glanced at Kaira and Graysen to see if they wanted me to toss Valencia off the field…literally. Kaira gave me a subtle shake of her head. So, I stayed where I was and exchanged glares with the Nats flanking Valencia.

"None of them is a significant threat," Smith said in my ear. "All of these degenerates have been in and out of prison for petty crimes."

I kept my eyes glued on Valencia. Just because Kaira and Graysen were all about freedom of expression, it wouldn't stop me from tackling her if she tried anything more than talking.

"The Nat Preservation Association," Graysen said in an amused voice. "I'm not familiar."

"We're fighting for Nat rights," Valencia said into her megaphone. "As you might remember, I used to be a Mag." Valencia made a dramatic show of shuddering. "I know how evil and corrupt magic is."

"Oh brother," A.J. groaned.

"Director Gald-ah, as Nats, we are connected on a deep level," Valencia persisted. "We have to stick together for the sake of all Nat-kind."

"Is she hitting on Graysen?" Yutika asked.

Kaira balled her hands into fists. "Have you forgotten that you put a ten-thousand-dollar price on my husband's head a few months ago?" she asked Valencia in an icy tone.

Valencia's upper lip curled in the perfect imitation of a snarl.

"You are nothing," Valencia told Kaira. "And Gald-ah will realize that soon enough."

"Kaira and I believe in equal rights for Magics and Naturals," Graysen said in a calm voice that was the perfect palate-cleanser to Valencia's crazy. "We have been clear—"

"We're called *Naturals* for a reason," Valencia interrupted. She tipped her head back to stare up into the filled bleachers. "I'm offering a reward for anyone who can get me enough Magical Reduction Potion to inject every Mag and Super Mag in the city."

And that was why we were destroying all the Agent S. No one had the right to take away someone else's magic.

Valencia continued, "Then, we'll all be equal. Then, Boston will be the way it was meant to be…Natural!"

There wasn't time for Graysen or Kaira to respond, or for the rest of us to react. A repeated popping sound filled the air. And then, out of nowhere, more people began to appear on the field.

"Super Mags," Smith shouted in my ear. "The Super Mags are here. Get the hell out!"

I saw one of the Super Mags point a finger in Valencia's direction. Lightning shot from his fingertip.

Valencia dove to the side. The jagged lightning bolt hit the ground, turning the grass black. The ground sizzled and smoked.

Valencia's people threw themselves at the Super Mags. Because they were idiots. No Nat could go up against a Super Mag and expect to win.

"Get the Directors out of here," I ordered my people, who were already surrounding Kaira and Graysen and herding them off the field.

I stayed where I was, making sure no one tried to come after the Directors.

"Stop saying magic is bad," a Super Mag told the group of Nats. He was at that awkward age where his voice was just starting to change, and it squeaked. The Nats laughed.

"I mean it!" The boy's face reddened. He started to close the distance between himself and the Nats.

I tensed but continued to use my body as a barrier between the Directors and anyone who might try to come after them.

"D-don't come any closer, freaks," one of the Nats told the Super Mags. He raised his hand to reveal a hunting knife.

"Are you insane?!" I shouted, but no one was listening to me.

I started forward, but I was too late. The Nat flicked his wrist in a quick, practiced move that I wouldn't have expected out of him. The Super Mag boy he was facing off with cried out.

The boy had turned just in time for the knife to miss his heart. It looked like it had sunk between his ribs, instead.

Relief that he was still alive quickly transformed to rage. That Nat had just attacked a kid. *What the fuck?!*

One of the Super Mag kids, who was wearing a daisy-patterned sundress, made a sound that could only be described as a war cry. She charged at the Nat who had thrown the knife. Just before they collided, the little girl twisted her hand.

The Nat's head snapped back so fast and so far that his chin was pointing up at the sky. And then he crumpled to the ground. His open, unseeing eyes fixed on the grass.

My mouth fell open in a silent scream.

"Oh my God," Yutika gasped.

Everyone was shouting. The ground thundered as thousands of people fled the stadium.

"Exits are all blocked by the crowd," one of my people said in my earpiece. "We'll have to get the Directors out a different way."

"Get them back here," I said into my mike. "Now."

Damnit. I should have made Kaira and Graysen leave the second Valencia showed her face.

"I'm on it," A.J. replied.

"Hey, what the—" Smith's surprised voice filled my ear.

Seconds later, our van was appearing…from the air. I squinted into the sunlight as the van drifted down like a metallic bird.

"Easy does it," Smith complained. "I'm getting sea sick in here."

"Complain, complain, complain." A.J. wiggled one of his hands, and the van did a pirouette in mid-air.

"A.J.!"

"Whoopsie." A.J. chortled in delight before bringing the van to a soft landing right onto the baseball field.

"No," Kaira said, fighting against Graysen, who was holding her in a bear hug to keep her from charging into the fight. From the looks of it, Graysen wanted nothing more than to do the very thing he was preventing Kaira from doing. "We have to help. We have to—"

"You go home and start figuring out how to undo this damage," I said, having to yell to be heard over the panicking crowd.

Kaira's gaze hardened, and I knew she was about to argue. The rest of her security detail knew it, too. They all closed around her and Graysen.

"Get in that van right now, or I'll toss you in," I told my friends.

Graysen put up his hands in surrender and got into the van, pulling Kaira in with him.

"Don't jostle my equipment," Smith snapped before the van door slid closed.

"Get them out of here," I told A.J., just as Valencia disentangled herself from the brawl and stumbled toward us.

The van lifted straight into the air. Muffled cries came from my friends inside the van. Within seconds, the vehicle was lost in the gray-blue clouds swirling overhead.

"A and B teams," I said into my mike. "Meet Kaira and Graysen back at the mansion. Make sure they stay put."

With my primary concern alleviated, I turned my attention on the disaster playing out in front of me.

"I'm stuck in the crowd," Michael said over my earpiece. "It's going to take me a few minutes to get down there."

"By all means, take your time," Smith said. "I'm sure nothing too disastrous will happen in the meantime."

"Be nice," Yutika told Smith. "You're just kicking back and relaxing in the van."

Smith's affronted response was cut off by a Nat's howl as she went hurtling through the air. I winced as she slammed against the Green Monster and fell back to the ground.

The Teleporter Super Mag—who was the one who'd gotten all of them to the baseball field in the first place—was transporting him and his friends in and out of the fight. They kept winking out of existence and reappearing elsewhere to tangle with Valencia's Nats. Just watching them was making me dizzy.

Valencia was shrieking at the top of her lungs, but aside from the piercing sound of her voice, she didn't have any defense against the Super Mags. There were already three dead Nats lying on the field.

Double shit.

I stopped gawking like an idiot and ran into the fight.

The Super Mags' power swirled around me in an intoxicating and terrible wave of heat. If I'd been in regular skin instead of titanium, I would have been drenched in sweat.

Their magic roiled in the air. It felt unstable and alluring at the same time.

"This isn't your fight," a ten-year-old girl with pigtails told me. Right before she held her palm against one of the Nats' faces. Her hand became translucent blue. The Nat screamed as his skin turned to ice and cracked beneath the girl's palm.

I dove for them, knocking them apart.

The little girl tried her skin-freezing trick on me, but I felt nothing. Her brow furrowed, like it had never occurred to her that she might meet her match. Before she could try her luck on someone else with actual skin, I thumped my fist on the side of her head. Not hard enough to smash her skull, but enough to give her a nice, long nap.

I tackled another kid to the ground. This boy couldn't have been older than ten, and he was drawing extra-long needles out of thin air and sticking a Nat full of them. The screaming, writhing Nat looked like a porcupine.

There were a few dull clinks as stray needles shattered on impact with my skin. The Super Mag took offense at my imperviousness to his magic. He screeched in rage, and then all of his needles were coming at me.

Clink. Clink clink clink clink.

What was left of the kid's needles shot straight into the air as A.J. joined the fight. While the Super Mag was distracted by the loss of his weapons, I tackled him. He fell to the ground like a sack of potatoes.

I wasn't a violent person by nature, but I also didn't lose sleep over other people hurting themselves on my skin. I didn't start fights if I could help it, but I did end them.

"Knock it off!" I shouted at the enraged, deadly children.

Predictably, they ignored me.

The lightning bolt boy was next. Purple electricity shivered up and down his bare arms and even cut down the center of his pupils. I would have been more impressed if he wasn't looking at me like he planned to fry me alive.

"Bring it, little man."

A lion sprinted past me. It roared and bared its teeth at the other Super Mags.

"Thanks," I told the Animalist.

The lion licked my arm with the biggest, stickiest tongue I'd ever encountered. It regarded me with bright gold eyes. And then it bounded back into the fray.

"Stop fighting."

I heard Michael's soft command in my ear. It never should have carried over the melee surrounding us, and yet, the Super Mags and Nats went still.

Eight dead Nats lay sprawled on the ground. Valencia wasn't one of them.

"You devils," Valencia croaked, getting to her hands and knees. "Barbarians…heathens! Nats will wipe you off the face of the earth!"

I strode up to Valencia.

With her runny makeup and billowing mumu, she looked far more barbarian than anyone else on the field.

"You piece of shit," I told her.

Today had been about Kaira and Graysen's efforts to make Boston a better, more inclusive home for all of us. Valencia had turned it into a senseless brawl that left eight people dead.

Not only would this whole disaster encourage the few lowlives who wanted war between Mags and Nats, it would spike fear in citizens who were just starting to trust their new leaders. The damage Valencia had done today might be irreparable.

Furious tears pricked at my eyes.

"I should kill you," I told the Mag-turned-Nat.

But if I did, it would reflect on Kaira and Graysen. As much as Valencia deserved to die, I didn't have the right to play the role of executioner.

"Go ahead," Valencia snarled, bending to stick her overly-large nose in my face. "It's just like you Mags to use your deviant powers to take advantage of us poor Nats."

It irked me beyond reason that she was taller than me.

"You were a Mag until four months ago," Yutika told Valencia, throwing up her hands in exasperation.

"You Mags are all the same," Valencia said, ignoring Yutika's comment. "You think you're better, stronger, and smarter than us. The truth is you're unnatural. *Wrong.*"

I gave Valencia my best impression of a crocodile smile. I blew on my fists so my skin lost its titanium sheen. And then, I punched her in the face.

A.J. and Yutika didn't bother stifling their laughter as Valencia dropped like a ton of bricks.

"There you go," I told Valencia as she wiped blood from her lip. "One-hundred-percent *natural* strength. Want me to do it again?"

I cracked my knuckles for effect.

While I had been born with the ability to make my body titanium, my reflexes and conditioning had come from training. My dad had helped me learn how to use my titanium skin to its full advantage. He was also the reason why I'd been the top Mag wrestler in the city during high school. I'd been the only female on my high school's team, and I'd gotten no end of pleasure at seeing the smirks on my opponents' faces when they first caught sight of me.

They were never smirking after we fought.

"Here's what's going to happen," I told Valencia and the mud-spattered and broken Nats who were staggering to their feet. "You're going to drive yourselves to the nearest Nat police station and turn yourselves in."

Technically, she was their jurisdiction now. I didn't want to cause any problems between the Directors and the cops by stepping on toes.

Valencia gave me a petulant look, flinching a little when I raised my arm to adjust my sleeve.

"You heard her," Michael said, narrowing his gaze on the Nats. "Except, instead of going to the nearest police station, you're going to go to the farthest. And you're going to walk."

Yutika nudged Michael in the ribs. "Let no one say Michael is completely humorless."

His mouth twitched in the approximation of a smile.

Without a moment's hesitation, Valencia and her remaining Nats began tromping across the field to do as Michael had said.

"What do we do about them?" Yutika asked, nodding at the Super Mags.

With the way they were placidly staring at Michael, I was almost fooled into thinking they were just a group of kids. *Almost.*

"Kaira and Graysen are going to want to talk to them," Michael said.

"That's a great idea." Yutika rolled her eyes. "Bring home a bunch of murderous, hormonal Super Mags. Ma will make a casserole, and then they'll kill us in our sleep."

I wasn't any happier about the prospect than Yutika. We'd gotten the upper hand on them because they'd been focused on the Nats. And because there were only ten of them here right now instead of the grand total of forty-seven.

The Super Mags were just too powerful.

As hard as Kaira and Graysen had worked to convince Boston society to accept them, the Super Mags had no interest in becoming law-abiding citizens. They needed a leader—one of their own to look up to. The problem was that the oldest of them was fourteen, and the Super Mags already had a lifetime of learning not to trust adults.

Kaira and Graysen were convinced that the Super Mags would come around. I wasn't so sure.

"I can Whisper to them," Michael told me with his usual quiet confidence, "since none of their magic is mental like mine."

In the three years we'd lived and worked together, I'd only seen Michael lose control once…when one of Valencia's people had held a gun to Yutika's head.

"I'll make a bus to get them back," Yutika offered, flipping to a blank page in her sketchbook.

A minute later, the Super Mags were filing onto the bus.

"Don't worry," Yutika assured me. "I can draw them some toys and snacks to butter them up before Kaira and Graysen read them the riot act."

The way she was talking, it was like we were about to chastise these kids for being naughty on the playground. The eight corpses on the baseball field told a different story.

As relaxed as she sounded, Yutika's hand visibly shook as she began to sketch. I noticed the way her gaze kept straying from her drawing to the bodies on the ground.

I wasn't particularly squeamish, but I still kept my gaze averted as I climbed onto the bus behind Michael. My clothes were splattered with mud, and I felt the kind of weariness that usually only came as I was dragging myself to bed.

And if the flurry of emails marked *Urgent!* in my inbox was any indication, my day was just getting started.

CHAPTER 7

It was late. My eyes were bleary from how long I'd been awake and on my feet. My stomach was growling. And I was in such desperate need of a shower that even Sir Zachary didn't want to come near me. I was just working up the energy to haul my butt up the two flights of stairs to my room, when Smith intercepted me.

He sniffed the air and wrinkled his nose.

"Oh, not you too," I warned him.

"We need to talk," Smith replied, taking a step back.

"I'm showering right now, okay?" I threw up my hands. "No need to stage an intervention."

Not that Smith was exactly the standard for hygiene, with his oily hair and three-day-old hoodie.

"What? No." Smith tapped the closed laptop he was cradling like a baby. "I have a lead."

"On the magic ripper?" I asked cautiously, not daring to hope that he might be referring to the other mystery far nearer to my heart.

Smith shook his head. "On the missing slaves."

My breath caught. I grabbed Smith's arm and practically dragged him back to the living room, where the rest of the Seven were gathered.

"Bri Hammond," A.J. whined. "You're still covered in dirt."

"I found someone who might be able to help us track down the slaves," Smith said, coming to my rescue.

Everyone sat up from their slouched positions at that.

"Talk," Kaira told Smith.

"Okay, so there's this blog I follow. It isn't exactly pro-Alliance." His gaze slid to Kaira and Graysen before he continued. "It's actually super anti-establishment, and you need to break a special code to even read it. It's kind of fun—"

"Smith!" Six exasperated voices said at once.

"Right." Smith cleared his throat. "Out of the blue, the blogger messaged me and said she had information about the location I needed."

I started. "The location?"

Could this blogger be referring to *the* location? If so, it was the piece of the puzzle the now-deceased interim Director, Dr. Pruwist, had taken to his grave. It was the last detail we needed to solve this stone-cold case. Anticipation shivered through me.

"I mean, we'll have to take whatever she says with a whole barrel full of salt." Smith's expression darkened. "She's a Clairvoyant."

"What's wrong with Clairvoyants?" Yutika asked.

"Aside from the fact that they couldn't give a straight answer if their lives depended on it?" Smith retorted.

"We need to go talk to her," I said. I didn't care what her magic was, just as long as she could give us the information we needed.

Except....

"Don't worry about the Super Mags," Kaira told me, already knowing what I was thinking. "Gray and I will deal with them when they wake up. The rest of you need to go see this Clairvoyant."

I wanted to argue. As their Security Chief, it was my job to *not* leave the two most important people in the city alone with a bunch of Super Mags. The ten kids we'd brought back from the baseball game were in the mansion now. They were sleeping off the effects of Michael's Whispering in various guest rooms in the mansion. But if they woke up before the rest of us got back and started tearing the place apart....

"Becoming Directors hasn't made us completely useless," Graysen said, giving me an amused look. "We've got this."

"I'll stay here," Michael said. "Just in case."

"Fine," Kaira conceded. "But the rest of you. *Go.*"

Having lost the small amount of willpower I had to argue, I nodded.

"Everyone meet at the van in ten," A.J. said before narrowing his gaze on me. "We've waited four months for answers. We don't want to scare this Clairvoyant away with the fierce and terrifying Mud Girl before she tells us what we need to know."

"That's Mud *Woman* to you," I retorted, already sprinting for the stairs.

* * *

Since it was close to midnight, we had no trouble finding a parking spot right outside the narrow brick building where the Clairvoyant had told Smith to meet her. We were on Newbury Street, which was full of high-end shops that were clogged with people during normal hours. Now, though, all the stores were closed and the street was quiet.

"Did you tell this Clairvoyant that we'd be dropping in after hours?" A.J. asked, as Yutika hung her freshly-created handicapped tag from the van's mirror.

We'd learned the hard way that being the new Directors' BFFs didn't exempt us from parking tickets. We probably should have felt guilty using Yutika's magic this way, but none of us claimed to be saints.

"We didn't discuss times," Smith replied.

"Do you at least have a phone number to call when this place turns out to be locked?" I asked as we climbed the short flight of stairs to the door. The windows were tinted, so it was impossible to tell if there were any lights on inside.

"Do you really think someone whose username is WorldEnds2070 is going to have a cell phone?" Smith asked, rolling his eyes at my apparently ridiculous question.

"Let's just hope her username isn't a premonition," A.J. pointed out, "and that she's simply an optimist like you."

"What's your username?" Yutika asked Smith.

He pointedly ignored the question as he tried the doorknob. Surprise and relief filled me when it gave. All four of us—four-and-a-half, including Sir Zachary—entered the building.

"Holy crap," Smith muttered.

It looked like a voodoo shop and one of those fake magic stores had gotten together and then barfed up their insides. Every inch of space was covered in stuff. There was a narrow, foot-wide path through the store. If I balanced carefully, I could avoid brushing up against anything.

The air was so full of incense it looked like a fog machine had been turned on. Strands of beads hung from the ceiling, and tribal masks hung on the walls. Glass cases were stuffed full of skulls, books about the occult sciences, and decks of tarot cards.

Burning candles balanced precariously on top of wooden figurines and dangled from iron holders nailed to the wooden wall.

"The Boston Fire Department would have a collective heart attack if they saw this place," A.J. said.

My hopes for getting useful information were fast dwindling. Anyone who owned a place like this had to be a real nut.

Sir Zachary sniffed everything, his tail wagging as he explored. He made cute little lapping noises as he drank from a bowl with a painted paw print that seemed like it had been recently filled.

"I can already tell this is going to be a waste of time," Smith muttered, echoing my thoughts.

"Isn't the owner worried about people stealing stuff?" Yutika asked. She petted a feather boa hanging around an Alaskan totem pole. "I mean, anyone could walk in here."

"But I knew they wouldn't," a soft, feminine voice said from the back of the shop.

We all went still.

"Except for the four of you, of course…well, five, if you include your dog."

"We do," A.J. said. "We definitely do."

Tinkling laughter came from the girl who emerged from the incense fog.

At first, I thought she was a teenager. She was shorter and thinner than me and didn't have much in the way of curves. But when I caught her eyes—a startling green—I could tell she was older than she looked. There was something fathomless in her gaze that I couldn't exactly pinpoint, but which told me she was no little girl.

The Clairvoyant cocked her head as we all sized each other up. With her breathy little laughs and the way her hands fluttered, she reminded me of a sparrow.

The Clairvoyant had boy-short blonde hair that was spiked on top. Rings, chains, and studs climbed their way up both her ears. A tiny emerald glittered on the right side of her nose, and she had about twenty bracelets on each wrist that jangled together every time she moved.

"Not what you expected?" She arched a brow at me, like she knew exactly what was going through my mind.

"I didn't know what to expect," I told her, embarrassed I'd been caught staring.

Frankly, I didn't care one way or another what she looked like, as long as she had the information we'd come here for.

"How's it going, WorldEnds2070?" Yutika asked in a bright voice. "And is the world really going to end this year?"

The Clairvoyant's lips curved into a full smile. "Not that I've seen, but it's always possible."

"Typical Clairvoyant response," Smith muttered.

The woman—who I had decided was probably around our age—arched a brow at Smith. Most people would be offended by someone questioning their magic. But instead of taking offense, her expression seemed amused.

"In case you were wondering," she said, "my name is Starlight."

"Of course it is," Smith said under his breath.

I elbowed him in the ribs. Hard.

"Don't be rude," Yutika hissed.

Starlight grinned, unperturbed. I liked that she wasn't as fragile as she looked. She gestured to us, leading the way through a curtain of beads at the back of the shop.

After exchanging a few skeptical looks, we followed.

We gathered in a circular room that was just big enough for the five cushions that were laid out on the floor. Starlight sat in a graceful motion, folding her legs up in what I thought yoga people called lotus position. She closed her eyes and breathed in the incense-filled air.

Exchanging glances and shrugs, the rest of us took our own cushions. Sir Zachary's collar jangled as he trotted into the room after us. He looked around, assessing his options. After only a second of consideration, he nestled into Starlight's lap.

The Clairvoyant didn't open her eyes or so much as twitch. She absently stroked our dog's ears as she hummed quietly to herself. Her easy acceptance of Sir Zachary made me like her even more.

"Dr. Pruwist died before he could reveal the knowledge he possessed," Starlight said, her voice coming out toneless and more formal than it had been before. "I cannot say what he might have revealed if he'd been permitted to live."

Starlight tilted her head to the side, as though she was listening to a voice only she could hear.

"But I saw an alternate future," she continued. "One where Pruwist survived and was made to recall the information."

I held my breath.

Starlight kept her eyes closed as she massaged Sir Zachary's ears.

"The location was given into his keeping without him ever knowing what it was. He kept the paper with the information somewhere secure."

"Do you know where he put it?" I asked breathlessly.

Starlight's eyes snapped open. She stared unblinking at me for several seconds. She didn't even seem to see me; it was like she was looking through me.

"I saw a closet inside the BSMU president's house. A false wall next to the shoe rack. Behind it, a safe. A sealed, brown envelope. That is where you will find what you've been searching for."

"Is that specific enough for you?" Yutika asked Smith.

Smith scowled.

Starlight blinked, coming out of her trance. She looked down at the dog in her lap and gave him a puzzled smile.

"Thank you," I told Starlight, feeling my blood surge with anticipation. I took her small hands in mine, feeling the cold metal of all her rings. "Thank you so much."

"Happy I could help." She cocked her head. Again, I was reminded of a bird listening. "Be careful of the bookshelf in the bedroom. There is a version of the future where it attacks you."

Okay….

Starlight lifted Sir Zachary and kissed the top of his head before handing him to A.J.

"Good luck," she said as she walked us to the door. "I'll be seeing you again, handsome."

I wasn't alone in my surprise when we all realized who she was talking to.

Smith.

"Uhh," Smith said.

Starlight just gave us a little wave and shut the door.

"I like her," A.J. announced.

"Me too," I agreed.

"Yeah," Yutika said, patting Smith on the arm. "Come on, *handsome.*"

CHAPTER 8

We drove straight to the BSMU campus on the other side of town. We called Kaira and Graysen on our way to update them. They were going to meet with the Super Mags as soon as Ma finished feeding them.

Ma's cooking was second only to Michael's Whispering when it came to ensuring a peaceful conversation.

We parked in the BSMU student lot, which was mostly empty given the late hour. Smith's research had revealed that Pruwist's widow was staying with her sister in New Hampshire, and the house she'd shared with her late husband was now vacant.

Getting in would be a cinch. I just hoped Starlight had been right, and that I'd find the information I needed inside.

"You all stay here," I told the others, blowing on my fists. It would be quicker and draw less attention if I went in alone.

"Take these," Yutika said, handing over an earpiece and mike. She sketched on her open pad, and a few seconds later, she produced a tiny camera. "And this."

I fitted the camera into the buttonhole of my shirt, glancing over at Smith's laptop to make sure the camera was working. It was.

"We'll keep our eyes on you, muffin," A.J. told me. "If you need rescuing, we'll be there in a jiffy."

"Watch out for the evil bookshelf," Yutika reminded me.

"Friggin' Clairvoyants." Smith rolled his eyes.

Pulling up my collar so the titanium of my skin wouldn't be so visible in the dark, I got out of the car. I jogged across the cobblestone path.

"Take a right," Smith said into my ear when I reached a fork in the path.

He continued to give me directions as I made my way to the other end of campus. After about ten minutes of this, Smith said, "It's the third building on your left."

The brick house was tucked behind two giant oak trees. The porch lights were on, but the rest of the house was dark.

"Try under the doormat," Smith told me before I just bashed my way into the house.

Stealth wasn't exactly my forte.

"Who actually keeps their spare key under the doormat?" Yutika asked across my earpiece.

The Pruwists, apparently.

"Know it all," I said to Smith's quiet chuckle as I fished the key out from under the mat.

I glanced around just to make sure no one was watching my break-in, and then I let myself into the house.

I paused in the entryway to listen, but the house was silent.

The air inside was stuffy, like the house had been closed up since Pruwist's death. I used the flashlight on my phone rather than turning on any lights.

"I didn't know people actually covered their furniture with sheets outside of movies," Yutika said in my earpiece as I entered the first room. "So creepy."

"Would it be tacky to turn this place into a haunted house and charge for admittance?" A.J. asked innocently.

"Found the house's blueprints," Smith announced. "Staircase is through the next room on your left."

I kept my steps as quiet as titanium on hard wood could be and moved deeper into the house. The musty smell didn't dissipate, and when I swiped a finger across a wooden table, it left a streak through the thick layer of dust.

Clearly, no one had lived here for quite a while.

I climbed the stairs two at a time and followed Smith's instructions to the master bedroom. Since all the curtains in the room were closed, I turned on the bedroom light.

I blinked several times as the room came into focus. It was as empty and abandoned as the rest of the house.

There was a bedframe at the far end of the room, which had been stripped of its bedding. A desk had been cleared of everything except dust. Double-doors opened up into what looked like an enviable bathroom. The closet was catty-corner to the bathroom.

"OMG people, this is it," A.J. said, loud enough that I had to adjust the volume on my earpiece. "I'm so excited I can barely contain myself."

"Try," came Smith's surly reply.

My own heart was thrumming against my ribcage. This was the break we'd been waiting for.

I paused on my way through the room when I caught sight of a bookcase. Could it be *the* bookcase…the one Starlight had warned me about?

I approached cautiously. When the bookcase didn't develop fangs and jump me, I poked it, ready for something illusioned. It was solid wood and glass—just a regular, inanimate bookcase.

"Maybe Starlight was referring to a different bookcase," Yutika said.

"Or she's just another quack," Smith said.

"What exactly do you have against Clairvoyants?" I asked as I headed for the closet.

"Yeah," Yutika echoed. "What do you have against them, *handsome?*"

"Will you let that go already?" Smith demanded as the rest of us tittered.

I flipped on the light in the closet, which was as big as my old bedroom. I headed for the shoe rack on the far wall.

"This dude had more shoes than Kaira," Yutika noted.

I wasn't sure I'd go that far, but it was close.

"Men's fashion is much more nuanced than most people assume," A.J. huffed.

I found the crack in the paint I'd been looking for and gave the loose board a yank. The board came away, revealing a small compartment built into the wall. A safe was nestled inside.

"Starlight was right," I said, hardly daring to believe it.

The safe was anchored to the floor, but it took little more than a tug for me to free it. I brought the safe into the bedroom, where the light was better.

Kneeling on the ground, I dug my titanium fingers under the lip of the safe. Then, I peeled the top off like I was opening a tin can.

I overturned the safe's contents on the floor. Papers, jewelry boxes, and keys tumbled out. Ignoring everything except for the papers, I sifted through the mess until I found what I was looking for: a brown, sealed envelope.

"Is that it?" Yutika asked in a breathless voice.

"It has to be," I said. "It's the only brown envelope."

I sat in the center of the floor. For several seconds, I just held the envelope.

"If Starlight was telling us the truth," I told my friends in a reverent voice, "we're about to find out where Agent S is made."

And then, we'd finally get answers about what had become of the slaves who were forced to produce it.

"What are you waiting for?" Smith demanded. "Open it!"

If I hadn't been in my titanium form, my hands would have been shaking. I slid my finger under the seal.

"Bri, watch out!" Yutika shrieked in my ear.

I turned to the side in time to see the bookcase move. And then, someone crashed into me.

CHAPTER 9

I was knocked to the ground. Either I was seeing things, or a human whose body was colored just like the bookcase was on top of me. My titanium head thunked against the floor forcefully enough to dent the hardwood. Before I could recover, the envelope was torn from my hands.

I heard my friends shouting across my earpiece, but all of my attention was on my attacker.

Magic, so powerful it took my breath away, filled the room. *Who was this person?*

A hard chest was pressed against mine. *Male…my attacker was definitely male.* The Mag felt human, but he matched the coloring and exact appearance of the bookshelf.

I didn't linger on that oddity. Regardless of how he looked, this man was normal flesh and bones. That gave me the advantage.

I grabbed the bookcase-man around his biceps and threw him.

There was a glimmer of color as the bookcase illusion—or whatever it was—disappeared. I waited for the sound of a body crashing through the wall.

The sound and corresponding hole in the wall never materialized.

There was a glimmer of color as the bookcase-person floated to a stop right before the wall…and disappeared.

Invisible? Was this some relative of Subject 6's we hadn't been aware of?

It didn't matter. Whoever or whatever this man was, he had my envelope.

I threw myself at the spot where I'd seen him phase out of sight. My fist grazed skin covered in bristly hair—a beard? I struck out for his nose, but the man had moved. My fist went right through the wall without encountering anything human along the way.

"He's a Chameleon!" Smith shouted in my ear. "Holy shit. I didn't know they could be this powerful. Bri—"

My earpiece fell out as a well-aimed punch made my head snap back. There was a muffled grunt, and I saw the faint outline of a man before he blended back against the wall.

"I think you broke my hand," the man complained. His voice was low and had a faint Spanish accent.

"No, *you* broke your hand," I retorted.

Following the sound of his voice, I struck out. Wood splintered as I caught the edge of the bedframe.

Male, husky laughter drew my attention to the opposite side of the bedroom. "Gotta be quicker than that to catch me."

I narrowed my gaze, searching for the man who was foolish enough to taunt a Steel.

"Why don't you show yourself," I challenged. "I promise not to hurt you…much."

"Tell me," the man said from behind me. I jabbed my elbow and caught nothing except air. "What will people say when they find out the famous Bri Hammond is breaking and entering?"

I was momentarily stunned that he knew who I was, before I remembered it wasn't surprising at all. As Kaira and Graysen's Security Chief, I was on TV multiple times a week. And with A.J.'s media pushes, I'd gotten a few magazine write-ups.

I hadn't thought much about it before, but now, it made me feel exposed. This man knew who and what I was, while all I knew about him was that he was a Chameleon.

It was a rare ability, but it shouldn't be enough for him to run circles around me like he was now.

"No one's going to find out I was here," I said through gritted teeth. "Because I'm going to smash your head into pulp."

More laughter. My blood boiled.

I delivered a swift roundhouse kick. It took apart the bedpost, but I also felt the give of human skin.

"Mierda," the man groaned. "That hurt."

"That was the point, moron."

I pounced. There was the distinct sound of flesh meeting titanium. I heard the rustle of clothes. The man bucked and writhed beneath me, but I was immovable.

If it wasn't for the smallest changes in his coloring, I would have sworn I was wrestling with someone invisible. My vision just caught the way his body made subtle adjustments to blend into his surroundings. His head, which was crushed against the wall, was the same green color as the paint. His feet were camouflaged perfectly with the floorboards.

"Give me the envelope," I demanded, roughly searching the man for the feel of paper.

"You know," he taunted, seemingly unconcerned that he was pinned by a Steel. "Normally, I'm all about the foreplay. But I'm in a bit of a hurry right now."

At that moment, I felt the crumple of the envelope. I yanked it out of his pocket.

"Ha!"

I slammed my fist at the Chameleon. Instead of connecting with the man's skull as I'd intended, my punch went right through the wall.

"Better luck next time," the man's laughing voice said. Impossibly, it sounded like it was coming from the ceiling.

"Come here," I ordered the insufferable Chameleon, not really expecting him to obey. *If I could just get a lock on his voice….*

"My pleasure, cariño."

I searched through the cobwebbed recesses of my high school Spanish vocabulary lists for the translation.

Darling? Oh, hell no.

The breath whooshed out of my body as the man's feet connected with my back. I slammed to the floor.

Wooden boards cracked beneath me. I felt no pain, unless a bruised ego counted.

"How did you—" I began, when the envelope was pulled from my hands once again.

I screamed in rage as the man's weight—and the envelope—were gone.

"That's mine, you bastard!"

I saw the man's profile as his body flickered from the green of the bedroom wall to dark shadows. He slipped out the door and into the hallway.

I don't think so, buddy.

Two leaps closed the distance between us. I tackled him.

We collided, but my momentum was too much for either of us to stop. We tumbled down the staircase, locked together.

A multitude of Spanish curses flew out of the man's mouth before we hit the ground floor. I came out on top, straddling the man who now blended into the oriental rug.

"Dios, you're heavy," he wheezed.

"I'll have you know titanium is far lighter than most metals, and forty-five percent lighter than actual steel." I settled my weight more firmly on my camouflaged opponent, making sure to put pressure on his lungs. "And haven't you heard it's the unwritten fourth high law to call a girl fat? Most women would tear your head off before you even finished your sentence. Lucky for you, I'm not most women."

"I'll say," the man replied, still struggling for breath.

I bent lower to feel for the envelope. That was when I caught a familiar scent on the man's skin. Cinnamon.

"It was you," I said in disbelief, as he squirmed and slapped ineffectively at me in a pathetic attempt to free himself. "You're the one who's been digging up the graves."

I felt, rather than saw, his surprise. For a second, he stopped fighting me.

"It's bad to litter," I informed him, taking advantage of his momentary stillness to reclaim the envelope.

As I waited for the man's comeback, I realized I was unnecessarily prolonging our fight…because I was having fun. I couldn't remember the last time I'd fought someone who could actually give me a run for my money.

It must have been Brent, when I was five and he was fifteen…and he only beat me because he took advantage of my ticklishness.

"What are you talking about?" the man replied. The teasing in his voice had been replaced by wariness.

"The gum wrapper you left in the cemetery," I told him as I got to my feet. I yanked him up with me by his shirt.

The man laughed.

"Pretty *and* clever. You are full of surprises, Bri Hammond."

"You forgot strong." I didn't wait before kneeing where I estimated his groin was.

I missed.

There was a tearing sound, and I was left staring at a scrap of black fabric in my hand.

"Too slow again," the man's voice taunted from the ceiling.

That was all the warning I got before I was shoved against a stone fireplace. The Chameleon grabbed for the envelope in my hand as I crashed into the cinderblocks. The envelope tore in half.

"Give that back!"

He shoved me again. My body surged straight through a support beam in the wall. The whole house shuddered.

"Ugh." I picked sticky, pink insulation off my titanium skin.

I'd just made it back into the ravaged foyer, when I felt the brush of the Chameleon's sleeve. I didn't wait. I shoved him.

Bricks crumbled, followed by a waft of cold breeze. A man-sized hole appeared in the side of the house.

Time to wrap this up, I told myself. Someone was bound to notice that a man had just fallen out of Pruwist's house…if they hadn't already heard all the crashing around.

The next time the Chameleon came at me, I stopped searching for him with my eyes. I felt for the crackling energy of his magic. I closed my eyes and breathed in the hint of cinnamon. Then, I lunged.

Before my limbs could connect with his vitals, the man caught my waist. He pinned me against the wall.

I could have thrown him off. Instead, I froze.

I couldn't see him, but I felt every place where his body pressed against mine. His warm breath fanned across my cheek. I smelled cinnamon and sweat.

"Lose the titanium," he said in a soft voice, his lips brushing my ear. "You'd enjoy this so much more if you could really feel me."

I didn't get hot or cold when I was titanium, and yet, a shiver went through me. Clearly, it had been a while since I'd been pressed up against a man.

"Ass," I told him.

I struck out with my fist and connected. The man slumped to the ground.

Two things happened at once. My friends burst through the hole in the wall. And the man on the floor lost his camouflage.

"Ohmygod," Yutika gasped, clutching her chest. "Are you okay?"

"Fine," I said. I was breathing hard, too. It was something that rarely happened to me when I was titanium.

"Who in the world is this guy?" A.J. asked, bending over to inspect the man on the floor.

I stared down at my attacker, getting my first glimpse of the Chameleon without his magic.

His golden-brown skin and dark, wavy hair spoke to Latino heritage. He had the shadow of a beard that couldn't mask the damage I'd done to his cheek and jaw. Blood trickled across skin that was already swollen and bruising.

I would have called him rugged, except his eyelashes were too long and his lips too full. His biceps swelled against the sleeves of his black T-shirt. The torn part of his shirt exposed a serious set of abs.

Damn.

I dragged my gaze away from his stomach. That was when I noticed his arms. I froze. The Chameleon's arms were covered in tattoos. There was more ink than skin. As I looked closer, I realized they weren't random designs as they first appeared. They were numbers.

The numbers overlapped and serpentined all the way from his wrist to his shirt sleeve. Feeling odd, I bent and shoved up one of his sleeves.

The tattoos went all the way to the tops of his shoulders.

A.J. crouched beside the unconscious man and started snapping pictures with his phone.

"Don't bother," Smith told A.J., staring in wonder at his computer screen. "I already know what they are."

We all turned to Smith.

"They're the IDs of every one of the Super Mags from MagLab."

I wasn't sure what I'd been expecting, but that wasn't it.

"Why?" I asked.

"Also," Yutika said, "what was he doing here?"

"Same thing as us, no doubt," Smith said. "The better question is, how did he know what to look for?"

I thought again about the cinnamon gum wrapper at the empty grave. Whoever this man was, he knew about Agent S. That made him even more dangerous than his strange magic.

"We could take him with us and have Michael make him sing," Yutika suggested.

We all looked down at the man. He was out cold.

"Or we can just let the cops have him when they show up," Smith said. "It'll give the police someone to pin the break-in on, and it'll keep him out of our way."

"Good thinking." I nodded. "If he tries to point the finger at us, we'll just deny we were ever here."

"Our word against his," Yutika said.

I crouched down to yank the envelope out of the waistband of the man's jeans. For a second, I wondered if he had put the envelope there deliberately to mess with me. Rolling my eyes at the unconscious man, I stuffed both halves of the envelope into my pocket.

Then, just for good measure, I grabbed a fireplace poker I'd noticed amid the mess we'd made of Pruwist's house. I bent the metal so it held the serpentine unconscious Chameleon's ankles together, just on the off chance he woke up before the cops arrived. Catching on, Yutika made a pair of actual handcuffs, which I took no small amount of pleasure in locking.

Good luck getting out of those, buddy.

"I'm just going to come right out and say it," A.J. said, putting his phone back in his pocket. "This one's a cutie patootie."

"Eyelashes like that should be illegal," Yutika agreed.

"He was trying to kill me," I reminded them.

"True." A.J. shrugged. "But that doesn't detract from his cuteness."

"He's more than cute," Yutika said. "He's seriously sexy." She thought for a minute. "I'm going to call him Sexy Cinnamon Man."

I was feeling increasingly disturbed by the direction this conversation was headed, not least of which because we were standing over the man's unconscious body and debating his hotness.

"You know," Smith said to Yutika. "If I started naming women Sexy This or Sexy That, you'd call me sexist."

"Ooh." Yutika nudged him. "You think Starlight is sexy, don't you? Do you want to start calling her Sexy Starlight?"

"That is *not* the point I was trying to make," Smith said, color rising in his pale cheeks.

The blare of sirens ended their argument.

"Time to go, folks," A.J. said, foregoing the front door and using the man-sized hole in the wall as an exit.

The rest of us hurried after him.

Once we were outside the house, it became obvious how much damage Cinnamon Guy—I refused to call him Sexy Cinnamon Man—and I had done. There was a giant hole in one side of the house. The roof was partially collapsed, which I didn't even remember happening. Dust was leaking out of the various holes we'd punched through the walls. And the chimney was smoking for no reason I could fathom.

What a mess.

I blew on my fists as we sprinted back to the van. If there were any witnesses around, I didn't want to make their job of identifying us easier by showing off my titanium skin.

"I killed the security cameras," Smith said as we ran. "It'll be like we were never here."

We were just pulling out of the parking lot when a fleet of police cars streamed past.

"That was a close one," A.J. said, fanning his face and tossing his shiny black hair.

"I'd like to see Sexy Cinnamon Man's face when he wakes up in police custody," Yutika said, craning her neck to watch the police cars as she drove.

"Yutika, focus." I pointed to the road in front of her.

Yutika wasn't the best driver when she was fully focused. She kept weaseling her way into the driver's seat by claiming she wanted to improve her skills…or lack thereof. I thought the real reason was because she enjoyed making all of us car sick.

"I can't find any records for a high-level Chameleon," Smith said, frowning at his computer. "I'll do a deeper search when we get home."

"Another unMarked Mag?" A.J. waved his hand. "What a cliché."

I turned on the overhead light and drew out the two envelope halves. The first half contained a single slip of paper. A GPS coordinate was hand-written across the page.

The tear mark at the bottom showed a pen line that had been cut off when the paper was torn.

I reached inside the envelope half I'd taken from Cinnamon Guy for the other half of the paper. My gut turned to stone.

The envelope was empty.

CHAPTER 10

Nothing," Smith said, pulling out his earbuds. "The cops have been all through the house and didn't say a word about the Chameleon."

"He must have woken up in time to camouflage himself," A.J. said.

"We left him in front of the front door," I seethed. "The cops would have tripped right over him whether he was camouflaged or not."

A.J. gave me a helpless shrug.

"I can guarantee he wasn't walking anywhere with that metal poker around his ankles," Yutika said.

I paced around Kaira and Graysen's study. My fury was a hot, living thing inside me. It didn't matter *how* the Chameleon had gotten away. The point was, he was gone...and he'd taken the information I needed.

The Chameleon must have taken the slip of paper out of the envelope and stashed it somewhere else. *Probably in his underwear, the bastard.*

"Stop blaming yourself," Kaira told me in a stern voice.

"If I'd gotten the envelope away from him sooner," I fumed, "we wouldn't be in this mess."

All of the *could'ves* and *should'ves* were racing around my brain in an endless loop. I wanted to scream. I wanted another chance to bash Cinnamon Guy's brains in.

"Cut yourself some slack," Graysen said. "This is a crazy situation no one could have anticipated."

I shook my head. It was precisely my job *not* to get thrown off by the unexpected. I could have taken Cinnamon Guy faster, if I hadn't been distracted by his obnoxious goading. If only I'd opened the envelope sooner, I would have realized what he'd done.

Damnit. Damnit. Damnit.

"The obvious first step is to start with the information we do have," Graysen said. "Smith?"

"GPS coordinate for a location in southern California," Smith said without looking up from his computer. "Satellite images aren't showing anything suspicious at that location. Just looks like uninhabited desert."

"We'd better go there and check it out, anyway," Kaira said.

A.J.'s face blanched. I tried to catch his eye, but he was staring at his shoes.

A.J. was from California, and I knew he didn't have happy memories of his life there. As close as we were, he'd never said much about the first sixteen years of his life before he came to Boston.

For as much as A.J. fake-complained, he was quiet about the things that bothered him the most.

It was something we had in common.

"Let's go in the morning," Yutika said, yawning. "The *late* morning. I'll handle our transportation."

Kaira nodded. "And we're going to need to track down the other half of this." She held up the torn page between her fingers.

I inwardly cursed myself again.

"I can't find anything on this Chameleon," Smith said.

"Sexy Cinnamon Man," Yutika corrected.

Kaira raised an eyebrow. I just shook my head.

"Like nothing," Smith continued. "He's not just unMarked…it's like he doesn't exist."

I started a rep of jumping jacks, because if I didn't, I was liable to bash my head through a wall.

And I'd already done that once tonight.

"I have an idea," Graysen said, taking the useless envelope half off the desk where I'd tossed it. "Come on."

We all followed him into the dining room. The Super Mags who had attacked Valencia and killed eight of her Nat followers were sitting at the table. Michael and the Hansley clan were interspersed among them. Each of the kids had a mug of hot chocolate in front of them. There were also mostly-empty bowls of mini-marshmallows, tiny chocolate chips, and homemade whipped cream.

Michael was speaking in a quiet voice to two of the kids. From their unglazed eyes, I knew he wasn't Whispering to them. Still, their expressions were quietly attentive in a way I knew they wouldn't be with anyone else.

Cora was reading *Charlotte's Web* out loud to a few of the youngest kids. Desiree was playing a card game with another. Ma was refilling mugs, and Grandma Tashi was presiding over all of them at the head of the table.

Looking at the Super Mags like this, they seemed more like regular children than the most powerful and deadly Mags in the world.

"00466," Graysen said.

The little girl sitting next to Cora glanced up. She returned Graysen's warm smile with a shy one of her own.

00466 was an Animalist and the sweetest of the Super Mags. She'd helped us during the Boston Enforcement Party and had been one of the few Super Mags to keep in contact with Kaira and Graysen after the magic ripper started going after them. The shocking gold color of her eyes was the same as the lion who had helped me at the baseball game.

I gave her a friendly wink that had her grinning back.

Graysen held up the piece of envelope in his hand. "I was wondering if you and Sir Zachary might be able to help us with something," he said to the little girl.

"What does Sir Zachary have to do with it?" A.J. demanded, speaking for the first time since the word *California* had been mentioned.

00466 was different from most Animalists. Not only could she communicate with any animal, she could also transform into them. All at once, I had an inkling about what Graysen was thinking.

"You should all give yourselves real names," Desiree said in a loud voice, making it clear her statement trumped all other conversations.

"Desiree's right," Graysen said, unoffended by the interruption.

The Animalist looked at the other Super Mags around the table, like she was waiting for permission.

"What name should I pick?" the little girl asked.

"Any name you want," Kaira said encouragingly.

The Super Mag's gaze went to the book in Cora's hands.

"I like Charlotte," she said shyly.

"That's a great name," Kaira said, bending down so she was at the child's level. As she and Graysen congratulated Charlotte on her choice of a name, I had a startling image of them as parents. They were only a couple of years older than me, but something about them seemed so much more mature.

I guessed it made sense. After everything they'd been through together, and living with the constant fear of being caught and executed, they must have been forced to grow up early.

Their situation was completely different from what I'd gone through with my family five years ago, and yet, the effect had been similar. It felt like I'd transformed from a carefree kid to an adult overnight.

"What do you need help with?" the Animalist—Charlotte—asked. She had to raise her voice to be heard over the other Super Mags, who were buzzing with excitement over their own choice of names.

"Do you think you and Sir Zachary can track someone down for us?" Graysen asked. "We don't have much to go on, except this." He handed her the envelope.

Charlotte took the envelope between her delicate fingers. Then, the little girl was gone. The envelope fell onto the table as a rust-colored moth fluttered above it.

The moth's furry antennae twitched as its little legs settled onto the envelope.

"Why a moth?" Graysen asked no one in particular.

"Silk moths have excellent pheromone receptors," Smith said, reading off his laptop screen. "And I imagine it was a more practical choice than an African elephant or great white shark, both of which also have great noses."

"Goodness," Ma said, pressing a hand to her heart.

"This family just gets weirder and weirder," Desiree said with a self-sacrificing sigh.

"Normal is overrated." Kaira leaned her head on Graysen's shoulder.

I was still trying to decide if the moth was more cute or gross, when the moth transformed into a small, black dog. Yutika jumped when the dog let out a bark that was way too loud for its small frame.

Sir Zachary's answering bark came a second later. His nails skidded on the tile as he ran into the room.

The two dogs faced each other, whining and wagging their tails. Using the chair as a launching point, Sir Zachary leapt onto the table and sniffed the envelope.

"You get your grimy paws off the tablecloth," Grandma Tashi ordered the two dogs, who were snuffling at the envelope.

Apparently, Grandma Tashi was as intimidating to dogs as she was to humans. Both dogs let out little whimpers and jumped back to the floor.

More dog talk ensued.

"I wish I had that kind of magic," A.J. said longingly.

"Being able to move objects with your mind is plenty cool," I assured him.

Charlotte reappeared as a little girl, crouching on the floor. I didn't know how it worked, but she was fully clothed, even though her outfit had disappeared when she was in animal form.

"We might be able to track him," Charlotte said uncertainly, brushing her fingers over the envelope. "The scent is really faint, though."

Before hopelessness could ensue, an idea struck me.

"One sec," I said, already running for the stairs.

I found what I was looking for at the top of my waste basket in my bedroom.

Good thing taking out the trash was perpetually at the bottom of my to-do list.

I raced back to the kitchen and handed Charlotte the gum wrapper Cinnamon Guy had left at the grave.

"Could you use this to track him?" I asked the little girl.

She took the wrapper and sniffed it. She wrinkled her nose.

"Whew, that's strong."

Charlotte offered the gum wrapper to Sir Zachary, who touched his nose to the paper. He sneezed.

"The man we're searching for chews this gum," I said, looking from Charlotte to Sir Zachary, since it seemed wrong to exclude our dog from the conversation. "He smells like it."

I knew it was a stretch, since Cinnamon Guy couldn't be the only person in Boston who chewed that gum. Still, it was something.

Dog and girl conferred. Then, Charlotte nodded.

"We'll do our best." She turned to one of the other Super Mags at the table. "That is, if it's okay with you."

I bristled at the way she was asking a boy for permission.

"00391 is the Super Mags' new leader, Kaira explained to me in a low voice. "He replaced the Pyro."

The boy in question was only twelve years old. With his twiggy arms and shaggy hair, he certainly didn't look like a leader. Then again, as I knew only too well, looks could be deceiving.

I remembered from our previous meetings and the files I'd memorized, that 00391 was a Level 16 Memory Reader and Level 14 Intellect. He acted and spoke more like an adult than a child, thanks to his Intellect magic. He was also on friendly terms with Graysen and trusted us more than the other Super Mags. Since he could see into our memories, 00391 knew how badly we all wanted to help them.

As a general rule, I avoided the kid. As nice as he was, I didn't like reliving my own memories if I could help it. I certainly didn't want anyone else mucking around in my mental black hole.

Regardless of whatever else I thought about him, the Memory Reader was a vast improvement over the now-incarcerated Pyro. Maybe if this kid was in charge, Kaira and Graysen would be able to convince the Super Mags to join the Alliance.

As soon as the idealistic hope passed through my mind, I knew it would never work. The Memory Reader might be brilliant and insightful, but that didn't make him the kind of leader who could wrangle all forty-six of the other Super Mags. I didn't think any of the kids had that capacity. They were all so young, and they'd barely spent any time in the world outside of MagLab.

"Actually," the Memory Reader said. "I think I'd like everyone to start calling me Emory." He flashed us a dimpled grin that made him look even younger. "You know, like *Memory*…except a real name."

"Great name, dude," Yutika said, holding out her palm for him to slap. After a second's hesitation, he high-fived her.

"And yeah," Emory told Charlotte. "You can go find this person." His eyes met mine as he said, "It's really, really important to her."

He was talking about me.

"We'll try hard," Charlotte promised me. "Between the two scents, we should be able to find him."

I swallowed and nodded, not really trusting myself to speak.

Charlotte turned back into a moth and perched on Sir Zachary's head. Our little dog let out a howl, and then he was skidding back across the tiles toward the doggy door Yutika had made for him.

"Thank you," I called after them.

As soon as I found Cinnamon Guy, I was going to tear him limb from limb until he gave over what he'd taken. The thought soothed the savage anger inside me.

"Okay, everyone," Ma said, getting up from the table and gathering empty mugs. She gave us one of her mamma bear stare-downs. "If you seven are flying to California tomorrow, then you're going to sleep. Now."

We all knew better than to argue with Ma.

Before we'd even reached the stairs, Kaira's work cell phone went off. She looked at the Caller ID, frowned, and beckoned for all of us to detour to her and Graysen's study.

"Yes?" Kaira said into the phone, as she closed the door behind us.

I looked at A.J., who was shamelessly tilting his ear toward the phone. After a few seconds, he shook his head at me in defeat.

"Are you sure?" Kaira asked the caller.

Her frown deepened.

"Okay. Thanks very much."

"What was that?" Graysen asked as soon as Kaira disconnected the call.

"The people from the Magical Marking Office," Kaira said. "They tracked down all the parents of the children on our list."

"And?" I asked.

Kaira gave me a puzzled look. "Every Mag on that list was a Steel above a Level 6 who was born in the last twenty-five years."

The information struck me like a physical blow.

Only the people high up in the Magical Marking Office would have noticed all those missing Steels, but only if they'd been looking for a discrepancy. And even if they had noticed, they'd all been working for Edwardian Remwald.

"What?" The word came out as a croak. "Why?"

"Agent S is attracted to Bri's skin," Michael said after a long pause. "Maybe there's something about Steels that make them able to handle it, or something."

"Or it's just too poisonous for anyone else to be around," Yutika said.

"Hold on," Smith ordered. He closed his eyes.

His laptop was open on the floor, but he wasn't touching it. The screen flickered as windows opened and closed in rapid succession.

We all waited in tense silence while Smith worked.

"Confirmed," he said after a few minutes. "There isn't a single Steel above a Level 6 born in Boston over the last twenty-five years. At least none in Alliance records."

"That can't be right," Graysen said before I could speak. "Bri fits that description, and she was Marked until she was—"

"Eighteen," I supplied.

"Yeah, about that." Smith shifted uncomfortably on his feet. "I had the same thought, so I did a little extra digging. And I have a theory."

Smith tugged on the cord of his hoodie. He flexed his long fingers.

"Out with it, Smith," Kaira ordered.

Smith looked at me. "You might want to sit down for this."

I leaned against the desk to appease him. I wasn't the fainting type. Smith waved his hand, projecting the image on his laptop screen onto the wall.

I stared at the enlarged document. It was my birth certificate.

"What's the problem?" I asked. I couldn't say I'd examined many birth certificates, but this one seemed legit enough.

"Look more closely," Smith said. "Specifically, at your magic designation.

Simultaneous inhales filled the room as we all made the same observation. There, on the dotted line, was a single word.

STEAL.

"Wait." Yutika held up a finger. "What's the problem?"

"Didn't you tell us you won your school's spelling B?" A.J. replied.

"That was elementary school," Yutika said. "And so what?"

"S-T-E-E-L." A.J. spelled out the word while frantically tapping on the rogue 'A' on the wall.

"Ohhhh." Yutika's furrowed brows smoothed out before scrunching back up again. "Wait, what's a Steal…with an A?"

"Nothing," Smith replied. "Unless you're trying to steal, with an 'A,' candy from a baby. I'm guessing it was just a typo that whoever was inputting the information made."

A typo. I swallowed.

Smith continued, "My guess is that Remwald had some kind of algorithm to alert him whenever a Mag matching his parameters was entered into the system. The algorithm didn't pick up Bri because of the spelling."

My mind reeled. I heard the others talking, but their voices sounded garbled and far away.

Lilly was a Steel. And if our intel was right, that was the reason why she'd been taken from our family. It's what would have happened to me if it hadn't been for a stupid spelling error.

What if that error had saved me and condemned my niece?

A wounded animal sound came out of my parted lips.

"Honey girl, don't do that to yourself." A.J. wrapped an arm around my shoulders, enveloping me in the smell of expensive cologne.

Kaira and Yutika joined us, enclosing me in a tight circle. Graysen, Michael, and Smith stood back. Smith's expression was shuttered, but I saw open sympathy on Michael and Graysen's faces.

To my horror, I realized everyone was blurry because I was crying.

I knew my friends were saying all the right things, but I couldn't make sense of any of their words. Everything was buried under the deafening, unending scream in my own mind.

My brother's baby daughter had been taken while I had been spared.

CHAPTER 11

After my breakdown in the study, it became apparent to all of us that sleep wasn't happening. So, we spent the last few hours of darkness getting ready for our trip to California.

My insides felt raw, but I forced my own emotions aside at the thought of what this impending trip would mean for A.J. I wouldn't be worth my weight as a best friend if I didn't make sure he was okay with all of this. So, after splashing cold water on my face, I went down to the master suite on the second floor.

A.J.'s door was open, so I let myself inside.

When we'd first moved into the house, there had been only one word to describe the master bedroom: beige. Beige walls, beige floors, beige furniture. That definitely wasn't the case anymore.

It felt a little like stepping into a different dimension. The textured wallpaper had a different pattern and color on every wall. Yutika and I had helped A.J. paint the ceiling to look like a stormy night sky. With all of the colors, it gave off cozy rather than sinister vibes.

There were racks for A.J.'s suits that didn't fit into the sizeable walk-in closet, as well as an alarming collection of statues, figurines, and stuffed animals that resembled Sir Zachary.

3D stars hung in thin air. I knew from trying to find their strings that A.J.'s magic held them in place whenever he was home. When he left the mansion, the stars dropped onto the floor.

The bed was canopied with red velvet curtains, like A.J. was some kind of Medieval king. The furniture scattered around the room was eclectic both in colors and style. There were rugs on rugs, as well as a criminal number of pillows.

"A.J.?" I called, moving farther into the room when I didn't catch sight of him.

A.J. appeared in the doorway that led to the bathroom. I blinked, almost not recognizing him.

His eyes were free of eyeliner. His hair was wet and uncombed. And he was wearing un-tailored jeans and a plain blue button-down.

"A.J.," I said uncertainly. "You're scaring me."

He gave me a tired smile that did nothing to ease my worry.

"It's all good, baby girl," he told me.

It clearly wasn't.

"You can talk to me," I pressed.

A.J. was always there for the rest of us. I hated the thought of him keeping his pain bottled up.

"I'm fine, precious." He patted my cheek in a way that could have either been paternal or patronizing…I wasn't sure which.

I could tell A.J. wasn't in a talking mood. So, I just said, "Just so you know, if we run into anyone from your past, I'm probably going to hang them by their toes and use them like a piñata."

I was rewarded with A.J.'s soft chuckle and an arm around my waist as we headed downstairs.

The rest of our friends were gathered on the front lawn. Ma was there, too, stacking up trays of food for us to take with us.

"Seriously, Ma?" Kaira said in exasperation as she looked at all the food. "This is enough food for a week. Besides, as bad as California's gotten, I'm pretty sure they still have restaurants there."

Ma shot Kaira a look that had my lips twitching in spite of the anxiety churning in my gut.

Kaira then leveled the famous Hansley glare on me. She was still miffed because I'd forbidden her and Graysen from coming to California with the rest of the Seven. The two of them might be in charge of the entire city, but when it came to their safety, I was the boss.

It was hard enough guaranteeing their safety in a civilized city like Boston. From everything I'd heard and read about California, it was one of the last places any right-minded person would go. If I could force all of my friends to stay behind, I would.

"With everything you and Graysen have to deal with," I told Kaira, "you'll barely notice we left. It's going to be fine."

"I remember the last plane I created," Yutika was telling Michael as her pen flew over her sketchbook. "I was only ten, and I had the idea that I would surprise my whole family by taking them to Disney World on a plane I'd created."

"I'm guessing it didn't work out the way you'd planned?" Michael replied, his adoring gaze fixed on her.

"Nope." Yutika added a few flourishes to her drawing. "I made the plane in our backyard without thinking about how big it would get, and the wings went through our house and the neighbor's." She laughed, shaking her head. "My parents were *pissed*."

Michael laughed softly. Yutika stopped drawing long enough to lean over and kiss him. Michael's cheeks turned pink.

Yutika tore the page out of her sketchbook and let it flutter onto the grass.

I looked around anxiously, measuring the distance to the house and surrounding obstacles in light of Yutika's recent story. Fortunately, the Directors' mansion had a really big front yard.

"So, this is the first time you're making a plane that's going in the air?" I asked, glancing down at the drawing on the grass. It had started to wiggle.

"Yuppers," Yutika replied, not seeming in the least bit concerned.

Michael and I exchanged a glance.

It was a cardinal sin among the Seven to question each other's magic, so we both kept our mouths shut.

The 2-dimensional drawing began to expand until it was the size of a model airplane. The crinkle of paper took on a tinny reverberation as the model airplane became metal.

Yutika kicked the tiny model away from us as it began to grow. We all backed farther away, knowing what was about to happen.

Metal creaked and groaned as the plane began to stretch. Tiny wings expanded. The plane grew upward and out. I craned my neck back so I could watch Yutika's creation turn into a full-sized jet. The plane's nose towered above us.

"I don't think I ever realized how big these are," Kaira said in an awed voice.

Smoke wafted up from the grass, where a new front wheel was rotating in place. A faint smell of gasoline filled the air.

The gardeners were going to have a fit.

Windows appeared on the plane's side, along with red lettering that said *Yutika Air.*

"Almost ready," Yutika announced. "Just finishing up its innards."

The rest of us jumped back as the turbine engines roared to life. The whole plane swelled, making it look like a breathing, metallic beast. I shook my head in utter amazement.

"Sweet," Yutika said. "Shall we?"

"Yutika," Graysen said in an awed voice. "You've seriously outdone yourself this time."

"I better illusion this plane until you're in the sky," Ma said. "You don't want any nosy reporters wondering what you're up to."

As soon as she'd finished speaking, the plane disappeared from sight. It was still there, but Ma had just made the plane blend into the rest of the yard perfectly.

"Follow me so you don't run into anything and knock yourselves out," Ma told us, leading the way to the invisible plane.

The smell of fuel and loud hum of an engine were the only proof that the plane really existed outside of my own imagination.

"Be careful," Ma ordered, taking my chin in her hand and kissing my cheek.

"Thanks, Ma," I told her as my foot fumbled for the bottom step.

"Call us as soon as you get to California," Kaira said.

The others behind me were still talking, but I had just gotten my first glimpse of the plane's interior, and my jaw was on the ground.

"What do you think?" Yutika asked, giving me a gap-toothed grin as she skipped up the steps behind me.

"I think your magic is way cooler than mine."

"Oh, stop." Yutika giggled. "But keep going."

"This is unbelievable," I murmured, taking it all in.

The plane was big enough for at least twenty people. The first part of the plane was taken up by couches that were long and wide enough for several people to stretch out for a nap. Gold and silver pillows were stacked on either end of each of the couches.

Large-screen TVs had been set up at the front and back of the plane. On one wall, portraits of each of the Seven—7.5, including Sir Zachary—hung above the windows.

In the center of the plush, egg shell carpeting, there was a circular table. Five recliner chairs were pushed against the table, which was set for dinner. There was a silver dome at each of the place settings, which were labeled with our names. There were two sealed cans of grape soda next to Smith's place card. The rest of us had crystal glasses filled with bubbling champagne. Out of curiosity, I took off the silver dome in front of my seat.

My mouth watered as steam rose from the plate of poached salmon, buttered sweet potato, and asparagus. It was my favorite meal, but I hadn't eaten it since I met A.J. and went vegan. I had no idea how Yutika had even known it was my favorite.

With great reluctance, I put the tray back in place.

"Holy moly," A.J. said, coming onto the plane and taking his first look around. His hollow expression brightened at the sight of so much awesomeness.

Michael was next. He had to stoop to keep from scraping his head against the plane's ceiling.

"This is really amazing, Yutika," Michael said in his serious voice.

"I was going to put in a hot tub," Yutika said, giving the space a critical look. "But I figured that might be impractical with turbulence."

I plopped down onto one of the couches and sighed.

"I'm never going back to commercial flying," I told my friend, swinging my legs and marveling at all of the leg room.

A.J. sat next to me and slid his feet into a pair of fuzzy slippers he'd pulled out of his bag. "I'll have a ginger ale, no ice."

"I'm not a flight attendant." Yutika scowled at A.J.

In spite of her words, A.J.'s drink appeared a few seconds later.

Michael and Yutika sat on the couch across from us. Michael said something in a quiet voice that made Yutika's cheeks stretch into an enormous smile. After a shy glance in our direction, Michael lifted Yutika's hand and pressed a soft kiss to her knuckles.

"Dear heavens," A.J. said, giving Michael a horrified look. "The scandal."

Michael's face turned red beneath his scruffy beard as he muttered something inaudible.

"Meanwhile," Yutika said, nuzzling against Michael's broad arm before turning to the rest of us. "I hope you people are aware that I don't know how to actually get this thing off the ground."

"But you're so good behind the wheel of a car," A.J. teased.

Yutika gave him the finger.

I was relieved to see A.J. bantering. As long as he was still doing that, he couldn't be in too bad of a place.

"If you can get us in the air," Smith told A.J. "I'll take care of the rest."

"You got it, sweet cakes," A.J. replied. "Seatbelts, everyone."

I whooped in surprise and exhilaration when, without warning, the plane started to rise. Instead of rolling out onto the street and racing down the pavement like a runway, the plane just went straight up.

I watched Ma, Kaira, and Graysen go from human- to ant-sized as we left the ground far behind. Clouds surrounded us. The rising sun spilled red-orange light across the sky.

I turned to A.J., only to see that his eyes were squeezed shut. He held both his hands out in front of him, gently waving them like they were fish riding a current.

Smith, who was sitting in the pilot's seat, also had his eyes closed. His lips were moving, but I couldn't hear what he was saying over the thrum of the engine.

Our group had been together long enough that I mostly took our magic for granted. At times like this, though, my friends' abilities blew me away.

"We'll be there in six hours," Smith announced once the plane had leveled out. "May as well get some sleep while you can."

CHAPTER 12

R ise and shine.”

I opened my eyes. A.J.'s face was about half an inch from mine.

“We're here?” I asked, coming instantly awake.

“Welcome to sunny and barbaric California,” A.J. said. His words were chipper, but his eyes held none of their usual brightness.

I wasn't sure if that was because of where we were, or because he'd just used his mind to land an airplane. It was probably both.

Smith was a little unsteady on his feet as he stood.

“Are you guys going to be okay?” I asked anxiously.

Here I was, all rested up, and my friends were on their last legs.

“I'm not sure I'm up for kicking any Californian asses at the present moment,” Yutika said, seeming slightly devastated about that fact.

“That's my department,” I assured her. “Now, let's go do this thing!”

“I can't handle your peppy cheerleader thing right now,” Smith grumbled.

“Psh.” Yutika waved a hand. “If you want to see peppy, give Bri a couple glasses of eggnog and a table to dance on.”

“The eggnog is superfluous,” I replied, grinning. “I just happen to be extremely light on my feet.”

“Focus, everyone,” Michael said.

The plane's hatch opened, and I shielded my eyes from the sunlight.

Compared to the crisp autumn air I was used to back home, it felt like I'd just entered a sauna. It kind of looked like it, too. We were in the middle of a desert.

"Are you sure these are the right coordinates?" Yutika asked, wrinkling her nose at the arid landscape.

"Have I ever been wrong?" Smith countered.

"Only about your choice in soda flavors," I told him.

We got out of the cool, comfortable plane and stepped onto dirty brown sand. Aside from mountains in the distance and a few scrubby bushes, there was nothing to see.

"There's no one around here," Michael said, his gaze searching the horizon.

"And thank the elves and wood sprites for that," A.J. muttered.

California wasn't the worst place to go, but it was definitely up there on the *do not visit if you value your life* list. It had gotten so bad that even the Enforcers had given up trying to instill law and order in the state.

After the Slaughters, all of the states broke up into territories led by whichever Mag or Nat could prove their dominance. The leader of this part of California was a Level 9 Telepath, and according to both A.J. and every news article Smith had pulled up before our trip, she was a few delusions shy of psychotic.

"What's going on over there?" Kaira's voice asked from Smith's laptop.

In answer, Smith shifted his screen so Kaira and Graysen could see the whole lotta nothing we were staring at.

"Take this," Smith told Yutika, handing her the computer.

"I'm honored," she quipped, giving the computer a slight bow before gently cradling it.

Smith didn't trust anyone with his technology.

Smith ignored her as he pulled his poison scanner out of his hoodie pocket. He flipped the switch and held it over his head like a sword.

Nothing happened.

It didn't make a terrible screeching sound like whenever Smith touched it to an open crate of Agent S vials. It didn't do anything at all. The only sounds were the wind and rustle of sand across the parched earth.

Yutika was drawing on her sketchpad as Smith walked around, waving his poison wand. A few seconds later, Yutika had a handheld GPS navigator. The numbers on the digital face shifted as she took several steps forward, to the side, and then back again.

She moved slowly, her gaze fixated on the screen.

"Right here," Yutika said, tapping her foot. "This is the exact location that Pruwist wrote down."

I held my breath as Smith came closer, his poison wand outstretched.

Smith squatted down to the ground. My heart lurched when the poison scanner gave off an anemic little bleep.

We all looked at each other.

"Are you sure that thing's working?" A.J. asked.

Smith pressed the tip of the wand into the sand.

Bleep. Bleep.

A flash of yellow light came from the scanner. Then, it went quiet again.

"Yutika, can I get a shovel?" I asked.

Maybe the Agent S was buried here, just like it was in the graves.

Yutika produced two shovels in a matter of seconds. I blew on my fists and got to work. Using all the strength in my titanium arms, I hauled sand faster than a construction machine. The other shovel dug just as furiously beside me, controlled by A.J.'s telekinesis.

Sand kept slipping back into the hole, so it took longer than usual to reach the same depth where the Agent S crates were buried in the Boston graves. We kept digging, even though our shovels came up against only sand and rocks.

Twelve feet later, I had nothing to show for my work except for tangled hair and pit stains.

I might not feel heat when I was titanium, but my body still functioned normally. I was sweating like a pig. Probably smelled like one, too.

"Bri," Smith called from the top of the hole. "Catch."

I lifted up my hand, closing my fingers around his poison scanner. I waved it around the way Smith had done. It continued its sad, sporadic bleeping. The yellow light flashed once.

"Come back up, lover," A.J. told me, his voice sounding as defeated as I felt. "There's nothing here."

"Maybe there was Agent S here at one time," Michael said as I climbed out of the hole. "There could be some trace remnants, which would explain why the scanner is detecting something."

"That would make sense," Smith said.

"Maybe we're missing something." Yutika tapped her chin in thought.

"Like the other half of Pruwist's paper?" I couldn't manage to hide the bitterness in my voice.

"Come home," Kaira said from the computer's speakers. "Once Charlotte and Sir Zachary track down our guy, we'll get the rest of the paper and work this out."

Graysen's face appeared beside Kaira's on the screen. "We're not going to stop until we've figured this out," he assured me.

I wanted to scream. I wanted to run ten miles and then do a thousand jumping jacks. My titanium skin felt too tight. I felt like a bomb waiting to explode.

"Back on the plane, everyone." A.J. clapped his hands. "Before we stay long enough to get a California welcome."

"What's that?" I asked, trying not to let my bad mood rub off on the others.

In answer, A.J. stuck out his thumb and index finger like it was a gun and put it to my head.

I wrapped an arm around A.J.'s waist. "Then, it's a good thing I'm bullet proof."

"People, we've got a problem," Smith announced.

I followed the direction of his gaze. An off-road jeep was bouncing along the uneven terrain and heading straight for us.

A.J.'s face went a shade paler. I cracked my knuckles.

"Should we just get out of here now?" Yutika asked, glancing at our plane.

"No," Michael and A.J. said at the same time.

"See that white stripe across the jeep?" A.J. asked.

We all nodded.

"That means these people work for this territory's ruler. If we just skedaddle on a plane that doesn't belong to any sanctioned airlines, they'll shoot us down before we make it over the border."

"I've got this," Michael said, his voice as calm as ever. "You all get back on the plane and be ready to take off."

I went with him, just in case he needed muscle to back up his Whispering. It never hurt to be prepared.

The jeep didn't slow down. I angled myself in front of Michael, ready to stop the jeep with my bare hands if necessary. During my angsty teenage years, I'd once beaten up Brent's new car after he tattled on me for sneaking out after curfew.

It wasn't something I was proud of, but it had taught me that in a girl versus car battle, I'd come out victorious.

The jeep skidded to a stop right in front of us. Sand flew in every direction, coating us in brown dust. Neither Michael nor I reacted. We just waited for the people inside the jeep to come out.

There were four of them. I sensed magic from each of them, but not much. They were all probably Level 1s or 2s. They seemed confident enough behind their assault rifles, though.

Their hair was matted, their faces sunburned, and their teeth rotten. In spite of the heat, they all wore actual fur capes. Even though we were too far away from the plane for sound to carry, I could have sworn I heard A.J. shrieking about animal rights.

"You are now on land that belongs to the Southern California Territory's ruler," the man who got out of the driver's seat said. His voice had a peculiar twang that made all of his words sound clipped. "You will—"

"Be quiet," Michael said. "And put down your weapons."

The four men complied without hesitation.

"Thank you." Michael said. "Now, you may go. You don't remember seeing us, our plane, or anything out of the ordinary."

"Okay," the driver said, giving Michael a goofy smile.

"You also decided you're animal lovers and will never, ever wear one of them again!" A.J. shouted at the top of his lungs, which meant his voice just managed to reach us.

Michael's lip twitched. He looked down at the guns on the ground and then back up to the men who were standing slumped in relaxed poses. Michael lifted a shoulder.

"You decided that you love animals and won't wear their hides anymore," Michael repeated.

The men were unfastening their fur capes before Michael had even finished his command.

"Go," Michael told them.

They got back in their jeep. With another spray of sand, the men were gone.

"You make everything so boring," I teased Michael. "I was really looking forward to beating some Californians up."

"Sorry to disappoint," Michael replied, returning my grin.

Maybe, by the time we got back to Boston, Charlotte would have discovered where Cinnamon Guy was hiding. When we did find him, there was no way I was letting Michael get a first shot at him. That pompous ass would be getting reintroduced to my titanium fists.

With that thought cheering me, I headed to the plane.

CHAPTER 13

It was dark when we got back to the mansion. A.J. and Smith landed the plane on our front lawn without fanfare. Ma was waiting outside for us, and by the time I climbed out of the plane, it was completely illusioned. The only way someone would figure out there was a plane parked in the middle of our property was if they walked right into it.

"I'll keep this illusioned until the next time you need it," Ma said as she gave each of us a hug. "Hungry, loves?"

"Definitely," Yutika said. Michael nodded.

Smith and A.J. slumped, exhausted from how much magic they'd used on our pointless venture.

"I've got lentil stew already warming for you," Ma told A.J. as she wrapped one arm around his shoulder. She put the other around Smith. "And I've got your ramen all ready to go. All you need to do is add the hot water and poison test it."

"Thanks, Ma," both boys said as Ma led them into the house.

Smith wasn't big on physical contact, but he didn't seem to mind when it came from Ma.

"You coming?" Yutika asked, when she realized I wasn't following the others into the house.

I shook my head. I'd spent the flight back from California working myself up to do something I'd been dreading.

"I need to go see my family," I said. I was relieved when my voice didn't waver or break. "They need to know what's going on."

"Want us to come with you?" Michael asked.

I swallowed around the lump that had formed in my throat.

"Thanks, but it won't take long. I'll be back soon."

Five years ago, my house had been the gathering place for all of mine and Brent's friends. We had a pool and a kickass game room, and my parents were far cooler than any of my friends' parents.

But that was before. I didn't bring other people home anymore.

"Do you have your phone on you?" Yutika asked. "Just in case you change your mind?"

I dug it out of my pocket and held it up for them to see.

"Get some rest," I told them. "I'll see you in a little bit."

❋ ❋ ❋

I parked in my parents' driveway and walked up to the front porch.

It had been a while since I'd been here, and nostalgia hit me like a brick to the face. I caught sight of my reflection in the polycarbonate windows at the front of the house and almost smiled.

It hadn't taken long into our childhood for my parents to realize that glass windows didn't mix with Combat Mag and Steel children. Even though Brent was ten years older, and thus should have been more mature, he took his duties as an annoying older brother to the extreme. Despite his superior age and size, we were well-matched. He was strong as a bull, but I was stronger—a fact I never grew out of reminding him. And Brent always retaliated by tickling me, which was my kryptonite no matter what skin I wore. Our wrestling matches that ensued were always lighthearted and came with the potential of bringing down the entire house.

For a few years, my parents had kept the window repair company's number on speed dial. Finally, they just replaced the glass with stronger and more durable polycarbonate.

I climbed the front steps and knocked on the door. I didn't need to knock, but it felt wrong to barge in when I hadn't been here in months.

Guilt fluttered in my stomach as I thought about how little I'd been around in the last couple of years.

Coward, that inner voice I despised whispered.

My mom's face appeared in the window, and then the door was opening.

"Bri!" My mom wrapped me in a tight hug. "What a wonderful surprise."

Her body was compact and petite like mine, but her hug was firm. She was a Level 5 Artist, and the proof of her magic was in the artwork covering our walls and her ink-stained fingers. There were so many paintings of our family that it was almost impossible to see the blue from the wall underneath.

"Hi Mom," I said against her shirt. I almost apologized for having been so absent, but I couldn't make the words come. Instead, I stepped back and looked at her.

My mom's hair was thin and gray, and there were bags under her eyes. Before everything with Lilly, she had spent hours fussing with her beautiful hair and doing her makeup. Now, she just looked pale. Tired.

"Look who it is," my mom said, taking my hand and leading me into the house that felt familiar but also completely alien.

It was the house I'd grown up in, and yet, nothing about it was the same anymore. Instead of my dad's oldies music playing on the speakers and my mom's homemade candles perfuming the entire house, it felt empty…even though four people lived here.

Brent and Sarah had moved in with my parents after Lilly died. Sarah hadn't been able to cope with the loss of their daughter, and Brent hadn't wanted to leave her home alone while he went off to work.

The inside of my family's house felt sadder than all the cemeteries I'd recently visited.

"Hey pumpkin face," my dad said, using my childhood nickname as he came to hug me.

My dad also looked like a shell of the man he'd once been. As a Level 7 Competitor, he'd always been in fantastic shape. We used to go for five-mile runs together every morning, and then he'd do it again at night. He'd also coached me in wrestling and Brent in baseball. Now, he had a receding hairline and beer belly.

My heart felt like a heavy weight in my chest as I gave my dad a bright smile and initiated our "secret" handshake we'd started when I was in elementary school.

"Hi, little sis," Brent said, giving me a smile over the couch.

I went into the living room where he was sitting on the couch. Even though it was only eight-thirty, Sarah was fast asleep with her head on his lap. In spite of all the noise the rest of us were making, she didn't wake.

I remembered when Brent and Sarah started dating. Since they were a decade older than me, I'd thought they were the coolest thing since sliced bread. Instead of getting annoyed with the little sister who was always around, Sarah had hung out with me. She'd done my makeup and curled my hair, and we'd had a tradition of going out to dinner every Friday night. We'd gossip about my brother and whichever boy I was crushing on at the time.

Brent had complained that his girlfriend liked me more than him, and she would tease back that I was the more fun Hammond sibling.

I hadn't spent any time alone with Sarah since Lilly's death. She'd shut down and shut out everyone in her life…except Brent.

"How are you?" I asked my brother, before inwardly kicking myself.

His only child was dead, and her death had been blamed on a fake disease. How did I think he was doing?

"Hangin' in there." Brent gave me the same tired smile both my parents had offered. "Tell me about you, Ms. Security Chief."

My parents came into the room bearing steaming coffee mugs. They surrounded me, watching expectantly as I started in on a story about a Mag who had convinced himself he and Kaira were married. The lunatic had tried to rescue his "bride" from the evil villain (Graysen) who was holding her captive.

My family shook with quiet laughter, conscious of Sarah asleep on Brent's lap, as I recounted half a dozen ridiculous stories from the last few months. My heart wasn't in it, but it was what my family needed. It was what they expected.

I talked to fill the silence. The tears rolling down my mom's face were from laughter, not from grief. It was all I could give them. And I hated myself for not being able to do more.

"Oh, pumpkin face," my dad chuckled. "You really are a barrel full of sunshine."

I bit my lip. *Stop stalling,* I told myself.

Sometimes, I wished all of the hardness in my skin could somehow seep into my personality and toughen me up.

"So, my friends and I have been investigating all the deaths that were blamed on DAMND," I said.

"No." My mom held up her hand to stop me.

My whole body tensed at her sharp tone. There was a wild look in her eyes.

"No, what?" I asked.

"Lilly died from one of those baby killers!"

My dad stroked a hand down my mom's back as her voice grew shrill, but she shrugged him off.

"One of those couples had a baby that was in the same neonatal unit as Lilly. The doctor told us so. She said they didn't realize the baby was one of *them* until it was too late."

"Come on," my dad said, tugging on my mom's arm. "It's getting late."

My eyes stung. I hadn't even reached the confession part…where I had to admit how little progress I'd made. I also needed to explain that the only reason I wasn't sharing in Lilly's awful fate was because of a spelling error on my birth certificate.

My dad gave me a defeated look as he led my mom out of the room. I felt like I'd betrayed him. My one job when I came here was to help them forget…and I'd failed at even that.

"They're not mad at you, you know," Brent told me in a hollow voice once they'd gone. "It's just been…hard."

"I'm sorry I haven't been around," I whispered, unable to meet my brother's gaze.

"I'm glad you haven't."

That made my head snap up.

"I want you to move on from all of this and live your life." Brent gave me a sad smile.

"I'm going to find out what really happened," I vowed. "Maybe the truth will help our family somehow—" I broke off, not wanting to sound callous by saying something like *move on*.

The truth was, Lilly would always be in all of our hearts. But I couldn't help but think that finding answers would let my family start to heal. Anything was better than continuing to live in this purgatory.

"It's been five years," Brent said. "I've made my peace with Lilly's death. It was awful at first, but I did my grieving. I feel…alright. It's just—" He looked down at his wife. "I just want her back."

I hurriedly wiped away the tear sliding down my cheek before Brent could see. I refused to add my grief onto the terrible load my brother was already carrying.

"How's she doing?" I asked in a quiet voice, nodding at Sarah.

Brent touched his wife's cheek with his fingertips.

"I…don't know how to help her," he whispered.

My fearless older brother looked at me, his expression lost.

I had no idea what to say. My throat felt too thick to manage speaking, even if I'd had the right words.

"It's her magic," Brent continued. "It's not just her pain she feels, but all of ours. She knows it's hurting me that she's so sad, and that makes everything worse for her. It's like a fucking emotional snowball of doom, and I don't know how to fix it."

They were the most honest, raw words my brother had spoken to me in years.

"Brent," I whispered, crouching down next to him and resting my head on his arm. "I'm so sorry."

Sarah was a Level 4 Bleeding Heart, which meant her capacity for empathy was seemingly endless. Her magic had helped her become a world-renowned child psychiatrist, back when she'd still been working. She'd quit her job after Lilly's death.

At that moment, my phone began to ring. Grateful for the distraction—and then guilty for wanting to escape—I pulled my cell out of my pocket. It was Kaira.

"I'm sorry," I told my brother, showing him my screen so he'd know why I was abandoning him. "I have to take this."

Stepping into the dark dining room, I answered.

"Hey," I said, hoping Kaira wouldn't notice my scratchy voice.

"Charlotte and Sir Zachary found him," Kaira said, her voice brimming with triumphant anticipation. "He's been at the Magical Solitude Cemetery for at least half an hour. Charlotte says he's digging up graves, so he should be there long enough for us to catch him."

I knew that cemetery. It was close enough to my parents' house that I could walk—or run—there.

"Gray's just finishing up some stuff with the Super Mags," Kaira continued. "We'll be in the car in a couple of minutes. Want us to swing by and pick you up?"

"I'll meet you there," I told her.

"Okay," Kaira said after a short pause. "But don't go after him alone. This man's too dangerous and too much of an unknown. Besides, I'll be able to illusion us all so we have the benefit of surprise. Thankfully, Chameleon magic actually changes the body's appearance while I just manage impressions, so his magic won't interfere with mine."

"Don't go in alone," I parroted. "Got it."

Kaira sighed. She knew as well as I did that there was no way I was going to sit around waiting for backup. I had half a paper to recover and a score to settle.

CHAPTER 14

The crisp night air helped to wash away my grief. I didn't turn into titanium as I ran, letting the cold air sear my lungs. I relished the burn of my calves as I sprinted to the cemetery.

By the time I reached my destination, I was feeling like myself again.

As far as cemeteries at night went, this one was at the low end of the creepy scale. All of the headstones were flat, so it looked more like an open field than a graveyard. A wide, paved road cut down the center of the grass. Bright lamps spaced throughout the cemetery made it look almost friendly.

I jogged down the paved road, which led up a gently-sloping hill. When I crested the hill, I looked around.

I didn't catch that overwhelming sense of Cinnamon Guy's magic the way I had back at Pruwist's house, but it didn't matter. The bright lamps illuminated a solitary figure in the middle of the cemetery. And unless there was another person digging up graves at night, then I'd found my prey.

There was a motorcycle parked under a nearby lamp, and hell if I didn't find that just a little bit sexy.

Shaking my head to rid myself of the ridiculous thought, I started to run. I didn't bother to hide the sound of my sneakers pounding the pavement. I wasn't going to give this Chameleon the chance to blend into the grass and slip away.

I blew on my fists and waited until my skin shone silver. Then, I pounced.

Cinnamon Guy let out an affronted *oof* as we hit the ground. I'd expected him to disappear from view immediately, but he didn't. I pinned him under me, allowing myself a moment of satisfaction that he was well and truly stuck.

"Bri Hammond." Cinnamon Guy quirked an eyebrow in a way that made it obvious he was making fun of me. "I'd say it was nice to see you again, but you know. It isn't."

"Don't worry," I told him. "I just have a few little questions, and if you answer them right, I'll let you go without messing up your pretty face…much." I gave him an evil smile I'd learned from my cheerleading days.

Most people assumed wrestling was the more vicious of my two sports. They couldn't have been more wrong.

"Aww, you think I'm pretty?" Cinnamon Guy batted his obnoxiously-long eyelashes at me.

The lamps surrounding us reflected in his dark eyes and illuminated his tattoos. I noticed that he had a tiny diamond stud in his left earlobe.

Cinnamon Guy's hair, which was longer in the front than on the sides or back, just brushed his forehead. I couldn't wait to beat that smirk off his full lips…right after he'd given me what I had come here for.

"How did you get out of Pruwist's house that night after we tied you up?" I asked, curiosity getting the best of me.

"You're not the only one with tricks up your sleeve." Cinnamon Guy gave me a *wouldn't you like to know* look.

I tightened my hold on him.

"Cariño," he purred in an accent that probably brought less discerning women running into his arms. "If you wanted to get me under you, all you had to do was say so."

I didn't validate that with a response. Instead, I glared down at his smug face.

"Where'd you put it?" I demanded. "That paper you stole from me?"

Cinnamon Guy smiled, showing off his even, white teeth. "Not on my person, sadly. Although you're welcome to frisk me for it."

Ugh. "What is your basic problem?" I demanded.

"You mean I have to pick just one?" he asked, clearly enjoying my growing frustration.

I was so tempted to knock him out and then let Michael pick his brain apart when he came to. So very tempted.

But it always took Michael longer to get information out of people I'd concussed. I didn't want to risk scrambling the few brain cells this guy had before we got what we needed out of him.

"What was on that paper?" I pressed, digging my knee into his ribs until he winced. "I know you looked at it, so don't try to pretend like you didn't."

"Sure, I looked at it." Cinnamon Guy shrugged the one shoulder I didn't have pinned to the grass. "There might have been some numbers or something. I wasn't really paying attention."

I didn't believe him as far as I could throw him. Actually, I could have thrown him a whole lot further than I believed him.

Fine. If he wanted to play it that way, I'd just wait for Michael.

"Why are you digging up graves?" I demanded, buying time until the rest of the Seven arrived.

I didn't say anything specifically about Agent S, since I didn't know how much he knew, and I didn't want to tip my hand.

Before Cinnamon Guy even opened his mouth, I could tell something sarcastic was going to come out. Sure enough, he said, "Because this is how the cool kids spend their Friday nights." He looked up at me. "And I'm definitely the cool kid."

This man wasn't the first asshole I'd dealt with, but seriously, enough was enough. I raised my fist to put Cinnamon Guy into a temporary and painful sleep, when a sharp whistle had me freezing.

"Is someone out there?" an unfamiliar male voice demanded.

"Mierda." Cinnamon Guy swore. All the amusement on his face vanished. "Mag Cop."

"What?" I looked around.

The beam of a flashlight was just visible over the crest of the hill.

"He sensed your magic." Cinnamon Guy made a sound of disgust. "Idiota."

"How do you know it wasn't *your* magic he sensed?" I shot back, defensive.

"Can you feel my magic?" he challenged.

I couldn't. That swirling heat of power I'd felt from him before was gone.

Well, shit.

I looked around, but there was nowhere to hide. I could run, but the cop would immediately notice my silver skin in the lamplight. And without my titanium, there was no way I'd be able to drag Cinnamon Guy with me.

It would take the cop about ten seconds to identify me in my Steel form. Five more, and I'd be on every major news network. The grave robbery would be pinned on me, and then Kaira and Graysen would have a thousand reporters hounding them.

Double shit.

"Lose your magic and get down," Cinnamon Guy ordered.

"He'll still be able to sense me," I argued.

"Do it!"

I bristled, but with no other option that would save me and my friends endless humiliation, I did as I was told. As soon as my skin was just skin again, I felt a small prick in my forearm.

I glanced to the side in time to see Cinnamon Guy pulling out the needle he'd just stuck me with.

"What the—"

"It's temporary," Cinnamon Guy said. "Ten minutes, and you'll be back to your kickass self."

That was when I felt my magic slipping away. It retreated deep inside me where I couldn't reach it. My power was still there, but it was like it was hidden underneath a heavy blanket. I couldn't call it to the surface.

"What the fuck, Cinnamon Guy?" I whisper-shouted, trying not to panic.

I'd never been unable to reach my magic before. My pulse began to race as thoughts of the Magical Reduction Potion flooded my brain.

No. No no no.

"Cinnamon Guy?" he repeated.

I wrapped my hand around his throat and squeezed. "What did you do?!"

"Ten minutes," he croaked. "I swear. It's in me, too. It's why you can't feel my magic."

I believed him, and not just because we both knew I could kill him. The past four months of dealing with criminals and people who might threaten my friends' lives had made me an expert at reading body language.

Cinnamon Guy was telling the truth.

While I was relieved, I was no less pissed off.

"You had no right," I said, barely able to stop myself from punching him in the face—magic or not.

If I could have done it without drawing the cop's attention, I would have.

"I'm trying to keep us both from getting arrested," Cinnamon Guy hissed. "I knew Mag cops were patrolling this area." He narrowed his eyes and glared at me. "The one factor I didn't count on was an angry little Steel messing with my plans."

I didn't have a chance to snap back. Cinnamon Guy grabbed my arm and yanked me down onto my belly, just as the cop's flashlight beam crested the hill. The light swept back and forth way too close to where we were hiding.

I tried to will myself into invisibility.

The cop's boots tapped the pavement.

If he came much closer, there would be nothing to hide us. *Turn around,* I silently begged the cop. *Nothing to see here.*

For a few seconds, I thought my desperate telepathic plea had been answered. The cop turned to the side, looking off into the distance. My stomach sank when I realized what had caught his attention. Cinnamon Guy's motorcycle.

We both cursed under our breaths—me in English and Cinnamon Guy in Spanish. The motorcycle was too far to be useful to us without revealing our position, but close enough to give us away.

I got ready to run, but Cinnamon Guy yanked me back.

"He'll taser you," Cinnamon Guy warned. "There's nowhere to hide out here."

I held back a retort about how the taser wouldn't have affected me if I'd still had my magic.

"What do we do?" I asked in a breathless whisper.

"Make out with me."

I gaped at Cinnamon Guy.

"It's the only way," he insisted. "Trust me."

"As if."

I managed a little squeak when Cinnamon Guy grabbed my shoulder and flipped me onto my back.

"Are you out of your goddamn mind?" I hissed.

Apparently, he was. Cinnamon Guy rolled on top of me. His lips hovered an inch above mine.

I reached up to his chest to thrust him off…and possibly break his sternum, when the cop's flashlight landed just feet from us. With no other choice, and hoping against hope the imbecile on top of me knew what he was doing, I let the situation play out.

I caught a hint of his spicy gum as he stroked his thumb across my cheek. And then, he angled his face to fit our mouths together.

His kiss was soft and unhurried. It was like he had all the time in the world and wasn't in jeopardy of getting an elbow to the kidney…or a taser to his back.

Just when I thought I had a handle on things, Cinnamon Guy ratcheted up the heat on the kiss index. He cradled the back of my neck with his hand, drawing my mouth more firmly against his. And…*damn*. This guy knew what he was doing.

"Open for me, cariño," Cinnamon Guy whispered. His tongue traced the seam of my lips.

I couldn't help myself. I kissed him back.

When I wrapped my arms around him, Cinnamon Guy let out a low, husky groan. Both of our hearts were hammering together in a fierce, staccato rhythm. I felt Cinnamon Guy's callused fingertips on the bare skin of my waist. I didn't even care that he was taking liberties I never allowed during first kisses.

This was not a normal first kiss. This wasn't a normal any kind of kiss.

I slid one hand up his back, feeling his muscles ripple beneath his thin shirt. My other got lost in his soft hair.

"Freeze!"

The shout punched through my foggy brain, and I jerked back on a gasp.

Oh no. The cop was standing directly over us, his flashlight blinding me.

Cinnamon Guy got to his feet, slowly, and put out a hand to help me up. He pushed me a little behind him so my profile was mostly hidden. I was sure he had his own nefarious reasons for hiding my identity, but I was grateful nonetheless. The last thing I needed was to be tomorrow's headline because of this.

"Sorry about that, Officer," Cinnamon Guy said, his voice betraying no hint of the storm raging inside me. "We thought we were alone."

"What in the heck are the two of you doing out here?" the cop demanded, his voice laden with suspicion.

Before I could even begin to come up with a response, Cinnamon Guy reached back for my arm, wrapping it around his stomach. He shifted very slightly, so the cop's line of sight was turned away from the desecrated grave.

"Do you want me to spell it out for you, Officer?" Cinnamon Guy asked. I could hear the smirk in his voice.

"It's illegal to be in the cemetery after hours," the cop said, sounding as out of sorts as I felt. "I'm going to have to call this into the Nat police."

He unhooked a walkie-talkie from his belt.

"We're really sorry, Officer," I said, surprising myself by speaking up. I even added a hint of a whine. To keep the cop from looking too closely at me, I nuzzled my face into the back of Cinnamon Guy's shirt.

"Yeah," Cinnamon Guy agreed. "It's just." He leaned in closer to the cop, as though they were two guys conspiring over a beer. "It's my girl's kink."

I choked.

"Cemeteries?" the cop asked, sounding embarrassed and a little intrigued.

"Don't knock it 'til you've tried it, Officer." Cinnamon Guy reached back to squeeze my hip. "And I'd try anything for my girl."

I dug my nails into his back to remind him that I was going to kill him as soon as our only witness left.

The cop scratched the back of his head. "Alright," he said on a sigh, tucking his walkie-talkie back into his belt. "But I'm going to need to take down your information and issue a small fine. Just covering my own ass, you understand."

I was panicking, but Cinnamon Guy gave the cop a sage nod.

"Of course, Officer. Let me get our IDs from my bike."

Cinnamon Guy lifted my hand to his lips and kissed it before he started to back slowly away toward his bike. I narrowed my gaze.

What are you up to?

In response, he winked at me. He got a few more paces. And then, he broke into a run.

"Hey!" the cop shouted.

The cop hurried after Cinnamon Guy. I joined in the chase.

We were too slow.

That slippery bastard hopped on his bike and revved the engine.

"No!"

"Get back here!" the cop yelled, chasing after the motorcycle.

Cinnamon Guy turned in his seat and blew me a kiss before leading the cop away.

I screamed in frustration.

At that moment, a new set of headlights came down the drive. I recognized Michael behind the wheel of our van.

"Stop him!" I screeched, pointing. The motorcycle raced across the grass, hopped a curb, and then slid neatly through a narrow opening in the chain-link fence.

I sucked in a breath as my magic came back in a rush. My skin shimmered titanium under the light of the street lamp. My magic had returned, but it was too late. Cinnamon Guy was gone.

CHAPTER 15

"Don't worry about it," Kaira said, after I'd finished explaining the situation. I was breathing heavily as I tried to rein in my temper. Kaira grinned. "Charlotte and Sir Zachary also found out where Cinnamon Guy lives."

"Seriously?"

My fury was instantly replaced with a seething anticipation.

"Yep," Graysen replied. "Should we head over there now?"

"Look at Bri's face," A.J. said. "Do you really need to ask?"

"Step on it, Michael," Yutika ordered.

On our way to Cinnamon Guy's apartment, I envisioned all the ways I'd kill him when I got my hands on him. It would definitely be a slow death, full of pain and screaming.

"You've got your scary Steel face on," A.J. observed.

"Just plotting," I replied.

Sir Zachary licked my hand, which helped cool my bloodlust. A little. Cinnamon Guy brought out something ugly and violent I hadn't known I had inside me.

I barely waited for the van to come to a stop before I was jumping out.

Michael sweet-talked a woman who had just gotten out of her car into giving up her excellent parking spot. Cinnamon Guy's apartment was on a busy street in Allston where a lot of BSMU students lived, and parking was scarce.

Kaira illusioned all of us to look like students, complete with backpacks. I caught a glimpse of my reflection in a glass windowpane and saw I had become an Asian woman with freckles and chin-length black hair. Even Sir

Zachary got an appearance makeover, since A.J. had made our dog as well-known as the rest of us.

The door to the apartment building was locked. I was eager enough to go wring Cinnamon Guy's neck that I would have just yanked the door off its hinges, but A.J. stopped me.

"Best not to draw attention to ourselves just yet," he said, patting my arm.

He then proceeded to press the call button for every single unit in the building.

A chorus of *Hello's* and *What do you want's* poured out of the speakers.

"We forgot our keyyyy," A.J. whined, pressing his mouth almost all the way against the speaker. "Help us!"

"What are you doing?" Kaira asked him.

"Aren't BSMU students drunk all the time?" A.J. fired back.

"Um, no," Graysen said.

A.J. gave us all a triumphant *Ha!* when the lock on the door clicked. Rolling my eyes, I grabbed the handle and let us in.

The building was nothing special…rickety elevator that could only fit half of us at a time, worn carpet, and that distinct college apartment smell. Not that I would know, since I hadn't been able to apply for college after I went unMarked. My only experience with higher ed was visiting Brent and Sarah when they'd been students at UConn's Magic Campus.

After Lilly died, I had been powerless to alleviate my family's grief. To keep myself from going out of my mind, I'd gotten involved with helping unMarked Mags who were trying to flee to Boston. A lot of them were stuck in dangerous situations and unable to defend themselves against the ones hunting them.

I had thrown myself into the work, needing the distraction. I'd become addicted to helping strangers, since there was nothing I could do for the people I loved most.

I helped enough people escape their homes that the Alliance started wising up to my involvement. My choices were either to stop cold turkey or make it impossible for the authorities to track me down.

So, during my senior year of high school, I decided to go unMarked. I was risking my life by breaking the second high law, which required all Mags to be Marked, but I didn't care.

I'd never regretted cutting out my tracker, but I also hadn't accounted for how isolated I'd become. I'd had no choice but to hide out in my parents' house until I encountered Kaira and the rest of our friends. It turned out they had the same goals as me, except they were a lot more effective. They'd needed muscle to rescue a Russian family that was seeking sanctuary in Boston, and I'd volunteered.

Becoming part of the Six had saved me. It had drawn me away from the despair that had been swallowing the rest of my family whole.

"You okay?" Yutika whispered, nudging me as we walked down the long hallway.

"I'll be better once we're done with Cinnamon Guy," I told her, following Sir Zachary around the corner as he led the way to the right unit.

"That makes one of us," Yutika sighed.

"You have a boyfriend," I pointed out.

"It doesn't make me blind," she retorted.

Sir Zachary stopped in front of a door with chipping paint. He wagged his tail.

"Should we knock," Graysen began, "or—"

I kicked the door in.

"Never mess with a Steel," A.J. said behind me. "Five words that could save your life one day."

I flipped the light switch by the door.

When Cinnamon Guy didn't come running with a deer-in-the-headlights look on his face, disappointment roiled through me.

I wanted a fight, and once again, this man had deprived me of what I needed.

What a jerk.

My friends filtered into the apartment behind me. Michael wrestled the door back into place while the rest of us spread out to look around.

It was a studio apartment, so there wasn't much to explore. There was a small kitchen, a slightly larger main room, and a separate bathroom. The place had a clean, almost sterile feel to it. There were no pictures on the walls, workout clothes strewn on the floor, or half-empty boxes of cookies like an intruder would find in my room. Cinnamon Guy didn't even have a real bed; it was just a mattress in the center of the floor with a plain blue comforter. Beside the mattress, there was a lamp with no lampshade. A black dresser against the wall completed the no-frills décor.

"There's no chocolate in here," Yutika said, her voice coming from inside the fridge. "But someone definitely lives here." She wrinkled her nose as she pulled out a bag of spinach and half gallon of skim milk. "I'm totally judging Sexy Cinnamon Man for his boring diet. Although, hey—are those ghost peppers?!"

"Are we sure this is his place?" Michael asked, looking around.

I picked up the pack of cinnamon gum on the counter.

"Yep."

"Everyone shut up for a second," Smith said.

We did. Our Techie closed his eyes and stood motionless. After a few seconds, he strode over to the mattress and pulled back the blanket. He tossed aside the pillow to reveal a laptop.

"Come to Papa," Smith said.

I waited impatiently for the computer to give up its secrets to Smith.

"Jackpot," Kaira called, closing the bottom dresser drawer.

"Did you find the other half of Pruwist's paper?" I asked, my pulse skyrocketing.

"No," Kaira replied. "But I found these." She held up a stack of stuffed manilla folders.

We all gathered around Cinnamon Guy's bed, with the exception of Yutika and Sir Zachary, who continued to explore. I ignored the way the blanket smelled like him and reminded me of what was inarguably the hottest kiss I'd ever experienced.

Kaira opened the folders and let the papers inside flutter out. We all stared.

"These are descriptions of all of the Super Mags," Smith said, spreading out the papers in front of us. "Looks like he included everything in the Super Mags' official files, plus a whole lot more."

Everything was written by hand. Grainy printer photos of each Super Mag were taped to the front of each packet.

"How did he get all of this information?" Michael asked. "Aside from us and the Super Mags, no one else alive has this information."

"So we thought," A.J. said.

There were pages and pages of information about each of the Super Mags. There was so much packed onto each page that it must have taken Cinnamon Guy years to compile all of this information. The papers were wrinkled and thin from how many times they'd been handled.

I recognized obsession when I saw it. For some reason, staring at these papers while I sat in this unloved apartment made me feel unbearably sad.

As we went through the hand-written pages, I noticed something else.

"Look at this." I tapped one of the papers.

Underneath a general description of the Super Mag's abilities, there was a section that Cinnamon Guy had labeled *Threat Assessment*.

As we leafed through the papers, we found that Cinnamon Guy had classified each Super Mag on a four-tier system, where Tier 1 Super Mags were the highest threat and needed to be "dealt with ASAP," while those labeled as Tier 4 were considered less deadly.

"Look at this," Graysen said. He held up several stapled pages. The cover page was a blown-up photo of the Pyro who had recently had his magic stolen. Beneath the photo, there was a single, hand-written word.

COMPLETE.

The two other Super Mags who had recently lost their magic were also marked as *complete*.

"Holy vegan baloney," A.J. said in disbelief. "If anyone wanted undeniable proof, we've got it. We found our magic ripper."

A dozen emotions went through me, the first of which was disappointment. I'd known the guy was a dick, but I hadn't gotten evil vibes from him.

Idiot, I told myself. What did I really know about him, besides the fact that he was a smart aleck and a fantastic kisser?

The lack of passion in my life was going to my head. I seriously needed to get laid.

Graysen said, "I wonder whether he's brewing the MRP himself or if he's got an Alchemist on his payroll."

"The former, most definitely," Yutika called from Cinnamon Guy's bathroom. "Check it out."

We crowded outside the bathroom and stared in. Yutika had shoved aside the white shower curtain to reveal the inside of the tub. In addition to body wash and shampoo, there was what looked like a professional chemistry set. Beakers, tubes ciphering liquid from one to the other, packets of various mystery powders, and vials of Agent S filled the tub. There was even a Bunsen burner on the counter next to Cinnamon Guy's toothbrush and razor.

"He's making MRP," Graysen said in disbelief.

We all gaped at the evidence in Cinnamon Guy's bathtub.

We knew the formula for the Magical Reduction Potion from our investigation into Subject 6, but we couldn't have done anything with it even if we'd wanted to. The formula was so complicated, and the ingredients so volatile, that the tiniest error could result in a brew toxic enough to take down an entire city block.

At least, that was what Smith had said after he'd researched the formula. He had a tendency to be a little alarmist, so it was possible only this apartment building would be destroyed by MRP gone wrong. Regardless, it wasn't the kind of potion an average chemistry enthusiast would attempt.

"Smith, who is this guy?" Kaira demanded. "I mean, aside from being the magic ripper we've been searching for."

"Assuming he didn't make it up for his laptop username," Smith replied, his attention still focused on the computer, "his name is Diego Agramonte."

Diego Agramonte. The name certainly didn't ring any bells.

"Can I still call him Sexy Cinnamon Man?" Yutika asked.

"Yutika," Michael said in a soft voice.

"What?" she turned a mischievous smile on him. "I don't need to call you Sexy Michael, since it would be totally redundant. You're the embodiment of sexiness."

Blushing, Michael just shook his head.

Smith shot Yutika an irritated look. "Whatever else *Diego* has done on this computer, he wiped it well enough that I can't recover anything."

Smith's expression was one of grudging respect.

"There's no record of anyone by that name in the Magical Marking Office's records," Smith continued. "There was a Rosa Agramonte born in Mexico City in 2017, though. She was a Level 8 Alchemist. I can't find anything else about her."

"UnMarked?" Graysen asked.

Smith nodded. "Had to be. Her only existing documentation is her birth certificate."

"Birth certificates are difficult to destroy," Kaira said, sliding a guilty look at Graysen.

"Well, I guess we know who taught Sexy Cinnamon Man how to play with chemicals," A.J. observed.

"I think we can call him Diego now," I pointed out. "You know, for simplicity's sake."

We all turned as Sir Zachary let out a plaintive whine. He scratched at the wall next to the dresser.

I exchanged a look with my friends before going over to investigate. That's when I noticed the grooves on the floor. It looked like the dresser had been repetitively dragged back and forth. I gave the piece of furniture a little shove, pushing it away from the wall.

"Holy shit."

"What?" six voices demanded at once.

Wordlessly, I stepped aside so the others could see.

"Holy shit," Smith echoed.

More curses and exclamations followed as my friends took in the scene.

Cinnamon Guy—Diego—had cut a hole in the wall. Inside the narrow space were rows and rows of stacked Agent S vials.

The green liquid gleamed luminescent in the dark. The liquid churned restlessly, straining against its glass confinement toward me.

Smith pulled his poison scanner out of his hoodie pocket and flipped it on.

Instantly, the room filled with the scanner's screeching cry. The red light flashed maniacally. My ears were ringing by the time Smith finally switched it off.

"Yeah, that's definitely Agent S," Smith confirmed.

"Time to call the police?" Yutika asked.

"No," I said quickly. "We have to find out what was on the other half of Pruwist's paper."

If the police got their hands on Diego first, I'd never find out what he knew.

"We could wait for him to come back here," Michael suggested. "I'll Whisper to him, and then we can hand him over to the police."

"Sounds reasonable." Graysen nodded.

"We could be waiting a while," A.J. said. He held up a piece of cardstock he'd fished out of the garbage. It was black and orange with gold lettering on it.

It was a Halloween party announcement…for tonight.

"Let me see that," Graysen said, reaching for the invitation.

"What's the matter?" Kaira asked.

"I have a bad feeling I need to confirm." Graysen pulled out his phone and dialed.

We all waited.

"Hey, Emory," Graysen said when the call connected. "Do you know anything about a party at a nightclub called *Liquid Magic* tonight?"

He listened for a few seconds.

"Yeah, that's what I thought." Graysen's brow furrowed as he shot us a worried look. "Tell your people to get out of there. We're heading over now, but the magic ripper may already be there."

"Gray, what?" Kaira asked, as soon as he disconnected the call.

"A bunch of the Super Mags are at that party," Graysen said. "I remembered them talking about it earlier."

"Shit," Kaira said. "We have to get them out of there."

On most nights, *Liquid Magic* was a slightly raunchy dance club. On the holidays, though, the place took a more family-friendly approach. I happened to know that they threw the best Halloween and New Year's Eve parties in the city.

"Oh goody!" A.J. clapped his hands. "Please tell me it's a costume party." He looked back at the announcement and squealed. "It is!"

"Hold your horses, cowboy," I told him. "What are we going to do about this?" I gestured to the Agent S stockpile.

If the vials had been filled with anything else, I'd just smash them. But Agent S would burn right through the floor and probably eat through the whole building.

"I'll take care of it," A.J. said. He flicked his hand, and the vials filed out of their hiding place.

The window opened, seemingly on its own, and the vials zoomed out and up into the night air.

"While you deal with that," Yutika said, flipping open her sketchbook, "let's talk Halloween costumes."

CHAPTER 16

Kaira had dared suggest simply illusioning all of us, and Smith had made the even more daring suggestion of going sans costumes altogether. But when it came right down to it, no one was willing to take on A.J. *and* Yutika.

"A party's a party," A.J. said, like he was spouting law or scripture. "The rules of engagement must be obeyed, which means we cannot cut corners."

So, while Michael drove to the dance club, the rest of us changed into our costumes.

Normally, I enjoyed parties as much as anyone. *Well, maybe not as much as A.J.* At the moment, though, I was too preoccupied with what we'd learned about Diego.

He was making the Magical Reduction Potion and injecting it into the Super Mags.

"Can we open our eyes yet?" Smith grumbled.

"Ready," Yutika, Kaira, and I said.

I was a little out of breath from squeezing into the outfit Yutika had made me. It was a mere inch or two away from sluttyville, but it was Halloween. Certain liberties were allowed.

"Looking good, Girlfriend," A.J. told me.

"Back atcha," I replied, grinning at our angel and devil costumes.

I was the devil. Yutika had even made me a headband with horns and four-inch red thigh-high boots. The red halter top dress was sparkly. I kind of loved it.

A.J. had a furry halo perched on his head and a white cape with attached wings. His black hair was full of glitter.

Kaira wore a sexy cop uniform. She claimed it was subtle commentary on the Alliance's legal system, but I thought the real reason had more to do with the way Graysen was practically drooling at the sight of her. He kept playing with the handcuffs on her belt and giving her *fuck me* eyes. The rest of us pretended not to notice.

Graysen was dressed up as the top Mag soccer player in the world—an Argentinian whose name I could never remember. Yutika went as a hamburger, because in her words, she liked to watch the world burn. A.J. seemed ready to blow a gasket at the sight of her.

"It's definitely a black bean patty," I consoled A.J., patting the relevant part of Yutika's costume. "Non-GMO and everything."

No amount of cajoling, pleading, and threatening had gotten Smith to agree to a costume. He would be staying in the van to monitor his tech and was generally opposed to fun.

And Michael, looking utterly miserable, had a French fries costume waiting for him as soon as he got out of the driver's seat.

Kaira illusioned herself and Graysen as soon as we rolled up to the club, but the rest of us were costumed up enough that no one was going to recognize us. Besides, *Liquid Magic* wasn't exactly the kind of place where reporters hung out.

"Try not to get into too much trouble," Smith said as the rest of us piled out. He sat back in his seat and stared at his computers.

"We never get into trouble," Yutika quipped as she squeezed her hamburger patty midsection out of the van.

It was close to 2:00AM, but there was still a line wrapped around the block. We went right to the front.

"Hey, Hank," I called to the scowling bouncer who was guarding the door.

"Bri, baby!" The giant man's face cracked into a wide smile. "You little devil, you."

Laughing, I reached over to give him a hug.

For a whole year before I'd joined Kaira and the others, I couldn't do anything that required a tracker and file…which was pretty much everything. Since *Liquid Magic* was less scrupulous about documentation, they'd given me a part-time job as a bouncer. The money had been nice, but the best part had been getting to talk to someone besides my family for a few nights a week.

"Come on in, Bri and friends." Hank swept his hand at the door. The people waiting impatiently behind the velvet rope let out an enraged cry.

Inside, the club was a madhouse.

"Now, this is what I'm talkin' about!" A.J. yelled over the pumping music.

"You're not in there to party," Smith said across our earpieces.

"Our priority is to find Diego and the Super Mags," Kaira said. "Let's split up."

"Kai and I will take the third floor," Graysen said.

"I'll do the rooftop bar with Yutika," Michael said.

"There are good camera angles on the second floor," Smith said. "Leave that to me."

"I guess that means you and me are down here, Devil Lady," A.J. said into his mike.

"Cool. I'll take the bar," I replied. "You start in the back."

My friends' chatter filled my earpiece as I moved deeper into the club. The combination of strobe lights and costumes made it next to impossible to see people's faces until I was on top of them.

The smells of perfume, sweat, and alcohol were so strong it gave me a headache. I was glad I'd convinced A.J. to leave Sir Zachary in the van instead of bringing him in.

"How are we supposed to find anyone in this mess?" Graysen complained. Even though his voice was in my ear, I could barely hear him.

"We dance!" came A.J.'s immediate reply.

Shaking my head, I pushed past a group of women dressed as vampires. I reached the bar, which was even more crowded than the dance floor. I leaned over the counter to try and get the bartender's attention, since everyone knew that was the best person to get intel from.

I yelped in surprise when cold liquid splashed down the front of my dress.

"Oh God, I'm so sorry!" The man standing beside me glared at his empty glass, like it was the drink's fault it had spilled all over me. He grabbed a handful of cocktail napkins and went to dab at the wet spot.

"I got it," I told him, taking the napkins from his hand and wiping up the spill myself.

I reeked of tequila. Awesome.

"Can I buy you a drink?" the man asked, ducking his head close to mine so I'd be able to hear him over the music.

"I think you already did." I gestured to my wet costume.

"Ah shit, you're right." The man put his glass down on the bar and gave me an apologetic smile. "Can I make it up to you on the dance floor?"

"Maybe later," I told him distractedly as I tried to wave over the bartender again.

"Just one dance?" the guy pleaded, clearly having missed my not-so-subtle dismissal. He reached for my hand.

"I said no."

I didn't want to turn titanium and blow my cover, but that wouldn't stop me from knocking out a few teeth if this guy didn't get lost.

Normally I was more polite, but I was on a mission.

"Have you guys found anything?" I asked into my mike.

No response.

I could still hear my friends' voices in my earpiece, but my mike wasn't working. I looked down at the wet spot on my cleavage, which included my mike.

Damnit.

I was contemplating whether it was worth trying to find Yutika and have her make me a new one, when the man reached for my hand again.

I was just about to introduce his face to my knuckles when an intense wave of magic surrounded me. At the same moment, a male body pressed against my back. I caught the faintest hint of cinnamon as his lips grazed the side of my neck. Goosebumps flitted down my bare arms.

"Sorry I'm late, cariño," Diego said, loud enough for everyone in the vicinity to hear. He draped an arm over my shoulders and gave the drink-spiller a cold look.

Diego was shorter than the other man by half a foot, but he gave off serious *don't test me* vibes. I had no doubt which of them would come out on top in a fight. Maybe it was the tattoos.

"You're not hitting on my girl, are you?" Diego asked the other man.

He didn't shout, and yet, his voice carried above the music.

"I, uh, was just going," my unwanted solicitor said, making a graceless exit as he scampered back into the crush of people.

"Twice in one night, Bri Hammond?" Diego quirked an eyebrow at me. "I'm beginning to think you can't get enough of me."

"Don't flatter yourself," I replied, removing his arm from my shoulders. "And I didn't need a rescue. I hope you weren't expecting a thanks."

"I'd settle for another kiss," he replied.

"Fat chance," I said, ignoring the reminder of how good his lips had felt on mine. "But since I have you here, you're going to give me some answers."

"Gladly," Diego replied smoothly. "But you'll have to earn them."

"I'll earn them," I said through gritted teeth, "by agreeing not to beat you into a bloody pulp."

"You could." The cocky bastard grinned and leaned closer. "But it'll be so much more fun to do it my way."

Without waiting for a response, he took my hand and pulled me toward the dance floor.

After a short internal debate, I decided to play his game. I could always get my answers and then beat him up. At the end of the night, the ordering didn't matter to me.

Besides, as long as he was with me, he wasn't shooting any Super Mags up with MRP. If that was in fact why he'd come here. In spite of all the evidence, I still didn't want to believe he was our magic ripper.

"I'm surprised to see you out partying," Diego said, leading me to a less crowded part of the dance floor. "Don't you have more important things to do?"

"I could ask you the same, Diego Agramonte," I shot back.

Surprise flashed across his face. I smiled to myself in satisfaction. So that *was* his real name. I filed that detail away to share with Smith later, since my mike was on the fritz. I could still hear my friends, I just couldn't talk to them.

"Where did you hear that name?" Diego asked. His voice was nonchalant, but there was an intense look in his eyes.

"From my Techie," I replied. "Now, it's your turn to answer questions."

"Nuh-uh, cariño." He wrapped his hand around mine. "You promised me a dance."

I'd done no such thing. Before I could tell him so, Diego spun me around and pulled me into the cradle of his arms.

All at once, there was nothing between us. The heat of his body and magic surrounded me until it was an effort just to breathe.

"She can fight," Diego said against my ear. "But can she dance?"

The tequila fumes must have gotten to me, because I didn't immediately put him in a chokehold and drag him to wherever Michael was.

I had no idea what it said about me that the first man to ever make my heart race was brewing MRP in his apartment and injecting it into Super Mags.

Nothing good.

"Okay, we're dancing," I said. "Tell me what was on that piece of paper you stole from me." And then, because I was feeling feisty, I added, "*Cariño.*"

I rolled my R like a native.

Diego's eyebrows shot up. "Hablas español."

Yeah, for four years in high school with a narcoleptic teacher who did more snoring than teaching. I knew some of the basics and pretty much all of the curses. My friends and I had downloaded and memorized a list of Spanish swear words while we were supposed to be reading *Don Quixote* in Spanish. We were so cool.

"Suficiente." I shrugged.

Diego leaned closer so his lips touched my ear. "Tell me something dirty. In Spanish."

From the way his grip on my waist tightened, I knew he expected me to pull away. I leaned closer. I licked my lips, giving him the most seductive look I had in my arsenal. Judging from the way his breath caught, it did the trick.

"Algo sucio," I said, giving him the literal translation for *something dirty.*

I never claimed to be mature.

Diego threw his head back and laughed. And then, eyes still twinkling, he started to dance to the music.

My body moved in time with his, like it couldn't help itself. I hooked one arm around his neck—mostly to make sure he didn't go anywhere until I got the answers I'd come for.

It had been a while since I'd been this close to another person, and I couldn't deny I was starved for the physical contact. I told myself it was that, rather than anything particular about Diego, that had me all hot and bothered.

There was also no denying Diego was as good at dancing as he was at kissing. Not that I'd ever tell him that.

"I like this," Diego said, his hand skimming down my spine and splaying across my lower back. "It's even more fun than fighting with you."

I scowled up at him, to which he responded with a smirk.

"Cute costume." Diego reached up to flick one of my horns.

"And where's yours?" I shot back, giving a pointed glare to his jeans and black T-shirt.

"Don't need one." He stepped back until he was pressed against the exposed brick wall. Diego blurred out until he was completely indecipherable from the wall behind him. He'd even replicated a small crack that went across a row of bricks. If I couldn't still feel his hands at my waist, I would have sworn he'd disappeared.

"Neat little trick," I told him.

The brick wall camouflage disappeared as Diego turned back into his normal appearance.

"I have lots of tricks," he said, drawing me so close our hips and chests were melded together. "Would you like to see some?"

"What I would like," I said, trying to get a handle on my skyrocketing pulse, "is for you to tell me what you did with that paper you stole."

Diego's lips quirked. "If memory serves, you were the one who stole it first."

"Where is it, Diego?" I demanded. I thrust my hands into his pockets, searching for the slip of paper that hadn't been anywhere in the apartment we trashed.

"A little to the left," he said as I dug my hand into his front pocket. "But no woman has ever had to ask me that before."

"Ugh!" I gave him a hard push. "Where. Is. That. Paper?!"

Diego grinned at me. "I threw it out as soon as I left the house."

I squinted up at him, trying to read his expression. All I saw in his eyes was amusement.

"Why were you in Pruwist's house, then, if not for that?" I asked, trying to stave off my panic at the possibility that he was telling the truth.

He gave me an inscrutable look. "No special reason."

"Mm." I stretched up on my toes until our lips were almost touching. Diego closed his eyes and tilted his head. His diamond earring winked in the club's strobe lights. "It wouldn't by any chance have anything to do with the MRP brewing in your bathtub, would it?"

Diego's eyes flew open. Fear, followed by anger, passed across his face. He took my upper arms and spun, so my back was digging into the brick wall.

"What have you done?" he demanded in a harsh voice.

All of his flirty teasing was gone, replaced by cold intensity. For the first time, I saw the obsessive person who had painstakingly compiled those information packets about all of the Super Mags.

"Destroyed all of it," I said casually. "Including the stack of Agent S vials you hid behind your dresser." I gave him a triumphant smile. "You're probably going to want to call in a cleaning crew, because—"

Diego moved so fast I didn't have a chance to react. His body blurred out until I could only feel rather than see him. Then, I became see-through, too. I felt Diego's arms like a vise around me. And then, I was flying.

Literally flying.

I shrieked as we shot straight into the air. Colors blurred as my appearance changed to match the purple-and-blue strobe lighting on the ceiling.

"What—" I gasped, just as I felt the brush of cold, clean air.

Diego's arms tightened around me as we spiraled straight through an open window behind the stage. And then we were in the sky, looking down at the club's roof.

I tried to shout at him to put me down, but I couldn't make the words come. I was surrounded by night sky and the Boston city lights. Freezing air rushed by, but I was sheltered by the heat of Diego's magic. He was so powerful.

As we flew higher, I remembered our fight in Pruwist's house. It had seemed like Diego was moving too quickly and silently for any normal person…even one who could camouflage his skin. I couldn't figure out why it had sounded like his voice was coming from the ceiling.

That's why he'd been so impossible to pin down when we'd fought. Diego wasn't just a Chameleon. The man could fly.

And that could mean only one thing. Diego Agramonte was a Super Mag.

CHAPTER 17

We were on top of the John Hancock Tower—the tallest building in the city.

I glanced over the edge and immediately swayed on my feet. If Diego's arms weren't locked around me, I might have gone right over. Heights weren't usually a problem for me, but then again, I'd never been this high up and at the mercy of a psycho Super Mag.

"What the hell?" I demanded, my voice coming out scratchy.

I blew on one of my fists. I had no idea whether I'd survive a fall from this height even in my titanium form, but I knew my chances if I was normal bones and flesh.

Well, at least now I knew how Diego had gotten out of Pruwist's house when we'd trussed him up like a wild boar. He hadn't needed his limbs because he could fly.

"What did you do with my Agent S?" Diego demanded. He kept an arm locked around my waist. Unlike before when we were dancing, this didn't feel like playing.

"I already told you," I said. "We destroyed it."

"Why?" Diego's dark eyes were molten fury. When I didn't immediately respond, he gave me a little shake.

If I'd been anyone else, I might have been a little afraid of him.

"I could ask you the same question." I met his furious gaze. "I'm curious why you've been taking away the Super Mags' magic. Especially because, you know, you're a Super Mag."

He didn't confirm or deny it, but I didn't need him to. I should have known the first time I felt his magic. My friends and I were powerful, but

Diego was in a completely different league. I just hadn't suspected what he was, since I'd never encountered a Super Mag outside of the MagLab kids.

Part of me had thought my awareness of his magic had something to do with my unfortunate attraction to this man.

"You had no fucking right," he began, his chest heaving.

"No, you had no right." I poked a titanium finger into his pec. "You don't get to go around taking away people's magic. Who do you think you are?!"

"Someone who understands that no person should have this much magic." He let go of me to gesture to himself. "You can't imagine what it's like. Someone like you could never understand."

"Someone like me? What the hell is that supposed to mean?"

Diego got right in my face, his eyes dark pools in the black sky surrounding us.

"I'm going to give them…us," his face contorted in disgust, "a chance at a normal life. I'm going to save hundreds…thousands…by stopping them before they snap like that Pyro."

"You're deranged," I told him.

"I'm right," he retorted. "That Pyro killed sixty-five people in the MagLab fire, and twenty-seven more at the retirement home.

"If I hadn't dealt with that kid, who knows how many more people would have burned? None of your precious Directors' new laws can save Boston from that kind of evil."

"Kaira and Graysen understand it isn't their place to play God," I shot back.

"I spent months learning how to make the Magical Reduction Potion," Diego said, his voice turning low and threatening. "Good people died for that formula, and I'm not going to let you get in the way of what needs to be done."

"Good luck with that," I told him in a frigid tone. "You're going to have a hell of a time making more MRP without any Agent S."

Diego's bronze skin paled a fraction. Then, all emotion fled from his face. He regarded me coolly.

"How's your memory?" he asked.

Startled by the abrupt change in topic, I said, "Uhh, good, I guess?"

"Then, remember this."

As soon as he started rattling off numbers, I decided my memory wasn't as good as the situation required. I batted Diego's hand off my waist and stepped away from the roof's edge so I could whip out my phone. Ignoring the dozen missed calls from my friends, I transcribed the rest of the numbers.

"GPS coordinates?" I asked, looking at my screen after he'd finished speaking.

"That's what was on the other half of the paper you were desperate enough to grope me for." His voice held that hint of mockery I'd come to associate with him.

"I thought you said you threw that paper out." I gave him a suspicious look.

This had to be some kind of trick.

"I did." Diego's lip twitched. "I just memorized what was on it before I tossed it."

"Uh-huh." I stared from the numbers on my screen to Diego's inscrutable face. "So, you're telling me this now…why?"

I was under no illusion that he was doing it out of the goodness of his heart. He'd just found out that my friends and I had disappeared his Agent S stockpile. And he didn't strike me as the forgiving type.

"Because." Diego leaned in close until his breath stirred the wisps of hair framing my face. "I need Agent S, and you're going to get it for me."

"Sure, buddy. Would you like overnight shipping or in-person delivery?"

He lowered his head to give me a sensual look full of dark promise. "In-person. Definitely in-person." His fingers curled around the hem of my dress. Fiery tingles shot up my thigh.

I forced myself to smack his hand away. I started to back up, before I remembered we were standing at the edge of a rooftop sixty-two stories above the ground.

"You're going to be arrested for what you've done," I told him. "You know that, right?"

Diego gave me a sardonic smile that wasn't at all friendly.

"We'll see, cariño. We'll see."

"Diego—" I began.

"As much as I'd like to while away my night on this rooftop with you, I came to this party for a reason."

Diego leaned in. For a heart-stopping second, I thought he was going to kiss me again. His lips stopped a centimeter from my own.

"Stay," he ordered me.

Then, he stepped off the ledge.

"You are *not* leaving me up here. Come back here, you bastard!"

I was talking to empty air. Diego was gone.

✳ ✳ ✳

"That piece of shit," Kaira fumed.

"Watch your mouth," Grandma Tashi snapped from the other room. "There are children about."

Kaira rolled her eyes, but only when she was sure her grandmother wasn't looking.

"It's five in the morning," A.J. said to Kaira's grandmother. "Why are you still awake?"

"Someone had to stay up and make sure you came back in one piece," Tashi grumbled. "Now get yourselves upstairs and to bed. Quietly. You'll wake the whole damn house."

"Did you just say damn?" Kaira asked, momentarily distracted from her Diego-induced fury.

"I said bed!" Tashi hollered.

Knowing we were beat, we did as we were told.

It had taken close to half an hour for me to stop cursing Diego at the top of my lungs…from the top of the tallest building in Boston. Afterward, I'd called my friends. With one bar of reception on my phone, it had taken a small miracle to convey the gist of what the Super Dick had done. It had taken even longer for us to figure out how to actually get me back to the ground.

In the end, Yutika had created a small cart, like the ones found on amusement park roller coasters. A.J. had flown it up to the top of the building, since he could only control inanimate objects with his telekinesis and couldn't just fly me to the ground. Then, once I was in the cart, A.J. was able to bring me back down. Kaira kept us all illusioned so someone from a neighboring skyrise didn't start spreading rumors about a flying person.

It hadn't helped my mood that the ride down was decidedly bumpier and more nausea-inducing than the flight up.

Diego Agramonte was a dead man. And I didn't mean that figuratively.

When we got back into the club, all of the Super Mags were gone except for one of the girls. 00545 was crying in the corner. It took Michael about three seconds to learn from the distraught child that she'd been injected with the MRP.

00545 had been a Level 16 Teleporter and was the Super Mags' primary mode of transportation.

Lower-level Teleporters could only manage quick jumps over a short distance. This girl could get from the US to Europe without batting an eye.

00545's only crime was that she was suspected in a drugstore robbery that had involved fifty bucks' worth of stolen goods—most of which were sour gummy worms. She was also eleven years old. And now, because of Diego, her magic was gone.

After we helped the girl get home, I told my friends about the fun fact that Diego was himself a Super Mag.

None of us could figure out how he'd managed to go this long without being detected. We also couldn't figure out why a Super Mag would be hunting down his own kind.

His explanation on the rooftop had made no sense.

I'm going to give Super Mags a chance at a normal life…. I'm going to save hundreds….

At best, Diego was delusional and a narcissist.

"At least tonight wasn't a total loss," Yutika said, interrupting my brooding. "We have the other set of coordinates."

As luck would have it, the location was right here in Boston.

"We'll check it out in the morning," Graysen said, yawning. "And by morning, I mean afternoon, since it already is morning."

"You all are looking extremely peaked," A.J. said, giving us pitying looks. "I become more exotic with shadows under my eyes, but the rest of you are getting a little scary."

"Thanks for the self-esteem booster." I patted him on the arm.

"Let's sleep until noon," Kaira said, leaning against Graysen as we climbed the stairs. "Then, we'll go check out those coordinates."

We all bid each other sleepy goodnights and headed to our respective rooms. Despite the fact that I hadn't gotten a decent night's sleep in longer than I could remember, I was oddly awake.

I did two reps of jumping jacks, a hundred sit-ups, and fifty push-ups. I didn't stop until my mind had quieted enough to give me a fighting chance at sleep.

I said good morning to Herbert, the window-tapping woodpecker, before pulling my blinds shut. As I stripped off my devil costume, I caught the hint of cinnamon on my clothes. I wasn't sure how that was possible after the tequila and everything else that had happened during the night, but the smell brought Diego's smug face right to the forefront of my brain.

I couldn't help but remember what it had felt like with our hips and chests molded together as we'd danced, and then as we'd flown.

We'd flown.

Granted, Diego had been pissed as hell and I'd been threatening him at the time. Those details aside, it had been the biggest rush of my life. The fear of falling, while somehow knowing he wouldn't let me go, made me want to do it again. And again.

Maybe I was an adrenaline junkie.

Since I was still too wound up for sleep or rational thought, I decided to take a bath. I hadn't used my amazing tub once in the four months since we'd moved in. I lit two vanilla candles and poured a frightening amount of vanilla-scented bubbles into the running water.

My skin naturally carried a faint smell of metal, regardless of whether I was using my magic or not. I didn't mind it, but I found that metal combined with vanilla made for a nice mix—sweet on the surface and hardness underneath.

I slid into the water, letting the bubbles close over me like a filmy blanket.

Vanilla and cinnamon, I thought hazily. Perfect combination for pastries, candles, and coffee creamer. But that was all.

I soaked in the bath until I'd washed away the day's adventures and purged all thoughts of a certain sexy, infuriating magic ripper.

CHAPTER 18

Six solid hours of sleep later, and I woke feeling like a new woman. Ma's brunch, which was hot and ready when we got downstairs, sealed the deal. I dug into a tofu scramble, hash browns, and fruit salad. I gave the cinnamon donut holes a wide berth. If I never got a whiff of that scent again, it would be too soon.

We spent the rest of the afternoon catching up on Alliance business. All I wanted was to race off to investigate the coordinates Diego had given us, but it wasn't like the city was going to pause everything else in the meantime. Besides, this whole thing was starting to feel more and more like a wild goose chase.

Kaira, Graysen, and Michael had been in meetings with Emory and the rest of the Super Mag kids for the last several hours. Kaira and Graysen had come up with the idea of starting a Super Mag-led coalition that would give the kids equal representation in the Alliance. The only problem was that after a lifetime in MagLab, looting and running wild on the streets was a lot more fun than being law-abiding citizens.

I couldn't really blame the kids.

Yutika was putting the final touches on a fairytale house for the Super Mags on our property to entice them to stick around. We had more than enough land, and it would make it easier for us to keep an eye on them.

The Super Mags hadn't agreed to live on our property yet, but I was sure once they saw what Yutika had made for them, they wouldn't be able to resist. Not to mention, with Diego on the loose and injecting them with MRP, the kids were feeling less invincible than they had before.

Smith was doing Techie things in his office, which was so full of wires and machines that there wasn't room for anyone except him inside. I had a sneaking suspicion he'd done that intentionally.

A.J. was busy doing damage control from the Red Sox game debacle. From the sound of it, he had also booked several photo shoots and TV appearances that Kaira was going to give him hell for once she found out.

I did my usual security rounds, checking in with all of my people. I also hired two new security guards…after they passed the Sir Zachary sniff test. I figured since he wagged his tail instead of barking fire at them, it was a good sign.

We reconvened for a quick dinner and meeting. Then, while there were still a couple of daylight hours, we headed out to the location Diego had given me the night before. After our failure to find anything useful in California, we brought Charlotte and Sir Zachary with us for extra olfactory support.

We piled out of the van in front of what was left of MagLab. The ground was covered in a fine layer of gray ash from the Pyro's fire that had freed fifty of the Super Mags…and killed sixty-five others.

The whole swath of ground was marked off with police tape and still carried the faint odor of something that was probably carcinogenic. Kaira illusioned all of into police as a precautionary measure, even though we were the only ones around.

We picked our way through the rubble as Smith's GPS tracker led us to the exact coordinates.

Acutely aware of Diego's reasoning for sharing the coordinates—that he thought I was going to bring the Agent S to him—I was on high alert for any hint of his presence.

I wasn't sure what I'd been expecting, but as we gathered amid the scorched rubble, my heart sank.

"Sexy Cinnamon Man screwed us," Yutika observed.

"Either that," Graysen said, "or this was the location we needed, but the fire destroyed whatever we were supposed to find."

"It's hopeless," A.J. groaned.

"Not necessarily." Smith, the pessimist of our group, held up a hand.

He closed his eyes.

"I can feel tech under here." He tapped his foot on the ashy ground. "Working tech."

"How far down?" Kaira asked.

"Hard to tell," Smith replied. "There's a lot of interference from the dirt and rubble."

"I'll go down and check it out," Charlotte said, her voice coming from the body of an overweight male cop.

Kaira dropped Charlotte's illusion just as the little girl transformed into a furry mole. I thought it was cute, until I caught sight of its paws. They were too big for the animal's body and looked like human skeleton hands…with nails. *Yuck.*

Sir Zachary gave the mole a tentative sniff and then wagged his tail.

"Be careful down there," A.J. said, unperturbed by the freaky little monster animal.

The mole's snout wiggled, and then it began to worm its way into the dirt.

I rescinded my earlier assessment of those creepy hand-paws when I saw how fast Charlotte-the-mole could dig. In seconds, all that was left was a small pile of dirt the mole had displaced.

The rest of us waited.

My legs were starting to cramp from standing in one place for so long, when Sir Zachary gave a happy little yip. Seconds later, a twitching nose emerged from the dirt.

There was a ripple of movement. Then, the furry mole with the creepy hands transformed into a little girl.

"Blech." Charlotte spat out a mouthful of dirt.

A.J. handed over his polka-dotted hankie.

"There's some stuff about ten feet down," Charlotte reported. "I can see where there was an entrance from inside MagLab, but it's all burnt and crumpled now.

"Can you show us where to dig?" Yutika asked, already sketching shovels on her pad.

In no time at all, we'd dug the hole. Yutika had even devised a pulley system so no one would break a leg coming in or out of the hole.

At the bottom, we found several blackened floor tiles and a metal hatch.

"It's stuck," Graysen said, his muscles straining as he fought to pry it open.

"Move aside," I said with a wink, blowing on my fists.

The metal hatch groaned and snapped. I hauled off the covering, which must have weighed more than I did, and tossed it to the side. We all looked down into a black, circular hole.

Aside from the top of the ladder that was attached to the hole, it was impossible to see anything.

"Who's going first?" Yutika asked, pressing a finger to her nose to indicate she wasn't it.

I didn't wait for anyone else to volunteer. I grasped the top rung and started lowering myself down.

Within seconds, I was surrounded by darkness. I couldn't see anything except for the dull silver gleam of my own skin. The air smelled dank and musty. I got an intimate preview of the life of an earthworm.

I didn't like it.

I heard voices and felt vibrations shimmy through the ladder as my friends followed me down.

I squeezed my eyes shut when a bright light flooded the hole.

"Yutika, you're blinding me," I yelled up.

"Oops," she replied, before angling the flashlight toward the wall.

We climbed. And climbed.

Hundreds of rungs turned to thousands. I lost count as the air grew thicker. An overwhelming sense of foreboding crawled across my metal skin. I was just beginning to wonder whether I'd climbed down some *Alice in Wonderland* black hole and would keep climbing forever, when my foot hit solid ground.

I immediately turned so my back was to the ladder and held up my fists, but no one jumped me. I pulled out my phone and turned on the flashlight.

I was in a circular chamber about ten feet in diameter. There was a tall, metal door opposite the ladder and nothing else. I was about to yank the door open, when I noticed a black box next to the door. It had a red blinking light and looked like one of those key card scanners. If there was some kind of alarm system rigged to this door, I didn't want to set it off by breaking in.

"Climbing back up is going to suck," Yutika noted as we all gathered around the door.

"Try doing it one-handed with a squirming dog in the other," A.J. said, shaking out his arm after he put Sir Zachary on the ground. "Thank goodness I'm at the peak of health."

"I can make a backpack carrier for Sir Zachary on the way back up," Yutika offered, getting to work on her sketchpad to do just that.

My friends were all sweating and panting from the climb. It must be hotter than hell down here, but I felt only the cool metal of my skin.

I loved my magic.

I held my phone flashlight over the black box while Smith inspected it.

"Good call not trying to muscle the door open," Smith said as he continued to examine the box. "This thing's rigged to blow if it isn't opened the right way."

"Can you hack it?" I asked.

I was expecting one of Smith's sarcastic and affronted replies. Instead, he frowned and peered more closely at the box. "It was designed by a powerful Techie," he said, all of his attention directed at the box. "They weren't as strong as me, but it would take days for me to find a back door."

Days? We didn't have days. I bit my tongue, knowing that Smith didn't need to be reminded of that fact.

"So, what do we do?" I prodded.

"Gotta go in the front door," Smith replied.

He pressed a button on the side I hadn't even noticed, and the bottom half of the box flipped down to display a keypad with letters, numbers, and symbols.

"Can I get some fluorescent powder and a brush?" Smith asked.

I had no idea what he was talking about. Fortunately, he wasn't talking to me. A few seconds later, Yutika handed over the items.

I should have been used to the way my friends operated by this point, but they never ceased to amaze me.

Smith carefully brushed powder over the keypad.

"Lights off," Smith ordered.

When we complied, I saw that seven buttons were lit up.

"So awesome," Graysen said, echoing my own opinion on the matter.

"Glad you think so," Smith replied without emotion. "But that doesn't tell us the right permutation."

With that, he punched each of the lit-up buttons. A warning beep emitted from the black box. A message scrawled across the screen.

Attempt 1/4.

Smith tried a different ordering.

Attempt 2/4.

I held my breath when Smith tried another.

Attempt 3/4.

"What happens if he doesn't get number four?" Yutika whispered.

"Kaboom," A.J. replied solemnly.

"Everyone be quiet and let Smith think," Michael ordered.

Smith hesitated, his fingers resting lightly on the keypad.

"Talk to me," he murmured. He closed his eyes and tilted his ear toward the box.

Another digital message appeared on the screen.

System shutting down in 5…4….

Someone cursed.

3…2….

Sweat slithered down between my breasts.

Smith plugged in another sequence. There was a mechanical whine, and then a panel slid out from the wall beneath the keypad.

We all let out simultaneous sighs of relief.

"How did you know that was the right order?" Kaira asked in a subdued voice.

Smith lifted a shoulder. "Techie instinct."

We all stared at the tiny table that had emerged from the panel. There was a long needle attached to clear tubing that disappeared into the depths of the wall.

"A blood sacrifice?" Yutika squeaked.

"I'll do it," Michael said, stepping forward.

"Wait," Graysen ordered. He squinted at the needle, but I could tell he wasn't really looking at it. He had his Level 10 Brainiac face on.

"I think—" he broke off.

I followed the direction of his gaze to Sir Zachary, who was lying at A.J.'s feet and licking the dirt floor.

"Oh," I said, following the line of Graysen's thinking. "Ohhh."

"The dog is the key," Kaira said in a quiet voice.

Those were the words Subject 6 had said to us four months ago. He hadn't figured out what Sir Zachary had been the key to, but now, looking at this needle and the locked door, it was obvious.

Ex-Director Remwald had transferred some of his own DNA into Sir Zachary and done who-knows-what experiments on our dog before he died. That was why Sir Zachary had crazy super powers. It would also explain why his blood could give us access to a secret location…his blood was the same as Remwald's.

"No way, José," A.J. said, scooping up Sir Zachary and cuddling him protectively. "You are not poking our dog without his consent. Nope, nope, nope."

"I can get his permission, if that would help," Charlotte offered.

"We're not stabbing my baby!" A.J. shrieked. His voice rose up in the metal silo and echoed back to us.

"It makes sense that Remwald would devise a system that only he could access," Graysen told A.J. "And if that's the case, Sir Zachary is the only one who can open this door."

"Not happening," A.J. said stubbornly.

"It's just a little needle," I said.

Normally, I was more sympathetic to A.J.'s animal obsession, but answers were waiting right on the other side of this door. We were so close.

"How about this," Yutika said, already drawing on her sketchpad. "We'll prick Sir Zachary this one time, and then I'll make a tiny doorstop that no one will notice. That way, we'll be able to get in and out without needing to hurt him ever again."

A.J. sniffed. Sir Zachary licked the tear that was trickling down A.J.'s cheek.

Taking advantage of his hesitation, Kaira plucked Sir Zachary out of A.J.'s arms and brought him over to the small table. She snuggled him against her chest as Graysen picked up the needle and hesitated.

"Um, anyone know how to do a blood draw on a dog?" he asked.

I didn't know how to draw blood from a human. It seemed to me that getting the needle into Sir Zachary, with all that fur, would be even more difficult.

"I'll do it," Charlotte offered.

"Have you ever done this before?" A.J. asked, his voice an octave higher than usual.

"No," she replied calmly. "But I know how his body functions. I promise I won't hurt him."

A.J. made a strangled sound. I put my arm around his shoulders, half for comfort and half so he didn't grab Sir Zachary and race back up the ladder.

Sir Zachary didn't make a peep as Charlotte pricked his paw. From the way he was busy nosing the table's surface, I didn't think he'd even noticed. I covered A.J.'s eyes as blood began to flow into the clear tubing.

I held my breath as the blood disappear into the wall.

A harsh beep made all of us jump. Then, the red light on the keypad turned green. The metal door in front of us swung inward without a sound.

CHAPTER 19

We stepped into a room that looked like some kind of futuristic train platform. A trolley-like vehicle was hovering over a dark hole in the ground next to the platform. It was like the vehicle had been expecting us.

The vehicle was bigger than a normal tram and made out of some material that looked like glass but was obviously far more durable. It was boxed in on either side by solid metal walls, which meant the only direction it could go was down.

"This was what I was sensing from the surface," Smith said in a reverent tone. "What a beaut."

"I guess the most pressing question is where will it take us?" Graysen asked, giving the train car a skeptical look.

"Only one way to find out," Yutika replied, pressing a button on the front of the cart.

The door slid to the side, revealing a wide entrance.

"Yutika, I think—" Michael began, but she just waved a hand at the worry on his face and settled herself on one of the long benches.

"I could have made these seats comfier," she said, squirming around on the flat bench. "But it's tolerable."

Shaking his head, Michael went after her.

Smith was next. He studied a panel at the front of the vehicle that had several buttons, levers, and gauges.

"Take Sir Zachary home," Kaira was telling Charlotte. "And can you tell Ma we won't be home in time for dinner, but that she shouldn't worry?"

I smiled at the way Kaira so seamlessly gave the little girl a job that made her feel important while ensuring she wouldn't be walking into whatever danger we were about to face.

I paused with one foot inside the vehicle. In addition to the smells of metal and dirt, I thought I caught the faintest trace of cinnamon.

It faded as quickly as it had come, convincing me that I seriously needed to get whatever this Diego thing was out of my system.

As soon as we were all inside, Yutika pressed another button to shut the door.

"I'm about to start this thing up," Smith said, still studying the panel. "And I have a feeling it's going to go fast."

There were no seatbelts or anything else to hold onto, so we just waited with baited breath.

It didn't take long. There was a shrill whistle, accompanied by a blast of steam from the vehicle's rear. And then, we were off.

The cart dropped straight down, leaving my stomach behind.

"Oh my God!" Yutika moaned.

I whooped.

Kaira shrieked. A.J. was holding onto my arm, like that might somehow slow his descent.

Down, down, down, we fell.

My racing pulse began to slow as the train car came to a gentle stop. We were all gasping.

"Well," Graysen said. "That was—"

The vehicle shot forward without warning. It went from zero to *fuck you* in half a second. Multiple screams filled the air as we hurtled at breakneck speed.

My head ached, like my brain was being sucked out from the sheer speed. My friends' shouts were overpowered by the rushing wind sound that filled my ears.

We were speeding through some kind of transparent tube, but there was nothing to see outside the clear walls except darkness.

We were hurtling through the earth. I had no concept of time or space.

As we continued to shoot along some pre-determined path, I began to relax. It was like a roller coaster…except so much better. It was like flying with Diego, except horizontally…and without Diego's arms wrapped around me.

All too soon, the vehicle began to slow. Lights filled the tunnel ahead, illuminating another platform that looked like the one we'd come from.

"What a rush," I said as we came to a gentle stop.

My friends gave me looks that ranged from incredulous to *Are you brain damaged?*

Since I seemed to be the only one in a good mood, I pressed the button for the door and hopped onto the platform. According to my phone, we'd been on the train for half an hour. Longer than I'd thought…since I was pretty sure I hadn't taken a breath the entire time.

Yutika tottered out after me, moving like she had sea legs. She bent over and promptly threw up. Michael held her hair and rubbed her back.

Graysen, Kaira, and A.J. were holding onto each other as they came onto the platform. Smith looked almost as thrilled as I felt.

"Do you people have any idea what kind of a feat this is?" he asked, motioning to the vehicle. "The technology and magic…it's unbelievable. I can feel the magnetic levitation. And then there's the technology countering the g-force. Do you know what would have happened to our bodies without it?! At that speed—"

"I don't want to talk about it," Yutika groaned.

"Where do you think we are?" Graysen asked, looking at the metal door that was the only way out of the chamber.

"California," Smith said.

"Very funny, Smith," Kaira said. "But seriously."

The train had been fast, but there was no way it had gotten us all the way across the country in half an hour.

We all turned to look at the Techie, but his attention was fixed on the GPS tracker in his hand. "We're in California."

CHAPTER 20

We were at the exact location that Pruwist's first set of coordinates had indicated…except we were hundreds of feet underground.

The metal door opened easily and without any blood sacrifices. We found ourselves in a tunnel that was so narrow even I couldn't stand up all the way. Michael had to fold himself practically in half to keep from scraping his head against the rough ceiling. There were no lights in the tunnel because none were needed. The entire place was illuminated in a hazy green glow. The color came from the crystals gleaming in the walls and ceiling.

"It's a mine," I said.

"Magically dug by the looks of it," Smith said, glancing around. "No normal construction equipment could have gotten down this deep."

When I looked back, I could no longer make out the door we'd come through. It blended in perfectly to the dark stone surrounding it; no one would ever find it if they didn't already know it existed.

"What have we here?" A.J. murmured, glancing around.

"Let's find out, shall we?" Yutika replied. She dropped a sheet of paper on the floor of the tunnel. A few seconds later, she handed a small walkie-talkie looking object to Smith.

"What's that?" Graysen asked.

"Mineral composition detector," Yutika said. "I could probably sell it to space exploration companies for a cool billion."

"Your sacrifice to our cause is truly noble," Smith said as he fiddled with a knob on the detector.

Yutika stuck her tongue out at him.

"Huh," Smith said a few seconds later. "This soil is almost completely metal dust." He held up the detector. "It's mostly titanium, but there are a whole lot of other metals."

I brushed my fingers over the green crystals. They didn't pop out of the wall and start molesting me like the liquid Agent S did, but I felt the same sense of familiarity around these stones as I did with the vials of Agent S.

"I think this is like the raw form of Agent S," I told my friends.

Everyone except me moved farther away from the walls and pressed their arms to their sides. None of us knew whether the raw Agent S was as deadly as the liquid, but it was better not to take any chances.

"I think you're right," Smith said, staring down at the screen on his instrument. "I bet if I poison scanned them—"

"Don't!" the rest of us said at once.

If Smith's poison wand started screeching, we'd alert everyone within a hundred miles to our presence.

"Let's keep going," Kaira said. "See where this tunnel leads."

We walked in silence for several minutes. The tunnel curved a few times, but there were no branches or other paths.

"Why does everything always have to be uphill?" Yutika panted.

"It won't be when we're headed back in the other direction," Smith pointed out.

"Says you," Yutika grumbled.

We all went motionless when a loud, unfamiliar voice echoed down the tunnel.

"Steel for Five!"

For several seconds, nothing happened. Then, I heard a rattling sound. It was faint at first but grew louder by the second.

"What is that?" Yutika whispered.

Graysen, who had gone ahead to peer around the corner, jerked back.

"There's a cart coming this way," he whispered urgently. "We have to get out of here before it runs us over."

We all looked back down the tunnel the way we'd come. Judging from the sounds echoing through the tunnel, we wouldn't make it back into the train platform in time.

"In here," Michael said, shoving his shoulder against a wooden door I hadn't even noticed.

The door gave way, and we slid inside just as a metal cart shot down the tunnel, narrowly missing Graysen's arm. Michael gently slid the door back into place, enclosing us in darkness.

"That was a close one," A.J. whispered.

The dark space filled with several beams of light as we turned on our phone flashlights. Dust particles swirled in the air, which carried an unpleasant, sour smell.

"Ouch," Yutika hissed, hopping on one foot and grasping her knee.

I shined my flashlight down at whatever she'd walked into. My breath caught.

The floor was covered with caskets. They were wooden and roughly made, but there was no question that was what they were. They were spaced in neat rows, going back farther than the beam of my flashlight could reach. Just in my line of sight, I counted twenty-five. But that wasn't the part that had turned all of our breathing ragged. We'd all made the same observation.

These caskets were too small to fit an adult. Every one of these caskets was child-sized.

I heard Graysen murmur something low and soothing to Kaira. Michael and Yutika were gripping each other's hands. Smith was standing stock-still with his head bowed. A.J. started toward me, his face pale as a ghost.

"I'm fine," I managed, before sinking to my knees.

My body couldn't hold itself up anymore, and I sagged against one of the rough-hewn coffins. Only a single thought filled my head.

Lilly.

Lilly had been taken to this underground mine. *Was one of these caskets hers?*

The thought of her tiny bones disintegrating in a splintered box, miles below the ground and far away from the cemetery Sarah and Brent faithfully visited, was too much for me. I pressed my fist to my mouth to hold back a sob.

At that moment, I realized just how deeply I'd been hoping that Lilly was still alive. I'd known the odds in theory, but it wasn't until this moment that it occurred to me how desperately I'd believed that she was alive and just…lost. Like she was just out of reach, and all I needed to do was hold out a hand and grasp her.

Now, staring at these rows and rows of coffins, reality crashed into me with the force of a physical blow.

I flinched at the sound of metal on rock coming from somewhere back in the tunnel. Whoever had come down in that cart was working nearby. I made the observation without reacting to it. I couldn't tear my eyes away from the child-sized coffins.

There were no names or inscriptions on the coffins, or anything else to indicate who might be buried inside. I ran my fingers along the unsanded edge of the nearest one, but I couldn't bring myself to lift off the top.

"Bri," A.J. said, reaching out a tentative hand but not touching me. "We don't know anything for sure, yet."

"We need answers," Kaira said, straightening her shoulders.

I was grateful for the way my friends were taking action. It helped ease the growing numbness inside me. It helped me get to my feet, when all I wanted to do was lie down on the hard ground and give up.

I felt weak in a way I never did in my titanium skin.

"I'm going to talk to whoever's out there and find out what's going on," Michael told me.

I nodded, not trusting myself to speak.

We all gathered behind Michael as he eased open the door and stepped back into the tunnel. After the staleness of the tomb, the air in the tunnel seemed almost fresh by comparison.

"I've got us illusioned as worms," Kaira's strained whisper said from behind me. "No one will see us until we want them to."

We silently stole back down the tunnel, closer to the clinking sounds I'd heard before.

I saw the metal cart first. At second glance, I realized it was plated in titanium. It also took up almost the whole width of the tunnel. If Michael hadn't gotten us inside the tomb, the cart would have crushed us.

I started when something plinked into the cart. When I peeked in, I saw it was a chunk of the raw Agent S crystals that were embedded in the walls.

There was a little girl a short distance away. Her skin was metallic, and she was gently prying chunks of green crystals out of the wall and tossing them into the cart.

Even though she was short enough to stand at full height in the tunnel, her back was slightly hunched. Her clothes were filthy and full of holes that had been badly mended. Her hair was a tangled mess.

My throat felt like sandpaper. It was an effort just to breathe. Every time I looked at the little girl, my heart sank all the way to my toes.

The only thing that kept me from scooping her up and carrying her away was the knowledge that she wasn't the only slave in this place. If the coffins in that tomb were any indication, there were more just like her.

"Bri," Graysen whispered, putting his hand on my arm so I'd know where he was. "Is that kid a Steel?"

"Yes," I whispered back.

"Then, how is her magic working right now?"

Excellent question. My skin was still titanium under Kaira's illusion, which meant that the girl's magic wasn't cancelling out mine. Magic didn't work when there was a higher-level Mag nearby with the same power. Since I was a Level 10, my power should negate any other Steels in the vicinity unless they had Super Mag-level strength, which this girl clearly didn't since my magic still worked.

Now that I was thinking about it, I felt strangely weak. My skin was still titanium, but I didn't have that *take on the world* attitude that came with my magic. Maybe it was a mental response to the sight of those coffins.

"I have no idea," I told Graysen.

"Kaira," Michael said in a low voice. "Can you make me look like one of them?"

A few seconds later, Michael appeared to be a small, dirty Steel dressed in rags. Even though I knew it was an illusion, the sight of his bony limbs and hollow eyes made me want to scream.

The little girl jerked to attention at the sight of Michael.

"I'm making quota," she said in a tremulous voice that broke my heart.

"Don't be scared," Michael told her in a gentle voice. "I won't hurt you."

If the slave girl was surprised by a man's voice coming from a child's body, she didn't say so. She let out a sigh as tension eased from her thin shoulders. She took a step closer to Michael.

"I don't know you," she said in a wondering voice. She poked his arm, her eyes widening in surprise. "You aren't a Steel."

"That's right," Michael replied gently.

"But then." Her face scrunched up in a frown. "How can you be down here? Only Steels can work on Level 5."

"And why is that?" Michael asked.

She displayed the chunk of Agent S in her hand. "Because if anyone else touches it, it explodes." She had a slight lisp, so the word came out sounding like *issplodes*.

"Only Steels are strong enough to get it out." The little girl puffed out her chest in a show of pride. "It likes titanium best, but any Steel can touch it for a little while."

To demonstrate, she tossed the chunk of Agent S she was holding into the cart and then dug her nails into the rock wall for more. She grunted as her fingers chipped off pieces of rock until she had a fist-sized crystal of Agent S. She threw it into the titanium cart along with the rest she'd collected.

The green stones clung to the titanium walls of the cart instead of settling to the bottom. I felt a gentle, magnetic-like tug toward the crystals all around me. It was a less intense version of the attraction the Agent S seemed to have toward my skin in its liquid form.

"What kind of Steel are you?" Michael asked, pointing to the dull metallic gleam of her skin.

"I'm an iron Steel." The little girl's eyes widened, as though she was waiting for Michael's reaction. When he didn't say anything, her face fell. "It'd be better if I was made out of titanium." She toed the wheel of her cart. "But there isn't anyone down here who's that strong."

I knew from my own research that there were only a handful of titanium Steels on the planet. I was the only titanium Steel currently living in the Northeast US. I was also the only recorded Level 10 Steel.

I'd embarrassed Brent to no end as a child, when I'd gone around telling everyone—including random strangers—about how special my magic was.

My blonde pigtails were probably the only reason I'd ever gotten away with all the bragging.

"We have gold Steels, too," the little girl was telling Michael. "And silver Steels and 'luminum Steels and nickel Steels—"

Michael pointed at the green crystals accumulating in the girl's cart. "Is this Agent S?"

The child looked at the green stones and then back at Michael.

"We just call it *stuff*, but sometimes Foreman calls it Agent Steel."

Agent S…for Steel.

I'd never wondered what the S might stand for before.

"Do you know what's being done with the stuff after you take it out of here?" Michael asked in a patient, unhurried voice.

"We bring it to the other levels for processing," the girl said. "We smush it." She clapped her iron hands together. "And then it becomes like water. No more issplosion."

"So, the raw Agent S is highly unstable," Graysen translated. "It stabilizes when it's in its liquid form, even though it's still deadly for non-Steels."

"Michael," Kaira said. "Ask her what the people here want with the Agent S."

Michael leaned close to the girl and repeated Kaira's question.

"Some of it gets put into the glass jars and sent away." The little girl shrugged.

Those were the vials that ended up buried in graves all over Boston.

"And the rest?" Michael asked.

"It gets put into *them*."

"Who's them?" Michael pressed.

"Monsters," the girl whispered.

She shuddered but didn't elaborate, and Michael didn't press her for more.

"Steel for Five!" a loud voice called from somewhere up the tunnel. The sound reverberated all the way down to us.

"Quick!" the little girl squeaked. "That means another worker is coming down. She dragged her cart into an enclave in the tunnel that I hadn't noticed before because it blended in with the wall. She gestured to Michael to get into the enclave with her.

"I see another one over here," Kaira whispered. She released her illusion just long enough to point out the carved-out section of wall, which melded into the rest of the tunnel so completely it was almost invisible. Together, we squeezed into the enclave.

"There are five levels," the little girl was telling Michael. "We're on the lowest one."

"What happens on the upper levels?" Michael asked.

"Lots," the girl replied sagely.

She didn't have time to elaborate. There was a whoosh of sound and air, and then another titanium cart came rushing down the tunnel.

The little boy perched inside hauled on a lever, bringing the cart to a screeching stop. He jumped out and immediately began carving out Agent S crystals from the wall and tossing them into his cart. From the color of his skin, he looked like a silver Steel.

"It's okay," Michael said, as he emerged from his hideout and the boy caught sight of him. The little girl glanced at the boy and hurriedly got back to work filling up her cart with the green crystals. "I'm a friend," he told the boy.

"Friend?" the boy asked, like the word tasted unfamiliar on his tongue.

My heart felt too big for my chest as I looked at these wraith-thin children with haunted eyes. I couldn't stop thinking about how these children's families believed them to be dead.

I couldn't stop thinking about Lilly.

Was this how she had died…down here in a dark tunnel, with no idea she was being mourned by a family who loved her?

Someone was gasping softly. It took me several seconds to realize the sound was coming from me.

I felt A.J. reach for my hand and squeeze. Someone else—Yutika, I thought—rubbed my back.

"What are your names?" Michael asked the children.

"641," the boy replied immediately, like he'd been rehearsing the number in his mind. He even straightened and linked his arms behind his back when he said the number.

"622," the girl said, linking her arms behind her back in the same way.

No names, just numbers. Just like the children kept in cages in MagLab.

"And we really gotta hurry," the girl continued, her worried gaze straying up the tunnel. "If we don't, Foreman'll put us in isolation chambers."

Both children shuddered in tandem.

Whoever this foreman was, I couldn't wait to get my hands around his neck. My whole body was trembling with the need to do violent damage to the one responsible for enslaving these children.

"Michael," I said, unable to hide the emotion in my voice. "Ask her about Lilly."

Kaira changed our illusions so our disembodied voices would be less strange. Instead of wriggling earthworms, we became dirty, bone-thin children in rags.

Just the sight of us like this made my stomach turn over.

"Do you know anyone by the name of Lilly Hammond?" Michael asked.

"She'd be five years old," I added, my voice coming out sand-papery and thin. "She—" I stopped myself before I started to describe her, realizing that I had nothing to say.

I'd seen my niece exactly once, and it was through the glass window of the neonatal unit in the hospital. I didn't know if she had Brent's smile or Sarah's freckles. I didn't know if she'd inherited my brother's stubbornness or my sister-in-law's kindness.

Both children looked at each other and shook their heads.

"Sorry," the boy told Michael, seeming crestfallen to be letting Michael down.

Both kids returned to their work, clawing out crystals and tossing them into their carts. I snapped out of my horrified stupor and began to help.

It was no easy task. It took a lot of finesse to claw the Agent S away from its natural metal cocoon, especially without shattering the crystals. It took me several attempts to get the lump of Agent S out of the wall without it disintegrating into dust. When I finally managed it, I was surprised to find how heavy it felt in my hands.

I jumped a little when the girl yelled in a shrill voice, "Steel up from Five!" She gave me a small smile of thanks, and then she began to lug her cart back up the tunnel.

The boy finished filling his cart with my help and then repeated the same call. I took the cart's handle for him and began to pull it up the tunnel in the direction the little girl had disappeared. The slave boy and my friends fell into step behind me.

As the cart creaked and groaned its way up the tunnel, I channeled my willpower into keeping my footsteps steady. All I wanted was to tear this place apart with my bare hands.

But we still didn't know what we were up against, and if I did something rash, I'd put all the kids in even more danger. So, I gritted my teeth and concentrated on pulling the heavy cart up the tunnel.

CHAPTER 21

I hadn't thought this place could get any worse…until we reached the end of the tunnel.

We stepped into a cavernous room with high ceilings. The walls were cement, and harsh white lights dangled from long chains overhead. There was a large, printed sign on the wall that read, *Level 5: Agent S Extraction and Processing.*

Everything was controlled chaos. Dozens of carts full of Agent S came out of various tunnels and headed for an open elevator on the far side of the room. The elevator transported the carts to the upper levels of the mine. But none of that was the reason why my feet were rooted to the floor.

I estimated there were a hundred people working in this one room, and all of them were children.

"I knew Remwald was a monster," Yutika said, "but this is so far past monstrous there isn't even a word for it."

I couldn't have said it better myself.

"We have to get them out of here," Kaira whispered, her voice tight with fury.

Desperation to do *something* boiled inside me.

The children worked at a feverish pace. They scampered to and fro, exchanging full carts for empty ones.

All around, the call of "Steel for Five!" rang out as more carts were sent down the mine tunnels.

The clanging, creaking, and shouting were enough to make even the sanest person crazy.

"Don't let him see you resting," a Steel kid hissed as he hurried past me with an armful of raw Agent S. "You don't want to go to the isolation chambers."

The little girl down in the tunnel had said something similar to Michael. I couldn't imagine how awful the isolation chambers must be if it was worse than this.

"Thanks," I managed, but the boy was already gone.

A piercing whistle cut through the other sounds. I felt a sudden urge to run and hide. Or at least to cover my ears.

The children stopped their work and hurried to the center of the room. They lined up shoulder-to-shoulder, leaving a few inches of space between them.

None of the slaves spoke. Without the movement of the elevator and carts, it had gone eerily quiet in the high-ceilinged room.

"This can't be good," A.J. murmured.

"Nothing about this is good," Smith hissed back.

"I hate to say it," Michael said, "but we should get out of here before we're noticed. We can come back with the police, and—"

"No." The word came out more forcefully than I'd intended. "I'm not leaving until I find out what happened to Lilly."

Whether she was buried in that tomb or not, I had to know what had happened to her. Brent and Sarah needed to know the truth, even if that truth would force them to begin their grieving process anew.

"Then neither are we," Kaira said in a firm voice.

No one else argued.

"I can bring reinforcements to us," Smith offered.

"Who would come?" Yutika said.

Graysen, illusioned to look like a wraith of a child, nodded in agreement. "We're not in Boston anymore. Alliance laws don't apply. If we try to bring in Boston cops, we'll have an inter-territory incident on our hands."

Graysen was right. And since California was essentially lawless, that wasn't a fight we wanted to start. We were on our own.

"We're sticking out like sore thumbs," A.J. whispered.

A.J. was right. We might look like the other slaves, but we weren't acting like them. The others were all standing in a line, while we were huddled at the mouth of the tunnel we'd come out of.

"I'm too worn out to do any more animal illusions," Kaira said. "The lack of natural light down here is making it harder for my magic to adjust, so this is the best I've got."

"Blend in," A.J. ordered.

My friends and I hurried to join the line. We got a few strange looks from the children on either side of us. I glanced to the side, and then linked my arms behind my back like everyone else.

I felt every kid in the line go stiff with fear as a set of heavy boots clomped across the floor.

"Did we meet quota today, kiddos?" a harsh, raspy voice asked.

"Yes, Foreman," the children chorused.

The man stopped at the other end of the line. He was large and barrel-chested. His metal skin had the rusty varnish of a Steel who was made out of copper. His matted hair and beard were the same color as the dirt floor—whether that was natural or due to lack of grooming, I had no idea.

Even from my spot at the other end of the line, I could see the bulge in the man's hairy cheek from what must be a wad of tobacco. His beady eyes roved up and down the line of children as he swung a titanium baton around his hand.

The foreman spewed out a stream of brown liquid onto the ground, inches away from the nearest kid. The slave didn't so much as blink, making it clear this was typical behavior.

My muscles quivered with the need to turn this man into pulp.

When the foreman stepped to the side, I noticed there was another adult standing behind him. The person wore a long cloak and had a hood drawn over their face. I couldn't see anything about them, but I could feel their magic. It wafted off them, just like it did around the other Super Mags I'd encountered.

"What's a Super Mag doing down here?" A.J. whispered, clearly sharing my thoughts.

"There's something wrong with that person's mind," Michael said in an urgent voice. "I can't—"

"Shut yer trap!"

The foreman tromped down the line toward us. The hooded figure retreated back into one of the tunnels, their cloak undulating behind them like a wraith.

The children around us shrank back as the foreman approached. They stared at him with dread in their hollow eyes.

Almost as one, my friends and I stepped forward. None of us wanted the foreman to take out his anger on the wrong target.

"Huh," the foreman grunted, looking us up and down. Kaira kept our slave children illusions in place, but it was obvious the foreman could tell we didn't belong. His mouth moved as his beady eyes flicked down to the other end of the line. "What the—there are seven too many of you's."

Well, so much for the wait and see approach.

I did the only thing I could. I threw myself at the foreman.

There was a harsh clang as our metal skin collided. The baton flew from the foreman's hand and struck Michael. If he'd actually been the scrawny little kid he was illusioned to be, the metal bat would have hit Michael's chest. With the way he groaned and crumpled in on himself, it had clearly connected with a more delicate part of his anatomy.

Michael stumbled to the side, his head striking against an overturned cart's metal wheel. His whole body went boneless as he slumped to the ground.

Yutika screamed.

I checked to see that Michael was breathing, and then I left my friends to focus on him. I turned all of my attention on the foreman.

I slammed my fist into his face.

The blow should have been enough to obliterate his skull. Instead, he just shook his head and came back for more.

The foreman struck back.

The fact that we were having a Steel-on-Steel fight right now defied every law of magic I knew. The fact that I was titanium to his copper meant I was the stronger Mag, and yet, his skin was still metal.

What the hell?

Something was definitely wrong with my magic. The foreman barreled into me, shoving me back several steps. Normally, I was completely unmovable.

The foreman blocked my next blow with his elbow. He spat out a stream of tobacco juice, which landed on my shirt.

"Pig," I snarled, wrenching his arm aside and head-butting him.

The foreman staggered back a step. One measly step…and then he was back for more.

"Little fucker," he huffed as he delivered a kick to my stomach.

"Where are the rest of the kids?" I demanded, strangely out of breath as we circled each other.

I was never out of breath in my titanium form.

"What you blabberin' about?" The foreman tried to kick me again.

This time, I ducked.

"All the kids you stole from the hospitals." My fists pummeled his copper shoulders. He slid back a few steps but was otherwise unaffected. "Where are they?"

Where is Lilly?!

"I don't answer to you!"

Clang. Crack. Thump.

We collided over and over again. No matter how hard I hit him, I couldn't get the upper hand. We were evenly matched.

Impossible, my mind shouted. He should be a mess of blood and shredded flesh on the floor.

As we continued our brawl, I became aware of a strange feeling inside me. It felt like a weighted blanket had settled over my insides. It was kind of like when Diego had injected me with the temporary Magical Reduction Potion, except this time, I could still reach my magic. It was just…dampened. I was still stronger than I would have been in normal human skin, but it was nothing compared to my usual titanium strength.

My friends must have realized something was wrong with me. With the exception of Yutika, who crouched protectively over Michael's crumpled form, the rest of the Seven joined the fight. Graysen, Smith, and Kaira grabbed onto the foreman, doing their best to pin his limbs while I pummeled him. A.J. used his telekinesis to throw sharp objects at the foreman's head.

"Don't just stand there!" the foreman bellowed. "Get them!"

Out of the corner of my eye, I saw the kids surround us. They yanked my friends away from the foreman. When I couldn't be manhandled so easily, they began to hit me with their metal fists.

"I'm trying to help you," I yelled. "Get out of the way!"

The kids ignored my pleas. They continued to hit, kick, and shout at me. The foreman stood just out of reach, panting and spitting brown tobacco juice onto the floor.

"I don't know where you seven came from, but I'm gonna find out," the Foreman growled. To the kids, he yelled, "Get them into the isolation chambers. Now!"

The kids swarmed my friends and me.

"Not good," A.J. murmured, swaying a little from the force of one kid's kick to his shin. "Not good at all."

If Michael had been awake, he would have resolved this whole shitshow of a situation in just a few words. Since he was still out cold, that left us with two choices. We could fight the kids, or we could give up and let them lock us up. Since none of us was going to raise a hand to a single one of the children, we submitted.

"Now," the foreman said, smiling nastily at us as he twirled a key between his dirty fingers. "Let's see how brave you are after a week in the isolation chambers."

CHAPTER 22

I had no idea how long I'd been sitting on the mud floor of my prison. After we'd been herded onto the elevator, the slaves had escorted us up to the next level of the mine. When we got off the elevator, I saw a rusted sign with the words *Level 4: Isolation Chambers*. There had been nothing else to see except metal stalls set up along a dirt-packed corridor. The slaves had locked each of us into our own cell.

I'd shouted myself voiceless before concluding that the cell was sound-proof. After that, I heard nothing except the *drip, drip, drip* of water on the metal wall and my own harsh breathing.

I had spent God-knew how long pounding at the door and walls of my prison to no avail. The enclosure was titanium, but even so, I should have been able to break through…or at least dent it.

I wasn't sure if it was my inexplicable weakness, or some other magic at work, that made me helpless to escape. After exploring every inch of the small chamber, which was four steps in length and five in width, I'd finally accepted there was no way out.

There was a thin slot in the door that was too narrow to even get my hand through, which I guessed was meant for passing food to the prisoners. No matter how much pressure I applied to the opening, I couldn't use it as leverage to break open the door. The cell was sealed tight around me.

I peered into the blackness, even though I couldn't see anything except the silver glow of my own skin. Finally, I just buried my face in my hands and did my best to hold onto the tattered remains of my sanity.

All my life, steel had been my ally. Now, it was my cage. It felt a little like being imprisoned in my own body.

I understood why all the children dreaded being put inside one of these chambers. I'd never felt more alone and helpless.

There was nothing for company except the dripping water and a bucket in the corner that I stayed as far away from as I could get.

My magic churned restlessly inside me. I still felt weak in a way I never had before, but I couldn't bring myself to care. All I could think about was the children who were forced to live and work in this nightmare of a place. I thought about Lilly.

Plunk. A silver tear hit the mud. *Plunk, plunk.*

My tears sparkled, looking like silver jewels nestled in the mud. Scowling, I kicked at the solid tears until they were buried. I blew on my fists, transforming myself back into regular skin.

I hated crying in general, but it was worse when I was titanium. The tears stuck around as permanent reminders of whatever had caused them in the first place.

I'd spent the last five years putting on a brave face so my family wouldn't have to deal with my grief in addition to their own. But I was alone now, with no one to see or hear me. So, with my tears dissolving into the mud, I cried.

There was a grating of a metal hinge. It was so soft I wondered if I had imagined it. Then, a tiny rectangle of dim light appeared as the food slot opened.

"Is that you, cariño?"

I leapt to my feet in the squishy mud.

"Diego?!"

"Shh," he hissed.

"What are you doing here?" I whisper-shouted.

So, it hadn't been my imagination when I smelled cinnamon before we stepped onto the flying train car. *Sneaky bastard.*

I could just make out the gleam of Diego's eyes through the food slot's opening.

"You followed us," I said. I was so relieved to see him, rather than the foreman, that I couldn't summon the energy to be annoyed.

"And aren't you lucky I did?" he replied. "I don't see anyone else busting you out."

"There's something wrong with my magic," I said, feeling the need to explain why I was stuck on the wrong side of a door I should have been able to tear apart with my bare hands.

"I like the damsel in distress look on you," Diego said. He sniffed loudly. "Although, I didn't imagine you smelling so foul while you did it."

"Can you get me out of here, or not?" I demanded. My relief at seeing him quickly morphed to my usual urge to start hitting things whenever he was around.

In response, Diego dangled what appeared to be the same key the foreman had been holding earlier through the food slot. Before I could reach for it, he snatched it back.

"Where did you get that?" I asked.

"Nabbed it off the foreman," Diego replied.

"Good for you. Now, stop talking and put that key to work."

"If you want out, it'll cost you," Diego said in that mocking tone I loathed.

"I don't have time for games," I seethed. "My friends are locked up, and I have someone I have to find."

"Lilly." His voice softened. For some reason, that pissed me off even more than his cockiness.

"Get me out of here, or I swear—"

"Not until you promise to do something for me."

"What?" I asked, wary.

"One favor. Whatever I ask, whenever I ask. You'll say yes."

"I'm not having sex with you, Diego."

A deep, male chuckle.

"Oh, I'll happily take that bet. But we both know I won't need to call in any favors for that."

"Diego—"

"Do I have your word?" All his teasing was gone. "Bri, look me in the eye and swear to me you'll keep your word. Whatever I ask, you'll do it."

"I won't kill anyone," I told him. "Or do anything that will hurt my friends."

"I'm not a monster," Diego replied.

I wasn't so sure about that. I thought of his bathtub full of MRP and those handwritten Super Mag files.

"So, do we have a deal?" he pressed.

I nodded before realizing Diego probably couldn't see me. I took a deep breath. "We have a deal."

CHAPTER 23

Even though the tunnel was only dimly-lit, it hurt my eyes after the blackness of the isolation chamber.

"Can you walk?" Diego asked.

"I'm not an invalid," I snapped back.

"Jesús, sorry."

I took the key Diego offered me and quickly unlocked my friends' cells. Their voices were as hoarse from screaming as mine.

"You okay?" I asked Michael when I got to his cell, noticing the streak of blood across his temple now that he was no longer illusioned.

"Nothing Oliver won't be able to fix," he replied, referring to Smith's Mender father.

Graysen and Kaira were holding each other like they would never let go, but neither of them seemed hurt. Smith, Yutika, and A.J. seemed fine, too. Aside from bumps and bruises, I didn't think there would be any lasting damage.

"Is everyone okay?" Yutika asked, hugging Michael.

"Never better," A.J. replied. He cocked his head at me. "What took you so long to get us out?"

I looked around at my friends. "Are any of you feeling…weaker than usual?" I asked. "Your magic, I mean."

My friends all shook their heads.

So, it was just me. Before I had a chance to consider what that might mean, my friends caught sight of the eighth person in our group.

"What is *he* doing here?" Yutika demanded, still holding onto Michael as she glared at Diego.

"Long story," I muttered. "But he's the one who got us out, so we have to play nice for the time being."

Diego gave me an angelic grin.

"Okay," Kaira said, giving Diego a suspicious look before cutting him out of the conversation. "We need a plan."

"What's to plan?" A.J. asked. "Michael tells the foreman to step off a tall ledge, we get the slaves out of here, and then we tear this place to the ground."

"Not gonna happen," Diego said. "While you were all twiddling your thumbs, I did some recon. The foreman is the least of your problems."

"What are you talking about?" Graysen demanded.

"The foreman answers to someone else. I don't know who, but I can tell you there's a whole operation going on here that's bigger than just the slaves. There are people with serious magic in here that you won't want to go up against."

"Care to elaborate?" Graysen asked.

Diego shrugged. "Not really. I just felt a shit-load of magic and saw some scary dudes in cloaks."

I thought about the figure who had been following the foreman around during the roll call.

"Super Mags?" I asked.

Diego nodded.

"Alright." Graysen ran a hand through his hair. "We have to go back to Boston and regroup. We won't be any good to those kids if we get ourselves locked back up."

The others nodded.

"I'm not leaving," I said in a quiet voice. "Not until I find out about Lilly."

Before my friends could insist on staying with me, I said, "You all need to go back to Boston and figure out how we're going to rescue the rest of the slaves." With my filthy clothes and titanium skin, I could blend in without needing Kaira's illusion.

"We don't leave people behind," A.J. said. "Ever."

The rest of the Seven nodded in agreement.

"I'll stay with her," Diego said, interrupting the tense face-off.

Kaira scoffed. "Somehow, that doesn't make me feel any better. And as soon as we get back to Boston, you're going to jail."

Diego crossed his arms and gave Kaira a bemused look. "Then, I guess you'll never find out what I learned snooping around in here."

"We could make you tell us," Graysen said, his voice dangerous.

"You could." Diego met Graysen's glare with one of his own. "But then you'd be no better than the last Director…taking what you want without any regard for civil rights." He smirked. "I'll escape wherever you try to lock me up, and then I'll make sure all of Boston knows how you treat Super Mags who don't play your little games."

Graysen's nostrils flared.

"You ass," Kaira spat, but she didn't say anything else.

I didn't know how I felt about Diego holding his own against my friends. I didn't know how I felt about him, period.

"You're right," Graysen grated out. The words seemed to cause him physical pain. "But once we have a handle on this," he swept his hand around at the dark tunnel, "we're handing you over to the cops. You'll get a fair trial, but you *will* be tried."

"I'd be honored, your majesties," Diego said, bending over in an exaggerated bow.

"And don't you forget it," A.J. huffed. To the rest of us, he said, "Look, how about we split our group in two. Yutika, Smith, Kaira, and Graysen can head back to Boston and start dealing with this mess on the home front. Michael and I will stay here with trouble and double-trouble."

He was referring to me and Diego. Or maybe Diego and me…I didn't ask for clarification.

Kaira opened her mouth to argue. After taking one look at my face, she sighed and shook her head. "Are you sure about this?" she asked.

"Positive," I replied. "Now, *go*. We'll meet back at the mansion as soon as I figure out what's going on here."

And find some proof about Lilly…one way or another.

"I'll send the train car back for you as soon as we get to Boston," Smith said. "I'll leave you a note talking you through how to make the thing run."

Kaira jabbed a finger in Diego's chest. "If any of my people don't make it back in one piece, I'm holding you responsible."

Unfazed, Diego gave her a salute.

We split off at the elevator. Kaira illusioned her group into slave children who waved to us as they got on the elevator. They headed down, back to the lowest level of the mine. The rest of us would be going up to Level 3.

"Allow me," Diego said, giving me a wink.

I sucked in a breath as Diego, Michael, A.J., and I turned almost invisible. Whenever one of us moved, there was a slight flicker as Diego switched our appearances to make us blend into our surroundings.

"Okay, that is kind of spectacular," A.J. said grudgingly.

We waited until the elevator returned, and then we headed up.

"Stay close," Diego whispered. "And follow me."

"Where are you?" I hissed back, trying to follow the sound of his voice.

In answer, Diego took my hand in his, threading our fingers together.

A jolt of heat spread up my fingertips. It unnerved me how natural it felt to hold his hand. I quickly fumbled for Michael or A.J. with my other hand to remind myself the contact was just about staying together…nothing more.

"Where are we going?" Michael asked in a low voice.

"Foreman's office," Diego said.

With my hand still linked in his, we took the elevator up to the third level. This space felt like less of a mine. The walls were wood-paneled, and the tunnel was lit with lamps instead of naked bulbs.

I paused to study a crude, hand-drawn map tacked onto the wall. From it, I could see the mine's five levels. The top level contained sleeping quarters and supply shaft to the surface. That must have been how the foreman got in and out of the mine without having to take the underground train to Boston.

Level 2 was the Alchemists' section of the mine. I assumed it was where the raw Agent S was converted into its liquid form. Level 3, where we were now, was marked simply as *Administration*. Level 4 was the isolation chambers…which I had no intention of visiting again. And finally, the bottom level of the mine was where the actual Agent S extraction took place.

I noticed that the underground train wasn't marked on the map. Probably whoever was in charge of this place didn't want just anyone hopping on the train and busting out of here.

"Bri, come on," Diego whispered.

He slid a key out of his pocket—a different key from the one he'd used to get us out of our cells—and opened the door at the end of the tunnel.

We let ourselves into a large, messy office. I held back a gag at the clear jar on the foreman's desk that was full of brown tobacco spittle.

Diego dropped our camouflage so we wouldn't bump into each other as we moved around the office.

A.J. and I went for the desk. Michael stayed near the doorway, keeping watch on the tunnel outside while he rifled through a file cabinet. Diego hung the keys he'd taken back on an empty wall peg.

The desk was a disaster of documents, paper plates crusted with smears of food, and hand-written notes that were barely legible.

I pulled a thick envelope full of receipts from one of the drawers and quickly thumbed through them.

"That's the main grocery store in California," A.J. said, looking over my shoulder.

I flipped the envelope over to read the writing on the back.

Remwald-These are October's receipts.

A.J. wrinkled his brows. "Remwald?"

"Maybe the foreman doesn't know he's dead?" I said, although that seemed unlikely. Ex-Director Edwardian Remwald had been dead for four months. The foreman might be dense, but he would have to notice if his communications went unanswered for four months.

"I found this when I was poking around earlier," Diego said. He held up a piece of stationary with an R embossed at the top. There was a list of supplies written in a flowing script that was nothing like the foreman's messy scrawl. At the bottom, there was a looping signature that looked like *Remwald.*

"Smith's going to love this," A.J. said. "A new conspiracy."

Michael took the paper and squinted at the signature. "There has to be another explanation," he said. "We all saw Remwald's body and the autopsy. There was even a DNA report, proving it was Remwald's body."

I looked more closely at the paper, which contained a list of hospital supplies and chemicals.

"Those are for the Magical Reduction Potion," Diego said.

"What are the spinal needles for?" A.J. asked, tapping the item on the list. "And why would our foreman need seventy-five of them?"

Diego shrugged. "When inhaled, the MRP is a poison that physically weakens us. When injected into the blood, it only affects our magic. I have no idea what would happen if it was injected into spinal fluid."

"You're awfully knowledgeable about this stuff, aren't you?" A.J. asked Diego.

"Someone has to be," Diego replied darkly.

I put aside the note and our questions about it. That mystery could wait.

"Look at this," Michael said, pulling a stack of print-outs from the file cabinet.

We all crowded around. My pounding heart turned to a dull throb when I saw there were no names, only numbers.

There were hundreds of children represented on this list—far more than I'd seen on the bottom level of the mine. There were also dates next to each number, which I thought was either their birth date or the date they'd arrived at the mine.

One of the numbers matched Lilly's birthday. *February 9, 2065.*

Hope—that cruel, fickle beast—surged inside me.

"Someone's coming," Michael said. "One of the slaves."

I noticed our bodies blending into the wood-paneled walls and shook my head at Diego. We didn't need camouflage when we had Michael.

A woman, wearing a dirty sack-dress and tattered shoes, came to the door. She was carrying a stack of papers and one of those TV dinners. She looked about our age, although it was difficult to tell from her emaciated figure.

"Don't worry," Michael said as soon as she came into the office. "We're not going to hurt you."

The woman gave Michael a shy smile. She deposited the papers and TV dinner on the foreman's desk as she regarded all of us with curiosity. Thanks to Michael, she wasn't afraid.

"You're older than the other slaves," I observed, cringing as soon as the indelicate words were out of my mouth.

The woman looked at the ground. "Our bodies can only tolerate so many years of abuse. Most…don't survive long down here." She leaned into Michael, as though his solid presence could give her more strength.

I thought about the caskets buried in the tunnel on Level 5. All at once, I felt unbearably cold.

"I'm so sorry," Michael said gently. "We're going to do everything we can to help you, okay?"

I could see the way the woman's whole body relaxed. She raised a tentative hand to Michael's arm.

"Thank you," she whispered, her eyes fixated on Michael in pure adoration.

I cleared my throat. "Can you help us with something?"

I held out the list of numbers to the woman, pointing to the one that matched Lilly's birthday.

"Do you know where I can find this…one?" I asked, my voice faltering. I couldn't make my mouth form the shape of the word *slave*.

The woman looked at Michael, and then took the paper from me to study it. She licked her lips. Her dirt-smudged cheeks turned pink.

"I—don't know how to read," she told Michael.

Michael patiently read the number and birth date, explaining to her that Lilly was five years old.

Michael pointed to me. "The child we're searching for might look like her."

"But she might not," I said, hating the way my voice wavered. "I…never met her."

A.J. linked his arm through mine, offering silent comfort.

I stood still as the woman regarded me.

"Your eyes are familiar," she said thoughtfully. "One of the slaves in the nursery has eyes like yours."

My pulse skipped. I had my mother's eyes…just like Brent. *Hammond hazel*, my dad called them.

"Can you bring us to this child?" Michael asked, since I was just standing there like an idiot.

The woman shook her head.

"The youngest ones are on Level 1, and only the master can get inside." She gave Michael an apologetic look.

"Where is this master?" I demanded, my voice on the edge of violence. "How do I find him?"

Fear flashed across the woman's expression at my intensity.

"I'm sorry." Her gaze flicked to Michael. "He isn't around much."

"That's alright," he told her gently, giving me a warning look. "Thank you for all the information. You've been a big help."

"Wait," I said, making a concerted effort to sound more civil. "Do you know why the strongest Steels in here don't cancel out everyone else's magic?"

The woman bobbed her head. "He does it to all of us. That way, we all get lowered to Level 6s and can work the same."

Level 6 Steels were strong enough to demolish a building with their bare hands. Depending on what kind of metal their skin was made out of, they were less flexible and quick on their feet than I was. Most Steels were better at brute force tasks than ones that required a lot of finesse.

"Are you talking about the master?" Michael asked. "Is that who's taking away your magic?"

She shook her head. "Energy Manipulator." She wrapped her skinny arms around herself. "Very powerful."

"Does he wear a cloak?" I asked, thinking of the cloaked person who had stuck close to the foreman.

The woman nodded her head.

It all made sense—why I was so much weaker here, and why my magic hadn't cancelled out the other Steels. The Energy Manipulator was sucking away just enough power from every Steel here so our magic became effectively identical.

It was infuriating, but at the same time, a tremendous relief. All we had to do was take out the Energy Manipulator, and then my magic would be back to full strength.

"Once we get rid of that pesky Mag," A.J. said, reading my thoughts, "you'll cancel out every other Steel in the mine. The foreman will be magic-less."

The thought brought a grim smile to my lips.

"There's something wrong with that Energy Manipulator's mind," Michael said. "I can't really explain it, except that his mind seemed blank of everything except his laser-focus on the Steels."

"Maybe he expends all his magic to keep the Steels at the same level and has no energy left for anything else," I suggested.

"Maybe," Michael said, but he didn't look convinced.

We all froze as the foreman's raspy voice filtered down the tunnel. The woman gasped.

"I have to go," she whispered. Without another word, she fled.

"I think we'd better skedaddle, too," A.J. pointed out.

"Come closer," Diego ordered all of us.

He took my hand again, and I grabbed Michael's. All of us blurred out of sight until we melted against the wall.

"This is really rather handy," A.J. observed.

"So glad you approve," Diego replied.

"Shh," Michael ordered as we slipped out of the office and back into the tunnel.

The foreman had disappeared, leaving our path to the elevator clear.

We were almost to Level 2, when someone's shout reached all the way to the open-air elevator.

"Oh, what now?" A.J. groaned.

Another panicked screech tore through the air. The hairs at the back of my neck stood up in warning.

An alarm began to blare.

CHAPTER 24

gent Steel spill on Level 2!" the foreman's voice roared over some kind of loudspeaker system. "All Steels to 2!"

The alarm continued to blare in the background.

"Bri, wait—" Diego shouted, his voice barely audible, even though he was standing right next to me.

I ignored him, jumping from the elevator and onto Level 2. Diego camouflaged me so I blended into the cement wall as I burst into the madness.

The room looked a little like the basement of MagLab, with black-topped tables covered with chemistry equipment. I wasn't really paying attention to that, though. The commotion was coming from the center of the room, where steam was billowing up from something on the ground.

A group of children were crowded around in a circle, trying to see the source of all the steam. I peered over their heads.

A woman in a stained white lab coat was lying on the floor. Her bare, normal-skin hand was clutching the remains of what looked like a broken Agent S vial.

The woman writhed and shrieked as gelatinous, green liquid oozed up her arm. Her skin pulsed a shimmery green. There was a sizzling sound, like frying meat. Then, her flesh turned black.

I couldn't look away.

The woman's charred skin peeled away, until the milk-white bone of her forearm was exposed. She cursed and cried as she tried to rid herself of the poison. She tore at her own skin with mangled fingers.

As I watched, her exposed bones began to sizzle. The woman was…disintegrating.

Nausea surged through my throat.

The Steel children congregating around her began to scoop up the liquid Agent S droplets into their cupped metal hands. From their methodical movements and relaxed posture, it was clear this wasn't the first time something like this had happened.

The alarm abruptly shut off, making the woman's screams even more hair-raising.

As one, the kids backed up from the burning woman. A second later, a panel opened up on the other side of the room. A group of people wearing those strange cloaks surged inside and surrounded the woman. A suffocating amount of magic filled the room.

Even though I was camouflaged, I backed away. Instinct told me it would be a really bad idea to attract these Super Mags' attention.

All at once, the woman's screams cut off. The quiet was deafening.

"Oh no!" someone gasped.

One of the children had knocked into a lab table as she tried to scramble away from the cloaked figures. Half a dozen kids hurried to right the unbalanced table.

A titanium tray covered with raw Agent S crystals wobbled. Several children reached out their hands to catch the stones, but they got tangled up in each other along the way. The tray clattered to the cement floor.

All of the crystals remained on the tray, except one.

"Run!" someone shrieked.

Everything turned to madness as Steel children, adults in lab coats, and cloaked Mags raced for the elevator. My friends and I had no choice but to let ourselves be carried along with the panicked tide.

A.J. shouted something, but his voice was lost in the pandemonium.

The four of us were crowded onto the elevator with about twenty others.

My heart was pounding, even though I had no idea what was going on. There were a few whimpers, and then all other sounds were eviscerated.

BOOM!

The elevator rocked. I would have gone right over the flimsy railing if Diego hadn't grabbed onto my arm and yanked me back.

The whole mine shuddered. The elevator swung dangerously. People screamed.

By some miracle, we made it down to Level 5 in one piece. Diego kept adjusting our appearances so we blended into our surroundings and were all-but invisible. When the elevator came to a jerky stop, my friends and I stumbled off. I wasn't sure about everyone else, but my legs felt like rubber.

"All Steels to Level 2," the foreman's voice called over the loudspeaker. "Now."

Children began to stream out of the tunnels as they ran in our direction.

"Bri, we have to go," Michael said from behind me. "Everyone is coming this way."

"No." I peered at the face of every child who passed, looking for familiar hazel eyes. "Not without Lilly."

"Sweetheart, we don't even know if she's here," A.J. said gently.

"Exactly," I snarled in a voice I barely recognized. "And I'm not leaving until I find out for sure."

"You're not going to do your niece any good if you get yourself captured," Diego snapped. "If we stay here, we're going to get caught."

"So go!" I retorted, starting back toward the elevator.

If Lilly was here, she would be heading to Level 2.

I tried not to think about the fact that none of the children congregating around the elevator were young enough to be the one I was desperate to find.

"That's not how this works," Michael said, as calm as I was frantic. "We'll come back, but right now, we have to go."

I was about to protest some more, when Diego lifted me up and threw me over his shoulder.

"Put me down!" I raged.

Diego cursed when my titanium fists struck his back, but didn't let go of me.

"You knock me out, and your friends will be completely exposed," he warned.

That stopped me before my kick hit home.

Diego was right, and that made me want to scream at the top of my lungs. As desperate as I was to find Lilly, I couldn't put A.J. and Michael in danger. I had no choice.

"Put me down," I ordered Diego, but there was no fight left in my voice.

Even when we made it back down to the tunnel that would lead us out, I couldn't stop looking back. We passed through the door that separated the mining tunnel from the high-speed train platform. Once the door was shut, my magic came back with so much force I would have collapsed if Diego wasn't still holding onto me like I was a flight risk.

It should have been a tremendous relief, but all I could think about was my enormous failure.

I was leaving the mine, and with it, the truth about Lilly. As I stepped onto the train car that was waiting for us just like Smith said it would be, all I could think was that I had failed my family.

CHAPTER 25

I was physically and emotionally drained.

I had gotten no joy from our speedy return trip to Boston, when every mile brought me farther from where I was desperate to be. Not even Smith's sticky note on the vehicle console that said "Push lever to full speed and hold on" got me to crack a smile.

A.J. was doing his best to cheer me up, but I just couldn't muster the strength to engage in his endless chatter.

As soon as we were back in Boston, above ground rather than below, I forced out the words I'd been dreading the whole ride back.

"I need to go see my family."

Ever since Subject 6 told us about the enslaved Mags, I had periodically lost myself in a fantasy where, one day soon, I drove up to my parents' house with Lilly in my arms. That fantasy had never felt further away than it did now.

I didn't have Lilly. I didn't have answers.

I didn't even have a car.

"We're going with you," A.J. said without hesitation. He held up a hand before I could protest. "No one should have to deal with relatives alone, especially when you're looking like a stiff wind might knock you over."

A.J. was right about the stiff wind part. The stranglehold on my magic might be gone, but so was my energy. I was beat.

"Mm, I get to meet Bri Hammond's parents?" Diego gave me a half-smile.

I rolled my eyes, already regretting my promise to Kaira that I would keep tabs on him. Diego stuck a piece of cinnamon gum in his mouth and sighed in contentment, clearly enjoying my discomfort.

Michael commandeered the first car we came across as we followed the access road from MagLab back into civilization. The driver was so eager to impress Michael, he offered to go home and get his wife's car for us, too. He seemed disappointed when Michael declined.

It took another five minutes to convince A.J. to ride in a car with leather seats.

"Must be nice to be adored by everyone you meet," Diego commented as we belted ourselves in.

"It can be," Michael replied vaguely.

He wasn't chatty on a good day, and we were all a little on edge with Diego.

If Diego noticed our discomfort, he wasn't bothered by it. He sprawled out across the backseat, throwing his arm over the back of my headrest and manspreading until his knee brushed mine. I glared at him and shifted farther onto my side.

The clock on the dash said it was 8:00. If the sky hadn't been dark, I wouldn't have known whether it was day or night. Our time in the mine was all jumbled together, and I had no idea whether I was coming or going. For all I knew, we'd spent days underground.

No one spoke except for when I was giving Michael directions to my house. I thought about asking Michael to babysit Diego in the car so I didn't need to invite him inside. If that wouldn't have made Diego even more curious about my personal life, I would have.

I hadn't brought anyone home to my parents' house since Lilly's death. My family had never met any of the Seven in person. The funeral parlor-vibe in my house wasn't really conducive to guests.

As I had the last time, I rang the doorbell, fidgeting from foot to foot as we waited. The door swung open to reveal my dad.

"Twice in one week, pumpkin head?" My dad stepped out to hug me. "Is everything okay?"

"I'm fine," I said, speaking into the front of my dad's *UConn Mags* sweatshirt. "But I need to talk to all of you."

"Brent and Sarah are watching a movie upstairs. Your mom and I just finished dinner. You hungry?"

"We already ate," I lied. "Thanks, though."

My dad did a double-take when he caught sight of the three guys standing behind me.

"Golly," my dad said. "Who are you fellas?"

Sometimes, my dad was such a dad.

"A.J., Michael, and Diego," I said, pointing to each one.

"Mr. Hammond," A.J. gushed. "Such a pleasure. I'm your daughter's bestie, and may I just say, she is a treasure."

"Why, yes she is," my dad replied. He was trying a little too hard not to stare at A.J.'s electric blue nail polish…which he'd "borrowed" from me and refused to return. The butt.

"Sweetie," my dad called to my mom in the falsely cheery voice he'd adopted since his real cheery voice disappeared. "Look what the cat dragged in." He gave me an exaggerated wink and thumbs-up before retreating into the house.

Michael and A.J. followed. Diego stood in the foyer, examining my mom's paintings.

"She's an Artist," I said, wondering why I felt the need to explain anything to him.

Diego's expression was inscrutable as his gaze lingered on the pictures of me and Brent as children. I wondered what he was thinking.

"Bri!" My mom hurried over to hug me. "Oh." She let go of me and stared at the three guys lingering in the hallway.

I went through the introductions again, and again, A.J. sang my praises while the other two stayed silent.

"Now, I remember," my dad said, scratching his chin. "I've seen the two of you on television with the new Directors." He pointed from Michael to A.J.

"Famous by association," A.J. chuckled. "I'll take it."

My mom was looking from Diego's earring to his tattoos with barely-concealed horror. My dad had gone from not-staring at A.J.'s nail polish to his violet shirt, which I'd bought for him on his last birthday. It had a picture of a cheekily-grinning sweet potato with a top hat and the words *I yam what I yam*. Both of my parents shrank away from Michael's towering height and unkempt beard.

My parents were good people, but they leaned toward the conservative and old-fashioned end of the spectrum. I had never asked their opinion on my friends, but I had to bite my tongue to keep from commenting on their judgmental expressions. I wasn't surprised about my protectiveness over A.J. and Michael, but I wasn't sure what to make of the fact that I was similarly bristling over the way my mom was assessing Diego.

Diego wasn't making things any easier. He was standing a little too close to me, which hadn't escaped my mom's notice.

"I need to talk to Brent and Sarah," I said, trying to cut through the obvious tension.

"I'll, uh, go get them," my dad said, giving the guys another once-over before heading for the stairs.

"We're Bri's friends," Michael told my mom in the soothing voice he used when he was talking to someone hysterical. "You don't need to worry."

"Oh, thank God." My mom pressed her hand to her heart and let out a short laugh. Her gaze slid to Diego when she said, "I was afraid my daughter had a boyfriend she'd neglected to mention."

I waited for Diego to make some obnoxious or inappropriate comment, but he didn't. He still had that strange expression on his face that made me think his mind was far away. His gaze was fixed on a painting of my brother and I when we were younger. Brent had me in a headlock, and we were both laughing so hard we could barely stand.

I wondered whether Diego had any siblings, and then wondered why I cared.

Thankfully, the clomp of feet on the stairs saved me from any more conversation or stray thoughts.

There was another round of hugs and introductions once Brent and Sarah arrived. We all sat down at the large dining room table that we didn't use anymore, since my parents had stopped entertaining.

I let out a breath as I met my family's expectant gazes.

A.J. found my hand under the table and gave it a squeeze. "You've got this, honey pie," he whispered.

Diego rested his arm on the back of my chair. I wasn't sure if it was out of solidarity, to show off his tattoos to annoy my mom, or if he just liked invading my personal space.

"I have to talk to you all about Lilly."

Sarah made a small sound and pressed her hand to her mouth. Brent started rubbing circles on her back. My parents' expressions darkened.

"What is it, Bri?" my brother asked, splitting his attention between me and his wife.

In fits and starts, I told my family about the slave mine. I told them about the list of children and the number that matched Lilly's birth date.

I didn't tell them about the tomb we'd stumbled on with all those child-sized coffins.

"I thought you'd all want to know," I finished lamely, loosening my grip on A.J. when I realized I had his hand in a stranglehold.

Sarah's whole body shook as she buried her face against Brent's shoulder. My parents were both wiping away silent tears. I felt like a monster for being the bearer of this news.

"I can't," Sarah was saying into Brent's shirt. "I can't survive—"

I couldn't hear what Brent said back, but the helpless look on his face shattered my heart.

"I'm sorry," I whispered.

I'd thought it would be kinder to tell them what I'd discovered. Seeing their faces now, I realized I had just torn open old wounds.

Michael leaned over A.J. to tell me in a low voice, "I can help her—your sister-in-law. If you want."

I looked at Sarah, whose slender shoulders were shaking from the force of her quiet sobs. I had seen what happened to people after Michael Whispered to them. They became enamored with him.

That would kill Brent, who was as obsessed with Sarah now as he'd been when they first started dating.

"Not Whispering, exactly," Michael said, like he could read my mind. "But I can give her some comfort."

I blinked back my own tears at the thought of Sarah and Brent getting a little peace. I gave him a grateful nod.

Michael got up from his chair and walked over to Sarah's side of the table. He moved slowly, like he was approaching a skittish animal. He crouched between Sarah and Brent's chairs and said something that was too quiet for me to hear.

The three of them got up from the table and went onto the back porch, where they were in sight but their conversation would be private. Whatever Michael was saying, I could almost see the way tension eased out of Brent and Sarah.

"How could you do this to them?" my mom demanded, bringing my attention back to my parents.

This time, A.J.'s hand tightened painfully on mine.

"Why do you insist on torturing us?" she continued. "We all know what happened to Lilly. She's dead, and to pretend otherwise is just—just—"

"I thought," I began, but my mom cut me off.

"If it turns out Lilly really is dead, Sarah won't survive. Have you thought about that? Have you thought about what it will do to Brent when she dies?"

She covered her face with both hands and let out a muffled sob. My dad looked from my mom to me, his expression miserable.

"I'm sorry," I whispered. "I was trying to help."

"No." The harsh word came from Diego. He was leaning forward, one of his fists curled on the table. The other was gripping the back of my chair. He gave me a hard look that held none of his usual sarcastic humor. "You are not the one who should be apologizing." He glared at my parents so fiercely they both shrank a little in their chairs. "You will not speak to her like that."

"Diego," I said, but he ignored me.

"Bri has risked her life to find out what happened to your granddaughter, while you sit here nice and safe in your little house."

"Diego—"

"Bri has lost just as much as you, but she isn't crying about it and wallowing in denial."

I felt a hard pressure on my shoulder, which Diego was now gripping. I wasn't even sure he'd noticed. He was really angry. He'd reacted the same way after I told him I'd broken into his apartment and taken his Agent S.

"Stop," I hissed at Diego, taking his hand and removing it from my shoulder.

"I hate to say it," A.J. cut in before I could say anything else. "But Diego's right."

It was the first time A.J. had referred to Diego by name, rather than as the Chameleon or Sexy Cinnamon Man.

"Bri has been running herself ragged," A.J. continued. "I understand you're in pain, but that's no excuse for behaving like heathens."

"Bri," my dad said through clenched teeth. "Your mother and I would like to speak to you. Alone."

The back door opened at that moment, and Sarah came in wiping her eyes. Michael and Brent were behind her.

Sarah gave us a wobbly smile.

"Thank you so much for coming," she said to me and the guys. She reached back and squeezed Michael's hand. "Thank you for everything. Truly."

"You're welcome," Michael replied, extricating his hand from hers.

"I'll, uh, call if I find out anything else," I said, getting up in such a hurry I almost knocked over my chair.

"Bri, wait," my brother said. He glanced from Sarah to our parents. "I want to come with you to look for Lilly. You're right about everything."

He was about to say more, but my parents' outcry made it impossible.

"You are not going to a slave mine," my father said, before turning his attention on me. "And neither are you. I forbid it."

"Call the police," my mom said, nervously tugging on one of her blonde curls. "They'll take care of it, I'm sure."

Diego and A.J. let out synchronized scoffs.

"Bri's right," Brent said. "If we can find out definitively what happened to Lilly, then it's my responsibility to do it."

An argument was heating up between Brent and my parents. I stood back, letting them duke it out. As much as I loved my parents, I hadn't asked for their permission for any of my choices since I decided to go unMarked. I certainly wasn't asking for their permission now.

"Brent, please."

Sarah's voice was soft, but Brent's head snapped around to give her his full attention. Her eyes were brimming with tears, but she looked more in control of her emotions than I'd see her in years.

She came over and clasped his hands. I looked away, feeling like I was intruding on a private moment between them.

"I can't survive without you. Please." She let go of one of his hands to press her fist to her heart. "I want to start to heal with you." She glanced at Michael before turning her attention back to her husband. "I want to move on with our lives. But I can't do that without you."

Uncertainty flickered in Brent's hazel eyes.

"Come walk us to the car," I told my brother, because I could see where this conversation was heading.

My brother kissed Sarah before following me out.

"I'll meet you in the car," I told the guys as soon as we were out of the stifling house.

Diego, A.J., and Michael exchanged a look. They were hovering protectively around me, like they might need to jump in and save me from another verbal assault.

I didn't need their support, but I couldn't pretend like I didn't appreciate it. I gave up on trying to get rid of them and shut the door behind Brent to make sure my parents didn't follow him out.

"I'm going back to the mine to find out what happened to Lilly," I told my brother. "But you have to stay here. Sarah needs you."

"Lilly's my daughter," Brent said. "I can't let you put yourself in danger for something that's my problem."

"Lilly isn't a problem," I replied. "And we both know I can take care of myself. Besides, my friends are the toughest Mags around. We've handled worse than a slave mine, trust me."

That last part wasn't exactly true, but the Seven were no strangers to life-threatening mysteries. And if anything happened to Brent, I'd never be able to live with myself.

A muscle ticked in Brent's jaw.

"Your wife needs you," Michael said, coming to my aid. "Trust us to do this for you."

Brent's broad shoulders slumped. He let out a long sigh.

"Okay," he said, glancing back in the direction of the house. "But please…promise me you'll be careful." He stooped until he and I were eye level. "Nothing is worth your life, baby sis."

I gave him a hug. "I'll be careful," I promised.

CHAPTER 26

By the time we drove up to the mansion in our borrowed car, I was on pins and needles. My phone had been blowing up for the last ten minutes as Smith and my security team updated me on the drama unfolding in front of our front gate.

"Just what we needed," A.J. groaned as we caught sight of our house…and the woman who was attempting to climb our unclimbable gate.

Michael parked at the bottom of the driveway and we all got out.

"I have rights!" a familiar and very unwelcome voice wailed.

Valencia Stark.

She had stopped trying to climb the fence, and was now facing off with five of my security guards. A Nat wearing a baggy suit and carrying a scuffed leather briefcase stood beside her, looking nervous and a little embarrassed.

"Valencia, this is private property," I said, when I was close enough that I wouldn't need to yell. "Did I not make myself clear the last time we talked?"

Maybe Kaira and Graysen needed to make our prisons a little less inviting, since Valencia was clearly so eager to be back inside one.

"My client is asserting her Alliance-mandated right to protest," the man next to Valencia said. He mopped his sleeve across his sweaty forehead. "Furthermore, it is our right as Naturals to—"

"Who are you, again?" I interrupted, even though Smith had already sent me a detailed file on the man.

"He's my lawy-ah," Valencia said, before the man could speak for himself. She pointed at me. "I'm suing you for assaulting me at the baseball game."

I laughed. Normally, I tried to maintain a higher level of professionalism. But it had been a long day.

By this point, Michael, A.J., and Diego had joined me. I wasn't sure if they realized it, but the three guys had their arms folded over their chests in identical poses. They were all glaring at Valencia. It was kind of adorable.

"Oh dear," A.J. said, screwing his face up into one of mock-concern. To me, he said, "We better get you a lawyer stat." He tapped his chin, pretending to think. He snapped his fingers. "I know who will want to represent you. Director Graysen *Gald-ah*."

The lawyer's shoulders straightened in indignation. "Director Galder is *not* a lawyer. He has no right—"

"Sure, sure," A.J. waved a hand. "You go ahead and make that argument to the judge. I'm sure they'll take your side when the *Directors* tell the judge what really happened on that baseball field."

"Not that they'll need to say anything," Michael added. "The whole altercation was televised. Have you seen it?"

Michael so rarely displayed any sarcasm or humor, I drank in the moment.

The lawyer's face blanched. A.J. reached over and gave him a pat on the arm.

I smiled sweetly at the man. "I'm sure clients will be lining up to hire you after this."

"Actually," A.J. said. "Let me make a quick call. I know some reporters who would love to get an early preview of your client's statement."

A.J. pulled out his phone.

The lawyer mumbled something about needing to reevaluate and fled to his car. Valencia shouted obscenities after him.

"Your five minutes are up," I told Valencia, making a shooing motion with my fingers.

Since she hadn't done anything illegal yet, there wasn't much more I could do.

Valencia glared at us, her eyes appearing magnified through the thick lenses of her glasses. "You'll be sorry, you filthy Mags," she spat. "But I'll have the last laugh." As if to demonstrate, she let out a maniacal chuckle.

"Begone, Wicked Witch of the West," A.J. said, yawning in Valencia's face.

When she didn't move, I blew on my fists. That was all it took. Valencia looked at my silver skin, muttered something about freak Mags, and scrammed.

"So, this is what it's like to be a big, scary security chief?" Diego raised an eyebrow at me.

"Pretty much," I replied. I pointed in the direction of Valencia's car, which was screeching out of our driveway. "And that's one of many reasons why we're destroying the Agent S. Can you imagine if she got her hands on the MRP?"

"I would never let that happen," Diego said.

"You might not have a choice," A.J. pointed out.

Diego looked like he wanted to say more, but after another glance in my direction, he kept his mouth shut. He'd been strangely quiet since we left my parents' house, and I was getting the disturbing impression that he felt sorry for me.

Obnoxious come-ons I could handle. Pity I couldn't...especially when it came from him.

Our little posse had barely made it into the house when another disturbance hindered our progress. It was raining in the front hallway. People were shouting. Sir Zachary, wearing a jack-o-lantern dog costume, was hiding under a table and shaking.

"What in tarnation?" A.J. asked, looking around before crawling under the table to rescue our distraught dog.

I hurried farther into the house, watching my step so I didn't wipe out.

The rest of the Seven were in the middle of the kitchen, which looked like a warzone. Kaira and Yutika were shouting at everyone to calm down. Graysen had a Super Mag child in a headlock. Desiree was standing next to Charlotte, who was now a golden-eyed tiger. And Smith was hunched protectively over a computer. Everyone and everything was soaked.

Out of the corner of my eye, I saw a purple streak of lightning crackle through the air. I moved, but before I could reach the source, Diego tackled the Super Mag child.

The child lashed out with another bolt of lightning, but Diego had been expecting it. He blurred out of sight, reappearing in full view near the ceiling.

He dodged the next bolt of lightning before hurling his body into the Super Mag's. They hit the floor with Diego on top.

Seeing how fast he moved, I understood how he'd taken me on in a fight. But speed would only get him so far.

I crossed the room between them. I was about to pull Diego off the girl, who seemed to be struggling to breathe, when purple lightning crackled along her palm. I threw out my arm, blocking the electricity from making contact with Diego's chest.

A small flame erupted on my sleeve, which caught fire before the lightning bolt shivered down my titanium skin.

"Ah." I squirmed. "That tickles."

The Super Mag girl scowled at me as she readied another lightning bolt. Diego pressed his forearm across her throat.

"Stop," Michael said in a clear voice.

The Super Mag pinned beneath Diego went limp. The lightning retreated back into her fingertips.

One by one, Michael went to the Super Mags in the room and Whispered to them.

"Desiree," Michael said in a calm voice. "Can you please go water the lawn outside?"

All at once, the pouring rain that had turned me into a wet rat stopped.

"That's it?" Diego demanded.

I ignored him, turning my attention on my friends. Kaira was inspecting Graysen's arm, which was bleeding. Smith was wiping his computer down with a microfiber cloth. The Super Mags were standing around the kitchen, looking a little lost.

"Well, I'd say we're making progress," Graysen said, smiling a little as he sank down into a chair.

"What happened this time?" I asked.

"Oh, you know." Yutika tried to blow her bangs out of her face, but they were plastered to her forehead from the rain. "The Super Mags were under the impression that living on our property meant they were exempt from rules."

Kaira surveyed the messy and water-stained kitchen with a glare that was almost identical to Ma's.

"You kids are going to clean this place up," she said in a perfect imitation of Ma's don't-mess-with-me voice. "And when you're done, you're going back to your house and cleaning that up. Just because you have more magic between you than the rest of Boston's Mags combined, it doesn't give you the right to behave badly. Now, get moving."

Some of the kids muttered apologies as they got to work. The rest quickly followed at a glance from Michael.

"What the hell is wrong with all of you?"

We turned at the sound of Diego's fury.

"Excuse me?" Graysen asked.

"Why haven't you locked them up?" Diego demanded.

"All of you, please go outside with Desiree," Michael said to the Super Mags.

We waited until it was just us in the kitchen before anyone else spoke.

"You mean, why haven't we imprisoned children who've spent their lives in cages?" Kaira replied. "Gee, I have no idea."

"They aren't just kids. This kind of power is monstrous and perverse."

A.J. stalked up to Diego.

Outside of animal rights discussions, I'd never seen A.J. angry. His whole body trembled as he faced Diego. For a second, I thought A.J. might hit the other man.

"You know," A.J. said. "Just because someone's different, it doesn't make them wrong."

"It does if it'll lead to death on a massive scale," Diego replied.

"They're children," Kaira said, her fury eclipsing both A.J. and Diego's. "They need love and attention, and to learn the difference between right and wrong. They're just like everyone else."

"Everyone else can't wipe out the city with their bare hands," Diego shot back.

"You're sounding like Valencia," I told him, caught between disappointment in his unwavering prejudice and defensiveness on behalf of my friends.

Diego scowled at me. "I'm not a bigot. I know firsthand what Super Mags are capable of, and I know that anyone who cares about the fate of Boston can't let them run wild. They have to be contained."

"Isn't what you're saying a little hypocritical," Yutika pointed out. "Since you're a Super Mag?"

"No." Diego crossed his arms. "I'm going to take away the Super Mags' magic, and then I'm going to take away my own. Nothing hypocritical about that."

"You're making a very dangerous argument," Graysen said in a deadly calm. "You're talking about taking away people's magic before they've even committed a crime. And you're giving people like Valencia and the Federal Security Enforcers the justification to go after regular Magics."

"I'm not saying there shouldn't be rules and that the MRP shouldn't be a controlled substance, but—"

"You don't have the right to make those kinds of decisions," Kaira snapped, her voice barely below shouting level.

"And you don't have the right to put the whole city in danger, just because your maternal instincts are all fired up," Diego retorted.

"That was very unsexy, Cinnamon Man," Yutika said in a frigid tone.

Graysen had his arms around Kaira, who looked ready to tear Diego's face off.

"Keep talking," Graysen told Diego. "I fucking dare you."

The two men glared at each other.

"Maybe we should all sit down," A.J. suggested. "This poor house can only tolerate so much testosterone." To Diego, he said, "Graysen already holds the alpha male role in our group. You're going to have to find your own pack."

Diego didn't back down.

"I don't have time for your idealist shit. What are you going to do when some Level 30 Earth-mover baby throws a fit because he didn't get his bottle and collapses the entire city?" Diego pressed on. "I'm the only one in this room who understands what so much magic is capable of. And that's why I have not only the right, but the responsibility, to do something about it."

Kaira let out a harsh laugh. "Yeah, you're a regular hero. Injecting little kids with poison." She turned to Graysen. "Maybe we should make a biggest bastard of the year award. We can make the trophy look like Diego."

"You're thinking about this all wrong," Diego said, ignoring Kaira's sarcasm. "When I take away their magic, they become a blank slate...people who aren't simply defined by their magic." He paused, and I got the sense he was struggling to contain his own emotions. "I'm not doing anything to them that I don't want for myself. Trust me when I tell you it will be a relief to be seen as a person, rather than a freak of nature."

I bit down on my lip as unwelcome sympathy flooded through me. Diego was a lot of things, but he wasn't a freak.

"Speak for yourself," Kaira told him. "The rest of the Super Mags are *not* freaks."

Diego looked from Kaira to Graysen. Then, very softly, he said, "Your future children might feel differently."

Kaira's chair screeched against the tile floor as she shoved to her feet, her hands balled into fists.

"You better get lost before my wife does something illegal," Graysen told Diego. "Or I do."

Diego wasn't cowed.

"The first time I interacted with someone in-person besides my parents, I was eighteen," he said. "And the only reason I could do it was because I had a low dose of MRP in my blood, which suppressed my magic enough for me to pass as a regular Mag."

All at once, Diego's reality struck me like a kick to the gut. My chest ached for what he'd been through...the life he must have led.

The year after I went unMarked had almost driven me insane. I couldn't imagine eighteen years of that kind of isolation.

I had to curl my hand into a fist to keep from reaching out to offer him some kind of comfort.

"I feel sorry for any child who had to go through that," Kaira said, less angry than she'd been. "But that's why Graysen and I are doing what we're doing. Under our version of the Alliance, no one has to feel like less, regardless of how much magic they have or don't have."

"That's ignorant," Diego snapped. "And completely irresponsible to the people of this city who are depending on you to protect them."

Graysen wrapped his arm around Kaira's waist. I wasn't sure if he was doing it to comfort her, or to make sure she didn't maul Diego.

"Everything you just said is enough of a confession for us to arrest you," Graysen told Diego. "We owe you for getting us out of the mine, so consider this your one free pass. Come back here again, and we'll arrest you so fast you won't know what hit you."

"You're welcome to try." Diego gave Graysen a taunting, *catch me if you can* smile. He winked at me. And then, he vanished.

A few seconds later, I heard the front door close. Diego was gone.

"Just goes to show," Yutika said on a sigh, "that looks aren't everything."

"They are when they're combined with a scintillating personality and prodigious intellect," A.J. said, brushing a speck of fake dust off his shirt.

The others headed upstairs to change out of their wet clothes, but I hung back, my feet anchored to the floor.

No one else was talking about the bombshell Diego had just revealed about his own background, but I couldn't get it out of my head.

Diego was our enemy. There was no doubt he was breaking just about every law and ethical code. He was also breaking one of my core beliefs…that it was wrong to punish a person for the way they'd been born.

But now that I knew his justification behind his actions and the childhood that had made him what he was now, I couldn't see Diego the same way.

He wasn't some psycho vigilante with a God complex like I'd thought. He was trying to save others from the life of isolation and self-loathing he'd led. He was trying to protect Boston from the possibility of a rogue Super Mag destroying all of us.

I still didn't agree with what he was doing, and I'd do everything in my power to prevent him from making any more of the Magical Reduction Potion. But for the first time, I was beginning to understand him.

CHAPTER 27

y the time we wrapped up for the night, it was three in the
morning. The living room floor was strewn with hand-drawn maps
of what we remembered from the mine, lists of information we'd
gathered, and law texts.

Graysen had gone through every relevant national law and inter-territory
policy before confirming there was nothing that could force the
Californians to dismantle the mine. The Alliance had no jurisdiction outside
of Boston, and the US Federal Security Enforcers hadn't gone into
California in decades.

That left us with only one option: diplomacy.

Graysen had an idea but wouldn't say anything more until he'd worked
it out. He and Kaira shut themselves in their study with the promise that
they'd have answers for us by the morning.

In the meantime, there was nothing to do but wait.

There was no way I'd ever be able to sleep. I couldn't stop thinking
about that underground tomb full of child-sized caskets and the empty-eyed
child slaves who had never seen the sunlight. My mom's words from earlier
in the night ran through my mind on loop.

If it turns out Lilly really is dead, Sarah won't survive.

I did jumping jacks until I was ready to drop. Then, I got in the shower
to wash off my ordeal in the isolation chamber. I soaped up twice, thinking
all the while about the slaves who had probably never had a proper
shower…or meal…in their lives.

I got into bed with a pile of Alliance work that had accumulated over the last day. I was just filling out my report on Valencia's most recent stunt when I heard a tapping at my window.

Usually, my friendly woodpecker came by in the morning. Then again, a glance at my clock revealed it was morning.

"Go to bed, Herbert," I called. "You're about two hours too early."

The tapping came again, more insistently this time.

I got out of bed and went to the window. I drew aside the blind. "Herbert—"

I let out a strangled scream. Diego was hovering outside my third-story window. While my heart pounded out of my chest, Diego opened my window and regarded me with his signature amused smirk.

"Who the hell is Herbert, and do I need to kill him?"

"What the hell are you doing here?" I demanded, clutching my racing heart.

Diego didn't answer. His gaze had dropped and was laser-focused.

When I realized what had captured his attention, I swore. I was wearing nothing except a skimpy tank top and panties.

"Don't look," I ordered, hurrying over to my dresser.

"You may as well tell me not to breathe."

Diego folded himself through my window without waiting for an invitation. The drawer I was opening slammed shut before I could extract a pair of oversized sweatpants. I spun around to find Diego only inches away. He caged my body with his, his palms resting on the wall on either side of my head.

"Oh no," I said. "This is so not happening."

"Oh yes." Diego leaned close enough for me to smell his cinnamon gum. "It so is."

Diego kissed me.

I meant to push him away, but I'd forgotten how good he was at this. My arms came around his neck before I even knew what was happening.

"Diego—"

He lifted me onto the dresser and deepened the kiss. And I was a gonner.

"You shouldn't be here," I murmured as his lips traced a line of fire down my neck. The bristles of his close-shaved beard teased my sensitive skin.

"Then tell me to leave."

Almost instinctively, I locked my arms around him to prevent him from going anywhere. His fingers dug into my wet hair, massaging my neck as he stole my breath.

"Mi pequeña diabla," Diego murmured against my lips.

My little devil. Smart-ass.

"You drive me crazy," he said as he slid his hands up my shirt.

"Ditto," I managed, gasping as his palm trailed across my ribcage.

"If you don't want this," Diego said, as out of breath as I was, "tell me now."

I should tell him to stop. Diego and I were enemies, and if my friends knew he was in our house, they would lose their minds…and then arrest him.

But Diego was making me feel more with just a kiss than anyone had made me feel…ever.

"I want this," I said.

"Good answer."

There was something predatory and possessive in the way he touched me. He wasn't rough, but he wasn't gentle, either. He was confident to the point of arrogant. It was sexy as hell.

He pushed my legs apart with his thigh, rubbing against me in just the right spot. Diego swallowed my moan with another hard kiss.

If things were this intense when we were both dressed, what would it be like to have sex with him?

I'd only ever gone all the way with Jordan, my high school boyfriend. Having sex with Jordan had been…sweet.

There was nothing sweet about Diego.

He whispered in Spanish as his hands explored my body. My brain was too occupied with sensation to translate, but I understood the tenor of his words. He was as turned on as I was.

Diego's fingers hooked around the edges of my panties, making me writhe against him. A sound I didn't even recognize came out of me. My body convulsed as pinpricks of heat lit up my insides, and a glass picture frame balanced on my dresser crashed to the floor.

"Bri?" a sharp knock at the door had Diego and I wrenching apart. "Are you okay?"

Yutika.

I could barely breathe, let alone speak.

"Bri? Ohmygod, did you faint? I'm coming in."

"No," I gasped, just as the doorknob turned. Diego gave me a devilish grin before blurring out of sight.

I threw myself across the room and into my bed, yanking up the covers. Yutika stepped into my room, her brow furrowed in concern.

"Sorry." Her frown deepened. "I thought I heard you cry out, or something."

"I—" I cleared my throat. "Just a dream."

I looked down at the comforter bunched in my fists. I'd never lied to any of the Seven before. And my reason for doing so now made everything even worse.

"Oh." Yutika came over and sat on the bed. "This must all be so hard for you, I can't even imagine. Want me to stay with you tonight? I could bust out my emergency jelly bean supply and we could binge a cooking show."

Now, I felt even worse.

"Thanks, but I think I just need to sleep," I said, feeling my cheeks grow hot as I stared my friend in the eye and lied to her.

Yutika nodded in understanding. "If you need anything, just shout."

She reached over and hugged me. I held my breath, terrified she would smell cinnamon and trouble all over me.

I didn't breathe again until Yutika had shut my door. I wilted, letting my head fall back against the headboard. I was like a teenager sneaking around with her boyfriend…except Diego wasn't my boyfriend.

Diego dropped his camouflage and stepped away from the wall.

"Next time, we'll have to go to my place," he said, smirking. "In the meantime, wanna get out of here?"

"Where are we going?" I asked warily.

Now that my lust had cooled, I realized what a horrible idea it would be to get close to Diego. Our chemistry might be through the roof, but that didn't mean we had any business being together. Not that we were…together.

"Put on some warm clothes." Diego watched me appreciatively as I wriggled out from under the covers. He grabbed the throw blanket at the end of my bed and tucked it under his arm. "I'm taking you flying."

CHAPTER 28

I was surrounded by black night sky, stars, and Diego. The air was crisp, becoming downright frigid the higher we went. I wasn't cold, though. Diego's magic wrapped around me like an inferno. And I didn't want it to ever stop.

He flew higher and higher. I had started out in my titanium form, but when I realized it would weigh Diego down, I turned back to regular skin. Besides, I wanted to feel the cold air on my face and Diego's heat pressed against me.

Below us, the city lights twinkled like tiny fireflies. Above me, the sky opened up in an endless expanse of stars and wispy clouds.

The wind stopped rushing past my ears, and I realized we were hovering in mid-air.

"Are you afraid?" Diego's low voice rumbled against my skin as he pressed his lips to my neck.

"No." I laughed.

"Do you trust me?"

That was a harder question to answer. "I trust you not to drop me," I said finally.

Diego chuckled.

I squeaked when he spun me around. I had a moment of weightlessness before his arms locked across my chest. Now, I was facing outward instead of looking over Diego's shoulder. It felt like I was the one who was flying. There was nothing in front of me except sky.

"So," I managed, a little breathless from the rush of flying and the male heat at my back. "This is how you get all the girls."

"I don't take people flying," Diego replied.

"What am I, a duck?"

"Trouble, cariño." He let go with one hand to tuck my hair into my collar. "A whole lotta trouble."

I tipped my head to the side, giving him more access to kiss my neck.

"Ready?" he asked.

"Ready for what?"

I turned in time to see Diego's devilish grin, and then we were plummeting back down.

I shrieked, which turned into a whoop that was stolen by the wind. We were flying so fast tears streamed from my eyes and my stomach was left somewhere above. It was *awesome*.

The city lights below came into focus, and then we were slowing. Disappointment pulsed through me at the thought that Diego was taking me home. Instead, he settled me on top of the John Hancock Tower…the same rooftop he'd brought me to on Halloween night.

"You're not planning to strand me here again, are you?" I asked as our feet hit the top of the building.

Diego chuckled. "No. I thought this would be a good place to watch the sunrise."

We sat at the edge of the roof, our legs dangling over. Diego draped the blanket he'd brought from my room over both of our shoulders. We sat with our sides touching as the sky began to turn from black to a hazy blue-gray color.

Diego pulled a pack of cinnamon gum out of his pocket.

"What's with the cinnamon?" I asked.

"I like it hot," he replied, holding my gaze as he put a piece of gum in his mouth in an exaggeratedly sensual move.

I laughed, shaking my head.

"What do you call your flying magic?" I asked.

"Levitator," he replied. "I'm a Level 15 Levitator and a Level 27 Chameleon."

Chameleons were incredibly rare, even at the low levels. Most of them worked in surveillance for the Alliance. They could blend into their surroundings, but it took a lot of time to get their camouflage right, and it was never as seamless as Diego's. Regular-Mag Chameleons needed hours to shift their appearances and could never change from blending into a painted wall to night sky in a second like Diego.

I'd met a Level 7 Levitator once. He'd been a performer for Brent's fifteenth birthday, and from what I could remember, the man couldn't go higher than a few feet off the ground.

"If you can fly, then why do you own a motorcycle?" I asked.

"For when I'm taking MRP." He gave me a little shrug, like it was no big deal. "And I'll need it once I don't have my magic anymore."

But you can fly! I wanted to shout. He had to be out of his mind to want to lose that kind of magic.

"Play your cards right, and I'll take you for a ride on my bike some time," Diego said with a wink.

If Diego were a normal man making the same offer, I would have jumped at the chance. But riding a motorcycle just didn't have the same appeal when the alternative was dangling hundreds of feet in the air, surrounded by the stars and Diego's magic.

"Flying is my weaker magic," Diego said, pulling me back into the present. "I can fly far and fast, but carrying anything besides my own weight exhausts me."

There was nothing weak about Level 15 magic, but compared to his Chameleon power, I guessed it must feel that way.

Diego wrapped an arm around me, drawing me tighter against his side. I glanced down at his forearm, corded with muscle and covered in black ink tattoos.

"Why do you have the Super Mags' numbers all over your arms?" I asked.

As soon as the words were out of my mouth, I realized the question might be too personal. Then again, Diego had seen me almost break down in front of my family and knew what kind of panties I wore. We were already personal.

"There's a backstory to these." Diego held out his forearm to display his tattoos.

I didn't say anything, hoping he'd share the story with me.

"My Amá was one of the few who knew DAMND wasn't real before I was born," Diego said. "So she knew I wouldn't be diseased in the way everyone had been led to believe."

I stayed silent, even though I had no fewer than a thousand questions. I could tell this was a painful topic.

"My parents started working on the MRP because they knew I couldn't have a normal life being what I was." Diego looked down at his tattoos. "I got these so I'd never forget how much danger my kind poses to the world." He held my gaze. "They're a reminder that, until our magic is gone, others will be at risk."

I swallowed down my arguments, even though all I wanted to do was tell Diego that he was wrong. Magic wasn't evil. *He* wasn't evil.

Instead of what I really wanted to say, I stuck to the less emotional parts.

"I thought Edwardian Remwald's Alchemist brother created the MRP before the Slaughters," I said, remembering what Subject 6 had told us months ago.

The Remwalds had been planning to use the MRP against any Mags who didn't help them in their war against Nats. Edwardian Remwald had mentioned once that his Alchemist brother was killed during the Slaughters. Edwardian had dedicated himself to his family's cause even when he was the only one left.

"My parents were the one who first developed that formula," Diego said, his voice taut. "They made it so I, and others like me, wouldn't have to spend our lives in hiding. When they found out what Remwald was planning to do with the MRP, they tried to stop him." His jaw tightened. "They might have succeeded, too, if it wasn't for—" He shook his head. "Never mind."

Before I could begin to work out how I felt about everything Diego was saying, he continued.

"That's why I was in Pruwist's house the night you broke in to steal the coordinates. My parents' notes were confiscated before MagLab was burned down, and I thought I might be able to access them through Pruwist's computer."

"Did you find their notes?" I asked.

Diego nodded. "Their last discovery was how to make the potion even stronger without needing as much Agent S." He gave me a sidelong glance.

"Great," I replied bitterly. "And then Valencia and her Mag-hating followers can get their hands on the MRP and shoot up whoever they please."

"You know how complicated the formula is," Diego said. "My mother was a Level 8 Alchemist and my father a biochemical engineer, and it took them their entire careers to figure it out.

"I destroyed all the digital copies of their research, so I'm the only one outside of the mine who actually knows how to make it." He gave me a pointed look. "Unless you and your friends go around giving out the formula, but even then, it would be almost impossible to get right without my parents' notes."

My friends and I hadn't mentioned the formula to anyone else. And I knew Diego was telling the truth about its complexity; Smith had gone on and on about how temperamental the ingredients were, even excluding Agent S.

"So, assuming you get your hands on more Agent S," I said, silently promising myself I'd never let that happen, "you're just going to spend the rest of your life making the MRP and injecting Super Mags?"

Diego quirked his lip. "I never said my life would be glamorous."

I slid out from under his arm, my pulse thudding in my rising anger.

I thought about Cora, Kaira's cousin who had lost her magic because a power-tripping Enforcer had shot her up with the Magical Reduction Potion. I thought about the Super Mags back at the house—of Charlotte and Emory.

I thought about Diego's strange, beautiful magic…and his desperation to be rid of it.

Diego's next words made my blood go cold.

"We've gotten to the point in the conversation where we discuss the favor you owe me, cariño."

I had almost forgotten the promise I'd made back in the mine, when I was locked in the isolation chamber.

"What is it?" I asked, my muscles tensing in anticipation of whatever he was going to say.

"The Alchemists in the mine keep the liquid Agent S locked in a titanium vault," Diego explained. "None of the keys in the foreman's office would fit, and I can't use Agent S when it's in the raw rock form. So, I need you to help me break into the vault."

For several seconds, my mind went completely blank.

"You want me to…what?!"

"Your stipulations were no sex and no killing," Diego said, giving me an infuriating smile. "And I'm not asking for either." His smile turned into something fierce. "You did swear to say yes to whatever I asked."

"This is going too far," I told him, trying to catch my breath. "My friends and I are trying to destroy everything connected to the MRP…not help you make more."

"You never would have gotten out of that cage without my help," Diego said, his tone going frigid. "Don't tell me that Bri Hammond's promises are empty."

I made a point of never promising anything I didn't intend to follow through on. But Diego had taken advantage of me when I was in a vulnerable situation. What he was asking wasn't just unfair…it was impossible.

"I'm not sure you're aware, but there are children being used as slaves in that mine," I said through gritted teeth. "There are a few more important things at work than your personal crusade."

"I disagree." Diego turned to look at me, his profile shadowed in the eerie pre-dawn light. "And I'm not saying you can't rescue your niece and the other children. I'm just saying you need to get my Agent S first."

I opened my mouth. Instead of the curses and accusations turning over in my mind, I asked, "Are you really going to inject yourself with a permanent dose of the MRP?"

"Yes," Diego said without a moment's hesitation. "I need my magic to get to the other Super Mags, but once all of their magic is gone, I'll lose mine, too. And I'll be glad for it."

"Won't you miss your magic?"

I couldn't fathom no longer being a Steel. I wouldn't know who I was without my magic.

Diego's laugh was dark and without any humor. "My whole life, my magic has been a prison for me."

The sun was just starting to peep up over the horizon, but I barely noticed.

"You think the MRP is a weapon," Diego continued, "but to me, it's a gift."

I shook my head, completely unable to wrap my head around what he was saying.

When Diego spoke again, his voice had lost its sharp edge.

"My parents loved me and gave me everything they could, but that didn't make up for the fact that I was in a prison of their own making."

"Where are your parents now?" I asked.

A muscle flexed in Diego's jaw. There was raw pain in his eyes, and for a second, I realized I was glimpsing the real Diego…the man behind the sass and sarcasm.

"They're dead."

He didn't explain how they died, and I didn't ask.

"I'm sorry, Diego." I put my hand over his. When he didn't pull away, I laced our fingers together.

"Things are different now, though," I said, my voice scratchy. "Graysen and Kaira are the Directors. They've already passed laws to protect Super Mags, and things are only going to get better. Our Directors' children are going to be like you."

Diego nodded slowly. "That just makes my kind an even greater danger. You've seen just a little of what we're capable of with that Pyrokinetic." His expression darkened. "I'm going to end it, Bri. And when I've lost my magic, I'll share the formula with someone else up to the task."

I didn't know what to say. I didn't know what to think.

Diego was wrong. It wasn't okay to punish innocent people just based on the possibility that they might one day commit a crime. And if I helped Diego, and his Magical Reduction Potion got into the wrong hands, everyone with magic would be at risk.

The sun was cresting the horizon, and its pink and orange rays were blinding. When I looked at Diego, tiny sunrises reflected in each of his irises.

"I need to get back," I said, letting go of Diego's hand. "My friends are going to notice I'm missing."

Diego didn't say anything. He just watched me, waiting for an answer to an unspoken question.

The words *I can't help you* were on the tip of my tongue when another thought occurred to me. With my magic weakened down in the mine, I needed all the help I could get. I might need Diego's magic to find Lilly.

"Alright," I said, getting to my feet. I didn't want to be near Diego anymore. "I'll do it. The next time we go down to the mine, I'll get you the Agent S." I turned to face him. "But after we get back to Boston, all bets are off. I'll do whatever it takes to make sure you never inject anyone else with the MRP."

When my friends discovered what I'd done, they might never forgive me. And if Diego managed to inject any more of the Super Mags before I found a way to stop him, I would never forgive myself.

CHAPTER 29

I slipped into the living room, fiddling with my scarf as I picked up on my friends' conversation.

"Morning, sleepy," A.J. said, giving me a strange look before turning back to Graysen.

My cheeks heated. With the exception of Ma, who didn't seem like she ever slept, I was always the first one awake. I picked at the fringes of my scarf and tried not to look guilty.

"Here's the situation," Kaira said. "Graysen got us a meeting with the California ruler who's in charge of the territory above the mine. We're going to try—"

"No." A.J. stood up so fast Sir Zachary, who'd been asleep on his lap, let out a surprised woof. "No no no no nooooo. Did I mention *no?!*"

We all stared at A.J.

"It's our best—really, our only option," Graysen said. "I've been through all the laws, and we have no right to do anything in her territory without her say-so. If we're going to get the slaves out and destroy the mine, we're going to need her help."

"Not to mention," Kaira added. "She's got a huge army—"

"Of cannibals!" A.J. shrieked, flapping his arms in agitation.

All of the books on our floor-to-ceiling shelves were fluttering around the room, snapping their pages like teeth as A.J.'s emotions made them swarm around us. The loveseat A.J. and I were sitting on started to lift off the ground.

"Isn't that just a rumor?" Smith asked A.J. "I couldn't find any accounts of her people actually eating…well, people."

"Cannibalism is one of the least heinous crimes Blade and her people have committed," A.J. replied with a shudder. "Trust me."

"Don't tell me the California territory ruler's name is actually Blade," Yutika said, smacking her palm to her forehead.

"Her given name was Leslie," Smith said.

I snorted.

A.J. snapped his fingers in Smith's direction. "Look up the Leslie Massacre of 2062."

The computer screen flickered. Smith raised his eyebrow at whatever he was reading.

"Care to share with the crowd?" I asked, sliding a worried glance at A.J., whose face was pale as a ghost. Flowers were arranging and rearranging themselves in a mad frenzy in their vase on the end table. Petals were flying through the air, which Sir Zachary was attempting to catch.

Smith waved his hand, and an image appeared on the wall we kept free of artwork or windows for this reason. There was a picture of an arid landscape. It looked much like what we'd seen when we stepped off the plane in California…except for the bodies.

Actually, there weren't even bodies. The picture taking up the entirety of our wall showed people's heads staked on the ends of spears. Bloody holes had replaced eye sockets, and purple tongues drooped out of open mouths. In the far corner of the picture, a crow was clutching the bloody sinews of an eyeball in its beak.

"That massacre started because one of her soldiers called her Leslie instead of Blade," A.J. said into our stunned silence. "I cannot emphasize how much we do *not* want to go near her."

A.J. flicked his hand, and the books replaced themselves on the shelves. Two brooms and dustpans came into the room, alone with dust rags, furniture polish, and about fifteen sponges.

When he was stressed, A.J. cleaned. Judging by how vigorously the cleaning supplies were working, A.J. was really stressed.

"Blade's also a Level 9 Telepath," A.J. continued. "And I *really* don't like people helping themselves to my thoughts. Those babies are worth more than just a penny."

"I'm with you, bro," Smith said, looking as sullen as A.J.

Lower-level Telepaths could speak directly into other people's minds, but the most powerful ones could also read thoughts and see into a person's past. One of my wrestling friends was a Level 5 Telepath, and he could see what a person had been thinking up to a week earlier. A Level 9 would probably be able to see all the way back to our childhoods.

"We're not planning to lie to her," Graysen said. "And there's one thing you're not taking into account. Blade isn't going to be happy when she finds out a whole organization is operating beneath her land. She'll want to destroy the mine as much as we do."

"Here's what *you* aren't taking into account," A.J. fired back. "Blade's unpredictable and downright certifiable. You can't reason with someone like that."

Graysen nodded thoughtfully. "Does anyone have any other ideas?"

No one spoke.

"What does everyone else think?" Kaira asked.

Kaira and Graysen might be the Directors, but they were still part of the Seven. They wouldn't make a decision that affected all of us without our input.

"If she tries anything, I can Whisper to her," Michael offered. "Telepaths don't interfere with my magic."

"We have to meet with her," I said, wilting under the look A.J. gave me. I mouthed *sorry* to him before continuing. "There's no way we can get all of those slaves out of the mine without Blade getting wise, and we may need her army's support."

"Besides," Yutika added. "She might be a nut case serial murder, but we're the Seven. Dealing with her kind is practically old hat for us at this point."

"Fine." A.J. made a violent gesture with his hand, and a broom snapped in half. "But when our heads are on stakes and crows are feasting on our eyeballs, I'm going to say I told you so."

✳ ✳ ✳

We didn't have any time to spare if we wanted to be on time for our meeting with Blade. Conveniently, we had Yutika's plane parked on the front lawn.

As we boarded the plane, A.J. regaled us with a *totally non-embellished* story about the last time someone arrived late to a meeting with Blade. I wasn't sure if any of us really believed him, but A.J. and Smith got us off the ground in record time.

We had wasted valuable time trying—unsuccessfully—to convince Kaira and Graysen to stay behind. I once again considered firing myself for being such a horrible security chief.

We congregated around the circular table in the center of the plane, where an extravagant breakfast was already waiting for us. There were eggs benedict and hot chocolate, with vegan alternatives for A.J. and me. We dug in while we discussed our upcoming negotiation with Blade.

I didn't think A.J. could get any more morose, but he pushed aside his avocado toast and stared at everyone else's eggs. He muttered, "Free range is still murder" under his breath.

To which Yutika replied, "My plane, my rules."

After we'd finished preparing as much as we could, we dispersed throughout the plane. Kaira and Graysen went to catch a few hours of sleep in the full bedroom Yutika had created onboard. Yutika and Michael were channel surfing on one of the giant flat-screen TVs. Sir Zachary, wearing a doggie pilot's cap, goggles, and blue tie, was asleep between them.

A.J. had expended enormous energy on getting the plane into the air, but he was still fidgeting and muttering to himself. Usually, Smith was the twitchy one in our group.

Even though the plane was spotless, A.J. had ordered Yutika to make him a vacuum, which was zooming back and forth across the carpet.

"Hey." I sat next to A.J. and gave him a nudge. "You okay?"

When A.J. looked at me, I saw the dark shadows beneath his eyes.

"'Course, butterscotch." He gave me a falsely-wide smile. Just as quickly, the smile turned to a frown. "Love bug, you're going to fry in that scarf. Not to mention, that shade of yellow doesn't do your complexion any favors."

"Don't—" I began, realizing too late what A.J. was doing.

My scarf unwound itself from my neck and folded itself up on the seat beside A.J. in a single motion.

A.J.'s mouth fell open.

"Bri Hammond, is that a hickey on your neck?!"

"Shhh!" I pressed my hand over his mouth, looking around to see if anyone else had heard. Luckily, the vacuum was loud enough that I didn't think they had.

"Mrrb wrrrb mrrrr!" A.J. said from behind my hand.

To which I replied, "Only if you keep your voice down."

I waited for A.J.'s nod before removing my hand. I hurriedly replaced the scarf, tying it tightly in case anyone else thought about trying to remove it.

"I thought you and Adam were done," A.J. whispered.

My confusion must have shown on my face. I didn't think I could blush any harder than I already was.

"Not Adam?" A.J. cocked his head at me.

Adam was my last hook-up before Diego, and the only other guy I'd been with in the last year. I chewed on my lip, unable to meet A.J.'s gaze.

"The coxswain is gay, so I really hope it wasn't him," A.J. said. He started going through all of Graysen's crew friends and discussing the likelihood that each one was the hickey-giver when I cut him off.

"It's Diego," I said, needing to put us both out of our misery.

"What's Diego?" A.J. replied. "Is he here?" A.J. looked around the plane, his suspicious gaze in place.

"No." I shook my head. "I made out with him."

"You made out with who?"

I groaned. "You can't possibly be this dense."

A.J. got right in my face and peered into my eyes. He touched the back of his hand to my forehead. His jaw dropped.

I hurriedly covered his mouth again as a torrent of exclamations hit my palm.

I waited until his tirade was over before removing my hand.

"Diego Agramonte? Our sworn enemy?" A.J. hissed.

"The one and only," I said, feeling like I was admitting to treason. "It's nothing serious," I added hurriedly. And then, because it looked like A.J. was in shock, I told him about our kiss in the graveyard, and then his visit at my window.

I wasn't ready to fess up to the promise I'd made Diego, and I left out the part about how we'd gone flying. A hotter-than-fire kiss was one thing, but flying and cuddling together during a sunrise was something more. A.J. might get the wrong impression that something was going on.

"Don't give me that look," I ordered A.J. "It was just a one-time—well, okay, two-time—thing." I thought again about the favor I owed Diego, and what my friends would say when they found out. No matter how attracted to Diego I might be, his request had reminded me that we were adversaries. Last night was never going to happen again.

I immediately squashed the quick stab of regret that accompanied that realization.

"Well, he does have very nice eyelashes," A.J. conceded.

He didn't say anything else on the matter. Whatever he was thinking, he kept it to himself.

"Get ready, people," Smith's tired voice called from the cockpit. "We'll be there in ten. A.J., look alive."

"Aye aye, Captain." A.J. saluted Smith, even though Smith's back was to us.

A.J. spread his arms out to the side like wings and dipped them gently. I felt the plane start to descend in time with the motion.

I blew on my fists and shook my head, clearing my thoughts of everything except our upcoming meeting with Blade.

The plane hit the ground with a gentle bump. Dust swirled around the windows outside. I whistled for Sir Zachary, who leapt off Michael's lap and joined me by the front of the plane.

I peered through the swirling dust outside the window.

"How many people did you say were coming to this meeting?" I asked Graysen, who had emerged from the bedroom and was straightening his tie.

"Blade and maybe a couple of her guards," Graysen said. "Why do you ask?"

"Because." I turned back to face my friends. "There's an army outside this plane."

CHAPTER 30

The 7.5 of us stayed close together as we crossed the stretch of desert that separated us from Blade. A few hundred people stood behind her, their eyes tracking our every move.

I glimpsed every weapon imaginable. Blade's soldiers carried everything from rusted knives, to crossbows, to machine guns. And that was in addition to whatever magic they were packing.

"I told you," A.J. whispered. "Didn't I tell you?"

"I'm making us bullet-proof vests," Yutika announced, drawing as we walked.

"Works for me," A.J. muttered.

"Blade," Graysen called when we were within earshot. "We're unarmed." He raised his hands, indicating for the rest of us to do the same. "Please tell your people to lower their weapons."

The California territory ruler let out a high-pitched, tittering laugh. She stalked toward us, leaving her army behind. Graysen moved protectively in front of Kaira, who poked him and pulled him back until they were side-by-side. Michael and I flanked them. A.J., Yutika, Smith, and Sir Zachary followed just behind us.

Blade wasn't much taller than me, although she looked bigger with all the weapons—and were those dead squirrels?—hanging off her belt. She held a leather riding crop, which she was tapping against her thigh.

I gave A.J. a warning look, but for once, he didn't go off on some animal rights diatribe. His face was deathly pale.

From the information Smith had gathered, I knew that Blade was forty-one. A combination of bad hygiene and the harsh California desert had turned her into a weathered thing that appeared decades older.

Blade's skin was sunburned and scaly, and her blonde hair was matted together into one clump. She had tattoos on her face that made it appear as though blood was oozing from her eyes and the corners of her lips. Her milky-gray eyes might have been her most disturbing feature.

"Well, well, well." Blade's voice was like honey mixed with cyanide. "Aren't you all adorable."

Sir Zachary let out a low growl. I moved to the front of our group, using my titanium body as a shield between us and Blade.

The territory ruler's milky gaze lasered in on me. I sucked in a small breath as I felt…claws inside my mind.

She wasn't controlling my mind the way Subject 6 had, but it felt just as intrusive…just as wrong. She was sifting through my thoughts and memories the way a child might flip through a picture book. Memories from my childhood flashed through my mind. I saw my dad pushing me on a swing, and my mom walking me to the bus on my first day of preschool.

"What are you doing to her?" Kaira demanded.

"Just say the word and I'll stop her," Michael told me in a low voice.

"It's okay," I muttered, even though it clearly wasn't. "I'm fine."

As much as getting my mind torn open by this wacko sucked, I would put up with it if it would get us into Blade's good graces. We needed her and her army to rescue the slaves. For that, I would put up with just about anything.

Blade dove back into my mind. She dug through my memories so quickly that I couldn't focus on what was happening outside of my mind anymore. I knew I was standing in the desert in front of Blade, but all I saw were the projections of my memories.

Boring, boring, boring, Blade's nails-on-chalkboard voice said inside my head.

The images in my head began to flip faster.

I glimpsed the first time Brent had brought Sarah home to meet the family. I felt our collective joy when Lilly was born, and then our despair over the news that she had died.

Ah, Blade's voice came as a delighted tinkle in my head. *This is yummy.*

Blade lingered on the memory of Lilly's funeral, forcing me to relive the darkest day of my life.

Such little shoulders to carry the weight of her whole family's happiness, Blade crooned. *Pretending to be so strong, when you're so lost.*

Blade giggled out loud. Then, before I could catch my breath, she went back for more.

I saw the inside of the mine and the tomb. I saw my hopes for finding Lilly dwindle. I heard my mom's warning about Sarah not surviving Lilly's death a second time.

So sweet, Blade crooned.

The images switched to Diego, pinning me against the dresser and kissing me…Diego flying me into the stars.

Well, hello, Blade's voice said.

Out loud, she said, "We have been a naughty, naughty. Haven't we?"

"Whatever you're doing to her, stop," Graysen ordered.

All at once, Blade's claw retracted from my mind. I staggered back a step, almost falling into Michael. I gritted my teeth as the worst headache of my life hammered around inside my skull.

"You okay?" Michael asked me.

I realized he was gripping my arm, which was the only reason I was still on my feet.

I tried to nod, but the motion sent a wave of nausea surging through me.

"Okay," I managed after the worst of the pain had dissipated. "Just…a surprise."

Blinking to clear my foggy vision, I saw Blade raise her riding crop to Graysen's face.

"Gray," Kaira said, but he gave her a small shake of his head. He had clearly made the same calculation I had—that a little thought-thievery was worth getting Blade's help. That, and there was no point in pissing her off when she had three-hundred soldiers waiting to tear us apart.

Blade drew the tasseled end of her crop across Graysen's cheek as they locked gazes. Blade's tongue darted out to lick her scaly lips.

Graysen's entire body went taut. His eyes were closed, his eyelids twitching as Blade searched through the recesses of his thoughts. Blade's lips moved, although no sound came out. I got the feeling she was speaking inside Graysen's head.

Kaira put a hand on his back as she glared daggers at Blade. Blade didn't notice.

"Awwww." She let out that horrible high-pitched laugh again. Her milky gaze snapped over to Kaira.

Graysen's eyes opened. He seemed disoriented for a second, but his attention focused the moment he realized Blade was facing Kaira.

"Sooo precious," Blade crooned. She placed the tip of her riding crop at Kaira's throat and dragged it down between her breasts.

Graysen's hand shot out and grabbed the crop.

"Touch my wife again," Graysen said on a low growl, "and you'll regret it."

"Mmm, possessive, aren't we?" Blade did that thing with her tongue again, and I had to stop myself from shuddering.

"Enough," Michael said. "We need your help, and you're going to give it to us."

Before coming here, we'd agreed it would be best to get Blade to willingly agree to help us. It was an ethical slippery slope to make other people do what we wanted just because we wanted it, but it was clear Michael was done playing nice with this woman.

"I…don't want to help you," Blade said, sounding puzzled.

"Her mind's really strong," Michael said without looking away from Blade.

"No one forces Blade's hand," the territory ruler said, referring to herself in the third person. Her eyes rolled back in her head, making her look even more unhinged. "Blade is strong. Blade is ruler."

Michael shook his head. "If I keep trying to influence her mind, I'll just make her more unstable than she already is. It's too risky."

When he broke eye contact, Blade shivered.

"Blade," Graysen said. His voice was polite, but his gaze was sharp. "You know why we're here. As I told your lieutenant over the phone, it will be in both of our interests to work together."

"There are hundreds of children down in that mine," Kaira said. "We have to get them out safely, and then we can destroy what's left."

Blade threw her head back and laughed. Even though her army was too far away to hear what we were saying, their laughter carried over to us, too. They clanked their weapons against each other, making a cacophonous riot of sounds.

When Blade spoke, her lips didn't move. I heard her voice in my head. *Remwald pays me well. Why should I do anything to hurt his operation?*

"Remwald's dead," Kaira said, making it clear Blade had spoken telepathically to all of us at once.

Blade opened up the front of her wrap shirt. I moved, putting myself between the ruler and my friends. Instead of the weapon I'd been expecting, Blade pulled wads of cash out of her bra. She giggled as she let the bills go, watching as the wind picked them up and drew them across the sand.

One of the bills passed me. It was for $1000.

"Holy shit," Yutika whispered.

There had to be $100,000 worth of cash flying off into the desert. And Blade didn't care.

"Are you seriously saying you aren't bothered by child slavery taking place on your land?" Kaira demanded.

Careful. Blade's telepathic voice had lost the honey. It was all cyanide now. *You do not want me as your enemy.*

"No, Blade," Graysen said. "You don't want us as yours."

"We're asking for your help," Kaira said. "But either way, we're going to rescue those children and demolish the mine. It's your choice which side you want to be on."

"I'm bored." Blade backed away from us, slapping her riding crop against her leg as she gave us a nasty smile. She kept going until she was halfway between us and her army. Then, she tipped her head back and howled like a wolf.

The three-hundred-or-so members of her army howled back. Then, they raised their weapons.

Yutika passed around bullet-proof vests to everyone except me. She bent down to fit Sir Zachary into his.

"And that concludes negotiations," A.J. commented.

I raised my fists as Blade's army surged toward us.

CHAPTER 31

Get back to the plane," I ordered the others, to which they responded with a simultaneous and emphatic *No*.

Blade's army swarmed her as they came for us.

I heard the now-familiar crack of guns being fired. I spread my arms out, trying to make myself as big as possible to intercept the bullets before they struck my friends.

A.J. pulled guns away from the front line of soldiers and turned them on their owners.

Seeing that their guns could be used against them, the Californians dropped their guns and reached for a multitude of other weapons they were carrying on their person…swords, hatchets, and other lethal-looking objects.

"There are too many of them for me to control all of their weapons," A.J. warned.

I broke into a jog, heading toward the oncoming army. Sir Zachary and Michael kept pace beside me.

"I've got Blade," I told Michael, before veering off to the side, where the territory ruler was surrounded by a mob of her people.

"Stop fighting!" Michael's voice was a roar that I felt beneath my feet.

The Californians in front obeyed. There were too many people for Michael to Whisper to all of them at once, so he used the ones under his control to form a protective ring around him as he moved deeper into enemy ranks.

My mind cleared of everything except the fight ahead. There was no time to second-guess myself or feel regrets. There was only the enemy standing before me.

I felt the tiniest bit sorry for these guys.

I pushed off the ground and threw my full weight into the front lines of Blade's defense.

There was a dull, metallic clang as people bashed into my titanium skin and fell limply to the ground. I had no pity for the broken noses and shattered wrists I left in my wake. These Mags were out for blood.

One of them raced toward me with his arms outstretched. His hands had turned to claws, and he was sprouting fangs.

Ew.

He raked his nails across my arm. Aside from shredding my sleeve, the claws had no effect.

"That was a mistake," I told the Mag. "I liked this shirt."

I launched myself into the air. I spun, delivering a backward kick to the man. I used my momentum to punch two other soldiers who were trying to get their hands on me. No reason why I couldn't be efficient.

I barely felt the swords and knives that broke apart against my skin.

I kicked, punched, whirled, and did it all again. All around me, bursts of magic struck my titanium skin and bounced off. The Californians' war howls turned to fearful whimpers.

"Stay away from the Steel!" I heard Blade's soldiers cry out to each other. "She's fuckin' strong!"

You have no idea.

Beside me, Sir Zachary locked his teeth around a man's pantleg. Our little dog flicked his head, and the grown man flew into the air. Two more Californians tried to kick Sir Zachary. Before their boots connected, our dog opened his mouth and barked fire.

The Californians screamed and fell all over each other as they tried to retreat. They knocked each other to the ground and trampled the injured. None of them stopped to help their fellow soldiers.

Loyal bunch, these Californians.

The only one on the battlefield the soldiers weren't abandoning was Blade.

I had left dozens of unconscious bodies in my wake and had almost reached the California leader, when a familiar shout turned my attention back on my friends.

My blood iced over at the sight of Californians encircling all of my friends except Michael, Sir Zachary, and me. Panic had me doubling back for them before I realized that the Californians weren't attacking my friends; they were defending them.

The question of why was cleared up when I noticed they kept their bodies and gazes angled toward Michael.

Other Californians who weren't under Michael's control beat their magic and weapons against their former-allies. The collision between the two was bloody and brutal. Corpses were piling up on the sand.

My friends might not have my Steel strength, but they were holding their own. Kaira was distracting our opponents by changing all of their appearances from illusions of us, to exact replicas of Blade, to hairless cats. I gagged when one of the Californians tried to take a bite out of a live cat…before realizing there was a person under the cat illusion. Then, the Californian bit the person anyway.

A.J. was controlling fifty-or-so weapons in mid-air, turning them to follow various people in the crowd and firing warning shots whenever the Californians got too close to any of the 7.5.

Graysen, Smith, and Yutika were wielding baseball bats, which they were using against anyone who got near them. Every now and then, I saw a burst of fire as Sir Zachary took care of a whole swath of our enemies.

Michael and I were working our way around the sides of the army, respectively turning them against their own comrades and knocking them unconscious. Blade kept retreating deeper behind her soldiers, but everywhere I went, I heard her horrible laughter.

My friends and I were stronger than anyone else on this field, but we were outnumbered forty-to-one, and we weren't the only ones with magic.

All around us, sinkholes were forming in the sand. We had to stay on the move to keep from being sucked underground.

A terrible, unnatural wind gusted up around only the 7.5. Sand particles sliced across our skin so ferociously that my friends' faces were raw and bleeding.

There had to be a high-level Animalist in the group, because we were swarmed by scorpions, coyotes, turkey vultures, and tiny bats with fangs.

I abandoned my hunt for Blade, wrestling the animals that bounded toward the Seven. All the while, I heard A.J.'s voice in my head begging me not to hurt them.

Sir Zachary sprinted between and around the Californians. He barked all-consuming fire and flung full-grown men dozens of yards away.

I had just caught sight of Blade again, when a deafening sound blocked out everything else. I looked up to see four helicopters heading our way.

Someone—Kaira, I thought—screamed.

A missile shot out from the first helicopter. It was coming straight toward us.

Panic lanced through me. A.J. waved one hand in the air in a frantic motion. The missile slowed, but it didn't change course. With all the other weapons A.J. was controlling, it was a miracle he was able to have any effect at all.

I ran toward the missile, not really having a plan other than needing to get to it before it got to us.

Clearly, Blade didn't care that her missile was going to kill her people along with mine. I could hear her maniacal laughter from somewhere nearby, even though I wasn't looking at anything except the missile.

It came closer. Closer still.

Come on.

I stretched up my hands and reached the missile's tip. Using my palms, I pushed against the missile's nose with every ounce of my strength.

If it hit the ground, we were done for.

The force of its propulsion dragged at me. Sweat streamed into my upturned eyes as the missile fought to go downward.

My arms trembled. I was losing this battle. The missile was going to explode.

With a stuttering gasp, I did the only thing I could. I said a little prayer and put everything I had into redirecting the missile back upward.

The sky rippled as the missile exploded overhead. My ears rang.

Debris hurtled back down. Burning chunks of the missile hit the ground. Fireballs and splinters of metal exploded all around me. I covered Sir Zachary's body with mine to protect him.

All around me, Californians were writhing in the sand. They screamed at the sight of their bloody, burnt skin.

I didn't have time to feel sorry for them or grateful for my titanium skin. The helicopters were releasing more missiles. Four of them were heading for the ground.

I couldn't get to all of them.

One seemed to be heading for Michael and A.J. Another was coming toward me and Sir Zachary. One was for Kaira and Graysen, and the last was targeted at Smith and Yutika.

For the first time in my life, I was paralyzed by fear during a fight. Out of the corner of my eye, I saw A.J. collapse from the effort of trying to slow them down.

I screamed his name and started for him, even as a missile rocketed straight toward me.

I hadn't even made it a step when all of the missiles halted in mid-air. They stayed poised for several seconds, and then they shot straight up.

Tiny bursts of flames went off so high in the sky I could barely see them.

"My missiles, now," Smith shouted.

I didn't have time to be relieved. I raced for A.J., who was just getting to his feet.

"Now I'm annoyed," A.J. declared as soon as I was near enough to hear him. All of the knives and guns he'd been controlling flung themselves far out of the Californians' reach. A.J. stretched both hands up toward the sky. He closed his fists around air, and then yanked his arms down.

The helicopters squealed in protest as they followed the motion of A.J.'s fists.

The Californians on the ground screamed and tripped over each other in their haste to get away. All four of the helicopters hit the sand at the same time. The ground rocked with so much force that we were all thrown several feet.

"Back on the plane!" I shouted to my friends.

Sir Zachary continued to bark fire at the Californians as we sprinted for our ride out of there.

I was at the back of our group, so I heard Blade before I saw her. Her laughter raised the hairs on my arms.

We were almost to the plane when Yutika screamed.

We all skidded to a stop. Blade and two of her people were blocking the entrance to our plane. And each one of them held a gun to one of my friend's heads.

CHAPTER 32

Blade had the muzzle of her gun pressed to Michael's forehead. The giant of a man on her right was digging his gun under A.J.'s jaw. And the third had his gun pointed at the back of Graysen's skull.

Kaira's mouth opened to scream, but no sound came out. Yutika took a step forward. She froze when all three Californians curled their fingers around the triggers.

A.J.'s eyes were wild as he looked from one gun to another. I knew the silent calculation he was making. He wouldn't be able to move fast enough to get full control of the weapons before the triggers were pulled. It was too risky.

The helicopter engines still rumbled, even as the metallic beasts lay crumpled in the sand. The sound was loud enough to keep Michael from Whispering or for any of us to try talking Blade down. Not that she looked like she was in the mood to negotiate.

There was actual blood splattered across Blade's face in addition to her blood droplet-tattoos, and her tongue kept darting out to taste it. She leaned closer to Michael like she might kiss him. Instead, she licked a line of blood across his scalp.

Kaira shouted something inaudible, but none of us moved for fear of what the Californians would do. As fast as I was, I couldn't get to any of my friends faster than the bullets just waiting to be released.

Blade was laughing. I couldn't hear the sound over the whine of the helicopter rotors that were still trying to turn, but I saw her body shaking from the force of her amusement. She was laughing so hard her gun shook against Michael's skin.

What was left of Blade's army had surrounded us, but I barely noticed. Three of my friends were about to die.

Puffs of smoke came from Sir Zachary's nostrils, but he seemed to understand he couldn't breathe fire without killing our people, too. We were utterly helpless.

The helicopters whirred their last and went still. The piercing whine of the blades cut off.

So fast I almost missed it, Michael thrust his head to the side. The violent motion knocked Blade's gun off-target a second before Michael bashed his skull against Blade's.

Blade stumbled back, clutching at her face and cursing.

Michael didn't hesitate. He reached down and grabbed the weapon she'd dropped. The gun in his hand cracked twice. It happened so fast, I didn't even see where he'd aimed.

A.J. and Graysen's captors released them and doubled over. That was when I saw the bloody circles in each of the men's right kneecaps.

Before I could marvel at Michael's incredible aim, he raised the gun again. Two more cracks, and the screaming men collapsed onto the sand.

Blood seeped out of holes in their foreheads as their lifeless eyes stared at the sky.

"Michael, what are you doing?!" Yutika started toward him, but Kaira gripped her shoulder, keeping her back.

A.J. staggered against me. His face was white as a sheet.

Blade howled and reached for another gun in her belt. The ragged remains of her army surged forward.

I was too stunned to do anything except watch as Michael's trigger finger twitched again.

Blade shrieked. She dropped the gun and clamped her hand over the bloody hole in her wrist.

Michael's face was completely, eerily blank. He aimed the gun at the Californians surrounding us, who seemed as stunned by the turn of events as us. They were mostly weaponless thanks to A.J., but they still had their magic. None of them attacked, though, thanks to the fact that we had their leader surrounded.

"Michael, stop," Kaira said in a hoarse voice.

Michael didn't stop. He didn't even seem to hear her.

"Don't move," Michael ordered the Californians.

Their eyes glazed over and their muscles slackened. Some of them even had slight smiles on their faces as Michael aimed at them.

Michael held the gun steady as, one by one, the Californians fell.

"Enough, Michael," Yutika said, flinching as the gun in his hand went off again. And again.

The Californians scrambled back as Michael dropped the ones closest to us. I was too shocked to do anything but watch as every one of Michael's shots hit its target. Horror mixed into the numbness.

"Michael, stop," Kaira said again, her eyes wide with panic.

"Please, Michael," Yutika begged, as Michael emptied a second gun. Tears were streaming down her face. Her voice warbled when she said, "This isn't you."

Michael didn't even look at her. He held out his hand.

One of the Californians stepped forward and, with chattering teeth, pulled out a gun that had been hidden beneath her fur cloak. Wordlessly, she handed it over to Michael.

Michael did something complicated with the gun without even needing to look at it. Bullets popped out of the back and fell harmlessly to the sand. Then, he passed the gun to Blade.

"What are you doing?" Graysen shouted.

Blade took the gun from Michael's outstretched hand. Their gazes connected for a long moment. Sweat broke out on both of their brows, and I knew there was some kind of mental battle raging between them.

When Michael spoke, I couldn't hear the words over Blade's whimpers and the roaring of my own pulse. But I could read his lips.

"Kill yourself."

She gripped the weapon and then put the barrel in her open mouth. She pulled the trigger.

I jumped. Kaira and Yutika screamed. Graysen looked like he was trying not to be sick.

Snapping himself into action, A.J. lifted his hand. Every gun in the vicinity shot into the air. The metal barrels winked in the sunlight as they arced through the sky and then disappeared from view.

Michael didn't react at all. His gaze was unfocused as he stared down at Blade's corpse.

"Time to go," he said, his voice as even and calm as ever. He stepped over one of the men he'd shot and headed for the plane.

The rest of us exchanged horrified looks. With no other choice, we hurried after him.

No one spoke once we were onboard the plane. I did a quick head count, making sure all 7.5 of us were present and accounted for. I stayed in my titanium form because I knew if I didn't, I would be shaking like everyone else on the plane. Except Michael.

He sat on the edge of the couch, straight-backed and unmoving. He stared at the floor without seeming to see anything at all.

"Buckle up, everyone," Smith called from the cockpit. His voice sounded too loud in the silent plane. "A.J. and I are fried, so this shit is going to get bumpy."

The plane lurched, and then we were leaving the ground and all those bloody corpses behind.

CHAPTER 33

As our plane carried us back to Boston, my mind kept replaying what had happened down on the ground.

I had seen people die before. But that had always been in the thick of a fight, when everything was happening too fast to process anything. This time, Michael had used his magic to hold the Californians in place while he executed them one by one.

My entire body was numb, even though Yutika had jacked up the heat on the plane. I couldn't seem to stop shivering, even in my titanium form.

Yutika sat beside Michael, trying to coax some kind of reaction out of him. He continued to stare off into the distance, giving no indication he knew she was even there.

In the years I'd lived and worked with Michael, I'd never so much as heard him raise his voice. Now, he'd just killed close to twenty people without batting an eye.

I grabbed a cloth napkin off the table that was still covered with our breakfast leftovers. I dipped the napkin in some water and went to Michael.

I started to wipe the dried blood from his skin. I tried to be gentle, even though he gave no indication he could feel anything at all. Yutika quickly sketched a new, clean shirt to replace Michael's blood-stained one. A.J. joined us, silently zooming first aid supplies from one of the overhead bins. Antibiotic ointment and bandages applied themselves to Michael's shallow cuts and sand-burned face without A.J. touching him.

It took both Yutika and me to get Michael's old shirt off and his new one on. He didn't resist, but he didn't help, either. If I didn't see his chest rise and fall as he breathed, he would have looked like a statue.

Sir Zachary lay down at Michael's feet. Kaira and Graysen joined us, sitting cross-legged on the floor beside Sir Zachary.

"We're all alive," Graysen said, breaking our silence. "For now, let's just be grateful for that."

Kaira leaned her head on his shoulder. He turned and pressed a kiss to her hair.

"I'm sorry you all had to see that," Michael said, speaking for the first time since we'd boarded the plane.

His unseeing gaze snapped into focus and pinpointed on Yutika. "I…I didn't want you to know that side of me."

Yutika's lips parted, but no words came out. I couldn't blame her. To say we were all shocked by what we'd witnessed would be an understatement.

After a few more seconds of silence from Yutika, Michael's gaze flicked to the rest of us. "I'll understand if you don't want me in the house or as a part of the Seven anymore."

"Are we in any danger from you?" Kaira asked.

"No." Michael's answer came immediately. "Never."

Kaira nodded. "That's good enough for me." She swept her gaze across the plane. "What about the rest of you?"

"We're the 7.5," A.J. said. "If members start dropping out, the name won't make sense anymore. And I already got bumper stickers printed up, so changing our name is not an option."

"Michael stays," I said. Whatever the fallout from killing Blade and decimating her army would be, we'd face it together. It was no less than Michael would have done for the rest of us.

Michael still radiated uncertainty. He couldn't hold any of our gazes. With a start, I realized he was ashamed.

I thought back to several months ago, after I'd accidentally killed Valencia's brother. Valencia had been trying to shoot Graysen, and when the bullet struck my titanium skin instead, it bounced off and killed her brother. I'd been a total mess afterward, and Michael had been the one to make me feel better. I still remembered the exact words he'd spoken to me.

"You were defending us," I told him, repeating the same words of comfort he'd given me. "You never need to apologize for that, no matter the consequences."

The tiniest smile flickered across his face.

Graysen and Smith nodded in agreement. Even Sir Zachary nuzzled Michael's hand.

The only one left was Yutika.

"Of course," she said, looking a little dazed. "Michael is one of us."

She didn't look at him when she spoke, though. She kept her arms wrapped around herself, trying to contain her shivers.

I couldn't begin to imagine what she was thinking.

Then again, I was mooning over a guy who hunted down Super Mags to take their power away. Compared to that, everything about Michael and Yutika's relationship seemed downright normal.

* * *

We stumbled off the plane, covered in dust and mentally spent. A strange sight greeted us on the mansion's front lawn.

All of the Super Mag kids were sitting in a circle. In their center, Grandma Tashi was perched on a lawn chair like she was a queen holding court. The kids were staring at her in rapt attention.

I didn't even think they'd noticed that a plane had just landed a few yards away from them.

"What's going on?" Kaira asked, giving the group a suspicious look.

I didn't blame her. I'd never seen all of the Super Mags sitting calmly in one place. It was unnerving.

"00445's momma visited Grandma Tashi," one of the children said eagerly. "We're waiting to see if the rest of our parents talk to her."

The unwavering hope on the kids' faces pulled on my already-stretched heartstrings. In that moment, I saw the Super Mags the way Kaira and Graysen always had—as children who had been deprived of the things every child deserved: a family and a home.

I wished Diego could see them now…not as wild creatures that could one day destroy the world, but as kids who just wanted to talk to their dead parents.

I wondered whether Lilly had ever dreamed of getting a message from her parents.

I blinked away the sting in my eyes.

"Now don't start fussing," Grandma Tashi said in a cranky voice. "I told you it doesn't work that way. The dead come when they wanna come, and they say what they wanna say. But if you stop your chattering, I'll tell you a fact. Your parents loved you. I'm a momma and a grandma, and I know there's no magic stronger than the love a parent feels for their child."

The Super Mags scooted closer to Grandma Tashi, hanging on her every word. The open longing in their gazes was too much for me. I turned my head.

Emory, who had just caught sight of us, got up from the circle and came to join us.

He had been steadily gaining weight over the last several weeks, and he was looking a little less gangly. His shaved hair had grown out into soft curls, and there was a brightness to his eyes that hadn't been there before.

"All forty-seven of the Super Mags have agreed to live here," he announced. To Yutika, he said, "We like the house you built us."

That was good news…mostly. Before today, only ten of the Super Mags trusted us enough to live with us. With all of them living on our property, we'd be able to keep tabs on them.

The challenging part would be for Smith and me to make sure they didn't become a security threat. While Kaira and Graysen were determined to make the Super Mags equal members of the Boston community, my first priority was my friends' safety.

"We're so happy to hear it, Emory," Graysen said, holding out his hand for the boy to shake.

"That's awesome," Yutika told Emory, offering him a weak smile. "I'll make some additions to the house so you won't have to share rooms unless you want to."

"Maybe we can talk about that Alliance group again," Kaira said, her voice rising in her eagerness. "You could help us draft the Super Mag laws, and—"

Emory yawned, before hurrying to cover his mouth. His cheeks turned pink.

"Sorry," he apologized.

Emory might be a Level 14 Intellect, but he was still a kid with an attention span to match.

"Or maybe not," Graysen said, chuckling a little.

Kaira nodded, trying to hide her disappointment. She wanted the Super Mags to have representation in the Alliance and not to feel so isolated from the rest of the city.

Meanwhile, I had promised to give Diego what he needed to take away their magic.

I'd never felt like more of a monster.

The front door opened, and Ma stuck her head out. She gave us that motherly up-and-down stare, like she was assessing us for injuries. Or hunger.

"When was the last time you Seven ate?" Ma asked, drying her hands on her flower-print apron and fisting her hands on her hips.

"We had breakfast like three hours ago," Kaira said. "We're not wasting away."

"It's lunchtime," Ma said, ignoring her daughter. "And with the time difference in California, you'll be extra hungry. I've got vegan mac and cheese and three-bean chili. Come and get it while it's hot."

"Ma isn't going to be happy until I'm obese," A.J. complained, rubbing his flat stomach.

"Tell me about it," Kaira replied.

Sir Zachary zoomed ahead of us, utterly unconcerned about what Ma's cooking was doing to our waistlines.

We were waylaid by one of the youngest Super Mags, a tiny wisp of a girl who was never seen without one of the numerous teddy bears Yutika had made for her. She was a Level 15 Phaser, which meant she could slip right through solid materials.

Her secondary magic was scary as hell. She could control people's internal temperatures and burn…or freeze…them from the inside out. Fortunately, she followed Kaira's cousins around like a lost puppy and didn't give off any violent vibes.

Now, she was crouched under the hydrangeas and crying.

"What's wrong, button?" A.J. asked her.

Instead of responding, the little girl just shrank deeper under the bush.

Michael crouched down beside the flowers. Even at that height, he still dwarfed the little Super Mag girl.

"Will you come out and talk to me?" Michael asked in a gentle voice.

The little girl wriggled out of the bush and went to him without a moment's hesitation. She wound her tiny fingers in his shirt as tears poured down her cheeks.

Michael scooped her up and sat down on the bottom porch step. He bent his head as the little girl whispered something to him. All I caught was *…stole Mr. Wiggles and tried to tear his paw off.*

Tears continued to roll down her cheeks, but her body wasn't strained in tension anymore.

"Tell them to go away," the girl said, giving the rest of us a fearful glance and burying her face in Michael's shirt.

"You can all go in," Michael told us, giving the girl a gentle pat on her back. "I've got this."

My brain struggled to wrap itself around the two halves of Michael…the one who comforted sad children and was the Seven's rock…and the one who had shot those Californians without batting an eye.

"Shout if you need anything," Kaira told him, before gesturing for the rest of us to head in.

I didn't know about everyone else, but I felt like a bow string ready to snap. Everything with Blade had gone to hell, and now I had no idea what we were going to do. We didn't just *not* have the Californians' support…we had made them our enemies.

And that meant we were on our own.

"It's good to be home," Graysen said, letting out a sigh as his stiff posture eased a little. He wrapped an arm around Kaira's waist as the two of them leaned into each other.

I breathed in the scent of vanilla wafting from the unlit candle I'd left on the hall table. The comforting smell helped ease some of my own anxiety. I listened to the familiar voices and turned my face into the fall air wafting in from an open window.

My stomach rumbled. Apparently, it was made out of stronger stuff than my brain. While my mind was still trying to come to terms with everything that had happened in California, my stomach had moved on to bigger and better things. The promise of mac and cheese and chili was too tempting to pass up.

Yutika turned off at the stairs. "I think I'm going to get cleaned up and take a nap," she said, her voice unusually toneless. "Unless you all need anything."

"We're good," Kaira assured her, her eyes full of sympathy. "Want us to bring you up some lunch?"

"No, I'm fine," Yutika said, already climbing the stairs. "Thanks."

That was bad. Yutika was always hungry, especially when Ma was the one doing the cooking. But I knew as well as anyone that sometimes, a person just needed to be left alone.

The rest of us followed our noses to the kitchen, where Sir Zachary already had his entire head buried in his food bowl. My gaze zeroed in on the huge pot in the center of the table and loaf of fresh-baked bread, before another sight erased all thoughts of food. My stomach did a somersault that had nothing to do with hunger.

Kaira's cousins and Oliver were already seated at the table, Oliver with a book and Kaira's cousins with half-eaten plates of mac and cheese. Sitting across from the two girls, telling them something that was making them both giggle, was Diego.

He had one arm thrown over the back of a chair and a huge bowl of chili in front of him. He grinned at me.

"Hola, mi pequeña diabla."

CHAPTER 34

hat the hell are you doing in our house?" Kaira demanded, since my throat had chosen an inconvenient moment to seize up.

"Kaira Hansley," Ma said, aghast. "Mind your manners."

"How did you get past security?" Smith hissed, once Ma had moved out of earshot.

"He probably just flew in from above," I said, giving Diego a glare that should have laser-fried him where he sat. The arrogant prick just winked and ate a bite of chili.

My face turned to flames as he locked gazes with me before licking his spoon. I drew my finger across my throat in response before shifting my attention to Smith.

"You and I need to talk about rewiring our security so this doesn't happen again," I said.

"Definitely," Smith replied, although he was giving Diego a look that was more intrigue than anger. I got the sense that my friend respected Diego's skill…and Smith didn't dole out respect lightly.

I couldn't decide how I felt about that.

"Stop being mean," Cora told us. "Diego's nice."

"Thank you, princesa," Diego said, making Cora smile and duck her head in bashfulness.

"Get out," Kaira said, keeping her voice low enough that she wouldn't incite Ma's ire.

"No," Diego replied. "We have things to discuss that will be of interest to all of you."

"So call," Graysen said. "You didn't need to drop by."

"I don't have a phone," Diego replied, completely nonplussed. "Too easy to track."

"Huh." Smith peered at Diego. This time, there was no mistaking his expression for anything other than respect.

A.J. gave me a sidelong glance but didn't say anything. The rest of us glared at the arrogant Super Mag making himself at home in our kitchen. I gave my scarf a self-conscious tug.

"I went back to the mine earlier today," Diego said. "I was poking around some more, and—"

"You went back to the mine?" I demanded.

Diego nodded.

"Why?" Graysen asked, his voice laced with suspicion.

"That light-speed train thing is fun to ride." Diego shrugged. "And I wanted to make sure I knew my way around so I'd be able to get out before you all blow me up along with the mine."

"Nonsense," A.J. said, before I could formulate a response. "You're too pretty to blow up. We might bury you, though."

"I'm flattered," Diego replied dryly.

I blinked at A.J. He only teased people when he liked them. It was his weird stamp of approval…and he'd just give it to Diego.

Somehow, in coming into our house uninvited and being as offensive as humanly possible, Diego had won over both Smith and A.J.

Go figure.

"No one said anything about blowing up the mine," I began, trying to get everyone back on track.

"But it's the obvious conclusion to all of this," Smith said. "Once we've rescued the kids, of course."

Diego and Smith exchanged a nod.

"You said you learned something useful yesterday?" I asked Diego, before he managed to befriend Kaira and Graysen, too. Although I didn't think there was any real chance of that.

Diego pushed aside his bowl. He pulled a folded paper out of his pocket and smoothed it out on the table. It was a bank statement.

There was a *Magic Bank of California* letterhead at the top of the page. Below it, there was an account number and a statement date from last week. The name printed below was Eugene Forrager.

"Who's that?" I asked.

"The foreman," Diego replied. "I did some digging into his background. He's from California and has always been involved in Nat-hating groups. He got pretty wealthy by scavenging and reselling scrap metal all over the state. He made regular appearances in local news for petty crimes and for generally being a dick, but all mentions of him stopped over a decade ago."

"Probably when he started working in the mine," Graysen said.

Diego nodded.

"Look at this." Smith tapped the top transaction on the page. It was for a million dollars.

A.J. whistled. "That's a lotta mulla."

In the description section next to the amount, it said, "Account Transfer In."

"Transfer from where?" Graysen asked.

Diego shrugged. "I tracked the money to a blind trust, but I couldn't figure out who was behind it."

"That's my area, Chameleon," Smith replied, opening his laptop and getting to work.

We all waited in silence while Smith tapped on his keyboard and muttered to himself.

"Did he fall asleep?" Diego asked several minutes later, when Smith closed his eyes and went still.

"Shh," we all replied.

Smith's eyes snapped open. "Huh."

"Talk, Smith," Kaira ordered.

"It's next to impossible to track the original source for these things, because the funds have been funneled through so many dark money trusts. These companies only work with super wealthy and shady people who don't want their money traced." Smith's lip quirked. There were few things he loved more than a technological challenge.

In the space of the dramatic pause he'd left, I asked the question Smith was waiting for.

"Were you able to find the original source?"

"You betcha." Smith gave us the closest thing he ever managed to a smile. He paused, relishing in the way the rest of us squirmed. "Felix Remwald."

I gave Smith a blank look.

"Do you mean Edwardian Remwald?" A.J. asked. "You know, the ex-Director who started the MagLab fiasco and then got murdered four months ago?"

"No," Smith replied, at the same time that Graysen said, "Didn't Remwald mention he had a brother? A Level 10 Alchemist, right?"

I nodded. "But we all heard Remwald say his brother died during the Slaughters."

"That's the part that doesn't make sense," Smith acknowledged, his face falling a little. "Felix Remwald was born in 2005 in Detroit, Michigan. He also died there."

Smith flicked his hand, and a news article popped up on the wall. It was a picture of a building that had been razed to the ground. Bodies were everywhere. The article was titled *Worst Slaughters Tragedy: Detroit Public's Magic School for the Gifted.*

"That was a school?" Kaira asked, pressing a hand to her stomach.

When I looked closer, I saw that most of the bodies on the ground were too small to be adults. Backpacks and books were littered among the corpses.

All at once, the smell of food was making me nauseous.

"What does this have to do with Felix Remwald?" Graysen asked in a tight voice.

Smith tapped the wall, underneath the article that described how a school had become the epicenter of a gruesome battle between Mags and Nats. There was a list of names…all of the victims whose lives had been claimed in the battle.

Hundreds of names, all crowded together. They looked like nothing more than words on a page, until I thought about all the lost lives those words represented.

My heart gave a painful squeeze.

I skimmed the article, which described how a nearby Slaughters battle got out of hand when a Teleporter accidentally brought himself to the school. Nats had tracked him there, and then the rest of the fighters had reconvened in the school parking lot. A combination of magic and homemade bombs had resulted in the horrific cover page photo.

Smith pointed to the list of faculty & staff. About a third of the way down the long list, there was a single name I recognized. Felix Remwald.

"This happened fifteen years ago," Smith said. "So, someone else must have access to Felix's money and is using it to fund the mine."

I remembered the note we found in the foreman's office that was addressed to *Remwald*, and the personalized notepad with the R and signature that looked like Remwald.

But both Remwald brothers were dead.

"Any chance of another Remwald relative we didn't know about?" I asked.

Smith shook his head. "Nothing that I could find."

"Okay, so we know someone is using Felix Remwald's fortune to pay the foreman's salary," I said. "I'm not sure how that helps us."

"Could be good to know at some point," Smith said, but even he looked dubious.

"There's something else," Diego said. "I was wondering about those spinal needles that we saw on the foreman's list, since there's no reason they should be needed for anything to do with the MRP."

"Did you figure it out?" Graysen asked.

In spite of his obvious dislike of Diego, Graysen couldn't disguise his scholarly interest. While I'd rather just go beat some people up, Graysen excelled at logic puzzles.

Diego nodded. "My parents tested a lot of the earlier MRP formulas on me, to see how different compounds would interact with so much magic."

"Monsters," Kaira whispered.

"I wanted it," Diego snapped, showing the first real emotion since this conversation started. "But that's beside the point. The point is that, during their experimentation, they found a way to make magic stronger."

"How do you mean?" Graysen asked, folding his arms across his chest and giving Diego a skeptical look.

"I mean, they theoretically figured out how to make a Mag's power more…well, powerful. They couldn't create Magic where it didn't already exist, but with a few adjustments to the liquid Agent S, they thought it might be possible to make a Mag stronger."

"So, are you saying—" Graysen began, but Diego cut him off.

"I'm theorizing that the reason for the mine isn't to produce shitloads of Agent S for the MRP."

"Watch your mouth," Oliver growled. "There are children present."

"Keep going," Desiree said, leaning forward to catch Diego's every word.

True horror stirred inside me as I began to process what Diego was saying.

"I think," Diego said, "the foreman and whoever's pulling his strings is planning to inject Agent S directly into Mags' spinal fluid. Kind of the opposite of the MRP, where their magic will be permanently enhanced."

"Synthetic Super Mags," Kaira whispered.

Diego nodded.

Holy shit.

All I could think about was Blade's army of psycho Californians, and what it would mean for the country if any of those people got enhanced magic.

Nothing good.

"That's insane," I whispered.

"Some Mags would do anything to become more powerful," A.J. said. "This could start another round of Slaughters."

Mags would want the magic-enhancing substance as much as Mag-hating Nats wanted the Magical Reduction Potion.

"There's an obvious solution to magic-enhancing and magic-reduction," Smith said. "Once we destroy the mine and all the Agent S in there, we won't have to worry about any of this stuff."

Out of the corner of my eye, I saw Diego's jaw tighten.

"You're right, Smith," Kaira said. "We have to get the slaves out, and then we'll obliterate the mine. We just have to figure out how to do it."

I could have sworn I heard Diego grinding his teeth. I ignored him, focusing on my friends.

"I don't want to be a Debbie Downer," A.J. said, raising a finger, "but it's going to take more than the 7.5 of us to rescue hundreds of slaves, deal with that maniac foreman and his boss, and destroy a five-level mine that's full of Agent S."

"I think I have an idea of where we can get some help," Graysen said, his brow furrowed in thought.

By now, we'd all come to recognize his Level 10 Brainiac face, and we just waited for whatever revelation he'd had.

"I'm going to talk to Emory and see if we can get him and Charlotte on board." He patted his pockets, which were empty, and then turned to Kaira. "Can you text Adam? We're going to need the crew team."

"Didn't Adam get a new phone?" Kaira asked, flipping through her contacts. "I don't think I have his number."

"I have it," I said, pulling out my phone. "I'll text him."

Diego's head snapped around at that. It probably made me a terrible person, but it warmed me to see him squirm. Just a little.

"Let's all convene first thing tomorrow morning," Kaira said. "That'll give us time to get everything together and then head to the mine." She started to get up from her chair before her attention caught on Diego. She'd clearly forgotten he was still with us.

"Thanks for the info," she told him stiffly. "You can go now."

"But I just got here," Diego said, stretching like a cat.

I tried not to notice the sliver of stomach he revealed when his shirt rode up.

"Besides." Diego gave me a shrewd look that instantly put me on high alert. "I'm not going anywhere until you keep your end of our bargain."

My stomach dropped out.

"What bargain?" Kaira demanded. She glanced from Diego to me.

I gave Diego a look that promised a slow, painful death. Then, I focused on my friends. I swallowed.

"In exchange for Diego rescuing us from the isolation chambers, I agreed to get him as much Agent S as he can carry before we destroy the mine." I said the whole thing in a single breath, with some of the words melting together.

I cringed as I waited for my friends' enraged responses. They didn't disappoint.

"Are you out of your goddamn mind?" Smith demanded.

At the same time, Kaira and A.J. screeched, "What?!"

Even Sir Zachary let out a little yip, not wanting to miss out on all the excitement.

Graysen didn't say anything, but his flashing turquoise eyes spoke for themselves.

"I gave him my word," I said helplessly. "But I swear I'll make it right." I pinned Diego with my gaze. He returned the challenge without blinking. "I won't let him get away with this."

"I feel faint." A.J. pressed the back of his hand to his forehead.

"I feel murderous," Kaira snarled. She rounded on Diego. "You took advantage of us when we were in a helpless situation, and now you're taking advantage of Bri's integrity. You are—" She glanced at her younger cousins, who were soaking up every word of our conversation, and sealed her lips tight.

I sat motionless, listening to Kaira defend me when I'd been lying by omission to the Seven for days. I should have told them about my bargain with Diego sooner.

Instead, I'd been busy sneaking out of my window to go flying with him.

"You don't owe him your loyalty," Graysen told me. "If our positions had been reversed down in that mine, any one of us would have helped Diego without demanding anything in return."

"I'm not going to apologize for going after what I need," Diego said. "From everything I've seen from all of you, you're no different."

My friends ignored him. All of their attention was on me. Their trusting gazes said they knew I would make the right choice.

The only problem was I wasn't sure what the right choice was. I understood Diego's reasoning behind his actions. I knew that he believed he was doing the right thing…not just for himself, but for all of the Super Mags. He'd spent his life obsessing over this mission.

If I sided with my friends as I knew I should, I'd be depriving Diego of all of that. If I took away his last chance at becoming a Nat, it would destroy him.

How could I do that to him, especially after I'd already given him my word that I would help?

"Actually," A.J. began, and then shook his head. "Never mind."

I gave him a questioning look, but it was clear that, whatever he'd been about to say, he'd decided to keep it to himself.

"What will it be, cariño?" Diego asked quietly.

"My friends are right," I said, ignoring the ache of regret that pulsed through me. "You did stop the Pyro before he could kill anyone else." I swallowed. "But you also took away the power of Super Mags who hadn't done anything wrong. There are too many ways Agent S can be used to destroy innocent lives. I'm sorry, but I can't let you do this."

An emotion flitted across Diego's dark eyes so quickly I would have missed it if I hadn't been watching him. *Disappointment? Betrayal?*

I felt awful.

"I thought you might say that," Diego said, his tone deceptively light. "So, I kept a little extra incentive tucked in my back pocket, just in case." He crossed his arms and looked straight at me. "You will do what I've asked…what you already promised…because I have something you'll be wanting in exchange."

"There's nothing that will make me change my mind," I said, feeling sick.

Diego raised an eyebrow at me. "Then, I guess you won't be interested in hearing that I found your niece." He stared straight at me. "I found Lilly."

CHAPTER 35

I leapt to my feet, already titanium. I grabbed Diego by his shirt and slammed him against the wall with so much force a crack shivered up to the ceiling.

"Where's Lilly? Where's my niece?!"

Diego didn't reply, his dark eyes holding mine.

"Sweetie, he can't breathe," A.J. said, giving my arm a gentle tug.

He was right. I loosened my hold enough for Diego to answer my question.

"She's alive?" My voice cracked.

Diego nodded.

"How did you know it was her?" Kaira cut in, her voice full of suspicion.

When Diego answered, he looked at me. "Ojitos bonitos. She has your beautiful eyes."

My throat felt like it was closing up. It was what the slave girl had said, too. Diego could be lying, since he'd been with me when the slave girl had spoken to me. One look at his face, though, and I knew he wasn't.

"Where is she?" I shook Diego hard enough that his head slammed back against the wall. "Where is she?!"

"All I'll tell you is that you won't be able to get her without me."

"Get Michael," I snarled without looking away from Diego.

"Bri," A.J. began uncertainly.

"Get Michael!"

"I'll do it," Kaira said, giving Diego a death glare before she left the kitchen.

Silver sparkled at the edge of my vision. I blinked furiously, refusing to let my tears hit the floor.

"Believe it or not, I'm not doing this to punish you," Diego told me in a low voice. "It's an even trade—what you want most for what I want."

I didn't say anything. I couldn't speak.

"It won't matter if your Whisper forces me to talk," Diego continued. "You won't be able to reach her without me."

"We'll see about that."

I was a Steel. I would tear apart whatever cage was holding my niece with my bare hands.

No sooner had the thought crossed my mind, I remembered what that slave girl had told us when we were searching the foreman's office. She'd said the littlest ones were on Level 1 and only the foreman could get to them.

"Bri." Diego leaned close enough so only I could hear him. "If you let your Whisper force the information out of me, you'll know I'm telling the truth. And you'll also be crossing a line you won't be able to uncross. You and me…we'll be finished."

"We already are," I said in a voice I barely recognized. I was shaking, even in my titanium form. I was so angry. "We were finished from the second you tried to use Lilly against me."

"I wouldn't have had to if you'd kept your word," Diego snapped, his anger rising to match mine.

"You're using a child to manipulate me," I said, unable to keep my voice down or stop my tears from falling. "My own family."

"And I'm trying to save all of us from a Super Mag losing their shit and destroying the whole city," he shot back. He jerked his head at my friends, who were poised to grab Diego if he tried his vanishing trick. "You all claim to care about Boston, but you're so obsessed with your idea of equality that you're blind to the threat my kind poses. I'm the only one who has the balls to do what needs to be done."

"Oh yeah." I laughed bitterly. "You're a real do-gooder."

Click. A titanium tear hit the tile floor and bounced off. *Click click click click.*

"Bri, honey." A.J. tugged on my arm, trying to get me to let Diego go. "Can I talk to you for a hot second?"

"I heard shouting," Yutika said, coming into the kitchen with a towel wrapped around her hair like a turban. "What are we—Oh, hey Sexy Cinnamon Man."

Diego didn't respond. His attention stayed locked on me as he and I continued our faceoff.

I let go of Diego when I heard Michael and Kaira's footsteps coming down the hall.

As soon as Michael stepped into the room, his gaze went straight to Yutika. His posture slouched, like he was trying to make himself less threatening. For several seconds, the two of them just stared at each other.

Michael's hands opened and closed at his sides. "Yutika, I—"

His attention flicked to the wall, where the image of the news article was still posted. All the color drained from his face. He staggered.

I managed to grab his arm before he fell.

"Michael?" Yutika asked anxiously.

"Smith, switch it," Kaira hissed. She planted herself in front of the wall, trying to block Michael's view of the massacre with her body.

The wall went blank, but the damage had been done.

"Why?" Michael asked, his stunned expression transforming to one of betrayal. He gave Smith an accusing look. "I thought we didn't pry into each other's pasts."

Smith began twisting the cord of his hoodie around and around his finger. "I was looking into Felix Remwald," he explained. "This has nothing to do with you."

Michael's chest rose and fell as his gaze searched all of us for the truth. I got the sense that we'd done something unforgivable…I just didn't understand what it was.

"Smith traced a million dollars that was paid to the mine foreman," Graysen told Michael. "It came from a blind trust that Smith linked back to Felix Remwald."

"And then, Gray remembered that Felix was dead, and so we were just trying to figure out what was going on," Kaira said quickly.

"What does that massacre have to do with Felix Remwald?" Michael demanded, his voice uncharacteristically harsh.

"He was a teacher at the school," I said, needing him to know we hadn't betrayed him.

"No, he wasn't." Michael shook his head.

"His name is on the list of faculty and staff casualties," Smith said.

"Show me a picture of him."

"Michael, what's going on?" Yutika asked. Her voice was gentle, but her eyes were wide. She seemed a little afraid of him.

At that moment, I thought we all were.

I glanced back to where I'd left Diego. A curse died before it passed my lips. The heat of his magic and scent of cinnamon were gone. He must have camouflaged himself and disappeared while the rest of us were distracted.

He'd be back, I thought bitterly. He still needed me for the Agent S. And right now, whatever was going on with Michael was more important than Diego.

An image popped up on the wall of a man who looked distinctly like Edwardian Remwald. Felix had the same shrewd, intelligent expression. His black hair was slicked back, and he wore a crisp suit. He had a moustache and a trimmed goatee. With the exception of minor feature differences, I might have mistaken him for his brother.

"He never worked at the school," Michael said.

"And you know this, how?" Yutika asked carefully, like she already suspected what he was going to say.

The same, awful assumption was growing in my mind, too.

"Because." Michael swallowed. "That was my school. And I was at that massacre."

CHAPTER 36

Michael had gone out with Sir Zachary, saying he needed to go for a walk. The rest of us stood in frozen silence as we tried to digest the twin bombshells Michael had thrust on us.

The first was that Michael's actions in California now made more sense. After what he'd been through, it was a miracle he'd managed to stay sane at all.

The second revelation was that Felix Remwald hadn't been an employee at the school. That meant either the newspaper had made a mistake, or—

"I guess it's possible he's still alive," Graysen said, tapping his fingers on the table. "He'd be in his sixties now."

"But there's nothing," Smith muttered from behind his laptop screen. "No credit card receipts, no bank accounts…nothing."

"Remember those receipts in the foreman's office?" I said. "Maybe Felix sends the foreman out through the mine's supply shaft to do all his shopping, while he stays hidden in the mine."

"It's possible," Kaira said thoughtfully. "But to stay down in that mine for—"

"Fifteen years," Smith said.

"I would say no one is nuts enough to do that," A.J. said, shaking his head. "But these are the Remwalds we're talking about. They're a special breed."

"Okay," Yutika said, drawing out the word. "But if his brother was alive and just chilling in the mine all this time, then here's what I don't get. Why did Edwardian bother with giving all those clues to Pruwist and the other board members? I get that he had his memory wiped so he could keep everything a secret when he was arrested. But couldn't his brother just have given him a call later to remind him what he forgot?"

"They probably figured Edwardian would be monitored and his thoughts might not be secure," Graysen suggested. "Felix would have had no way of knowing when it was safe to reach out to his brother. Edwardian must have thought the only safe route was for him to be the one who made contact after he put the pieces back together."

Kaira held up a finger. "But that would only make sense if Felix Remwald is actually alive and behind all of this."

"It doesn't really make a difference whether he's alive or not," I said, feeling antsy. All I could think about was Lilly.

"Kaira."

The single word came from Oliver.

We turned to Smith's father, who I was pretty sure we'd all forgotten was even in the room. He marked the spot in his book, closed it carefully, and stood up.

"I need to talk to you."

"Now?" Kaira asked, still looking like she wanted to punch someone…namely Diego.

Get in line, I wanted to tell her.

"Now," Oliver agreed. "In your office."

When Graysen started to follow, Oliver added, "Alone."

"What's wrong?" Graysen demanded, looking from Smith's dad to Kaira.

"Nothing," Oliver said. He left the kitchen without another word, heading for Kaira and Graysen's study.

Kaira and Graysen looked at each other. They seemed to have an entire, silent conversation in the space of a few seconds. There was something strangely intimate about it, and I looked away.

"Do you know what this is about?" Kaira asked Smith.

The Techie shook his head.

"Alright, I'll be right back." Kaira brushed her hand down Graysen's back as she stood up.

"So, I guess there's nothing else to do right now. We'll enact operation mine take-down in the morning," Smith said.

"Uh, yeah," Graysen said. He didn't even look at Smith. All of his attention was on the hallway where Oliver and Kaira had disappeared. His expression revealed nothing, but his fingers tapped incessantly on the table.

A minute later, Oliver reappeared in the doorway. I couldn't read anything from his expression.

"She wants you," he told Graysen before disappearing again.

Graysen was gone without another word.

"What do you think's going on?" Yutika asked in a hushed voice.

The rest of us exchanged worried looks.

"Okay, all of you," Ma said, coming over and pursing her lips at the sight of our still-full bowls. I didn't think I'd have an appetite again until I had Lilly back, and the rest of my friends seemed just as uninterested in food. "You all need to get some sleep before you collapse." She made a shooing motion with her dish towel.

There was no way I'd ever be able to sleep with tomorrow looming over all of us, but there was no bucking Ma when she was in one of her moods. So, we helped clear the table and headed upstairs.

There was a light on under Kaira and Graysen's bedroom door, but I couldn't hear anything that would offer a clue about what had happened. I would have been more worried, but my mind was at capacity for horrible thoughts for the day.

As I mechanically went through my workout routine and got ready for bed, my only lucid thought was that Lilly was alive. Well, that, and the fact that I was going to wring Diego's neck for using my niece to control me.

Even as fury ate through me, I couldn't help the niggling guilt that was there, too…that I'd forced his hand because I'd gone back on my word.

But preventing MRP from getting out into the world was worth betraying a single person's trust.

I idly tossed my phone from hand to hand as I lay in bed. After I'd come down from my initial rage at Diego, my first instinct had been to call Brent and tell him that Lilly was alive. But then I'd remembered what my mom had said about Sarah not surviving. I couldn't give them false hope.

The only thing that would help now would be to get them their daughter back. And I would…or I'd die trying.

A soft knock came at my door.

"Come in," I called.

I'd learned my lesson from Diego's unexpected visit the other night and was now fully dressed.

The door cracked open, and Yutika poked her head in. She was wearing flannel pajamas and fuzzy socks.

"Hey, what's up?" I asked before noticing Yutika's puffy eyes.

"Can I—" Yutika's voice cracked. "I don't really want to sleep in our room…alone."

"C'mere," I said quickly, flipping back the blanket and scooting over to make room for her.

Yutika settled back against my mountain of pillows and rested her head against my shoulder. For several seconds, we just sat like that. I wasn't sure what Yutika needed to hear right then, so I kept quiet and waited for her to speak first.

"Michael thinks I'm avoiding him because I can't cope with the violence of what he did in California."

I'd assumed the same.

"That's not it, though," Yutika continued, nestling deeper under my covers. "I mean, it was shocking and gruesome, but our lives were in danger. He acted to protect us, so I can't really fault him for that, can I?"

I shook my head, recognizing that Yutika just needed to talk through her feelings without interruption.

"I love him." Yutika toyed with a loose thread on my blanket. "So much it hurts." She pressed her hand to her heart.

"I know." I wrapped my arms around her and squeezed. "He loves you, too."

There wasn't a single doubt in my mind about Michael's feelings. He and Yutika might not be as openly affectionate as Kaira and Graysen, but their love was just as obvious. It was there in the way they looked at and spoke to each other, and in the little touches they thought the rest of us didn't notice.

"It's not enough though, is it?" Yutika's gaze searched mine.

"What do you mean?" I asked, puzzled.

Yutika wipe away an errant tear.

"I was never cool with him keeping his past so secret, but I thought it was something we could work through. I thought he would come to trust me enough to open up. But he never did." Yutika scrubbed at her eyes. "I learned more about his past today than in the whole time we've been together."

"I think," I said carefully, "if I'd been through something like that, I would be doing everything I could to forget. Talking about it would make me relive it over and over again."

It was why I hadn't even mentioned Lilly to my friends until I'd been with them for more than a year. And I was a social creature. Michael was much more reserved.

"I understand that," Yutika said. "That's what makes this so hard. I'm not mad at him or disgusted or scared. We talked a little while ago, and I told him I didn't need anything from him this second but that I had to know we could move forward at some point." She huffed out a breath, making her bangs fly off her face. "I even told him he could write it all down if he didn't want to talk about it."

Yutika turned her face away from me as she wiped away more tears. I passed her the tissue box on my nightstand.

Yutika blew her nose loudly before saying, "He said he didn't want to drag me into that bloody part of his life. He said he couldn't give me any more of himself than he already had."

"He's trying to protect you," I said, hating that two of my best friends were in pain.

"I get that, too," she said. "But I realized that, emotionally, we've gotten as far as we're going to get." She laughed darkly. "I know more about Diego's history than I do about Michael's. How messed up is that?"

I started a little at the mention of Diego.

Yutika reached for the channel changer and switched on the TV, making it clear she didn't want to talk any more. We cuddled up together and hunkered down for a marathon of *Magic Bachelorette* reruns.

"Your bed's really comfy," Yutika said half an episode later. She yawned. Yutika had less appreciation for *Magic Bachelorette* than A.J. and me.

A few minutes later, her snores cut through the drama unfolding between the bachelorette and her ex-boyfriend, who had shown up unannounced. I lowered the volume but kept the TV on, just in case shutting it off would wake Yutika.

I pulled the blanket up to her chin and turned over, wishing I could fall asleep so quickly. I'd be needing all of my strength in the morning. I closed my eyes and tried to empty my mind.

It was hopeless. Yutika snored like a banshee. She was also a terrible blanket hog.

After about fifteen minutes of watching the clock and shivering, I got up and tiptoed out of the room. There were plenty of spare bedrooms in the house, but I wasn't tired. I padded downstairs, planning to make hot chocolate and curl up on one of the couches to finish my TV binge session alone.

Clearly, I wasn't the only one of the Seven with insomnia. Smith, Michael, and A.J. were sitting at the kitchen table. Sir Zachary, who was wearing a doggie bathrobe and had been asleep in one of his extra-fluffy beds, trotted over to greet me.

A.J. and Michael had mugs of coffee in front of them and were talking quietly. Smith was sitting apart from them, a can of grape soda in one hand and his laptop balanced on his knee. His headphones were in and his back was turned to Michael and A.J.

When I glanced at the laptop screen, it was dark. Smith was staring at the blank screen, his gaze unfocused.

I didn't think I'd ever seen him *not* doing something on his computer. I wasn't sure what to make of it, but I knew better than to try to ask him if he was okay.

Smith shied away from emotions the way most people avoided the flu.

"Is she okay?" Michael asked when he caught sight of me.

I nodded. "Sleeping now."

Michael let out a sigh and hung his head. A.J. patted his arm and said something too quiet for me to hear. Michael dragged a hand down his face. He looked terrible.

I sat down next to him. My butt had barely hit the seat when Smith yanked out his earbuds and stood up.

"Someone just tripped one of my motion sensors in the backyard."

"Could be one of the Super Mags," I said.

Smith shook his head. "None of them have left the house tonight. And whoever it is knows exactly where to go to stay out of my cameras."

I got up from my seat, my pulse hammering as I blew on my fists. The three guys followed as I headed for the back door.

We kept our footfalls quiet and stayed in the shadows as we slunk around the side of the house. Sir Zachary stayed by my side, but he didn't growl or bark fire the way he would if there was real danger.

I heard muffled sounds at the same moment Michael put out a hand and said, "Wait."

When I listened harder, the sound was unmistakable. A man was crying.

My stomach cramped at the reminder of my dad's sobs after we'd been told Lilly died. It was the first time in my life I'd seen an adult cry, and it had scared me senseless.

"We should go back," Smith said, a nervous kind of helplessness reflected in his wide eyes. "It's not a threat."

That was when I saw movement under the big oak tree.

Ma and Oliver were sitting with their backs to the trunk, their hands clasped. Oliver was sobbing with enough force that his entire body shook.

I could see tears glistening on Ma's dark skin from the garden lights on the grass.

I backed away, keeping my silver skin out of the light and softening my steps so they wouldn't hear me. My friends and I didn't make a sound until we were back in the house.

Without discussion, we went into the living room and sat down.

"Does this have to do with what he told Kaira earlier?" A.J. asked Smith.

"I doubt it." Smith lifted a shoulder. "It's just, ah—" He tugged on a lock of greasy hair and glanced at the door, looking like he was considering making a break for it. "My mom died ten years ago today."

My heart lurched.

"Smith," I gasped, at the same time A.J. said, "Oh, honey."

"Do you want me to talk to your dad?" Michael asked Smith. "I can make it easier for him."

Smith shook his head. "It's not something we talk about…ever. Except with Ma, apparently."

I wasn't sure if I imagined a twinge of bitterness in Smith's voice.

"I don't like to talk about it either," Smith said quickly.

"We know," Michael assured him.

For several seconds, we were all quiet.

A.J. cleared his throat. "I'm having a hankering for some ramen," he said. "Anyone else?"

A.J. never ate anything with artificial ingredients…including ramen.

"I'll have some," I said, catching on.

Michael and Smith nodded.

"I was thinking," A.J. said as a pot filled itself with water in the kitchen. "I've been meaning to watch that new documentary on Alliance cover-ups. I'm forgetting the name."

"*Overreliance, Compliance, and Defiance*," Smith said immediately.

A.J. snapped his fingers. "That's the one."

"I'll get it going," I said, grabbing the channel changer to download the movie.

"Do you want a cold or room temp grape soda?" Michael asked in a gruff voice as steaming bowls of ramen floated in from the kitchen.

We spent the next four hours watching all sorts of experts talk about Alliance conspiracy theories. The only sound aside from the movie was our slurping of ramen noodles and Sir Zachary gnawing on a bone.

My eyes were starting to close when Smith's voice startled me awake.

"Thanks for this," he said quietly.

"We'll do it again next year," I said.

"Yeah," A.J. agreed. "Maybe by then, they'll have a conspiracy movie about us. It'll be totally meta."

Smith chuckled.

Lulled by each other's company, we drifted off. The last thing I remembered was A.J. pulling a fleece blanket over me and tucking a pillow under my head. Sandwiched between him and Sir Zachary, I finally fell asleep.

CHAPTER 37

We were all a sorry state the next morning. We picked at our breakfasts because Ma wouldn't let us leave the house until we ate something. None of us spoke.

We all snuck peeks at Kaira and Graysen for some sign of what Oliver had told them the day before. Their expressions revealed nothing and they offered no explanation. They kept exchanging furtive looks, and it was clear they were having one of their silent arguments.

When Graysen narrowed his gaze at her, Kaira snapped, "If you're going to start treating me like a china doll, then I'm taking up skydiving lessons."

"I'll come," I said immediately.

"I'm not going to apologize for being obsessed with you," Graysen shot back. "Deal with it."

He and Kaira exchanged a fiery look. I shook my head and went back to my coffee.

Yutika and Michael avoided each other, although I caught them both stealing glances at the other when they thought no one was looking.

Sir Zachary was doing his best to cheer everyone up. He offered Michael his favorite stuffed elephant, licked Yutika's hand, and then fell asleep with his chin resting on Smith's foot.

Even Ma was quiet as she moved around the kitchen with none of her usual enthusiasm.

Emory and Charlotte joined us a short while later. I was grateful they were coming with us. Of all the Super Mags, they were the most trustworthy and least likely to do something unexpected.

Graysen tore his attention away from Kaira. "Once we get that Energy Manipulator Super Mag out of the picture," he said, as though we'd been in the middle of a conversation, "Bri will be the only working Steel."

I took great pleasure in thinking about the copper, tobacco-chewing foreman without his magic. We'd see what a tough guy he was when he couldn't hide behind his Steel strength.

"Sir Zachary and I will find him," Charlotte said, tapping her nose. Sir Zachary wagged his tail at the mention of his name.

Graysen smiled at Charlotte. "That will be really helpful."

"I've been thinking," I said. "Kaira and Graysen should stay here—"

"Oh, no." Kaira pointed a finger at me. "Not you too."

Graysen chuckled.

"Just saying." I put my hands in the air. "I'm going to have to fire myself for being the worst Security Chief ever. What if this whole thing goes down in flames?"

"Then we go down together," Kaira snapped. "And the next person who tries to exclude or protect me for this mission is getting illusioned into a blobfish."

"What's a blobfish?" Yutika asked, perking up a little.

In answer, Smith projected an image on the wall. The pink, gelatinous creature looked more like something that belonged inside an animal's body than outside of it.

"Ugly little sucker," Yutika said with a shudder.

"All animals are pretty," Charlotte said, crossing her arms.

"Amen, sister." A.J. lifted his glass of pomegranate juice at the image on the wall in salute.

"Crew guys are here," I said, texting Adam back as I shoved a spoonful of cashew yogurt into my mouth to appease Ma.

"You all be careful," Ma said, following us out.

"We will," we chorused back.

Ma pulled Smith aside and gave him one of her bear hugs. She whispered something to him before pulling his face down to kiss his cheek.

Smith swiped a hand across his eyes before hurrying out the door.

The weather outside was cold and bleak. The October sky was full of dark clouds heavy with the promise of rain. A frigid wind swept across the lawn, dragging dead leaves off the trees.

Even though I wasn't titanium, the cold didn't bother me. We were going back to the mine, and that meant I was only a few hours away from rescuing Lilly. Anticipation filled my skin with pinpricks of heat.

My mood took a rapid turn for the worse at the sight of Diego, lounging on a stone bench on our lawn like he didn't have a care in the world.

My friends mostly ignored him. They had all been quick to agree that saving Lilly was the priority, and we could deal with Diego and the Magical Reduction Potion after we had my niece safely out of the mine. But that didn't stop Kaira and Yutika from throwing him dirty looks. Diego either didn't notice or didn't care. He was glaring at Adam, who had just gotten out of his truck and was jogging up to me with a huge grin on his face.

I made sure to greet Adam with an extra-long hug.

Normally, I was above those kinds of petty games. But Diego brought me to a new, unapologetic low.

We all congregated on the driveway while Yutika handed out earpieces and mikes to all of us…minus Diego. Kaira reviewed the plan while we geared up.

Charlotte and Sir Zachary were in charge of finding the Energy Manipulator who was making all the Steels a Level 6. The Nats on the crew team would knock him out, which would leave me as the only working Steel in the entire mine.

Emory and Michael were going after the foreman. Between Emory's Memory Reader magic and Michael's Whispering, the two of them would be able to learn everything about the mine that we didn't already know, including whether Felix Remwald was really still alive and in charge of the mine.

I would go with Diego first to get his precious Agent S, and then to free my niece.

I still had no idea what Diego had meant when he said only he could get to Lilly, but I didn't want to take any chances. My friends had all agreed that we would play Diego's game for the sake of getting Lilly back. But as soon as I had my niece, all bets were off.

The Mag half of the crew team and the rest of the Seven were on rescue detail. They would get all of the slaves out of the mine using both the underground train and the supply shaft on Level 1 that led up to the surface. Then, after everyone was out, we'd destroy the mine.

Once we were all clear on our roles, Yutika started to create a bus that would be large enough to get our whole group across town.

While she worked, and my friends discussed last-minute details, I took Sir Zachary over to his favorite pee spot to take care of his business. It was a good excuse to get away from everyone for a few minutes and just collect my thoughts.

A light breeze surrounded me with a familiar and unwelcome smell. Cinnamon.

"Stop creeping and show yourself," I ordered.

Diego materialized in front of me. He had a large duffel bag slung over his shoulder and was leaning against the trunk of my favorite tree on the property. The towering maple looked like it was on fire with its red, orange, and yellow leaves.

"I have nothing to say to you," I told Diego.

"I get it," he replied, his usual smirk nowhere in sight. "But I don't want you to think I'm a monster for no reason."

"It makes no difference to me," I told him coolly. "Once we have what we need from each other, we'll go back to being enemies."

Diego grabbed my arm and spun me around to face him. He recoiled a little at my expression, but he didn't loosen his hold.

"So stubborn. Will you just listen to me for a second?" Diego went to touch my face, but stopped when I flinched away from him.

"Fine," I grumbled, sitting down at the base of the tree.

As much as I wished it were otherwise, I wanted to hear what he had to say.

Diego sat down next to me, leaving plenty of room between us. For several seconds, we watched Sir Zachary dig a hole next to a row of hedges the gardener had just put in.

"My parents gave their lives to discover the MRP formula."

Those words startled me out of my brewing fury. I'd known his parents were dead, but he hadn't said before how they'd died.

I looked at Diego.

"My parents were in MagLab when the Pyrokinetic burned it down."

He spoke the words so quickly it took several seconds for my brain to register their meaning. When it finally did, I gasped.

"The Pyro murdered my parents." A storm raged in Diego's eyes. "For the entire last year of their lives, they spent day and night in MagLab. My parents tried to tell Remwald how dangerous Super Mags were, and that they deserved to live normal lives without the burden of their magic. He didn't listen." Diego's fingers dug into the grass. "And then, that Pyro burned MagLab to the ground." He turned his fierce gaze on me. "That fucking psycho murdered my parents."

"Diego." My voice came out hoarse.

I bit my lip hard enough to taste blood. I wanted to tell him I was sorry, but the words seemed too inadequate.

Diego hadn't had anyone in his life except his parents. If I'd been in his place, I wouldn't have just injected the Pyro with MRP. I would have ripped him limb from limb.

"I wanted to kill that Pyro," Diego said softly, like he could read my thoughts. "But I knew that kid's magic drove him to do what he did. No Mag can resist using their power, but for Super Mags, it's just this constant explosive force inside us. There's just too much magic."

I swallowed hard. What could I possibly say to that? All of my earlier arguments felt weak and insensitive in light of this new information. All at once, it struck me that if I had been in Diego's position, I'd probably feel the exact same way.

Dizziness swept through me at that troubling revelation.

"After my parents were killed, their mission became mine." Diego flexed his forearm, drawing my attention to the Super Mag numbers tattooed on his skin. "I'll never make the mistake of underestimating what my kind's capable of."

When he put his hand over mine, I didn't pull away.

"Damn you, Diego Agramonte," I whispered.

He was making it so hard for me to hate him.

"This changes nothing between us," I said, getting to my feet.

Diego didn't follow me right away, but the smile playing at the corner of his lips said it all.

We were still on opposite sides, but we understood each other. And in spite of all my efforts to the contrary, I respected him.

CHAPTER 38

Michael drove the bus right up to the ruins of MagLab and the trap door that led down to the high-speed train.

The crew guys did their best to creep each other out as we climbed down the endless ladder. Their teasing turned to complaining when Diego just flew straight down and let his sardonic *I'm waiting...what's taking so long?* echo back up the chamber.

The doorstop Yutika had made the last time we came was still in place, so we didn't have to do battle with A.J. to prick Sir Zachary again.

We all piled onto the waiting train car. The crew guys just about blew my eardrums out with their shrieks as Smith put the vehicle in gear.

As soon as we reached the other end, our light moods transformed to deadly seriousness. The sheer magnitude of what we were about to do settled on all of us.

"Okay," Kaira said. "Anyone have any questions?"

No one did.

We put in our earpieces and mikes, exchanged solemn nods, and opened the door to the mine.

I'd thought it would be easier now that I knew what to expect, but the sight of two little Steels pulling chunks of Agent S out of the wall made me sick to my stomach. I saw the crew guys' horror as they took in this place for the first time. Charlotte let out a little whimper and cuddled Sir Zachary against her chest, while Emory moved closer to Graysen and Kaira.

The slaves shrank away from us until they caught sight of Michael.

Michael crouched down in front of them, and a few seconds later, the kids were hurrying back up the tunnel to collect the other slaves.

Kaira illusioned all of us so we'd blend in with the other kids as we made our way up the tunnel. Our progress was hampered several times when voices calling *Steel for Five!* preceded a cart that came zooming down the tunnel.

I was titanium, so the oppressive underground heat didn't bother me, but everyone else was huffing and puffing.

"Good luck, everyone," Kaira whispered when we reached the end of the tunnel. She squeezed my hand before the rest of our group split off, leaving Diego and me alone.

Diego's slave illusion blurred out as he camouflaged himself to be indiscernible from the cement wall.

"Take my hand," he said, making me jump a little at his unexpected proximity.

"No, thank you," I replied stiffly.

"I don't need to expend unnecessary magic because you're feeling stubborn." Diego laced our fingers together.

Rolling my eyes, even though he couldn't see me, I let Diego lead me from the tunnel. We entered the massive, brightly-lit room where carts and people were moving back and forth to the elevator. Diego and I stood hand-in-hand against the wall and waited.

My magic was inside me, but it was dull. I knew I had to wait until the others took care of the Energy Manipulator, but I could barely contain my fidgeting.

I wanted to find Lilly *now*.

I scanned the face of every slave who passed us, searching for my hazel eyes in one of the thin, dirty faces.

"Soon, cariño," Diego murmured. "Just relax." His thumb stroked a soothing pattern across my knuckles. I didn't want his touch to comfort me, but at the moment, it was all I had.

"Stop," Michael's calm, commanding voice said across my earpiece. "Come here."

A few seconds of silence passed before Michael spoke directly into his mike. "Emory is taking the foreman's memories now. We're going to keep him alive to use as leverage once we find Felix."

"Good," Graysen said. "When you're done with that, Michael, we could use your help in the third tunnel from the left. I'm not sure these kids are going to come with us willingly."

"Will do," Michael replied.

"Sir Z and Charlotte just found the Energy Manipulator," Adam's voice said across my earpiece. "He hasn't seen us yet. We're hiding behind—

"Oh. Oh shiiitttt."

"Adam?" I hissed into my mike. "Adam, what happened?"

Adam started to answer, but Charlotte's high-pitched voice interrupted.

"There's something seriously wrong with this guy," she said, her voice a little shaky. "He looks like he has the Plague or something."

"I seriously doubt that," Smith said. "But my dad can heal you if he does have something communicable."

"Maybe he has cancer," Adam suggested. "There's this tube hanging out the back of his neck. It looks like the one my grandma had in her chest when she was going through chemo."

"Chemo ports don't go in the back of a person's neck," Smith said.

"Well, this one is," Adam said.

"He smells funny," Charlotte observed.

"Like he's sick?" Graysen asked.

"I don't think so," Charlotte replied uncertainly. "He's got too much magic. I'll have to get closer to know for sure."

"Alright," Graysen said. "Adam, knock him out. Whatever's going on with him, we'll figure it out later."

"Um." Adam let out a nervous little laugh. "Sir Z kind of just torched the Energy Manipulator."

"Is he dead?" Kaira asked.

"Oh yeah. Like, really, really dead. Sir Z, you're a beast."

He'd barely finished speaking when magic flooded back into my system.

I staggered from the force of my power coming back all at once. If Diego hadn't caught me, I would have been sprawled on the ground.

Slaves were running every which way, shouting to each other as the message spread that they were getting out.

"We've got a problem," Yutika's voice said over my earpiece. "There's a door blocking all the important parts of Level 1. We're not going to be able to get to the supply shaft to get the kids out."

"I'll break down the door as soon as I'm done with Diego," I said.

"I'm not sure you're going to be able to," Yutika said uncertainly. "The door looks *really* thick."

We'd see about that.

"Oh crap," Yutika squeaked. "Some of those creepy Mags in cloaks are heading this way."

"Don't panic," Kaira said firmly. "Come back down to Level 5. We'll just have to use the train. It'll take longer, but at least we won't have to deal with the Californians."

That was going to be a problem, since only twenty-or-so people could fit on the train at once. It was going to take way longer to empty the mine than it would have if we could have transported the kids out all at once. And that meant we had to keep a low profile for longer than we'd hoped.

The Seven were good at a lot of things. Keeping a low profile wasn't one of them.

"No sign of Felix Remwald," one of the crew guys announced. "If the guy actually exists, we've seen no sign of him."

I chewed on my lip. Right now, the question of who was actually in charge of the mine was at the bottom of my list of concerns. In fact, aside from finding Lilly, I had no concerns at the moment.

"Kaira and Graysen," Yutika said. "I'm sending the first batch of slaves your way."

"We're ready," Graysen replied.

"I've got the train fired up and ready to go," Smith said. "I think we can fit at least twenty-five of them in here at a time."

"Okay?" Diego asked me, his lips brushing my ear.

"Yeah." I sucked in a breath. "Let's go."

Diego tugged me onto an elevator that was occupied by a couple of kids with carts full of Agent S crystals. We pressed ourselves against the far handrail and kept silent so we wouldn't be noticed.

The elevator went up to Level 2, where I'd witnessed a woman be burned alive by Agent S. The kids pushed their carts off the elevator, leaving Diego and me alone.

Alchemists and slaves were back at work, transforming solid chunks of Agent S into the usable—and deadly—liquid form. At the far end of the room, I caught sight of the titanium vault Diego had described.

Diego shifted slightly. The rough material of the huge, empty duffel bag on his shoulder brushed against me.

"How do you want to do this?" I whispered.

I could break into the vault without a problem, but as soon as I did, no amount of camouflage would hide the fact that there was thievery in progress.

Diego didn't say anything. His breathing had gone ragged, and his hand was cold and clammy in mine.

"You're going to have to let me get me closer if you want me to actually get the vault open," I said irritably.

Diego swore quietly to himself in Spanish. He was holding my hand tightly enough that if I hadn't been titanium, he'd be crushing my bones.

"Diego, what?" I demanded.

Kids with empty carts were heading toward the open elevator. If we didn't get off now, we'd be stuck going back down with the slaves.

"I can't do this," he said.

"What can't you do?" I demanded, having to raise my voice to be heard over the squeal of the elevator cables.

"I was wrong to use your niece against you to get what I wanted," Diego said. "I'm sorry, Bri."

I opened and closed my mouth, too startled to form a response.

"Atta boy, Diego," A.J. said into my ear, even though Diego wouldn't be able to hear him.

"That's a step in the right direction, anyway," Kaira muttered.

I asked Diego, "Aren't you afraid I'll go back on my word again?"

I felt his shrug. "I'm going to trust you not to dick me over. Now, let's go get Lilly."

"Thank you," I managed in a choked voice.

Diego hit the button on the elevator that would bring us to Level 1. This was the only level I hadn't been to yet. We passed through a narrow, empty hallway before we came up against a floor-to-ceiling titanium door. The door blocked me from seeing whatever was on the other side.

Yutika had been right. This door was too big and heavy for me to easily muscle through. I would attract every bad guy in the place if I tried.

Diego pressed his hand to mine. I felt the shape of a key between our palms.

"Had to steal it from one of those cloaked Mags," he explained. "He's a Spider and lives at the top of the elevator shaft, so I really wasn't lying when I said I was the only one who could help you reach Lilly."

My hand was shaking so badly Diego had to help me fit the key into the lock. We turned the key together, and the door swung inward.

I went motionless at what I saw on the other side. We were standing in a nursery.

Everything was metal, from the cradles and tiny beds, to the few toys scattered across the floor. The oldest child in the room couldn't have been more than seven, and yet the kids who were big enough to walk were clearly in charge of caring for the babies.

The older children moved up and down the rows of metal cradles, reaching up on tiptoes to hold bottles to the babies' mouths and change diapers. The room was oddly quiet. None of the babies cried. They had probably learned it was pointless to do so.

A few of the children looked up when the door opened. When they saw no one, they went back to work.

I whispered into my mike, "The first level is full of babies and toddlers. We're going to need help getting them out."

"Roger that," Kaira replied. "We'll be up as soon as we get the rest of the slaves on Level 5 onto the train."

The silence in the nursery was broken when one of the kids looked down at himself. He tapped his arm, his forehead puckered in confusion. He squeezed his eyes shut, opened them, and then tapped his skin again.

"Where's my magic?" he whispered.

Now that the Energy Manipulator was gone, the rules of magic were back in play. Since I was the strongest Steel in the place, my magic cancelled out everyone else's in the vicinity.

The other children were trying to access their magic, to no avail. Their dirty cheeks turned red from the effort of calling on magic that wouldn't come. Some of them made little whimpering sounds when their skin didn't turn to metal. They didn't understand what had happened to them, and they were terrified.

The kids all looked so distraught that I almost asked Diego to take away my camouflage so I could explain it to them. I didn't say anything, though, because I didn't want my presence to freak them out even more.

My friends' chatter continued across my earpiece, but I didn't hear a word they said. Because I had caught sight of a familiar set of hazel eyes.

I'd found Lilly.

CHAPTER 39

Lilly," I whispered.

I almost lost my footing because my legs had turned to mush. Diego steadied me with a firm grip around my waist.

My niece had Sarah's curly brown hair and Hammond hazel eyes. She was standing next to one of the cribs, trying to summon her magic like the rest of the older children.

"Let her see me," I told Diego without taking my eyes off Lilly.

There was a flicker of color, and then my camouflage was gone.

The children stopped furiously tapping their non-metal skin as they noticed me. My heart stuttered at the expressions in all of their too-wide eyes. They were afraid of me.

"It's okay," I said quickly, wishing Michael was here to calm the kids down. Some of their faces were turning purple from how hard they were trying to reach their magic.

I locked gazes with my niece.

"Lilly," I said, my voice breaking.

She looked at me, but not with any recognition at the sound of her own name. I saw the same fear on her face that all the other children wore. I hadn't expected her to come running into my arms, but it was still a kick in the gut to look her in the eye and know that all she saw in me was another adult who might hurt her.

"Please," I said, trying to hold back my emotions so I didn't scare her any more. "We're here to help you."

"You're not in trouble," Diego said, appearing beside me.

The kids cringed away from the two of us, huddling behind metal cribs and against the metal walls.

I crouched down to make myself less threatening. When that didn't seem to help, I blew on my fists until my magic retracted. I reached out a shaking hand toward my niece.

"Lilly," I tried again. I pointed to my eyes and tried to give her a smile that wouldn't terrify her. I kept my movements slow and careful, when all I wanted to do was pull her into my arms and never let go.

"I'm your family," I told her, not sure if she would understand the words *aunt* or *niece*. "I'm going to take you home."

It was that last word that undid me. A strangled sob escaped me.

Diego knelt beside me. At the same time, Lilly took a hesitant step closer. She pointed at my face and then tapped her tiny index finger beneath her eye.

"Yes." A choked laugh bubbled up from my throat. Tears rolled down my cheeks, but I didn't try to wipe them away. "Come here, love."

Lilly took two more steps toward me and stopped. She glanced down at the floor and then back at me. The fear was back in her eyes as she hopped back.

"No, wait," I began.

There was a soft sound of metal moving back on well-greased hinges. I followed Lilly's gaze to an almost-invisible seam in the floor. Two metal panels slid back, revealing a hole in the ground that led to the level below.

A sleek, mechanical platform rose up from the lower level. The platform stopped once it was perfectly aligned with the floor of the nursery. All the children pressed themselves away from the center of the room as three people stepped off the platform.

The room filled with magic…far more than three Mags should have between them.

Two of the Mags were wearing cloaks like the Energy Manipulator. Their faces were shadowed, and there was a strange wrongness to their magic. It felt slimy.

The man standing between the two cloaked figures wore a black suit, black shirt and tie, and black patent leather shoes. The only part of his attire that wasn't black was a silver chain around his neck. Three keys dangled from the chain and stood out against his solid black shirt. His hair and goatee were pure white, but other than his hair color, he was a dead ringer for the photo Smith had plastered on our wall.

"Felix Remwald," I said. "So, you didn't die in that Detroit massacre then, did you?"

My friends' voices filled my earpiece, but I tuned them out. All of my attention was focused on the three people standing between me and Lilly.

"I've kept that secret from everyone except my inner circle for fifteen years," Felix said, his voice disturbingly similar to his actually-dead brother's. He gave me a curious look. "How did you figure it out?"

Beside me, Diego blurred out of sight. There was a whoosh of air, and then Felix was stumbling backward.

I took that as my cue. I darted around the group.

"Lilly," I called, as the children cowered deeper into their corner. Before I made it another step, something lashed out at me.

I dove, but the barbed, metallic rope followed me. It fastened around my waist and yanked me back with so much force I slammed into the metal door.

I leapt to my feet in time to see that what I'd thought was a rope made out of metal was actually a tail. It shot out of one cloaked figure's backside, expanding and retracting.

That was some messed up magic. I blew on my fists and got ready to brawl.

The tail snapped back across the room, curling around a spot directly in front of Felix. Diego shimmered back into view, groaning as he struggled in vain against the metal tail. Blood dripped onto the floor as the barbs cut into his skin.

"Let him go," I shouted, throwing the full force of my body at the Mag with a tail.

As we collided, the wrongness of his magic washed over me again. I shoved him with all of my strength. His tail unwound from Diego as the Mag sailed away from me. The Mag crashed through the open doorway. He let out a bloodcurdling screech as his momentum carried him into the empty elevator shaft.

"Get Lilly," I ordered Diego as I ran to meet the next obstacle in my path.

"Bri." Diego caught my arm. "They're like me. They're Super Mags."

I didn't give a shit what they were.

"Lilly," I told him. And then I attacked the other cloaked Mag.

Instead of coming up against flesh and bone, my fist struck…water.

The man's chest rippled and dissolved at the place where my fist had connected.

What the—

I didn't have a chance to finish the thought. The cloaked man transformed into a puddle on the flood, sucking me down with him.

I had no idea what kind of magic this was, but I was helpless against it. I plunged head-first into inky water that surrounded and engulfed me. It rose up around me, rippling and undulating. No matter which direction I tried to move, the water just clung to me.

There was no surface, no bottom to push up from, and no way out of the darkness.

I was drowning.

My lungs were burning. If the water hadn't already been pitch-black, my vision would be going dark. I was going to die here.

Strong, solid arms closed around me, drawing me up and out of the watery depths.

I coughed and blinked water from my eyes.

"Breath, cariño."

Diego.

"Get Lilly," I choked.

We were hovering near the ceiling, looking down as the puddle of black water reformed into a cloaked man.

"That is enough." Felix's cold voice cut through the room like a knife. He snapped his fingers at the children, who were whimpering. They fell silent. Even the babies in their cribs stopped wriggling.

I saw red.

"Don't," Diego said, wrapping his arms around my waist.

I wrenched free, my mind empty of everything except Lilly. But Felix knew where I was heading and got there first. A soft cry came from me as Felix strode over to Lilly. He yanked her roughly to her feet.

"No," I gasped.

"You look too young to be her mother." Felix offered me a cruel smile as he held Lilly. "An older sister, perhaps?"

"My niece, asshole."

I wanted nothing more than to tear her away from him at that very second, but he had both his arms wrapped around her, and his water Super Mag was standing between us. There was no way Diego or I could get to Lilly faster than Felix could hurt her.

"I am not cruel without purpose," Felix told me, his shrewd gaze tracking my every move. "So long as you never return to the mine or reveal my existence to anyone, your niece will survive."

A harsh laugh barked out of me. "What about all those children you buried in the tomb? Did you promise to keep them alive, too?"

"I did not," Felix replied. "With the difficult nature of the work here, deaths are inevitable. I would use adults if I could, but to my deepest regret, infant Steels are easiest to disappear from the world above without prompting questions."

I took a step closer. The water Mag moved with me. His cloaked arms turned to rippling water and split off into tendrils that hovered menacingly in front of my niece.

Lilly closed her eyes and turned her face into Felix's sleeve.

"Okay." I put up my hands in surrender and backed up.

The rest of the Seven had to be on their way. They could hear everything that was happening through my mike. *Where were they?*

"You look familiar," Felix said.

I stiffened, but he wasn't talking to me. His attention was fixed on Diego.

"Can't imagine why," Diego said cautiously, like he was expecting some kind of trap.

Felix shrugged, like it didn't matter to him either way. He kept Lilly firmly against him as he backed up. With the hand that he didn't have locked on Lilly's arm, he fumbled at the wall. He pressed some invisible button, and then a panel was sliding back.

"No," I began, as Felix disappeared behind the wall with my niece. Felix barked out a harsh command, and then the rest of the Steel children who were big enough to walk followed. The wall panel slid back into place behind them.

"No!"

The cloaked Mag remained, his body expanding until it made a watery barrier between me and where I needed to be.

"Bri!"

Kaira's voice wasn't just in my ear. My friends were coming through the door. Relief slammed into me with so much force tears leaked from my eyes.

"Keep that thing busy," I told them, gesturing at the water Mag. "I'm going after Lilly."

"Allow me," the coxswain said, rolling up his sleeves and putting out his hands. All at once, the floor-to-ceiling human wall of water began to churn. The coxswain could control water, and his magic must have been different enough from the cloaked Super Mag that it wasn't cancelled out. The two of them battled for control of the water.

"Watch the babies," Yutika cried. She pointed to the water, which was getting dangerously close to a row of cribs.

"Jesus, this bastard's strong," the coxswain gasped.

He was spinning his hands in a circle, making the water Mag transform into a waterspout that was slamming itself into the wall and bursting over and over again.

"I can't Whisper to that Mag," Michael said, his voice barely audible over the rush of swirling water. "His mind's not normal."

I took my chances and ran, hoping the others could keep the Mag's attention long enough for me to chase Felix down.

Someone screamed out a warning.

I skidded to a stop as the middle of the floor opened up again. A dozen Mags in cloaks stepped off the platform and started for us.

276

CHAPTER 40

A dozen hellions were blocking my path to Lilly.

"They're all Super Mags," Diego called as the cloaked figures surrounded the group of my friends. The Seven were here, in addition to the Mag half of the crew team. I didn't have a chance to ask where Sir Zachary and the rest of our group had gone.

We were surrounded.

The room teemed with magic. I was aware of the infant Steels wailing in their cribs, but I couldn't see anything beyond the Super Mags' cloaks.

"Come on, pendejos," Diego growled. "Come and get it."

The cloaked Mags all lifted their hands at once. The movement was so coordinated it threw me off guard. I braced for an attack, but instead of coming for us, they lowered their hoods.

Yutika let out a muffled cry. I gasped.

"Joder," Diego cursed.

Fuck, indeed.

We were surrounded by monsters.

They were the size of adults, but they didn't look human. Their skin was scaly and gray, more corpse-like than any living creature I'd ever seen. Their hair was patchy and spotted with blood. Their unfocused eyes were so bloodshot it was almost impossible to see their pupils. And their pointed teeth carved long, blood gashes at the corners of their white lips.

"Agent S," Diego whispered.

I didn't have a chance to ask him what he meant.

The…creatures…attacked.

The Mag with the barbed metal tail reappeared and joined the fight. The tail lashed back and forth, searching for a target. It missed Michael's head by inches, striking the wall and shearing right through the metal.

"Mine," Diego growled, flying up to the height of the Mag's head and levelling a kick at his hideous face.

The rest of us chose our own opponents, and the fight was on.

I punched, kicked, and headbutted every one of the evil creatures I could get near. I smashed my fist into one of them that kept dissolving into puffs of smoke and then reappearing on the other side of the room. I finally connected with him while he was in solid form.

The Mag struck the wall head-first and slumped into unconsciousness. His hood fell all the way back, exposing his wrinkled and bloody skin. I noticed there was a few-inch-long tube sticking out from the base of his neck.

"My magic isn't working on them," Michael said helplessly, thrusting Yutika out of the way when one of our enemies dove right for her.

"Mine works," Kaira said, "but they don't give a shit what we look like. They're going to kill us either way."

Graysen was managing to keep one of them back with a metal rod, but he was quickly losing the fight. So were the rest of my friends. A.J. and the crew guys had retreated until their backs were against the wall and there was nowhere else for them to go.

"Bri, they've got too much magic," Diego panted, shooting into the air to avoid something heinous that spewed out of one of the Mag's mouths. "We can't fight them."

"Watch me," I snarled, crouching down in a fighting pose.

I lunged at the nearest Super Mag. I hit him hard enough to make a human-sized dent in the wall. He bounced right off as his body began to expand like a balloon. He grew and grew until he was easily twelve feet high and six feet wide. The Super Mag roared in pain wherever my blows landed, but with his sheer size, I couldn't do much damage. If this creature got any bigger, he'd reach the cribs that A.J. had carefully relocated to the far side of the room.

"Get the babies out of here," I yelled to anyone who could move.

"Get them where?" Diego shouted back.

The giant balloon Mag had grown so much he was now blocking the door out of here.

Double shit.

"Get me up to his head," I shouted to Diego, as the monstrous figure continued to grow and grow.

Diego wrapped an arm around my waist, and then we were in the air.

As I stared into a bloodshot eye that was almost as big as my fist, I was reminded of the monster movies Brent and I watched as kids. Thick blood dribbled around the creature's pointed fangs. Resisting the urge to shudder, I pulled back my fist and punched the enormous Mag. My fist got him square in the eye.

"Ugh!"

Blood and goopy eye matter splattered across my titanium skin. The Mag screeched and began to deflate.

"Ew," Diego complained.

I was about to tell him to take me to the Super Mag who had just torn Graysen's metal rod out of his hands, when the whole room began to shake.

I looked around. The magic didn't seem to be coming from the cloaked Super Mags. What was left of the deflating balloon Mag burst apart in a spray of blood and guts as a rhinoceros with golden eyes obliterated it.

Diego cursed and flew us higher.

"It's Charlotte," I yelled, wresting myself free from Diego's grip and falling back to the floor.

Charlotte-the-rhino turned her enormous head from side to side, spearing the cloaked Mags on the end of her horn and flinging them into the walls.

A.J. zoomed the babies' cribs around the Super Mags and straight out the door.

One of the cloaked figures rose out of a crouch and came at Charlotte from behind, a giant scythe-like weapon extending from his misshapen hand.

"Charlotte!"

Before I could get to her, fire engulfed the cloaked man and his weapon.

Sir Zachary raced through his own fire, completely untouched by the flames that were engulfing the Super Mag. He tilted his head back and barked fire up at our enemies.

"Coolest dog ever," Diego said, staring at Sir Zachary in amazement.

"Bri, Diego, come on!"

Kaira and Graysen were gesturing frantically from the door. The rest of our group was already piling onto the elevator.

"Not without Lilly," I said, leaping over the charred bodies of the mutated Mags without feeling a shred of pity. These monstrous Super Mags would have killed me without batting an eye. And they had tried to keep me from Lilly.

"No time," Michael said. "The foreman told Emory—"

Whatever he was about to say was drowned out by a deafening alarm.

CHAPTER 41

Blue lights pulsed from bulbs in the ceiling. And then, as quickly as it had started, the alarm ended. There was a gentle hiss as cloudy white smoke came out of nearly-invisible vents in the walls and floor.

Diego swore. He yanked off his shirt and threw it at me.

"Cover your face!" He made a frantic gesture. "It's MRP gas."

The rest of my friends had their noses and mouths buried in their collars as they crowded onto the elevator.

A.J. was shouting at me to hurry up.

"Not without Lilly!"

I ignored the way my heart had begun to race. Weakness was stealing over my body.

I felt woozy…like I'd had a few too many of A.J.'s peach-pomegranate martinis. Those things were delicious.

"You look awesome without a shirt," I told Diego. The words came out sounding like one. My tongue felt fat and dry. I tried to take a step forward, but my feet gave out and I sank onto the floor.

It was a really comfy floor. And I was really tired.

"Oh no, you don't."

I made a grumbly sound when Diego lifted me up and cradled me in his arms.

I knew there was something I was supposed to do…someone I needed to find…but I couldn't remember. Diego smelled good, and he felt even better.

My eyes rolled back in my head as the floor became the ceiling, and I was flying down an elevator shaft. My friends were there, but they were all blurry.

"Sir Zachary!" A.J. shrieked. His voice was right in my ear, even though I didn't see him next to me.

"I'll come back for him," Graysen's voice replied. "As soon as I get Kaira out."

My foggy brain remembered that MRP couldn't hurt Nats, since they didn't have any magic.

"Why…you…okay?" I asked Diego. Whatever was happening to me and the rest of my Mag friends wasn't bothering him.

"High tolerance," he replied. "Keep my shirt over your face."

I noticed my dangling arm was no longer titanium. No matter how hard I tried to call on my magic, my skin remained normal.

Tendrils of panic wrapped around me when I couldn't sense my magic.

"Diego—" I gasped.

"I've got you, cariño. Trust me."

I didn't want to, but it wasn't like I had a choice. I was dead weight in his arms.

The elevator containing the rest of the Seven reached the bottom floor just after Diego and me. The Nat members of the crew team came running from a different direction. With my double-vision, it seemed like there were a lot more of them.

As my head bounced against Diego's chest, I was dimly aware that the Nats in our group were each carrying an unconscious Mag. I felt the cold stirrings of dread when I remembered that our team had more Mags than Nats, and I couldn't see anyone carrying Yutika, A.J., or Michael.

"Help," I began, but I couldn't get the rest out. My lips had frozen. It was taking all of my concentration just to stay awake.

Diego followed the direction of my unfocused gaze. His grip tightened around me.

"Please," I managed.

I could see Michael on the elevator platform on his hands and knees, retching as he tried to lift Yutika.

Diego said something in Spanish, and then he lowered me to the ground behind an overturned cart.

"Stay," he ordered me.

Like I could do anything else, I tried to say, but the witty retort got stuck somewhere between my brain and throat.

Diego went to Yutika, tossed her over his shoulder like a bag of potatoes, and flew down the tunnel that led back to the train platform.

I thought I saw dozens of the cloaked Super Mags moving silently to and from the elevator, but I wasn't sure if there really were that many or if I was just seeing triple.

Five times Diego came back to carry A.J., Charlotte, Emory, Sir Zachary, and the coxswain. On his last trip to the elevator, Adam went with him. It took both of them to heave Michael down the tunnel, each of them supporting half of the bigger man's body.

When I was the only one left, I finally lost my battle to stay awake. My last thought was that I was going to have one hell of a hangover tomorrow. And then my world went black.

CHAPTER 42

"What time is it?" I groaned, trying to bully my eyelids into opening.

"Seven," Diego's voice replied.

"AM or PM?"

Was I blind? Oh god—I was blind!

My eyelids peeled back, showing a room that was familiar but not my own.

Okay, not blind. Phew.

Diego chuckled. "PM."

I sat up, the last of my grogginess fading away. A delicious smell was coming from the other room, and it helped bring me the rest of the way back to full consciousness.

I was in Diego's apartment. The lamp next to the bed threw off a warm glow. That, combined with the rain drumming on the windowpanes, made for a cozy setting. All I was missing was a fire and smores.

"How did I get here?" I asked.

"You flew." Diego stirred something on the stove, wiped his hands on his jeans, and came to sit on the mattress beside me. "Well, technically, I flew. You just hung on for the ride."

"Are you calling me a parasite?" I grumbled.

"A very sexy parasite," he corrected.

I could live with that.

Diego's hair was wet, and he smelled more like his shower gel than his usual cinnamon. I wondered if I'd be able to taste cinnamon if I leaned forward and brushed my lips against his.

"Holy shit." I sat up so fast my head swam. Images and memories blasted into my mind at full force.

Lilly…Felix Remwald taking her away…those zombie Super Mags…the MRP gas that downed all the Mags in our group….

"Relax, cariño," Diego said, scooting down onto his side and pulling me with him. We were face-to-face and sharing a pillow. "Everyone else got on the underground train. They were at capacity with the last batch of slaves Kaira and Graysen loaded up, so I told them I'd take you back."

"Lilly?" I asked, already knowing the answer but needing the confirmation.

Diego shook his head. "I didn't see Felix again, and those zombie Super Mags were all over the place. We barely got away."

The smell of food wafting over from the kitchen no longer smelled good to me. Acid churned in my stomach.

"She's safe," Diego assured me, reaching up to push a strand of hair behind my ear. "Felix knows how important she is. He's going to keep her as leverage."

"And that's supposed to make me feel better?!"

Diego lifted a shoulder. "We're the only ones who know he's still alive. He isn't going to want a secret he's kept for fifteen years to get out, which means he won't let anything happen to her."

"I have to go back." I was here while my niece was still stuck in the mine.

"Whoa, mi pequeña diabla." Diego pressed me back onto the bed. "You need to call your friends and tell them I didn't murder you, since I vaguely remember A.J. threatening me before he passed out."

I reached for my earpiece and mike, but both were gone. They must have fallen off during the flight from California back to Boston. I dug my phone out of my pocket. Incredibly, it had survived the trip. I called Kaira.

She picked up on the first ring.

"Are you okay?" she demanded.

"Yeah, you?" I switched to face time, and Kaira's haggard but unharmed face filled my screen.

"We're fine," she assured me. "The 7.5, Charlotte, Emory, crew team…all good. We got three train-loads of slaves back to Boston. It was everyone we could find on Level 5, but we didn't have time to search any of the other levels before everything with Felix. And then with the MRP gas…." Kaira faltered. "Bri, I'm so sorry about Lilly."

My fists tangled in Diego's quilt as I thought about how close I'd come, only to have my niece wrenched away from me again.

"I'm sorry," Michael's voice said from somewhere nearby. "If I'd known the foreman was going to do that, I would have stopped him. I was hoping the foreman would bring us to Felix, but then I got distracted by the fact that I couldn't Whisper to those Super Mags."

"It wasn't your fault," I told him, my throat thick with a sense of failure and loss.

More voices on the other end of the line assured him of the same.

"Mag cops are trying to locate the kids' families," Kaira told me. "It's not easy because all of their records were destroyed and they never met their parents, but we'll figure something out."

I nodded, trying to be grateful. Objectively, we'd saved dozens of children from a horrific fate. I should be glad.

Instead, all I could think about was Lilly's wide, terrified eyes as Felix disappeared with her.

There was more chatter on Kaira's end of the line. Kaira balanced her phone against the wall so I could see everyone's faces. The rest of the Seven crowded in around her.

"Sweetums!" A.J. cried, shoving his face right in front of the camera.

"I'm so glad everyone's okay," I said. "I have to—"

"We know what you're going to say," Yutika said, cutting me off. "So, I'll save us all some time by telling you *no*, you're not going back alone, and *yes* we're going to save Lilly ASAP…together."

"I have some ideas for how we can get her back," Graysen said.

"And there are other issues we need to discuss," A.J. added. "Because I, for one, have no desire to die at the hands of a Synthetic."

"Synthetic?" I asked.

"That's what we're calling them," Kaira clarified. "Those freaky creations that have tubes hanging out of their skulls and don't respond to Michael's Whispering."

I shivered, remembering their bloody skin and pointed teeth.

I put my phone on speaker so Diego didn't have to strain to hear everything. After what he'd done for all of my friends, I figured he deserved to hear what they were saying.

"Tell her what Emory saw in the foreman's memory," Smith told Michael.

My friends moved aside to give Michael more access to the camera.

"Emory learned that the foreman—Eugene Forrager—came across Agent S while he was scavenging the rubble of a crashed plane. He knew the Remwalds from various anti-Nat rallies they'd been to, and thought Felix might be able to use the Agent S because of his alchemy."

Michael paused and inclined his head. "Am I getting all of this right, Emory?"

The Super Mag boy's face appeared on the screen next to Michael's.

"Yep," Emory said. "Felix figured out that Agent S could do crazy stuff, and that there was a huge deposit of it in the California desert.

"The foreman helped Felix Remwald set up the mine, while Edwardian Remwald took care of everything at MagLab. Edwardian funneled money to the mine from the Alliance, and Felix sent the MRP back to MagLab."

"Thanks to the formula my parents developed," Diego said under his breath.

Emory continued, "The foreman has been Felix's eyes and ears down in the mine for the last fifteen years."

I realized I was clutching Diego's blanket in a death grip and forced my fists to relax. After everything the foreman had done to those kids, I would personally make sure he never made it out of that mine ever again.

"In good news," A.J. said, "since Sir Zachary torched the Energy Manipulator, all we have left to take care of are the Synthetics and the MRP gas. Well, and the foreman and Felix, of course."

"Yeah, real piece of cake," Smith grumbled.

"I don't think we'll have to worry about tracking down Felix and the foreman," Kaira said. "I'm pretty sure they'll come to us at some point."

And I'd be ready. I cracked my knuckles in anticipation.

"I'll make us gas masks," Yutika offered. "So when that slime of a foreman tries that dirty trick a second time, the only one he'll poison will be himself."

"Excellent idea," Graysen said.

"The Synthetics aren't affected by the MRP gas," Diego said. "Felix has probably been building up their tolerance."

"We already thought of that," Kaira said. The look she leveled at Diego was somewhere between suspicious and tolerant. It was a marked improvement from the *I'm going to kill you* glares she'd given him before.

If that wasn't progress, then I didn't know what was.

"Emory thinks he might be able to convince the rest of the Super Mags—the real ones—to come with us," Graysen said. "We figure with all of us, we'll be able to deal with the Synthetics without endangering Lilly and the rest of the slaves."

That sounded reasonable.

"Well, can we talk to the Super Mags now?" I asked, trying not to let my impatience come through too much.

"That's the only hiccup," Graysen said. "Ma took all of them to the Blue Hills for an overnight bonding thing. Their cell service is shit, so Kai, Emory, and I are going to drive up there to talk to them. If they agree, we'll bring them back here first thing in the morning."

No way. There was no way I was waiting twelve more hours to go back for Lilly.

"I can't wait that long." I got up from the bed, shrugging off Diego when he tried to pull me back down.

"Bri, honey pot," A.J. said in his soothe-the-wild-Steel voice. "We're going to get steamrolled if we try to go back there without help."

"Besides," Graysen added. "Oliver said the only way to fully recover from the effects of MRP gas is to sleep." He glanced at Kaira before turning back to me. "We're going to go back for Lilly, but we won't do her any good if we're operating at partial-strength."

I knew he was right. But how could I snuggle up in my bed, safe and cozy and surrounded by my friends, when Lilly was still down in the mine?

If I insisted on going now, though, my friends wouldn't let me go alone. I didn't have the right to put them at that kind of a risk.

"Okay," I relented. "Tomorrow morning."

"It's a date," Adam said, poking his head in front of the camera and winking at me.

Diego scowled.

"I'm sending your security team to the Blue Hills with you," I told Kaira and Graysen, already texting my people. "You're not driving all the way down there without backup."

"Fine," Kaira said on a heavy sigh.

Graysen gave me a thumbs-up.

I rubbed my face, picturing my niece's terror as Felix dragged her out of my reach.

I'd been so close. So damn close.

"Bri, we're going to get her back," Kaira said. She was wearing that fierce expression that promised she wouldn't rest until we finished what we'd set out to do. "We just need to regroup, and then tomorrow, we're going to tear that place apart."

I nodded.

"Is Diego bringing you home, or should we come scoop you?" A.J. asked.

"She's staying with me tonight," Diego said.

"I—" I stuttered.

Diego wrapped an arm around my shoulders, like this was all perfectly normal.

I saw Yutika's mouth drop open before A.J. elbowed her in the ribs.

"Okey dokey, artichokey," A.J. said amiably.

Apparently, he had just given Diego his stamp of approval. That irked me, since I distinctly remembered having to try a lot harder to work my way into A.J.'s good graces when we first met. I thought it had something to do with him not trusting blondes.

"Are you sure?" Kaira asked me, furrowing her brow.

I knew she was thinking about Diego's tiny apartment and the one bed. I was certainly thinking about it. My cheeks felt feverish all of a sudden.

"Have you seen the frightful weather out?" A.J. demanded. "We're all staying put until this storm blows over."

As if on cue, the rain pound harder against the window.

"I have my truck," Adam offered. "A little rain won't stop me."

Diego stiffened beside me.

"Uh, I'm good here," I said. "I'll meet you back at the mansion first thing tomorrow."

I wasn't exactly sure why I was agreeing to this, except for the fact that spending the night alone in my room seemed like the worst kind of torture.

We said our goodbyes and disconnected. And then, Diego and I were alone.

CHAPTER 43

I emerged from Diego's bathroom half an hour later, free of Synthetic eye goo and drowning in Diego's clothes.

He hadn't been idle in my absence. There was a picnic laid out on his bed.

"You can fight, dance, *and* cook?" I teased. "Now I'm really impressed."

"You forgot kiss," Diego reminded me. He plucked a cherry tomato from his plate and made deep eye contact with me while he ate it.

Laughing and blushing, I grabbed a seat on the floor next to him.

"I like seeing you in my clothes," Diego said.

"What's for dinner?" I asked, a tad louder than necessary.

Smooth, Bri.

Grinning, because he knew he'd unsettled me, Diego nodded at the plate in front of me. There was a piece of grilled chicken slathered in black beans and avocado chunks, with a spinach salad on the side. I hadn't realized until this second that I was ravenous.

"You didn't have to do this," I told him, even as I dug into the salad.

Normally, I avoided meat for A.J.'s sake, but I didn't want to be rude by snubbing the food Diego had cooked for me. Besides, it wasn't like not eating this chicken would benefit him or her now.

Muttering a quick apology to the chicken gods, I took a bite.

Spice flooded my tongue, making my eyes water. I barely managed to swallow before I started to cough.

"Like it?" Diego asked, his lip twitching.

"Hot," I said, quickly stuffing some spinach leaves in my mouth to put out the fire.

Diego got up and came back with a glass of milk. "This'll help cut it," he told me.

I noticed that Diego's food had slices of chili peppers in addition to whatever edible lava he'd already put in.

"I guess you really do like it hot," I said, remembering his explanation for why he chewed cinnamon gum.

"Boy do I." Diego dragged his gaze lazily from my bare feet up to my eyes.

"*Diego.*" I gave him an exasperated look.

He retorted with an unapologetic grin.

"How's your leg?" I asked, inclining my head at the bandage around Diego's calf.

Diego cringed. "Can we *not* talk about the fact that I got slapped by a tail?"

I snorted at that. "Yeah, I'm actually a little embarrassed for you."

Diego humphed. From his lack of an obnoxious response, and the way he was staring at the rain streaming down the window, I could tell his mind was elsewhere.

"What are you thinking?" I asked.

Diego took a long time to respond. When he did, there was no hint of levity. "I'm thinking I need the Agent S now more than ever. If those Synthetics ever get loose, it'll be a nightmare."

I couldn't disagree with him there, and yet, I couldn't stop a flare of disappointment. After Diego brought me up to find Lilly instead of going after the Agent S, I'd thought we hit some kind of turning point.

"I'm never going to change my mind on this, Bri," Diego said, like he was reading my thoughts. "You know that, right?"

I stabbed another bite of chicken.

Instead of agreeing with him, I asked, "What was it like, growing up the way you did?"

"It wasn't so bad." Diego rearranged the food on his plate with his fork. "For the first eighteen years of my life, I only left the house at night to fly. I had to stay high enough that no one would see me or sense my magic, so I never interacted with anyone. My parents taught me everything from chemistry to poetry to mandarin." He raised an eyebrow at me. "I'm fluent in six languages, and I can seduce you in all of them."

"Maybe some other time." I rolled my eyes, and then took a sip of milk to hide my smile.

"After my parents discovered a temporary version of the MRP, I could start going out," Diego said, getting serious again. "It was…strange to actually be in the world, instead of just observing it from books or TV.

"I think my parents assumed I would go visit some historical monuments or museums or something."

"Where did you go?" I asked, curious. I had no idea where my first stop would be if I'd spent the first eighteen years of my life sequestered in my parents' house.

"Underground boxing rings and sex clubs."

I choked on my milk. For several seconds, it was touch and go whether it would come back out through my nose. Finally victorious, I asked, "Sex clubs?"

"What do you expect from an eighteen-year-old who can get in anywhere he wants without an ID?" Diego retorted.

Point taken.

Diego shrugged. "I could only be out for a couple of hours at a time before the side effects of the MRP got to me. Too much of the temporary formula has a sedative effect, and it wasn't like I could tell anyone what I was."

What…not *who*. Like Diego was a thing rather than a person. I wanted to correct him, but he spoke first.

"I honestly don't remember a whole lot from that year." Diego's smile turned sad. "If I'd known how little time I had left with my parents, I would have done things differently."

For several seconds, the rain beating on the glass was the only sound in the small apartment. I knew Diego didn't want my pity, but I couldn't help but feel sorry for him.

Diego had become very interested in his food, and I got the sense he regretted telling me so much. I didn't want him to close himself off, though, so I decided to return the favor.

"I get it," I told him. "I only lived that life for a year after I took out my tracker, but it was awful. My brother spent every minute with his wife, and I barely saw him. My parents were so sad it felt like a viper was squeezing the life out of me every time I talked to them."

It took me a few seconds to compose myself as I reopened my box of memories from that year.

"I spent most of my days watching shit daytime TV," I admitted. "The high points of my week were when I got to bounce for *Liquid Magic.*"

Diego's attention was so intent on me that I found it difficult to hold his stare. He seemed like he was about to say something, but then he just shook his head.

"Are you finished?" he asked, nodding at my plate.

"Oh, right," I said, feeling a little foolish. "You probably want to get some sleep." I glanced at the bed.

Diego's chuckle was deep and rich.

"Cariño, I have no intention of sleeping tonight."

"Presumptuous of you, don't you think?" I gave him my best attempt at being scandalized. In truth, I was just grateful to be back to our sarcastic sniping.

I'd begun feeling unbalanced by the personal turn our conversation had taken.

"Presumptuous is my middle name," Diego replied, taking our plates to the kitchen and putting them in the sink. He turned back to me and crossed his arms. "What's between you and the blonde oaf?"

"His name is Adam," I corrected, a little thrown off by the unexpected question.

"Okay. What's between you and the blonde oaf named Adam?"

I shook my head in exasperation. "We messed around a couple of times. There was nothing there, so we decided to just be friends."

"I don't believe any man could just be friends with you."

"Believe it," I replied, pulling my knees up to my chest and wrapping my arms around them. "I'm more cut out for friendship than romance."

Diego gave me a slow, predatory smile. "That changes here and now, Bri Hammond."

I believed him. He hadn't even touched me, and he was driving me crazy with the tenor of his voice and the sensuous promise in his eyes.

"What happens now?" I asked, feeling a little winded.

"Now," he said, scooping me up and depositing me on his mattress. "I'm going to get you naked. And then, I'm going to see if the rest of you tastes as sweet as your beautiful lips."

"Diego," I managed, but that was as far as I got. He pulled me on top of him and drew my face down to his.

If I'd thought our other kisses were passionate, they were nothing compared to this. I was instantly on fire. The torrential rain pounded against the window, drowning out the embarrassing moans I couldn't hold back as Diego dragged his tongue across mine.

I pulled his shirt over his head and tossed it across the room. I drank in the sight of his copper skin and tattoos, which seemed to come alive as his muscles flexed.

Diego slid his hands up the too-big shorts I was wearing to grasp my hips. He pulled back from our kiss, his chest heaving. When I opened my eyes, it was to find him staring at me in amazement.

"No panties?" he asked in a husky voice.

"Excuse me for not packing an extra pair in my nonexistent overnight bag," I said, a little defensively.

"Fuck, that's hot," he growled. He freed his hands to tug my sweatshirt over my head.

Rolling us over so I was beneath him, he looked at my chest and said something in Spanish I didn't catch, but I didn't need to be fluent to know that he liked what he saw. A lot.

Instead of going for what was left of our clothes, he brought his scorching gaze up to mine.

"I've never done this before," he said, his eyes darting away from mine.

If I didn't know him better, I'd have thought there was a vulnerability to his expression.

I barked out a laugh. "Right. Because sex clubs are for board games."

"No." Diego shook his head. "I mean, I've had sex, but not like this."

Now, there was no denying that Diego's expression had gone deadly serious. I searched his face, trying to understand.

"Every other time, I was shot up with MRP," he explained. "I set literal timers to make sure I was long gone before it wore off. It was always get in, get off, get out. I've never even bothered with names."

I winced at the crudeness of his words. At the same time, I ached at the thought of how lonely he must have been. Even when Diego had been able to go out in public, he'd still been alone.

"Trust me, cariño," Diego said, misreading my silence. "None of them ever complained." He gave me a cocky smile. "Except for when I didn't stick around for seconds."

I reached up to cup his face and pressed a soft kiss to his lips.

"I want you, Diego Agramonte," I told him, staggered by the truth of those words. "You and all of your magic."

Diego's expression softened. "That—" He cleared his throat. "That's the hottest thing anyone has ever said to me."

"It's the truth," I told him.

He gave me a long, searing kiss. When he pulled back, the tenderness in his eyes had been replaced with the arrogance that was all Diego.

"In that case," he said, easing his hand beneath the waistband of my shorts, "I'm going to spend the rest of the night seeing how many times I can make you scream my name."

"I'm not really the screaming type," I told him, lifting my hips to help him get my clothes off. Not that he seemed to need any help in that department.

A smirk played at the corner of Diego's lips. "We'll see, cariño. We'll see."

✳ ✳ ✳

I had no sense of time, but I thought it was probably close to dawn. The rain had stopped. I was surrounded by the smell of cinnamon and the scorching heat of Diego's magic. Even asleep, his arms stayed locked around me. When I nestled deeper into the crook of his shoulder, he made a rumbly purring sound.

My hair was still wet from the shower we'd taken together. The blanket was crumpled in a heap on the floor. It was cold in the apartment, but I felt like I was on fire.

Diego had kept his promise about making me scream, and I was pretty sure I'd have no voice in the morning. Tonight had been everything I'd always wanted…everything that had been missing in all of my other relationships.

At one point, I'd glanced away from Diego and realized we were levitating two feet off the bed. We were so into each other neither of us had noticed.

But tonight hadn't just been the most passionate I'd ever felt in my life. It had been so much more.

For the first time, I thought I understood the way Kaira and Graysen looked at each other. I hadn't thought I wanted the emotional part of that connection, but I was beginning to see the appeal. This was all too new to even think the L-word, but as I watched Diego's eyelashes flutter and heard him whisper my name as he dreamed, I felt myself falling.

And after everything that had gone down between us, I could sense Diego tumbling over the edge of that precipice right alongside me.

CHAPTER 44

When I woke, the apartment was dark. The blanket had been tucked around me and there was a pillow under my head. And I was alone.

"Diego?" I croaked.

My voice sounded like a smoker's.

"Go back to sleep, cariño. It's still early."

I stretched, luxuriating in the unfamiliar soreness. My body would need to get used to this new kind of workout.

The thought brought a smile to my lips.

"Come back to bed." I held out my arms for him.

"I wish I could," he replied.

I heard the rustle of clothes and Diego's soft footsteps as he moved around the apartment. I fumbled for the lamp beside the bed.

I flicked it on in time to see Diego pulling a shirt over his head. There were two empty duffel bags next to the door.

A horrible feeling replaced my elation from a few moments ago.

"What are you doing?" I asked, my voice coming out far calmer than I felt.

"I need to make my move before you and your friends destroy the mine," he said as he pulled on his socks. "I don't want to get caught in the crossfire when you and your Super Mags storm the place."

"Wait. What?"

Diego looked at me. "I can drop you back at the mansion on my way if you want, or you can hang out here until you're ready to go. There's food in the fridge—"

"I thought you couldn't get the Agent S without me," I spluttered.

Diego dug into his pocket and pulled out a silver key.

"I took this off Felix yesterday," he explained, giving me a sheepish look.

Those few minutes with Felix had been a blur, but I remembered Diego disappearing and then reappearing.

"You stole that key while he had Lilly?" I hissed, anger starting to permeate my shock.

Diego shook his head. "It was before he grabbed her."

"Why didn't you get Lilly if you were going to steal something?" I demanded, my voice rising. "You could have gotten her away from him. You could have gotten her away from that monster!"

Regret passed across Diego's face before his expression hardened.

"You saw those Synthetics," he said, buttoning his jeans. "Making MRP is more important now than ever. They're even more dangerous than my kind."

My kind.

"I thought you were done with this self-loathing bullshit," I said, not trying to hold back the bitterness in my voice. "After last night—"

I want you, I'd told him. *You and all your magic.*

When he'd reacted so strongly to those words, I'd thought that meant he accepted himself and what he was.

I'd thought we were on the same side.

"I care about you, Bri." Diego stopped fiddling with his clothes to look at me. "But I told you yesterday. The only thing that changed was that the Synthetics made me more committed to taking away our magic."

"It's not that simple!" I threw up my hands in frustration. "You can't just lump people together like that. You don't have the right to pass judgment on people who haven't committed a crime and likely never will. Just because someone is strong, it doesn't make them evil."

"I have to do this," Diego replied. "I'm going to make enough MRP for the Synthetics and other Super Mags, and then I'm going to inject myself."

"Go, then," I said, sneering in disgust. "Run away, just like you did after all your other quickies."

Hurt flashed across Diego's eyes.

"That's not what this is," he said. "And I think you know that."

I did know. And part of me understood I wasn't being fair. Diego had never deceived me or led me on. I just hadn't wanted to believe him. Hell, I'd wanted to fix him.

"Whatever," I muttered, feeling that awful, telltale sting at the back of my eyelids.

"We can talk about this tomorrow," he said. "Once you have Lilly back and I have what I need."

"No, you know what?" I snapped. "I'll make this easy on you." I grabbed the pile of my dirty clothes from the day before and dressed faster than I ever had in my life.

If I was going to do a walk of shame at four in the morning, I'd do it in my own clothes, thank you very much.

"I'll get out of your hair so you can finish your planning…alone." I gave him a scathing look. "That's how you prefer it, right, Diego? Just you and your obsession. I'm sure all those Super Mag files keep you nice and warm at night."

I left him, standing in the middle of his kitchen with his jaw clenched hard enough to break. I wrenched open the door, pausing when I caught sight of the key hanging on a lanyard around the knob.

I could call any of my friends to come get me, but I had no interest in talking about tonight…ever again.

"I'll have A.J. send your motorcycle back," I said, grabbing the key and slamming the door behind me.

Or maybe not, I thought viciously. The motorcycle could be like my prisoner of war, or something.

I raced down three flights of stairs, unwilling to wait for the elevator.

Diego's motorcycle was parked outside, and even though I'd never driven one before, it didn't take a genius to figure out how to get it going.

A few seconds later, I sped away from the curb. I didn't look back.

✳ ✳ ✳

I cut the engine at the bottom of the driveway so I wouldn't wake anyone. It was a true mark of how upset I was that I hadn't even enjoyed speeding along empty streets on a sort-of stolen motorcycle.

I left the bike and walked around to the back of our property, where the fewest security cameras and guards would see me come in.

I smiled at the guards on duty, said all the right things, and hurried past before anyone got a good look at my face. I didn't need anyone realizing I was about two minutes away from breaking down.

I was halfway across the lawn when I stopped in my tracks.

"Damnit, Diego!"

He stood in front of me, his arms crossed.

"Who do I see about stolen property?" he asked, his lip twitching.

I was so *not* in the mood for his lighthearted, flirty bullshit.

"You can fly," I pointed out. "You don't need it."

"After I lose my magic, that won't be true." Diego's teasing smile faded. "But that was really just my excuse. I didn't like the way we left things."

I laughed bitterly.

"Bri, is everything okay?" one of the guards on duty asked.

"Fine," I said quickly, dragging Diego into a dead zone between two cameras. Smith and I really needed to do something about that.

"I'm not going down with your sinking ship, Diego," I whispered, not wanting to draw any unwanted attention. "You're so determined to be the bad guy. I'm done trying to convince you you're not the monster you think you are."

"You're one to talk." Diego uncrossed his arms and closed the short distance between us. "Tell me you aren't the same."

"I'm nothing like you!"

"Right. Then look me in the eye and tell me you don't blame yourself for Lilly's situation. Tell me you aren't carrying the weight of your entire family's grief on your shoulders."

"You piece of shit—"

"Tell me I'm wrong," Diego challenged.

I couldn't, and we both knew it. In that moment, I hated him for seeing my vulnerabilities and throwing them in my face.

"You want to be the one who spent her life down in that mine." Diego threw his hands in the air. "You think if you punish yourself enough, it will somehow make up for something that was never your fault in the first place!"

"It is too darn early for all this hollerin'," a voice that was neither Diego's nor mine huffed.

Grandma Tashi, followed by Kaira and Graysen, was crossing the lawn toward us.

Great. Just great.

"Problem?" Graysen asked, giving Diego a cold look.

"No problem," I said. "This *pendejo* was just leaving."

"Language," Grandma Tashi snapped at me.

Too late, I remembered Kaira's father had been Mexican. Clearly, her grandmother had picked up at least some of the language.

"Sorry, Tashi," I began, but she wasn't paying attention to me anymore.

"I know you," Grandma Tashi said, stalking over to Diego.

Diego shook his head. "I don't think we've ever met."

Tashi reached up, grasped his chin in her bony hand, and pulled his face down until it was level with hers.

"Grandma," Kaira began, and then gave up when her grandmother held up a hand to hush her.

"Boy, you do look like your daddy, don't you?"

I heard Diego suck in a surprised breath.

"You knew my father?" he asked.

Tashi shook her head. "But your mamma came to visit me a few months back, and I could see your father through her."

Diego's face clouded over in confusion. As much as I hated him at that moment, I couldn't stop myself from explaining, "Kaira's grandma is a Medium."

Diego swallowed. "My Amá…came to see you?"

"Twice," Tashi replied, still studying Diego. "She was talkin' to me about the slaves down in that mine, and how their bodies weren't buried the way they shoulda been."

I thought about all the empty graves and biohazard containers I'd dug up over the last few months, and then I thought about that tomb in the mine. I wrapped my arms around myself, suddenly aware of the chilly air.

Diego bowed his head, hiding his expression.

Tashi said, "She came to see me a second time soon after that."

Diego jerked his head back up. "What—"

"She didn't say anything, but I could sense her sadness for you. She felt responsible for whatever you've been going through. She was…conflicted."

Grandma Tashi's brow wrinkled, and for a second, her brown eyes turned cloudy.

"She loves you deeply, and that love is also mixed with deep regret," Tashi said. "I believe she wanted more for your life than what she felt she gave you. She felt like she failed you."

"No. Never." Diego reached out a hand to Kaira's grandma, as though he could get to his mother through her.

I looked away, unable to bear the anguish on Diego's face.

Kaira and Graysen were turned into each other, pretending like they couldn't hear what was being said.

"Please," Diego said in a rough voice. "I need to tell her—I just—" He braced his hands on his knees. "Can you tell her something for me?"

I had to stop myself from going to him.

Just as she did whenever someone asked her a similar question, Tashi shook her head. There was sympathy in her usually-hard features.

"It doesn't work that way, but I'll tell you what. I know your Amá loved you very much."

She stroked her thumb across Diego's cheek, nodded to the rest of us, and then headed back the way she'd come.

"Diego," I began, having no idea what to say, only knowing I couldn't let him suffer alone.

"Don't," he replied. He stayed where he was for several seconds. Then, he straightened.

Diego walked away without another word.

Kaira cleared her throat. She gave Diego's retreating figure an inscrutable look before turning her attention on me.

"Bri, we hit a wall with the Super Mags. I'm so sorry." Her eyes watered as she reached for my hand.

"What?" I asked, my mind still reeling from everything with Diego.

Out of the corner of my eye, I saw Diego stop to listen to what Kaira was telling me.

"We tried," she said, her grip tightening on me. "I swear, we tried."

"They're scared," Graysen added, giving me an apologetic look. "After everything they went through in MagLab…well, they're afraid of getting locked up again."

"I get it," I said, dully. And I did.

If it wasn't Lilly's life at stake, I'd be relieved. Super Mags or not, I didn't want to drag a group of kids into a dangerous situation with me.

But that left us back where we'd started.

"We have a plan, though," Kaira said quickly, following the direction of my bleak thoughts.

"Okay," I sighed. "Let's go gather the troops."

I glanced back once as the three of us made our way to the house. Diego was gone.

CHAPTER 45

Even though it was barely 5AM, the 7.5 were awake and gathered in the living room. A.J. gave me a questioning eyebrow raise. At whatever expression crossed my face, he nodded in understanding. He plopped a very excited Sir Zachary in my arms and said he had a new nail polish color that would look divine on me.

I bit my lip until I tasted blood, because all I wanted to do was lean on A.J.'s shoulder and cry.

"You're all in for a treat," Yutika said by way of greeting. "Check these babies out."

She held up the most intense-looking gas masks I'd ever seen.

"I'd like to see any of the MRP gas get inside these," she said, knocking on the hard-plastic exterior. "They'll block out any toxins and even pump fresh oxygen inside if the air is contaminated."

"Why are they pink?" Smith asked, frowning over the top of his computer screen.

"Because I wanted them to be," Yutika replied, at the same time A.J. asked, "What's wrong with pink?"

"So, Kai and I were thinking," Graysen said quickly, before the conversation could devolve. "Since we don't have the Super Mags' help, we decided it would be better if we didn't have to waste time fighting the Synthetics. If we can keep them distracted long enough to get the slaves out—"

"—then we can blow up the mine with all the bad guys still inside," Kaira said.

"I can't Whisper to them," Michael said. "Their minds are porous, or something. As soon as I Whisper, it's like whatever I told them filters right out of their brain again."

"We'll figure something else out," Graysen said.

"Maybe Sexy Cinnamon Man could help with the distraction part," Yutika suggested. "Like, he could fly around and make the Synthetics chase him, and then he could go all Chameleon before they kill him."

"Diego's not an option," I said shortly.

I had decided that I wouldn't stop him from getting his Agent S. I owed him that much, since he'd already have it if he hadn't helped me go after Lilly first.

Once we were all out of the mine and I had Lilly, Diego and I could go back to being enemies. Then, I wouldn't feel even a shred of guilt about hunting him down and destroying whatever Agent S he'd salvaged.

But for now, I owed Diego a debt.

"It wouldn't hurt to ask," Yutika said. She narrowed her gaze at me. "And by the way, you never mentioned what it was like spending the night with him."

Queasiness roiled through me.

"Flying buttresses," A.J. said quickly.

"What about them?" Michael asked.

"Nothing," A.J. replied. "I just like the sound of it."

"The first time I heard that term," Kaira said, catching on, "I thought it was referring to literal flying butts."

"I love Kaira-isms," Graysen said fondly.

The conversation spiraled from there, sparing me from any more mentions of Diego.

I noticed the way Yutika and Michael were staying on opposite sides of the room and making a point of not looking at each other. Between the three of us, there was enough heartbreak in this room for the whole place to combust.

Before I could expend any more mental energy on that pitiful thought, Smith jerked to his feet. His eyes were closed, and I instinctively reached out to steady him before he knocked into his chair. A.J. rescued his computer, which was about to crash to the tiles. Instead, it floated carefully onto the center of the table.

"Smith, what?" we all asked.

"We've got a situation outside." Smith's eyes snapped open. "Valencia's here."

I was titanium before he'd even finished speaking. All 7.5 of us moved in a flurry of curses and magic.

I hurried out first, making sure there wasn't a security threat before I let the others follow.

"No weapons," the head of my security team said, meeting me halfway across the lawn. "She's claiming her right to gather in a public place."

I saw the reporters first, who were setting up camp all along the street. A few of them were even trying to climb our fence to get a better vantage point.

Valencia was standing in the street as close to our property as she could get without touching the grass. She stood on a precarious stack of crates and had a group of her Nat bigot friends in front of her. All of them were working together to hold up a banner that read "Make Boston Natural."

"Can we buy the whole street and arrest her real quick?" Yutika asked from behind me.

"I'll look into it," Smith replied.

I was going to kill Valencia. We were supposed to be on our way to the mine to rescue Lilly, and now, there were two dozen reporters standing right outside our gate. We weren't going anywhere until we got rid of them.

"Director Gald-ah," Valencia called into a megaphone. "I have solved our city's biggest problem. You'll thank me when I tell you that I've found a way to make your wife normal."

Kaira's eyebrows flew up. Graysen's friendly gaze turned colder than ice.

"I'll take my wife exactly as she is, thanks," Graysen said.

To prove his point, he took Kaira's face in his hands and gave her a long, slow kiss. The reporters' cameras flashed.

"Ooh, one of those is going to look great on the Globe's front page," A.J. said.

When Graysen came up for air, he turned to face the reporters.

"I'm sorry," he said, glancing in Valencia's direction and giving the reporters a puzzled look. "Were you still here, Valencia?"

The reporters tittered at that.

"I've called the press here this morning to share an exciting new discovery my *Nat* scientists have made," Valencia said. She wobbled a little on her stack of crates before righting herself.

That was when I noticed the small group of nervous-looking people in white lab coats standing behind Valencia.

Valencia snapped her fingers at one of them, and the woman passed her a syringe.

"My scientists have recreated the Magical Reduction Potion," Valencia announced as she held the syringe over her head. "It's so easy and effective, anyone can make it at home. Once I share my recipe, we'll be able to make Boston what it should be—Natural!"

"What's she talking about?" Yutika said, nervously looking around.

I clenched my hands into fists so I didn't go across the street and rip Valencia's head off her body in front of all these cameras. She was basically inviting Nats to brew their own concoctions and inject it into any Mag they could find.

"I want to be very clear with the entire city of Boston," Kaira said in a clear voice that somehow carried farther than Valencia's, even though she wasn't holding a mike. "It is illegal and unethical to attempt to remove a person's magic."

"The Alliance's Report of Laws calls for a minimum five-year sentence for magically-motivated attacks of any kind," Graysen added. "I speak for the Alliance's Magical Law Office when I saw we will prosecute anyone found attempting to make or utilize MRP to the full extent of the law."

"We're Bostonians," Kaira said. "Our city is a haven because Magics and Naturals are equal."

"Woo!" A.J. shouted, clapping his hands. The rest of our friends and most of the reporters joined him.

"Director Gald-ah," Valencia said. "I invite your wife to be the first to come forward and accept this gift."

"That's it," Graysen growled. "I'm going to kill her."

He started forward, but Kaira pulled him back. Her gaze darted to the cameras in warning.

"Kaira," Michael said in a quiet voice. "Let me take care of this."

He stepped behind a tree where only we could see him. Then, he was gone. My eyes caught on the movement of a tiny bunny on the lawn, right where Michael had been.

"OMG adorbs," A.J. whispered.

If any of the reporters had been looking at the ground, they might have noticed a bunny walking on its hind legs. Fortunately, Valencia was doing all the work of captivating everyone's attention.

"It's *scientific*," Valencia said, emphasizing the word like she'd just learned it. She held the vial right in front of her face, letting the cameras capture the yellowish liquid inside. She turned to the white-coated Nats at her back, who were looking more nervous by the second. "Tell the report-ahs how it works."

The white-coated man who now held the megaphone in his trembling hands gave the cameras a deer-in-the-headlights look.

"Hello," he said awkwardly. "The thing is, we're not yet ready for the trial stage. The serum Ms. Stark is holding is more of a concept rather than an actual, usable—"

Valencia snatched the megaphone from him before he could finish. The reporters' snickers grew louder.

"The serum relaxes the magic muscle," Valencia said with great confidence, "and so their pow-ah just slips right out. It doesn't even hurt."

Her lip curled in distaste at that—clearly, she would have preferred it to be an agonizing experience as one's magic was being stolen away.

"What a crock of shit," Smith said. "That makes no sense."

"Which begs the question," Graysen said grimly, "what the fuck is in that serum?"

All at once, Valencia's expression turned placid. She tilted her head to the side.

To anyone who didn't know what was happening, it would probably seem like she was just gathering her thoughts. To the Seven, it was obvious Michael was Whispering to her.

Valencia cleared her throat and brought the megaphone to her mouth. "I'm going to prove my serum is perfectly safe and works as intended," she announced. "By injecting myself."

The scientists behind her erupted into a flutter of lab coats and frantic whispers. One of them tugged on Valencia's arm, trying to pull the syringe away from her.

Valencia batted the scientist away. With a smile for the cameras, she plunged the needle into her arm and squeezed the plunger.

The small crowd went silent. Almost at once, Valencia's face contorted. Her cheeks reddened and her shoulders hunched. She made a strange grunting sound.

"Ugh," one of the reporters standing closest to her said. "*What* is that smell?"

"Her pants," Yutika gasped, holding her stomach as she started to giggle. "Look at her pants."

We all did.

"Ho-ly shit," I said. "Did she just—"

"You got the shit part right," Graysen said, grinning.

The scientists and reporters were backing away, but the video cameras were still rolling. The reporters who weren't busy holding their noses were explaining the situation to everyone who was watching the broadcast live.

The Seven of us looked at each other. Yutika snorted, and the rest of us were done for.

It felt good to laugh, and even better to see the look on Valencia's face as she hurried away from the reporters. A dark streak marked her path on the road behind her.

"Fecal incontinence," Smith read off his laptop, wiping away a tear of laughter. "It happens from a loss of bowel control—"

"Stop," Kaira begged, hanging onto Graysen as she tried to stifle her giggles.

"She did say something about relaxed muscles," A.J. pointed out, slapping his thigh as he chortled.

"So brilliant," Yutika whispered, her face alight with pride.

The only one who wasn't in hysterics was Michael. When Kaira pulled his bunny illusion away, it was to reveal him standing beside us again with a gloomy expression on his face.

"You're my new hero," I told him.

Michael ignored me and scowled at Kaira.

"A bunny?" he demanded. "How about a hawk or a snake?"

Kaira was still laughing too hard to respond.

"How did you know that would work?" Smith asked him.

Michael lifted a shoulder. "I Whispered to a couple of the scientists. They weren't sure what would happen if it got injected into a person, but they all seemed confident the effects wouldn't kill her…but also wouldn't be pleasant."

"Incredible," Yutika said. "Seriously brilliant."

For the first time since our fight with Blade's army, Michael smiled.

"Thanks," he said, ducking his head as a flush spread down his neck.

"I don't think anyone's going to be trying to make their own version of the MRP anytime soon," Graysen observed, still chuckling.

Now that the crowd Valencia had attracted had dispersed, we were free to go back to the mine without anyone asking questions.

Two cars pulled into the driveway at that moment. The crew guys piled out, yawning and holding coffee travel mugs.

"Did we just pass Valencia on the road?" one of the guys asked. "She had all of her windows down and was screaming something about natural bodily functions."

The Seven of us looked at each other and devolved into hysterics.

CHAPTER 46

The train car glided to a stop at the California end of the long tunnel. We clipped on our earpieces and mikes. All of the Mags in our group also had a pink mask in case the MRP gas was used against us again.

I wasn't sure if I was relieved or disappointed that I hadn't caught the hint of cinnamon or the heat of Diego's magic since he left the mansion.

"Our priority is getting Lilly and the rest of the slaves out," Graysen reminded everyone as we got off the train and hovered around the door that led into the mine. "Once that's done, we're going to destroy this place."

We all nodded in agreement.

"Thank you," I told all of them, catching myself before my voice hitched. "I can't tell you—"

"You don't have to, hon," A.J. said, gently. "This is what we're here for."

Nodding, I wiped the back of my hand across my eyes before any tears could fall.

"Don't go getting soft on us now, Hammond," Adam ordered with mock seriousness. "Put your Steel pants on, and let's go kick some ass."

In response, I blew on my fists.

We left Smith behind in the train car so he could do Techie stuff. The rest of us went on to the tunnel that led up to the main part of the mine.

The tunnel was eerily quiet and empty. I wasn't sure if it was because my friends had managed to get so many of the children back to Boston during our last trip here, or because some new horror was lying in wait for us.

Knowing the way the Remwalds' minds worked, I assumed the latter.

"Good news," Smith said, his voice coming through our earpieces. "I've hacked into the mine's electrical system. I'm going to install a virus that'll bring this whole place down once I activate it."

"How are you going to manage that?" Yutika asked.

"My malware will get into the electric grid and short-circuit the system," Smith explained.

At our dumbfounded silence, he said, "You know, like how your phone or computer can overheat, only a million times more intense. I figure once it catches fire, it'll ignite the Agent S and *kaboom*."

"Good thinking, Smith," Graysen said, clearly impressed.

"There's just one issue," Smith said. There was something in his voice that made my hopes sink. "This malware will be enough to bring the whole mine down, but once I put everything in motion, there's no way to stop it. It'll take ten minutes from the time I set the virus for the electrical fire to catch onto the Agent S and ignite."

"So if we want to destroy the mine," Graysen said, "you have to set up the malware exactly ten minutes ahead of time?"

"Yeah," Smith confirmed. "And once it's going, I won't be able to do a thing to reverse it. So we need to be damn sure we're out of there by the time it blows."

We all stopped talking when we reached the end of the tunnel. The open room was as busy as ever, except it wasn't crowded with kids and carts brimming with Agent S the way it had been before. It was full of Synthetics.

Their cloaks undulated around them with every movement. They didn't make a sound, which made their presence even more eerie. Their magic felt slimy and unstable.

The Synthetics congregated around the elevator, like they knew where we were headed…like they'd been waiting for us.

Yutika gulped audibly.

"Okay everyone," Kaira whispered. "Here we go."

Our normal appearances vanished and were replaced by exact replicas of the Synthetics.

"I left our hands looking normal," Kaira explained. "That way, we can easily tell us from them."

I glanced at the silent, cloaked Super Mags. Sure enough, their hands were gnarled, cracked, and bloody. A little shudder passed through me when I caught sight of the tubes sticking out of the backs of their necks. There was something creepy and distinctly non-human about them.

"Are you sure you're up for this?" Graysen asked Charlotte, who stood between him and Emory.

Charlotte looked down at Sir Zachary, whose fur was standing on end as he growled quietly at the Synthetics.

"We've got this," she said.

Her golden eyes flashed, and then the little girl was gone. In her place was a beautiful black-and-white Border Collie. Unlike our appearances, which were illusions, Charlotte had really become what she appeared to be. She whined softly to Sir Zachary.

The two dogs looked at each other. Then, they both shot off like bullets.

Charlotte and Sir Zachary split off in opposite directions, their bodies hunched low as they raced around the Synthetics. They bared their canines and snapped at the Synthetics' ankles.

The Synthetics all turned their hooded gazes onto the two dogs. One of them opened his mouth, displaying double rows of pointed teeth.

"Oh my—" Kaira began.

The Synthetic screeched.

The sound was like nothing I'd ever heard before. The cement walls reverberated. Cracks appeared between my feet. I felt something wet and sticky trickling out of my ear. When I reached up to touch it, my fingers came away stained with blood.

My friends' mouths were moving, but I couldn't hear more than a jumble of senseless words. Blood streamed from their ears.

"Sir Zachary!" A.J. shouted.

Relief at discovering I wasn't deaf turned to terror. Sir Zachary was facing off against a line of Synthetics.

When Sir Zachary reared onto his hind paws, the rest of us got the hell out of his way.

Sir Zachary opened his mouth. Fire spewed out.

The Synthetics let out harsh wailing sounds as a wall of fire surrounded them. Some of them allowed themselves to be herded by Charlotte, moving wherever they could to avoid the fire. The rest fought back.

A wall of ice appeared between Sir Zachary and the Synthetics.

Border Collie-Charlotte transformed again. This time, she became an enormous polar bear.

Charlotte rose up on her hind paws and roared.

The sight of her was almost as terrifying as all of the Synthetics combined. The creatures must have agreed, because they tripped over their cloaks as they hurried to get away from her…and ran right into Sir Zachary's flames.

The only problem was that there were only two of them against all of the Synthetics. And the ice-wielding Synthetic was a match for Sir Zachary's fire.

"What do we do?" Yutika asked in a panicked voice.

"Sir Zachary and Charlotte can hold their own," A.J. said. "For a little while, anyway. Let's get moving. I've got a trick up my sleeve, but it'll only work once."

We didn't waste time asking him for details. We ran to the elevator on the far side of the room.

We went up to the isolation chambers on Level 4. With my magic no longer impeded by the Energy Manipulator, I had no trouble wrenching the doors off every single one of the cells. My friends hurried in after to help the kids back out to the elevator. Most of the kids were hysterical and too weak to walk on their own.

Their skin was covered with grime and their clothes were in tatters. Some of them were even barefoot. I took one look at the cowering, bone-thin children and saw red. These kids were afraid of us because they'd had a lifetime of learning to fear adults.

What kind of monster did this to children?

Michael Whispered to the kids, calming them enough so they trusted us to carry them out.

We worked quickly. We focused on the job so we wouldn't all succumb to our fury over how these kids had been treated. We couldn't afford to lose our heads…not yet, anyway.

I promised myself that the ones responsible would pay.

"First group coming your way, Smith," Graysen said, lifting a straggling little boy in his arms and carrying him after the others.

It was especially slow going, because with my magic interrupting theirs, the kids didn't have their Steel strength. Some of them scrabbled on hands and knees because their legs were too weak to support the rest of their bodies. Charlotte and Sir Zachary kept the Synthetics occupied while the rest of us carried, dragged, and cajoled the children down the tunnel that led back to the train.

Given what had happened on Level 1 of the mine last time, we decided not to push our luck with trying to find the supply shaft that led all the way up to the surface. We figured it would be safer to take the kids straight back to Boston. Besides, none of us was especially interested in ending back up in California territory, only to have to battle Blade's insane followers to get the kids the hell out.

It wasn't a perfect plan by any means, but it was the best we had.

"Go," I told Smith, once the train car held as many as we could fit.

There were a few whimpers from the kids as the door to the train slid shut. I felt badly that we couldn't explain to them what was happening, but there wasn't time.

Michael stayed with the next batch of kids who would board the train as soon as it came back, keeping them calm while they waited.

"The isolation chambers on Level 4 are cleared of slaves," Adam announced. "We're gonna go check the offices on Level 3."

"The rest of us can deal with Level 2," Graysen said. "I saw a bunch of kids heading up that way the last time we were here."

"No," I said, thinking about the vault full of liquid Agent S vials on that level. I didn't know whether Diego had already come and gone, but I'd promised myself to let him take what he needed. "Start at the nursery on Level 1."

"On our way," Kaira said.

I felt like a traitor to my friends and everything we stood for, but there was also relief. I was no longer in Diego's debt.

"Sir Z's exhausted," one of the crew guys said. "And Charlotte isn't looking much better. They're not gonna make it much longer."

"Get Charlotte and Sir Zachary back to the tunnel," A.J. ordered. "I'll deal with the Synthetics."

"A.J., what—" I began.

Before I could finish, I heard a sound like tinkling bells. I barely had time to press myself to the side of the dark tunnel as dozens of glass vials came zooming my way. The vials shimmered with the liquid green Agent S inside.

They had come from the train tunnel and were clearly being controlled by A.J.'s magic.

"A.J., what?" I began.

"Oops," A.J. replied. "Did I forget to mention to Diego I kept these?" He cackled to himself.

"Where did you hide all of this?" Kaira asked.

"In the train tunnel," A.J. replied. "I figured no one would accidentally discover them there."

"You little genius!" Yutika shrieked.

"Damn, A.J.," Graysen said. "Good thinking."

"You could have mentioned it to me," I grumbled. "Would have saved some time dealing with Diego and the vault."

"Oh honey," A.J. said. "First, we both know keeping secrets isn't your thing."

I was about to express my deep resentment on that unfair statement, but A.J. continued.

"And second, we had to get Diego back to the mine to help rescue Lilly. I was afraid if he knew I still had the stash from his apartment, he'd try something crazy pants, like kidnapping you."

I humphed. A.J. was right, but he didn't need the confidence boost from hearing me spell it out for him.

A trail of glittering Agent S vials led the way to the main room on Level 5. From my position at the mouth of the tunnel, I could see the vials hovering in mid-air over the Synthetics' heads.

"Seven, make sure you're out of the way," A.J. said calmly.

My position gave me a clear view of the green vials when they overturned. I backed farther into the tunnel as the Agent S splashed down, and the Synthetics' screams began.

The Synthetics writhed and screeched as the Agent S burned straight through their cloaks. Some of them were rolling on the ground as their skin dissolved and turned to steam. Nausea surged through me at the sight of white bones beneath shredded skin.

Perversely, the Synthetics' agony was making them seem less zombie-like and a whole lot more human. The smell of burnt flesh filled my nose. I hurriedly put on my gas mask to get some fresh air before I threw up.

Less than a minute later, the Synthetics were gone. Their clothes, skin, and bones had completely dissolved. The only evidence that they had been here at all was a giant hole in the ground where the Agent S had eaten through the floor.

"You had to, A.J.," I said in a hoarse voice, knowing how he must be feeling. "They would have died when we collapsed the mine, anyway."

"I know," A.J. replied heavily. "But I'm guessing these Synthetics had as little choice in what they'd become as the slaves. And a life's a life."

I wanted to hug him right then, but more children were coming down the elevator with the crew team.

I scanned their tiny, scared faces, looking for hazel eyes.

The older kids struggled to carry the infants. The crew guys helped by using an empty cart to move as many of the kids out of the elevator as fast as they could.

"I don't see her up here, Bri," Kaira said into my earpiece. "We haven't done the very back yet, but I don't think she's here."

As soon as the elevator was free of children, I jumped on with Michael. We went up to the nursery on Level 1, where Kaira and Graysen were already waiting.

It looked nothing like it had the day before. The metal cribs had been tipped over and kicked to the side of the room. The metal toys strewn across the floor looked disturbingly like little corpses.

I went straight to the panel in the wall where Felix had taken Lilly. When I didn't see a door, I punched through the wall.

I stumbled into another room that was slightly smaller than the nursery. Metal, child-sized beds were lined up in neat rows. The beds, along with the rest of the room, were empty.

"We haven't checked everywhere yet," Graysen said, coming to join me. "We'll find her."

Swallowing the lump in my throat, I started back for the elevator, feeling like thousand-pound weights had attached themselves to my legs.

"Oh shit," Yutika said across our earpieces.

"What?" the rest of us asked at once.

"Yutika, what's wrong?" Michael demanded, his cool demeanor unraveling. "Are you hurt? Where are you?"

"Level 3. The—"

A loud thump traveled across our earpieces. Michael shouted Yutika's name.

We all raced to the elevator.

Michael leapt off before we came to a complete stop. I was right behind him. What we saw made us both freeze…until Yutika screamed again.

CHAPTER 47

Synthetics were everywhere.

Their cloaks swirled around them as they encircled Yutika.

"Michael, no," I gasped.

He ignored me. He didn't even try to Whisper. He just barreled right through the rows of Synthetics to Yutika's crumpled figure. He fell to the ground beside her, cradling her in his arms as he hunched his body protectively around her.

"Hey!" I shouted, waving my hands to get the Synthetics' attention.

They gnashed their teeth and started for me.

"A.J.," I said, crouching down into a fighting position. "I could use some more of that Agent S."

"There is no more," A.J. said in a panicked voice.

I didn't hear anything else, because the Synthetics were on me. They lashed out at me with ice, teeth, blades, and fists. I struck back.

My limbs were a blur. I let my magic take over. Everything else faded away as I punched and kicked.

One of the Synthetics opened his hand. A swarm of mechanical bees leapt off his palm and surrounded me. Aside from their annoying buzzing, the little creatures had no effect on me. Their enlarged stingers simply broke off against my titanium skin.

The Synthetics might have more magic than me, but they were still made out of flesh and bones. I was not.

Nothing they did could hurt me. They were also slow and awkward, like they were just learning how to function in their bodies. Their magic was powerful, but it wasn't a part of them the way mine was a part of me. They were hesitant and uncertain, and I was steadily pushing them back, away from my friends.

The only problem was that my energy was waning. The Synthetics didn't pass out as easily as normal people, and they weren't afraid of pain. They kept getting back up for more.

I couldn't hold my own against them forever. And every second I was fighting them meant I couldn't go searching for Lilly.

The others were helping as best as they could. The coxswain's waterspouts swirled around the room, drenching the more powerful Synthetics. Graysen's Nat friends shouted curses and delivered blows tough enough to impress my old wrestling coach. They managed to distract the Synthetics, while the rest of the Seven threw everything they had at the creatures.

"Get back," I shouted as a torrent of acid spewed out of one Synthetic's mouth. I positioned myself in front of the others, wincing more from disgust than anything else as the gunk covered my torso.

"Blech."

It smelled as disgusting as it looked.

"Get out of here," I ordered the others. "Find Lilly."

The Synthetics were stronger than all of us, but my magic would keep them from killing me.

I heard Smith shout something across my earpiece, but I was too busy trading punches with three of the Synthetics at once to pay attention. I wasn't sure how much time passed, but my body was aching and my reflexes were getting slower and slower.

An icicle-blade *shinged* across my titanium skin, barely missing my eye. I ducked away from the next blow instead of trying to deliver one of my own. I was on the defensive, slowly being backed toward the wall. The Synthetics, sensing my weakness, closed in around me.

No, I thought desperately. *Not yet. Not until I find Lilly....*

The next thing I knew, people were crowding into the room with me. Magic surged through the space, making me feel a little drunk.

I was so worn out that it took my mind a few seconds to catch up.

The Super Mags...the real ones...were here.

The kids we'd left happily sleeping in their fairytale house in Boston flocked around the Synthetics. The Synthetics, already flagging from everything I'd done to them, didn't stand a chance. There were fewer of them, and they were less powerful than the real Super Mags.

"Where did you come from?" I asked, confused and relieved.

"I've been trying to tell you," Smith said across my earpiece. "They were waiting on the platform when the train got into Boston."

"But why?" I asked, watching as the kids hurled their magic at the Synthetics.

"He convinced us to come," one of the older Super Mags, who had never really taken to the Seven, replied.

"Smith?" I asked, not understand how he could have had time to go back to the mansion for a heart-to-heart with the Super Mags between ferrying the slaves from the mine.

"The Chameleon," the kid said, frowning in irritation at my slowness.

The Chameleon. It couldn't be….

"He said they had someone in your family," another one of the Super Mags told me, "and that we should help you because you would do anything to help us." The little kid shrugged. "He also told us there were fake Super Mags down here, and if we wanted to kill them, this was our chance."

Diego. Diego had convinced the Super Mags to come.

"Go," the kid told me. "We'll take care of these things."

"Thank you," I managed.

With one last look in their direction to assure myself the Super Mags had everything under control, I leapt onto the elevator and went to the last unexplored level, where the raw Agent S was turned into a liquid. I'd saved this one for last because of Diego. If he hadn't already gotten his vials out of the vault, he was out of luck.

My friends were already there. The Alchemists were helping to ferry the few children on this floor toward the elevator. Their glazed eyes kept straying to Michael. One of them even touched his elbow and asked, "Am I doing a good job?"

"She's not here," Kaira said, gasping for breath as she carried a large boy to the elevator. "She has to be in that locked part." She motioned to the door at the other end of the chamber.

I noticed the titanium vault in the corner was open and empty. My stomach did something funny at the realization that Diego had most likely flown in, gotten what he'd needed, and left again.

"Our Super Mags locked the Synthetics up in some kind of barbed wire thing," A.J. said across our earpieces. "They're all exhausted, though. I'm sending them back."

"Any idea how long the Synthetics will stay out of commission?" Graysen asked.

"Not long," A.J. replied grimly. "They're very…determined."

"Once we find Lilly, Smith'll start the malware," Kaira said. "We just need to keep the Synthetics contained until we can bury them along with the mine."

"Get everyone to the train," I said, leaving my friends to finish loading the elevator as I went straight for the locked door.

I wrenched it hard enough that the hinges groaned and cracked. The door fell inward and slammed onto the bare floor.

The room was empty. There were some lab tables and shattered glass beakers, but no Agent S, and more importantly, no people.

"Lilly's not here," I said in a broken voice.

"Bri, I sense some tech behind the wall on your right," Smith said. "Elevator, I think. It's on the move. Worth a look."

I ran over to the far wall, which as far as I could tell, was just more steel.

I was about to punch my way through, when I caught sight of a small keyhole. There was no handle or any other indication that this was a door, but Smith had never been wrong before.

I hooked my titanium pinky finger in the keyhole and gave it a mighty tug.

A door-shaped panel came away from the wall to reveal a huge, open area. I experienced a moment of vertigo as I found myself in the midsection of a giant metal cylinder. It was at least thirty feet in diameter, and it reached above and below me farther than I could see.

"I found the supply shaft," I announced. My voice sounded strange as it bounced off the metal walls and came back to me.

A crude kind of ladder, which was really just rusted metal rungs nailed to the wall, climbed up the closer side of the cylinder. Naked bulbs were spaced at regular intervals along the metal wall. A yellow light was flickering.

I gripped the side of the wall and looked down, but I couldn't see the bottom. It seemed to go down forever.

I looked up. What appeared to be an elevator without sides was moving slowly away from me. It was crawling up the far side of the supply shaft, leaving at least twenty feet of space between it and the ladder on my side of the cylinder.

The elevator.

"Bri, talk to us," Kaira commanded.

"Smith, stop that elevator," I said before quickly describing what I was seeing.

The elevator ground to a halt far above me.

"I fried the electric motor," Smith said, "so that baby's not going anywhere."

"Bri, don't go for it until we get to you," Kaira said. "We're headed your way."

My earpiece filled with my friends' voices, but all of my attention was on the elevator. I couldn't say how I knew, but I just had a feeling Lilly was on it.

I jumped off the edge of the floor where I was standing and grasped the nearest ladder rung on the wall. I began to climb.

The elevator platform was about a hundred feet up and as many metal rungs away. I had no idea how I'd cross the twenty feet of space between my side of the shaft and the nearest edge of the platform without jostling it hard enough that Lilly might fall off. I'd figure that out later, though.

I climbed quickly, my titanium limbs making short work of the task.

"That's enough," a sharp, male voice called out when I'd covered just about half of the distance. His voice echoed through the cylindrical shaft rather than coming from my earpiece. "Stop what you're doing."

The elevator was close enough now that I could see it was just a long platform with flimsy handrails. Naked cables attached to the sides were hauling it up to the surface. There were no walls to prevent whatever was on the slow-moving elevator from falling off.

Clearly, safety inspections weren't a priority down here.

Six Synthetics stood motionless around the railing, blocking the rest of the platform from view. They moved aside to reveal the man who had spoken. Felix Remwald.

His white hair gleamed in the light, contrasting sharply with his black suit. The foreman stood beside him. There was a large crate at his feet. Cowering on the platform beside it…was Lilly.

"Lilly," I gasped. And then, louder, "Lilly!"

My niece's head jerked up. She was too far away for me to see her face, but I knew it was her. She was curled into a ball, as though she was trying to make herself smaller. She glanced fearfully from Felix, to the foreman, to the Synthetics towering over her.

Panic punched straight through my gut.

"What do you want me to do?" Smith asked me.

At almost the same time, the foreman said to Felix, "Want me to toss her off, Boss?"

The question echoed in the circular chamber.

"No. Don't do anything." My hoarse words were for both Smith and the foreman.

I couldn't risk Felix hurting Lilly.

I continued to climb slowly so I wouldn't spook Felix.

"I just want my niece," I called, my voice coming out muffled from behind my gas mask. Clinging to the metal bar with one hand, I pulled the mask off and looped it around my arm. I repeated what I'd said before, and this time, my voice echoed off the metal walls.

"You and your friends have ruined more than two decades of work," Felix called back. "You have taken everything from me. Why shouldn't I do the same to you?"

"Please." I climbed faster. I reached for the next rung. In my haste, I grasped it with too much force.

The metal tore away from the wall. I fumbled, momentarily losing my balance. I dangled by three fingers.

I steadied myself against the lower rung and dropped the useless piece of metal.

It struck off the metal wall. For several seconds, the echo of its descent carried up to where I was perched. I listened for the sound of it striking the bottom. What felt like forever later, I finally heard a dull clunk reverberate back up through the walls.

"It's a long way down," Felix said, sensing my thoughts. "Even with your powerful magic, I don't think you could survive that kind of a fall."

I didn't disagree. Worse, Lilly couldn't become steel at all. With my magic interrupting hers, she was completely vulnerable.

"She's takin' my magic away," the foreman growled to Felix. "Kill her. Kill her right now."

"No," Felix replied in a bored voice.

The foreman spat a stream of brown juice off the side of the elevator. It missed me by inches.

"What do you want?" I asked Felix. I didn't bother with the foreman, since it was clear who called the shots around here.

I yanked myself up to the next rung.

If I'd been in my regular skin, I'd be sweating bullets. As it was, nervous energy was shooting through me like electrical jolts.

"I want your Mag friends to return my slaves and leave my operation in peace, for starters," Felix said.

"They already left," I lied. "I'm the only one who's still here."

Felix's chuckle sounded even more evil with the way it ricocheted through the metal chamber.

"One of my Super Mags tells me that he can sense the heat of other bodies heading this way."

"If I tell them to leave," I said, "will you let me have my niece?"

"No," Felix replied. "But I'll agree not to throw her to her death. For now." He put a hand on Lilly's shoulder, making white bursts of fury explode across my eyelids. "This elevator is very crowded, after all."

"Fine," I said quickly. I stopped climbing and wedged my toes into one of the rungs. I measured the distance, trying to decide whether I'd be able to catch Lilly if she fell from the elevator.

It was possible, if she fell just right. But even then, I wasn't sure the rickety metal rungs would hold me with her added weight.

I held up the small microphone clipped to my shirt, making a show of speaking into it.

"The Synthetics can feel your body heat," I told my friends in the calmest voice I could muster. "I need all of you to leave. Give me those ten minutes."

I held my breath, silently praying my friends would understand what I was trying to tell them.

For several seconds, there was silence in my earpiece.

"You want Smith to initiate the malware, don't you?" Graysen asked.

"That's right," I said loudly, awash with relief. To Felix, I said, "They're leaving now."

All I had to do was get Lilly. Then Felix and his creations could go down with the rest of the mine.

"I can't stop it once it starts," Smith told me. "Are you sure?"

"Go back," I said into my mike, conscious of the fact that Felix was listening to everything I was saying. "I'll be able to get out of the mine through this supply shaft."

Translation: Take the train back to Boston so the Synthetics won't have another way out of here once the mine collapses.

Only two people were making it out of this supply shaft…and it wasn't going to be Felix and the foreman.

"We're not leaving here without you," Kaira said.

"You have to go," I said. "If you don't, he'll kill Lilly."

"We'll wait in the train and have it ready to go as soon as you get down here," A.J. said.

"No." I glanced up at the cloaked figures clustered on the platform above me and thought about the dozens of Synthetics still on the lower level of the mine. "I don't want the Synthetics to get you."

Or get out before we collapse the mine.

"Synthetics?" Felix chuckled darkly. "I suppose that's an accurate description. Have you figured out what I'm doing down here, then?"

"You're trying to make Super Mags," I said, slowly resuming my climb upward.

Felix nodded. "Agent Steel is truly a remarkable substance. When it's distilled and combined with other ingredients in just the right way, it creates a solution that removes magic. But if the undiluted liquid is injected directly into a Mag's spinal cord, it enhances magic."

"It also makes them look like zombies," I pointed out, trying to buy time while I inched higher.

Felix hmmed. "Yes, well, there are adverse effects on the subject's epidermal layers. I was working on a potion to rid them of that discomfort before you disturbed my entire operation."

"Just out of curiosity," I said. "Did these Mags know what you were doing to them?"

Felix and the foreman shared a laugh at that.

The foreman was the one who answered. Even though I was too far away to see his face, I could hear his sneer. "I 'pecifically found Mags who were down on their luck and didn't have nobody to miss 'em."

"And the Agent Steel spinal injections have a secondary effect of warping memories," Felix added. "It's rather beneficial, as it makes my creations' minds pliant and submissive. Combine that with the addictive properties of Agent Steel when it's injected into the spinal fluid, and I've found a recipe for ensuring they obey me and no other."

So, that was why the Synthetics didn't respond to Michael's Whispering.

"I guess after enslaving children, taking away adults' free will must be no sweat off your back," I said, unable to stop myself.

I knew I'd be better off if I didn't goad him, but I couldn't help myself.

"An unfortunate consequence of needing Steels for my work," Felix said. "Sacrifices must always be made for the sake of progress. The same has been true throughout history.

"I need Steels to extract the solid form of Agent Steel, since it is volatile. And only Steels can handle the liquid safely."

"Also," the foreman said, letting out a raspy chuckle. "Us Steels are the only ones strong enough to work a mine."

The pride in his voice, as well as that word *us*, made me sick.

"Eight minutes," Smith said into my earpiece.

I started to climb faster, the rungs blurring as I got into a rhythm. Reach, reach; step, step. Repeat.

"Forgive me," Felix said, his voice completely devoid of apology. "But I think that's quite close enough."

I couldn't be more than twenty feet from Lilly. So close. *So damn close.*

I was near enough to watch Felix take a small, metal box out of his pocket. The foreman bared his rotten teeth in a feral grin as Felix overturned the box's contents over the side of the open elevator.

White dust sprinkled down and then dispersed, creating a cloudy haze as it filtered toward me.

"Bri, what's going on over there?" Kaira demanded.

Instead of answering her, I fumbled for my gas mask as instinct told me I was about to need it. I had just wrestled the mask over my face when the first specks of powder touched my bare arms.

I hissed as my titanium skin was immediately engulfed by a tingly, burning sensation. It wasn't unbearable, but as I watched, my titanium body turned back to normal skin.

I reached for my magic. Nothing happened.

"Alchemy really is the most potent of all magic," Felix boasted as he observed my distress. "And Agent Steel is so versatile."

"What have you done to me?" I demanded, even though it was obvious.

"Magical Reduction Potion," Felix replied. "It's very concentrated and starts with the surface of the body. It is quite effective in a place filled with Steels."

Felix ignored the foreman's growl.

Terror clawed up my throat. He hadn't said whether it was permanent. What if I'd lost my magic…forever?

A small sound from the platform brought my attention away from myself and onto the tiny, huddled figure beside the crate.

"Hush, you," the foreman ordered, striking the bottom of the crate with his boot. Lilly whimpered and then went silent.

I'm coming, Lilly, I silently begged her. *Just hang on.*

My magic didn't matter. All that mattered was getting to Lilly. And I didn't need my magic for that.

I resumed my climbing, but I was slower now. My every movement felt sluggish. It felt like my body was fighting against itself. If it hadn't been for the gas mask Yutika had made me, I was pretty sure I would have passed out and fallen to my death.

"Fifteen years," Felix said, as I labored up the side of the tunnel, one rung at a time. "I haven't left this mine in fifteen years."

I was finally close enough that I could see distinct facial features. I tried not to look too hard at Lilly, because if I did, I would get us both killed in my frantic attempts to take her away from these monsters.

"That's some serious dedication to your cause," I said, breathing through a burst of pain across my palms. My skin, weak and raw from the powder, was blistering against the repetitive motion of grabbing the rungs.

My legs felt like lead. It was taking all of my energy to raise each foot to the next rung. My arms were trembling from holding up my own weight.

"I began work on this mine when I discovered Agent Steel and the possibilities it contained," Felix said.

"I brought you the Agent S, don't forget," the foreman reminded Felix, sounding like a petulant child seeking a parent's approval. He spewed out a mouthful of brown tobacco juice that hit the side of the metal shaft.

"And you needed a Level 10 Alchemist to unlock its potential," Felix snapped back.

Clearly, this was an argument the two of them had had before.

"Edwardian built MagLab, while I created the mine," Felix told me. "My brother was breeding an army of regular-born Super Mags. I was creating a force of my own down here.

"We knew it would behoove us for the rest of the world to believe I was dead, so I committed to never leaving the mine."

"You faked your death at that school," I said, thinking about Michael's stricken expression when he saw the news article about the battle.

"There were so many deaths that day." Felix shrugged. "My brother and I didn't think anyone would notice if another name was added to the list."

"You really had this thing planned out for a while, then," I said.

A little closer.

I tried to catch Lilly's eye, but her face was downturned.

My arms trembled. Sweat poured down my back and ran into the open blisters on my palms. The burn brought tears to my eyes.

"My brother and I were going to avenge our parents' murders at the hands of Nats.

"Edwardian and I planned to combine our forces to destroy the US Federal Security Enforcers. I was going to use the Agent Steel to enhance Mags' powers, and my brother would use the Magical Reduction Potion to encourage any unwilling Mags to fall into line with our new regime."

Felix held his hands out to the Synthetics standing on either side of him.

"While we have failed in every other regard, I will succeed in this. Behold the weapon that will dismantle the Nats' control over our country."

"Six minutes," Smith said into my ear. "Bri, you've gotta get moving. It's going to take you at least two minutes to get down here to the train."

I didn't bother responding. I wasn't leaving without Lilly.

My arms were shaking violently, and my legs were refusing to move.

Please, I thought, willing my limbs to obey, but it was hopeless. It was taking all of my strength just to hang on.

As my panic reached a fever-pitch, I felt the brush of air against my skin, and then a familiar scent somehow permeated the shield of my gas mask.

Cinnamon.

CHAPTER 48

iego. He was here. I couldn't see him, but I felt his arms around me, helping to support my dead weight.

"Dios, Bri," he murmured.

"Lilly," I whispered, turning my head so Felix wouldn't see my lips move. "He has her."

"You're hurt," Diego whispered back. "Where's your titanium?"

Forget about me! I wanted to shout, but I never had the chance.

One of the six Synthetics held out his arm and pointed a long, deformed finger down at the spot to my left…right where I could feel Diego hovering beside me. The Synthetic made a guttural sound. Blood dripped from his nail-less finger.

"Ahh." Felix came to the edge of the platform and stared down at me. "The real Super Magic has arrived. Show yourself, Chameleon."

With no point in staying hidden, Diego dropped his camouflage.

He swept one arm beneath my knees and used the other to support my back.

"I've got you, cariño," Diego said, taking my weight.

"How delightful," Felix said, his eyes glittering as he stared down at us, like we were specimens in a lab. "The Agramontes do have such big hearts." He stared like he was trying to puzzle Diego out. "Are you as blinded by love as your parents?"

"You need your head examined, pendejo," Diego said.

I wasn't sure if he even noticed that, even as he spoke, Diego pulled me tighter against his own body. It didn't escape Felix's notice.

"I was in love once, too, you know," Felix said. All humor disappeared from his expression. "A very long time ago."

"Bri," Smith said. "Bri, what the fuck are you doing? You only have five minutes."

I didn't bother responding. There was nothing to say.

"What have you done to my girl?" Diego demanded, his whole body radiating fury.

"Interesting," Felix murmured. "I thought you'd be wondering about what I did with all of the Agent Steel you've been so desperately searching for."

Diego tensed, his grip tightening on me.

A strangled scream came out of me as the foreman yanked Lilly to her feet. He didn't throw her off the platform like I'd been expecting, though. He just pushed her roughly behind him so he could kick off the lid of the crate she'd been huddling beside.

The foreman grunted as he tilted the crate toward us, just enough to reveal its contents.

Diego sucked in a breath. The crate was packed with rows and rows of glittering green Agent S vials. There had to be hundreds of them.

The foreman tipped the crate back onto the elevator. The whole platform trembled as the heavy load settled.

Even though Lilly was blocked by the foreman's body, I could hear her crying.

"This is all that's left of the Agent Steel," Felix told Diego. "The rest has been destroyed."

"Why would you do that?" Diego demanded.

"Insurance," Felix replied. "I knew that once you learned the truth, you would attempt to kill me. I also knew that if you were anything like your parents, you wouldn't be able to resist the only way to get more of your precious Magical Reduction Potion."

"What truth?" Diego asked in a flat voice. He was grinding his teeth hard enough that I heard them squeak.

"Your parents didn't die in the MagLab fire," Felix said. "I killed them at least a week before that Pyro set flame to the lab."

All the color drained from Diego's face.

Felix's mouth twitched into a cruel smile. "After my brother's death, your parents learned what he'd really been planning to do with the Magical Reduction Potion. They found out about the Steel slaves and lost their heads. They were threatening to destroy all of their research unless I agreed to release the children. So, I sent one of my people to dispose of them."

"What?" Diego's mouth made the shape of the word, but no sound came out.

All this time, Diego had believed the Pyro was responsible for his parents' deaths. And not only had Felix killed the only people Diego had ever had in his life, the Alchemist possessed the ultimate bargaining chip…the one thing Diego wanted most.

"Bri, you've got three minutes," Smith shouted into my ear. "Wrap this shit up. Now."

"That's it," Kaira said. "I'm going to come get you."

An argument erupted across my earpiece, but I didn't hear any of it.

Felix had just admitted to murdering Diego's parents. And he held my niece's life in his hands.

"I will survive this," Felix said. "But I am curious to discover what you care about most, Diego Agramonte." He smiled cruelly. "Will you try to avenge your parents' death by attempting to kill me? Or will you prioritize the Agent Steel, since your parents gave their lives in pursuit of the Magical Reduction Potion formula, and this crate is your last chance to make more of it? Or, will you choose to save a single life of value to no one except your little Steel?"

Before Diego or I could speak, there was a commotion on the platform. The foreman kicked the crate once, twice, three times…until the entire thing went over the side.

At almost the same moment, Felix lifted my niece by her armpits and flung her off the platform.

I screamed.

Diego flew straight up. Before I could utter a word, I was airborne, and Diego's arms were no longer around me.

Diego had thrown me high enough that my hand connected with the elevator's handrail. My skin was sweaty, but I clung on and managed to hoist myself onto the platform.

My momentum thrust one of the Synthetics over the side. His gnarled fingers wrapped around the bottom of the platform for a second before his weight and gravity did their job. He plummeted down.

"Lilly!" I screamed.

Ignoring everything and everyone else, I looked over the side of the platform. I couldn't see Lilly or the crate.

All I saw was Diego, shooting down.

CHAPTER 49

Lilly and the last crate of Agent S were in a race to the bottom, and I was powerless to do anything.

My friends were shouting across my earpiece, but I couldn't hear anything over the crash of my pulse.

Diego had told me his Levitator magic was the weaker of his two abilities, and that he couldn't carry much more than his own weight. He wouldn't be able to catch that heavy crate and Lilly. Not to mention, the awkward shape of the Agent S container would make it impossible for him to hold them both.

Diego's words from our fight came back to me.

The only thing that changed was that the Synthetics made me more committed to taking away our magic.

A broken sound tore free from my lips.

"Get rid of her," Felix ordered the foreman. To the remaining five Synthetics, he snapped, "And get us out of here."

Two of the Synthetics began to haul on the thick cables, drawing the platform up by hand. The other three stood protectively around Felix and the foreman. The Synthetics' magic simmered just below the surface.

"Bri!" My friends shouted my name until my ear rang.

The metal walls of the supply shaft began to vibrate. Dimly, it occurred to me that whatever Smith had done to the mine's electrical system was starting to take effect. Once the Agent S stones were disrupted enough, the explosions would begin.

The foreman spat what I swore to myself would be his last mouthful of tobacco juice.

Hope you enjoyed it, asshole.

"Go!" I shouted into my mike. And then I threw myself at the foreman.

The MRP powder must have been temporary, because I could feel it wearing off. Some of my strength was coming back.

I didn't have time for gratitude.

I elbowed the foreman in the face, making him stumble to the edge of the platform. He wobbled for a second before righting himself. He plowed toward me like a charging bull.

Two things happened at once. My skin transformed back to titanium. And Diego appeared beside the platform. He was cradling Lilly against his chest.

My knees went weak with relief.

Before I could say a word, the walls shook again, more forcefully this time.

"Get her out of here," I begged Diego.

"I can't carry both of you."

There was a wild look in Diego's eyes. He might not have my friends' frantic voices in his ear, but he understood. The mine was collapsing.

"It's okay," I told him. "Please. Just get her out."

The foreman launched at me again. I moved out of the way with inches to spare.

"Diego, go!"

Diego looked sick. He wrapped a protective hand behind Lilly's head. And then he was gone.

Relief like I'd never experienced washed through me. I dodged another one of the foreman's blows, letting his momentum carry him forward. I waited for him to turn around and face me. I let him see his death in my eyes. Then, I struck.

One well-aimed punch sent him sprawling backward. For what felt like forever, he wobbled on the platform's edge, his arms pinwheeling. His terrified gaze met mine right before he went over the side.

The foreman howled. There was a horrible thud as his body struck the metal wall. The two sounds bounced up and down again in a chilling cacophony until they faded completely.

Another tremendous boom rocked the entire shaft, making the platform tremble violently.

"Kill her," Felix ordered his Synthetics.

The ones pulling up the elevator kept at their task, which left three to come for me. They were stronger and more powerful than me, and I was exhausted. I couldn't take them down.

I wasn't useless, though. I might not be able to save myself, but I could at least prevent Felix and his Synthetics from getting out of here alive.

"I love all of you," I said into my mike, hoping my friends would hear me over their panicked screams.

I let out a startled gasp as the full force of my magic slammed back into me. A grim smile tugged at my lips as I met Felix's gaze.

The Synthetics attacked, but I was ready. I jumped straight up, grasping onto one of the thick metal cables. I pulled with all of my strength.

Felix shouted. The cable snapped. And then, we were all falling.

CHAPTER 50

I fell for what felt like forever.

All around me, the mine was collapsing. Debris rained down. Deafening booms ricocheted through what was left of the metal cylinder. Something heavy and metal struck the side of my face, hard. I felt my jaw crack.

Lilly is safe.

Those words echoed through my mind, giving me peace even as I fell and the mine exploded around me.

The air was filled with shattering sounds. Stone and metal crumbled. And still, I fell.

Lilly is safe.

My grasping hands caught on the metal rungs, tearing them free from the collapsing wall. The interruption slowed my descent just enough for me to truly understand how screwed I was.

I saw no sign of Felix or the Synthetics as I fell, but that was fine with me. It gave me no comfort to think of their bodies entombed in here with mine.

Lilly is safe.

I closed my eyes and tried not think about whether the impact or suffocation would be what killed me.

* * *

I must have fallen hundreds of feet, and yet my magic kept me from dying on impact. The dirt floor of the mine was molded around me.

Stone, metal, and other debris struck me on their way down. I held my hands up, protecting my face as I watched what had to be miles' worth of dirt raining down.

Through everything, I could see a small circle of light. It was so high overhead it might as well not exist, and yet, it was a comfort. I didn't want to die alone in the dark. That little patch of sunlight reminded me of everything good that would exist even once I didn't. Lilly and the rest of my family. The Seven. Diego.

I thought I was hallucinating when a very human-shaped piece of debris came zooming down faster than all the rest. I gasped, trying to form words. Panic flooded me until there wasn't room for anything else.

Diego.

"No," I managed. He wasn't supposed to be here. He was supposed to be safe.

Even though I was half-buried by falling rocks and metal junk, Diego managed to zig and zag his way through everything. His hand closed around mine, hauling me out of the pile of rubble that was covering me.

I felt his whole body convulse as something heavy hit him. He sank to his knees.

"Get out of here!" I tried to tell him, but my ears were too full of the mini explosions going off all around us to hear my own voice.

I crouched down beside him. Diego reached out with a bleeding, trembling hand to touch my cheek.

"Go!" I shouted.

There was still time. He could fly fast enough to avoid the falling rubble. He could make it out.

Diego shook his head. He reached for me again, yanking his arm back when a shard of metal sliced across his forearm.

I let out a muffled scream as blood gushed from the wound.

"Get out," I begged. I didn't know if he could hear me, but he saw my lips moving and must have known what I was trying to tell him.

Diego shook his head again. I understood he was as weak and exhausted as I was, and that he wouldn't be able to get us both out. And he wasn't going to leave me.

When my wild eyes went back up in the direction he'd come from, the patch of light was gone. Now, the only reason I could see anything was because of my skin's silver sheen.

Diego winced as a huge stone came barreling toward us.

I rolled myself on top of him, using my titanium body to shield as much of him as I could. The stone shattered across my back. Jagged pieces sprayed around us, hitting against the metal wall and bouncing back. There was one dull thud after another as debris struck my back. With their momentum, even small rocks would be deadly if they hit the wrong part of Diego.

I looked down at him. He was trying to say something, but he was coughing too hard to get the words out. Not that I could have heard him, anyway. The only sound in my ears was the crash of the mine all around us. I felt Diego's body shaking, though. His face was turning purple. He couldn't stop coughing as he inhaled the swirling dust.

My lungs were clear and my breathing easy. In the midst of my panic, it took me too long to figure out why.

The gas mask Yutika had made and I had completely forgotten about was still over my face. She'd said something about it blocking out toxins and pumping in fresh oxygen.

Using one arm to hold myself over Diego so the rubble accumulating on top of us didn't push me down and crush him, I tore off the mask. I fumbled with it until it was tight over Diego's nose and mouth.

He coughed and writhed for another few seconds before his breathing evened out. I felt his body relax, just as mine seized up.

It felt like there was sand in my chest, swirling around and rubbing against my insides with every breath. Now, I was the one coughing.

Diego took another breath and then passed the mask back to me.

We went back and forth like that for several minutes. Our gazes stayed locked the whole time, even though we didn't say a word. All of our efforts were focused on staying alive.

The explosions had stopped. Dust was still swirling around us, but everything else was darkness and quiet. My arms trembled as I fought against the weight of the entire mine. My body was all that kept it from crushing Diego.

I couldn't last like this much longer. Titanium tears dropped out of my eyes and pattered onto Diego's torn shirt. He reached between us, passing back the gas mask and cupping my cheek.

His hand shook, but the expression in his dark eyes was serene.

I didn't know how he was so calm. My mind was in turmoil. I wanted to scream at him for coming back. I wanted to kiss him. Instead, I gave him a feeble nod, letting him know it was his turn to take back the gas mask.

Diego took the mask off me, but instead of putting it on himself, he leaned up to touch his lips to mine.

I choked back a sob. My whole body shuddered under the weight I was holding up. My body and magic were exhausted. My arms were failing me, and as soon as they did, we'd be flattened under the weight of the entire mine.

Dark spots flitted across my vision. I could no longer see the reflection of silver in Diego's irises.

I knew I had reached the end when the weight pressing down on my back lessened and light began to crowd out the dark. People always talked about going into the light, right?

It wasn't what I would have pictured if I'd ever given my own death serious thought, but I recognized it for what it was. There was no other reason why sunlight would be filtering in through the dust and debris when we were miles underground.

I looked down at Diego, expecting to see him fracturing into shards of light as my life drained away. Instead, I saw confusion and amazement in his eyes.

A deafening sound filled the silent tomb. A beam of light pierced the darkness. I felt Diego's arms come around me. And then, we were flying.

CHAPTER 51

The next time I had any awareness, everything was dark. I couldn't open my eyes, but it didn't bother me. I felt comfortable. Safe.

A woman was crying. Someone was trying to comfort her. Their voices, which had started out hushed, got louder.

"My patients, my rules," a gruff voice said. "Get out if you can't handle it."

"She's our daughter, and that boy—"

"Has thirteen broken bones and has been unconscious for hours. He's not moving an inch until I say so."

"Move him to a different bed or I will," a familiar male voice ordered. "That's my baby."

"Mom, Dad, be reasonable," another voice said.

Brent? What was he doing here?

Come to think of it…where was *here?*

"Bri's friends said he's the only reason Lilly and Bri are alive," Brent continued. "If Bri didn't want him in her bed, she'd find a way to beat him up even in her sleep."

I shifted a little, holding back a moan as pain shot through every inch of me. I instinctively moved closer to the smell of cinnamon and magical heat.

Diego.

I snuggled closer and let myself drift off again.

* * *

"Bri. Pumpkin face. Can you open your eyes for us?"

"Dad?" I croaked.

Muffled sobs filled my ears. Then, there was intense pressure against me. At first, I thought it was the mine collapsing on me and that the voices had just been a hallucination, but then my eyes cracked open.

My mom was draped over me, sobbing as she petted my hair. My dad was holding one of my limp hands and saying "Thank God," over and over again.

I blinked, bringing the room into focus. I was in my room at the mansion. My gaze fixed on a family photo taped to my wall.

"Lilly," I said, as my memory started coming back. "Where's Lilly?"

"Right here."

I twisted my head, trying to get free of my mom's mass of blonde curls.

"Mom, you're crushing her," Brent's voice said.

"Oh." My mom let out a muffled sob. "Of course."

She moved enough for me to get a view of the part of my room her body had been blocking.

Brent was leaning against my desk, his eyes crinkled in the first true smile I'd seen on him in as long as I could remember. Sarah was sitting on my rolling chair. She held a beautiful little girl on her lap.

"Lilly," I whispered.

I barely recognized her. She was still too thin, but there was a brightness in her hazel eyes that reminded me so much of Brent's and my own. The similarity took my breath away. Lilly's hair, which had been dirty and matted down in the mine, was a shiny brown. Soft curls framed her tiny face. Instead of the awful sack-like uniform she'd had in the mine, she now wore a pretty red dress and sparkly shoes.

"Aunt Bri," my niece said tentatively, looking to her mother to see if she'd said it right.

Sarah buried her face into Lilly's back, her shoulders shaking as she cried silently. Brent put an arm around Sarah's shoulder and leaned down to kiss the top of Lilly's head. He looked at the two of them with so much tenderness it made my heart swell like a balloon. Then, he turned to me.

"Thank you," he rasped, coming to perch on the edge of my bed. He wiped his sleeve across his eyes. "Bri, how can I ever thank you for this?"

"You don't need to," I replied. My voice sounded strange, like my vocal cords were grating against sandpaper. But I barely noticed. I was still trying to figure out how I was here at all.

Before I could form my mind around the question, Lilly slid off Sarah's lap and shyly deposited a mangled daisy on top of my blanket.

"Thank you, sweetheart," I told her, feeling my own eyes begin to sting.

I took the flower and tucked it behind my ear. My niece's face lit up with the most gorgeous smile I'd ever seen.

Sarah came over and knelt beside my bed.

"Bri," she whispered.

"You don't even need to say it," I told her. I didn't want gratitude for this. Lilly was my niece, and I'd do anything for her.

Sarah nodded. She leaned over and gave me the gentlest of hugs, like I might shatter.

"Oh, Bri." My mom burst into tears again.

Sarah had to scoot out of the way as my mom threw herself across me again.

While I patted my mom's back and reassured her that I was okay, I looked around the room. I remembered Diego being here, but there was no sign of him now. *Had I imagined his presence?*

"Where's Diego?" I asked.

My mom sat up, her chin wobbling. "That boy with the awful tattoos?"

I bristled.

"*Mom*," Brent said, rolling his eyes at her back for my benefit. To me, he said, "He left with your friends when you started waking up. I think they wanted to give you some time alone with us."

"Pumpkin face, are you in a relationship with him?" my dad asked. "Because I'm not sure—"

"Alright everyone," Brent said, scooping Lilly into his arms. "Bri's friends are going to want to see her now. Let's give them some privacy."

Thank you, I mouthed to my brother. Brent winked at me as he ushered our parents out.

They were barely out the door before A.J. and Yutika poked their heads in. They let out simultaneous squeals and charged me.

The two of them jumped on my bed. Kaira and Sir Zachary quickly followed. Charlotte and Kaira's two cousins squeezed on, too.

Graysen, Smith, and Michael stood, since they weren't really the bouncing-on-the-bed types. Not that there was room for anyone else, anyway.

"Bri!" A.J. wrapped his arms around my neck and tried to squeeze the life out of me. I almost had to turn into titanium to avoid being strangled, before Kaira pointed this fact out to him and he released me.

Sir Zachary was trying to drown me in slobbery dog kisses, and Yutika was shrieking so loudly my ears were throbbing.

Oliver poked his head into my open door and shouted, "Have you idiots lost your collective minds?!"

"Oops," Yutika whispered, scrambling off the bed along with everyone else.

"You almost died," Smith's dad said, pointing an accusing finger at me. "I know for a fact there's a brain inside your head. Use it."

With that, he spun on his heel and stalked down the hall.

"That's his way of saying he's happy to see you awake," Smith said, nonplussed.

"Aren't we all." A.J. swatted me with his polka-dotted handkerchief. "If you ever do something like that again, I'll kill you."

"I'll keep that in mind," I said, searching the sea of faces in the room.

My friends looked back with expressions ranging from relieved to ecstatic. As happy as I was to see all of them, I didn't see the one face I was looking for.

"Diego," I said, interrupting more threats from Kaira about what would happen if I ever scared them like that again.

Had I imagined him being here this whole time?

"He left, love bug," A.J. said gently. "About fifteen minutes ago."

"He didn't leave your side the whole time you were out, though," Yutika said. "Even Ma couldn't lure him out with food."

So, I hadn't imagined his presence. But, why did he stay all that time just to leave?

"He was saying the mushiest stuff to you in Spanish," Desiree said, rolling her eyes and clicking her long nails on my bedframe in irritation. "I got this app that translated everything."

"Ma told you not to do that," Cora said to Desiree, aghast.

"I thought he was cool before," Desire continued, ignoring her sister. "But he's actually as bad as Graysen."

"Why, thank you, cuz," Graysen told Desiree, giving her a bright smile.

"How long have I been out?" I asked, because I didn't want Desiree to start going into details in front of a room full of people.

"Two days," everyone replied at once.

"Two days?" I managed.

"You were buried alive," Smith mumbled. "You should be dead."

At that, there were a lot of hard swallows, sniffles, and more suffocating hugs.

"What happened?" I asked.

I remembered everything up to the part where light was coming into the mine and I thought I was dying. What happened after was a blurry haze.

"Finally," A.J. sighed. "We get to the good part of the story." He stole my pillow and tucked it under his own head. "I was obviously the hero."

He made an affronted sound when Yutika lightly smacked his arm. "You were only a partial hero," she said.

"Why don't we actually tell her what happened," Graysen suggested. "We can do a dramatic retelling later."

"Party pooper," A.J. muttered.

"We were trying to get to you," Kaira began, "but the explosions had already started, and the whole mine was coming down."

"We barely made it out," Yutika said. "The tunnel back to Boston started to collapse, too. We would have been crushed, except Smith detected the air shaft that was used to blast the Agent S gas through the mine.

"A.J. used his magic to pull the train car through the rubble and right into the air shaft so we could climb out without being crushed."

"You're kidding." I stared at A.J. in utter amazement.

Even with as strong as A.J.'s magic was, I couldn't imagine how much that had taken out of him.

Looking more carefully at his face, I saw that he had burst blood vessels in both eyes. I leaned my head on his shoulder and gave him a squeeze.

"I pulled a few hustle muscles, but we weren't going back to Boston without you," A.J. replied with a little shrug.

"We got to the surface at the same time Diego came out with Lilly," Michael said, taking up the story. "Diego brought us to the entrance of the supply shaft you were in, but it was already collapsing."

"I'm sorry, Bri," Smith said, looking anywhere except at me.

"Don't," I told him firmly. "It was my call to blow it up. You warned me exactly what would happen. You did everything perfectly."

Smith gave me a jerky nod.

"Diego went back in after you, even though it was suicide," Yutika said, her lip trembling.

My stomach did something between a somersault and freefall.

"It was the worst ten minutes of our lives," Kaira said.

Everyone was quiet for a few seconds until Michael spoke.

"Yutika made a giant dirt digger machine," he said.

The two of them exchanged a complicated look and hesitant smiles.

"And Smith and A.J. made it pull rubble out of the supply shaft at record speed," Graysen said. "You should've seen the thing."

I shook my head in amazement. I didn't think I'd ever get used to my friends' general awesomeness.

"The two of you were down there for almost twenty minutes," A.J. said in a hushed voice.

As I looked around at the group, I saw the toll those twenty minutes must have taken on them. I was about to start apologizing, when A.J. said, "You were holding up the literal weight of the entire mine on your shoulders, Girlfriend."

"And then Diego flew you out as soon as we had a path clear," Kaira said. Her tone was full of respect, which I took to mean that she didn't hate him anymore. "You were unconscious, and he was in seriously bad shape. Yutika made another plane, and Michael held off the Californians long enough for us to get out of there. We brought you back to Oliver as fast as we could."

"Wow," I whispered, trying to make sense of it all.

"But we did it, right?" I asked. "All the slaves are safe, and the Synthetics are dead?"

"Yay to the first," A.J. said. "Nay to the second."

At the questioning look I gave them, Graysen said, "One of those Synthetics was a Teleporter. Someone in California reported seeing five of them with a white-haired man wearing a black suit.

I jerked upright. "Seriously?!" I demanded.

"Small potatoes," A.J. assured me. "Believe me when I tell you they were the least of our concerns." He cuddled a squirming Sir Zachary for comfort.

The rest of my friends nodded in agreement.

I rubbed my eyes, trying to digest everything my friends had just told me. I dropped my hand and looked up as a new realization struck me.

"Diego saved Lilly instead of getting the Agent S."

"He's got it for you bad, honey girl," A.J. said, making my face turn uncomfortably hot.

"We misjudged him," Graysen said solemnly, saving me from having to respond to A.J. "I'm sorry about that."

Kaira nodded. "After what he did for you, Ma practically tried to adopt him."

"Why did he leave?" I asked, my other emotions being eclipsed by frustration.

I looked around the room, as though he might appear.

"We tried to stop him," Yutika said. "He said he didn't know if you'd want to see him."

"What a dumbass," I muttered.

I swung my feet over the side of the bed and stood up. My friends erupted as I swayed on my feet.

"Are you out of your ever-loving mind?" A.J. shrieked.

"I have to go talk to him," I said, catching a glimpse of myself in the mirror and wincing.

Maybe I'd shower first and then go chase down my man.

"He said he was leaving Boston," Kaira said apologetically.

"What?!"

"When we talked to him," Michael said, "I got the sense that he feels lost. Everything he's been working toward is gone."

Because he chose to save my niece instead of going after what he'd wanted more than anything.

"I have to stop him," I said, raking my fingers through my hair and pulling a sweater over my tank top.

The boys in the room graciously averted their gazes while I tugged on a pair of jeans. Kaira and Yutika held my arms while I got dressed to keep me from keeling over.

"He only left a little while ago," Yutika said. "I'm sure he hasn't gotten too far."

I didn't wait to hear any more. I ran out of my room, only pausing once at the top of the stairs to catch my breath before racing down to the first floor.

"Bri!" Yutika shouted.

I looked up in time to see something shiny fall out of the air. I caught the object and felt a smile break out over my face.

It was the key to Diego's motorcycle.

"Bri, wait up," A.J. called as he came bounding down the stairs behind me. Kaira and Graysen were on his heels.

The three of them had to jog to keep up with me. The cold air that greeted me when I opened the door recharged me faster than a whole night's worth of sleep.

"Gray and I have an idea," Kaira said, a little out of breath.

"And you're going to have wait a hot second," A.J. told me, using his magic to pluck the key out of my hand and dangle it out of my reach. "There's something I need to tell you."

CHAPTER 52

I parked right outside Diego's apartment building. I didn't even bother finding an actual parking space. If the motorcycle got towed, Yutika could always make Diego a new one.

I slipped in the door behind a woman who gave me a strange look, probably because I was somewhere between frazzled and frantic.

What if Diego wasn't here? He didn't have a phone or any other easy way to track him down.

My heart was thundering as I hauled ass up the three flights of stairs to Diego's apartment. I was breathless by the time I made it to his door. I knocked a tad aggressively, bending the metal frame of the door in my enthusiasm.

I was about to break in when Diego wrestled the door open. His eyes widened at the sight of me.

"What are you doing here?" he asked.

All of the little speeches I'd rehearsed on the way over evaporated from my mind, leaving me gaping like a fish.

Diego was so handsome. His black T-shirt was molded to his sculped chest, and his tattoos shone starkly against his bronze skin. I noticed a long, white scar across his forearm that hadn't been there before. I swallowed, remembering the piece of metal that had cut him as he flew back into the collapsing mine to be with me.

Diego raised his eyebrows at me.

I cleared my throat. "You're packing," I said, noticing the duffel bags that were stuffed full of clothes instead of Agent S.

"Very observant." He gave me a little smirk that was a shadow of his characteristic arrogance.

"Where are you going?" I asked, deciding to let his sarcasm slide.

Diego lifted a shoulder. "Mexico City, at least until I figure out what I'm going to do next. It's where my parents are from, and I've never been."

"Oh." I glanced from the packed clothes to Diego.

"Why'd you do it?" I blurted out. "Why pick Lilly instead of the Agent S?"

Diego folded his arms and leaned against the warped door frame. "I'm pretty sure you already know the answer to that."

I was pretty sure I did, too.

"I want you to tell me," I said, my voice barely above a whisper.

Diego searched my face. He leaned close enough for me to catch his intoxicating scent and gave me a cocky grin.

"I figured it was my best chance of getting you back in my bed."

I laughed. Diego's lips curved up, and this time, it was a real smile rather than his sardonic approximation.

"I actually had a reason for coming here," I said in the awkward silence that followed. "Well, four, actually."

"That's a lot of reasons." Diego moved farther into the apartment, inclining his head in invitation.

I closed my hand around the glass vial in my pocket before meeting Diego's curious gaze.

"My first reason is that I wanted to thank you. Not just for what you did for Lilly and me." I bit my lip as the memory of Lilly falling down that endless black hole came back to me. "But also for convincing the Super Mags to help us. If it wasn't for you, we all wouldn't have made it out of there." I paused to take a breath. "I know that if you'd gone straight to the mine like you were planning, you might have been able to get the Agent S. So, thank you."

"You're welcome," Diego replied, his face a complete mask.

"That brings me to a second, related point," I pushed on. "Kaira and Graysen want to offer you a job."

I rushed on as skepticism overtook Diego's features.

"The Super Mags listened to you when they wouldn't listen to anyone else."

"I'm also the one who was hunting them down to take away their magic," Diego pointed out.

I nodded. "But you're one of them, and that matters more than anything else. The kids also think you're cool because you let them beat up the Synthetics. So, Kaira and Graysen want you to be in charge of the new Alliance Super Mag coalition."

Diego scrutinized me. It was really starting to irk me that I had no idea what he was thinking.

"You would be their voice in the Alliance," I continued, babbling in the wake of his silence. "You would be involved in any legislation relating to Super Mags. You'd oversee the Boston Mag police in any Super Mag-related crimes. Also, you would be in charge of all rules and procedures relating to Super Mags…you know, so they don't get themselves into trouble." I paused to suck in a gulp of air. "And you'd go to a lot of boring meetings."

"I'll take it into consideration," Diego said.

Disappointment coursed through me, even though I'd known it was a total long shot. I'd actually expected a flat-out no, so this was better than nothing.

I stalled a little, not wanting to get to my next point.

A.J. had given me the vial now burning a hole in my pocket. He told me he'd saved it in case we needed it, and that it was my choice whether or not I wanted to give it to Diego.

I pulled the vial from my pocket and held it out. The green liquid shimmered in the dim light of the apartment.

"This is the only one that survived our ransacking of your apartment," I said, unable to meet his gaze.

The vial I was offering was as close to an apology as he was going to get from me. It was also enough for a single dose of the Magical Reduction Potion.

"If you still want to take away your magic," I told him, "you can."

Diego reached out and took the vial. My heart sank as he rolled it around on his palm. All of his attention was fixed on the Agent S, like he was mesmerized by the sparkly green liquid. His gaze flicked toward his bathroom, where he kept his chemistry set.

I tried to swallow down the knot in my throat.

I started when Diego took my hand and uncurled my fingers. He placed the vial in my open palm.

"I'm not going to be needing this, after all," he said in response to my puzzled look.

"I…don't understand," I stammered.

"Well." He reached up to brush his knuckles across my cheek. "If I'm going to be in charge of the Super Mags, then it'll be useful if I'm still an actual Super Mag."

My heart felt light as a feather.

"Are you saying," I began, but Diego didn't give me a chance to finish.

"And it's not just that." He gave me the classic Diego smirk. "If I lose my magic, then how am I going to fly my girl up to see the stars and creep on her when she's showering?"

"You wouldn't dare," I said, pressing my hand to my chest and acting aghast.

Diego gave me an unrepentant shrug. "It's not my fault she's a goddess."

"Wait," I said, giving him a suspicious look. "Just to clarify, we're talking about me, right?"

Diego laughed.

"Si, mi pequeña diabla. We're taking about you."

I was grinning like a fool, but I didn't try to stop. I glanced down at the vial in my hand and then slipped it back into my pocket.

"Why the change of heart?" I asked.

I couldn't imagine Diego giving up on the dream he'd been chasing for most of his life. That kind of obsession didn't just go away.

I wasn't fooled by his careless shrug. I waited while he gathered his thoughts.

"Part of it was what my Amá told that Medium…Kaira's grandmother," he said.

I remembered the grief-stricken look on Diego's face after Grandma Tashi has passed on his mother's message.

"And the other part?"

"You know how they say when you're about to die your whole life flashes before your eyes?"

I nodded.

"Well, when Felix told me he'd murdered my parents, and then he dropped that crate, I saw everything I'd worked for disappearing. But in that moment, none of it mattered. All I could think about was how you wouldn't leave the mine without Lilly. And I wasn't leaving without you."

I stared very hard at the floorboards. When I'd finally pulled myself together, I said, "We're going to make Felix answer for what he did to your parents. He's not going to get away with any of his crimes."

Diego nodded slowly.

"What's the fourth?" he asked.

"What?" I replied, confused.

"You said you had four reasons for coming here."

"Oh, right." I gave him my best *little devil* smile before launching myself at him. I moved so fast he barely had time to bring up his arms to catch me before we both went over. Our faces were only inches apart.

"I wanted to do this," I said.

And then, I kissed him.

CHAPTER 53

The next week that followed was a complete blur. Between catching up on all of our Alliance work that we'd neglected, dealing with the fact that we'd created a two-mile deep trench in the middle of California, and moving Diego into the mansion, we'd barely come up for air.

According to Kaira and Graysen's contacts in the Inter-State Magical Cooperation Initiative, Felix had inserted himself into the vacancy left by Blade. He was now calling himself the Southern California Territory ruler.

I wasn't sure the Californians would take kindly to a suit-wearing, smooth-talking Alchemist as a replacement for their barbaric former-leader. But if the Californians didn't take care of Felix first, we would. Kaira and Graysen had already submitted legal summons to extradite Felix from California to Boston to stand trial.

Graysen, in his infinite brilliance, had found a legal loophole that would allow us to prosecute Felix in Boston. Since the mine was technically connected to MagLab through the underground train system, Graysen had been able to argue that Felix's crimes were also committed in Boston, and thus, the Alliance had jurisdiction to arrest him.

The panel of inter-state judges had agreed.

Legal, but with a twist.

I'd been spending my free time with the rest of the Hammonds at Brent, Sarah, and Lilly's new house. Sarah had gone back to work, using her Bleeding Heart magic and connections to other top child psychologists in the world to help all of the slaves we'd rescued. There were almost two-hundred in all, and Brent and Sarah were leading the Alliance group that was in charge of them. Brent had quit his office job to take over the logistics of tracking down the children's families and reuniting them. Sarah was helping all of the children and families get the counseling they needed.

My family's healing wasn't finished after everything we'd been through. Lilly was emotionally and academically far behind where she should be. But no challenge seemed insurmountable now that we had her with us.

Every day, my family was getting back pieces we'd lost over the last five years. Just yesterday, Sarah had suggested she and I start our weekly date nights back up. I'd responded by jumping up and down like a little kid. Later, as I'd been heading to my new motorcycle, which I'd been gifted/stolen from Diego, my mom had hurried out after me. She told me she was having a big welcome-home party for Lilly, and she wanted to invite Diego.

I had helped Diego move the last of his stuff into the mansion this morning. In the afternoon, he'd been officially sworn in as the head of the newly-created Alliance Super Mag Special Relations Division. He had his own room in the mansion, since I hadn't wanted him to think his position was contingent on being with me, but neither of us had been interested in him using it. The Seven had accepted him, and the fact that he and I were dating, without batting an eye. The only exception was A.J.'s friendly threat that he would cut Diego into tiny pieces if he ever hurt me.

Diego's position in our growing family had been cemented by Ma, who now kept a condiment basket on the table by his seat that contained bottles of hot sauce, siracha, and chili flakes. There was also an airtight container in the fridge full of small orange ghost peppers. Ma had drawn a skull and crossbones on the lid, along with the message *Danger, for Diego only!*

The week had passed without us noticing, and tonight we were hosting Thanksgiving dinner. The actual holiday was still a few weeks away, but after everything we'd been through, we decided a celebration was in order.

Ma had been cooking for two days straight in preparation of the feast, and she'd been ordering the rest of us around like a drill sergeant. I had done so many dishes in the last two days, I'd needed to turn my arms titanium before my skin actually fell off.

"What's your rush, cariño?" Diego asked me, chuckling as I pulled on the off-the-shoulders sweater dress Yutika had made me for tonight.

"We're half an hour late." I scowled at him. "Everyone's totally going to know what we were up to."

"They will with that hairdo," he replied, grinning as he helped smooth out my bed hair.

"This is all your fault," I grumbled as we hurried downstairs hand-in-hand. "I'm implementing a rule that you can't walk around shirtless within an hour of any important engagements."

"Are you saying you wouldn't have mauled me if I'd been fully clothed?" he asked, clearly missing the gravity of the whole situation.

"I did not maul you," I hissed as we cut through the empty house and headed for the backyard.

I kind of did.

Diego wrapped an arm around my waist as we walked through the open French doors.

"Ohmygod," I breathed as I took in the sight before us.

"Wow," Diego said.

Yutika and A.J. hadn't let anyone into the backyard for the last day-and-a-half, and now I knew why. The place had been transformed.

A rainbow-shaped tangle of branches hung over the longest table I'd ever seen. Pink roses and white lights were interwoven through the branches. Candles and small bouquets of roses lined the center of the table, which was covered with so much food there was barely room for the plates. Instead of chairs, there were long, wooden benches.

Fortunately, everyone was in the process of sitting down and didn't notice Diego's and my late entrance.

It was a cold, clear night, and so Yutika had set up heat lamps around the table. She'd also created tiny fires in glass jars that lined the table as added centerpieces. Paper lanterns hung from the large trees in the yard, and more white lights were artfully draped over the bushes. It was like I'd stepped into some kind of fairy world.

Diego and I grabbed seats with the rest of the Seven in the middle of the table.

"Where have you two been?" Yutika asked, waggling her eyebrows at me.

"Shh," I ordered her, and then glared at Diego, who was looking inordinately pleased with himself.

The two of them were silently conspiring to say something that was bound to make me blush, when Michael tapped Yutika on the shoulder. He pressed a sealed envelope into her hands, letting his fingertips linger as they trailed over hers.

Yutika slipped away from the table, holding the envelope to her chest. The next time I glanced around for Michael, I noticed he had disappeared, too.

Somewhere down the table, I heard my dad's deep-belly laugh that was coming out more and more now that our family was back together. Brent had Lilly on his knee and his arm around Sarah's shoulders. He lifted his wine glass to me in a toast, grinning from ear to ear.

The crew team was making enough noise for at least three times their number. Whatever they were saying had Kaira's cousins doubled over in laughter and Grandma Tashi scowling.

A.J. and Sir Zachary were holding court across from me. They were wearing matching tuxedos with red bowties.

Smith sat on my other side, grumbling about all the security threats that came with inviting so many people for dinner.

"I don't think anyone here is a threat," I told him, reaching over to yank a plate of turkey out of Sir Zachary's reach before he dove in.

"Minus the fifty hellions," Smith muttered, nodding his head in the direction of the Super Mags.

As if on cue, one of the Super Mags made all the nearby kids' hair stick straight up in the air with his electricity magic. The little girl sitting next to him began to cry when she couldn't flatten her hair back down.

Diego leaned back on the bench and made eye contact with the perpetrator.

"Hey Simon," Diego called out to the Super Mag, who immediately released his magical hold over his friends' hair. "What did I tell you?"

"Don't be a pendejo," the Super Mag replied, sinking glumly back into his seat.

"Are you serious?" I gave Diego an incredulous look.

"What?" he replied.

The rest of the Seven just snickered.

The Super Mags had taken to Diego more easily than I would have guessed. It turned out that none of them had liked the four kids whose magic Diego had stolen. In fact, rumor had it the four kids were bullies with serious anger management issues. The rest of the Super Mags had been secretly relieved when their magic was gone. And Emory had been more than happy to cede his position as the Super Mag leader to Diego. With an actual adult to look up to who was one of them, the Super Mag kids had fallen into line mostly without protest.

Michael and Yutika rejoined our group. They kept glancing at each other, and I even caught a few hesitant smiles being exchanged.

"Is everyone here?" Graysen asked, looking around.

"Yuppers," A.J. replied. "Time to get this party started!"

"Not so fast," Graysen said, exchanging a look with Kaira. "Kaira and I have an announcement to make."

"Why do there always have to be boring speeches," Desiree complained, staring morosely into her glass of sparkling grape juice.

Cora elbowed her in the ribs. "Don't be a pendejo," she whispered.

Graysen chuckled. "Well then, I guess we'd better keep it short." His turquoise eyes gleamed in the candlelight as he turned to Kaira. "Tell 'em, babe."

Kaira's entire face lit up. She laced her fingers through Graysen's before announcing, "We're pregnant!"

For several seconds, we stared dumbly at her as those words sank in. And then the table erupted.

Kaira and Graysen were mobbed. There were tears, laughter, and shouts of joy. Ma was crying as she hugged the two of them at the same time.

Sir Zachary zoomed around, leaping in and out of various people's arms. I noticed a leg of turkey disappear from the table during the confusion.

"Twins," Oliver said, amid the ruckus. "A boy and a girl, if I'm not mistaken."

A worry that had been gnawing at the back of my mind evaporated. Ever since the night Oliver pulled Kaira aside to talk to her, I'd noticed Graysen being even more protective.

Now, it all made sense.

A.J. was jumping up and down, shouting, "I'm gonna be an uncle!"

As soon as their family moved aside, the 7.5 gathered together into a giant group hug. While I hung onto Kaira with one arm and A.J. with the other, I looked over at Diego. His gaze was already locked on me.

I stepped back from Kaira, opening up a space in silent invitation.

Diego swung his legs around the bench and came to join our group. He leaned in to kiss me before taking his place between Kaira and me, wrapping an arm around each of us.

Our circle was whole and complete. And so was I.

THE END

* * *

Because reviews are so important for a book to be successful, please consider leaving a brief review on your favorite retailer if you enjoyed *Steel for 5*. Many thanks!

* * *

Sign up for Stephanie Fazio's e-Newsletter to learn about upcoming books at: https://StephanieFazio.com/subscribe/

Acknowledgements

I am so grateful to all of the people who helped bring this book together.

To Andrew Brodsky, Keith Tarrier, and Ellen Schaeffer. Thank you for being part of the team that made this series so much more than it would have been without you. You all are so talented at what you do!

To my amazing ARC team. Thank you so much for your time, encouragement, and advice.

To the friends and family who have been there with me every step of the way.

To my fantastic readers, who are the inspiration behind these books.

To all the incredible musicians who got me through this book…one song at a time. Two Steps from Hell, Tones and I, and Walter Bergmann…I owe you much.

To my amazing husband, Andrew Brodsky, for being my biggest champion.

About the Author:

Stephanie Fazio is a fantasy author. She grew up in Syracuse, New York, and prior to writing full time, she worked in the fields of journalism, secondary education, and higher education. She has an undergraduate degree in English from Colgate University and a Master's degree in Reading, Writing, and Literacy from the University of Pennsylvania. Stephanie lives in Austin with her husband and crazy rescue dog. When she isn't writing, she's getting lost in parks, hosting taco nights, or ironically and miserably losing at word games, but having fun while she does it.

Connect with Stephanie Fazio:

Visit her Website: https://www.StephanieFazio.com
Sign up for her newsletter: https://StephanieFazio.com/subscribe/

Discover other books by Stephanie Fazio

The Fount Series

The Prince's Chosen

The Forsaken's Choice

The Chosen Union

Opal Contagion Series

Opal Smoke

Opal Slayer

Opal Storm

Bisecter Series

Bisecter

Halve Human

Dusker Dark

Captain Harkibel

Mags & Nats

The Nat Makes 7

Mag Subject 6

Steel for 5

www.ingramcontent.com/pod-product-compliance
Lightning Source LLC
Chambersburg PA
CBHW051203190726
48288CB00006B/1795